The Grammar of Carnatic Music

This book argues that Carnatic music as it is practiced today can be traced to the musical practices of early/mid-eighteenth century. Earlier varieties or "incarnations" of Indian music elaborately described in many musical treatises are only of historical relevance today as the music described is quite different from current practices. It is argued that earlier varieties may not have survived because they failed to meet the three crucial requirements for a language-like organism to survive, i.e., a robust community of practitioners/listeners which the author calls the Carnatic Music Fraternity, a sizeable body of musical texts and a felt communicative need. In fact, the central thesis of the book is that Carnatic music, like language, survived and evolved from early/mid-eighteenth century when these three requirements were met for the first time in the history of Indian music.

The Grammar of Carnatic Music

K.G. Vijayakrishnan

with an MP3 CD

Munshiram Manoharlal
Publishers Pvt. Ltd.

ISBN 978-81-215-1233-6
First Indian edition 2012

Originally published by Walter de Gruyter GmbH & Co., Berlin, 2007

PRINTED IN INDIA
Published by Vikram Jain *for*
Munshiram Manoharlal Publishers Pvt. Ltd.
PO Box 5715, 54 Rani Jhansi Road, New Delhi 110 055, INDIA

www.mrmlbooks.com

To my Gurus

Kappumma and Akka

'eṉṉum eẕuttum eḍupiḍiyaay nirkkum'

'thought and word will stand by attentively'

Table of Contents

Acknowledgements

A book can never be written without the help of a host of people contributing their mite to the success of the project. Being of a logical bent of mind, I shall start at the very beginning. My first thanks goes to my Dad whose love of Carnatic music kept the music gene alive in me; my Mom and my brother, Ananth, whose implicit faith in me and my worth kept me in the Carnatic music world on which I would have turned my back long ago but for their staunch belief in my destiny; the project got realized solely because of my wife, Raji, who is my manager, conscience keeper and severe critic; my late night trysts with the laptop, struggling with the recalcitrant chapters owe a special thanks to Raji's understanding and adjustability.

When I began working on the project I had no idea what I would do once I had the finished manuscript on hand! A giant of a 'thank you' to my friend Aditi for offering to publish the book as part of her series Phonetics and Phonology (which is very appropriate in hindsight) with Mouton de Gruyter, Germany and her generous funding which allowed me to approach Sanjay Subrahmanyan and the Charsur Digital Workstation, Chennai for the making of the accompanying CD in MP3 format. Of course, I am immensely grateful to Sanjay for immediately agreeing to do the demo for me and Suresh Gopalan, Charsur Work Station, Chennai, for being very patient and understanding with me during the recording sessions (where a thorough professional had to deal with a scatter-brained professor).

I owe a great deal to Srinivasan Pichumani and Arvindh Krishnaswamy for extended email discussions on issues pertaining to the '22 srutis' in Carnatic music which clarified my own stand on the matter. Of course, errors of understanding are my own.

Finally, writing of this sort, which is aimed at a mixed audience of music lovers and linguists, requires to be constantly vetted so that neither the music nor the linguistics get taken for granted leaving the poor reader in the lurch. I owe a special thanks to Francois Dell, Annie Rialland, Nick Clements, Aditi Lahiri and her colleagues and my 'Carnatic music discussion group' at CIEFL for patiently giving me a hearing and quizzing me whenever I had taken too much for granted either in Carnatic music or linguistics; my thanks to Geetha Durairajan, Rajiv Krishnan, Deepti Ramadoss, Saumya, Bharani and Malathy for constantly insisting on more explanation. I am very grateful for the interaction with the CIEFL group when I presented my chapters 6 and 7. I am specially grateful to Jayaseelan and Amritavalli for some very insightful comments which set me on the right course. My gratitude to Vineet and Deepti for helping me with the staff notation and the diagrams respectively.

My special thanks to N. S. Srinivasan, a musicologist of standing, who prodded me into thinking about matters musicological with his insightful, provocative comments. I am extremely grateful to Aruna Sairam, a very popular performer and Prof. Paul Kiparsky, Stanford University, a great linguist and a Sanskritist for agreeing to write forewords for my book. I am doubly indebted to Prof. Paul Kiparsky for he not only wrote the foreword but also went through the first draft of the manuscript with great care and provided me with detailed, critical comments which helped me reformulate the main ideas in the book. A very big thank you to all of you!

I am grateful to Deepti Ramadoss, Hemalatha Nagarajan and Bharani for helping me in proofing the manuscript. The book would have suffered without their timely help as my proofing abilities are almost nil. And finally a big thank you to my editor Peter Gebert for being so very patient with me through the entire, painful process of long distance editorial consultations.

Of course, long before I planned my book, unknown to me, every detail about the execution of my book had been thought out by my guru, Pujyasri Mathioli Saraswathy, who knew where the funding would come from for my book long before I did! My heart felt thanks to her. The best I can do is to dedicate this book to her.

Foreword by Paul Kiparsky

Vijayakrishnan approaches his subject from two perspectives which are rare in themselves and almost never joined in one individual. He is a veena player who is keenly aware of the principles and practice of his art, and can explain them clearly to others. He is also a linguist specializing in the study of speech sounds and their linguistic function and organization. Collaboration between the musician and the phonologist in a one-man interdisciplinary project has resulted in the ambitious account of Carnatic music presented here, certainly the first which aspires to the status of a testable scientific theory.

The book can be enjoyed at many levels. The casual reader and music lover will appreciate the wealth of information about how Carnatic music is performed and received. We learn especially about the author's own "chamber music" style of veena playing, whose characteristics he exemplifies throughout in the accompanying MP3 collection. But he also paints a vivid picture of various other styles and schools of vocal and instrumental music, including the more flamboyant "concert hall" style, again with illustrative analyses of performances by various well-known (but mostly unnamed) artists. Vijayakrishnan's discussion is generous and even-handed, and he never lapses into proclaiming guidelines for musicians and their audience to follow; indeed his only strong words are directed against the hegemony of normative orthodoxy in Carnatic music circles. Thus the book provides a fascinating inside view of the current state of one of the world's great classical musical traditions. But this information serves a larger purpose in the book. It situates, and forms part of, the rich empirical evidence for the formal characterization of the Carnatic tradition's musical "grammar". In other words, Vijayakrishnan's treatment of Carnatic music is neither prescriptive nor merely descriptive: it is analytic and explanatory. The reader who makes the effort to accompany him all the way on this intellectual journey will be well rewarded.

Musical competence is seen as a cognitive system that distinguishes potential "grammatical" performances from "ungrammatical" ones and assigns them a musical structure. It constitutes the internalized musical knowledge that participants in the tradition acquire through experience and training, on the basis of their innate capacity for processing combinatoric systems. Musicians must have such knowledge in order to perform, even when they may not be able to articulate it, and even if parts of it may be beyond intuitive introspection, accessible only through theoretical reflection. The goal is to model this implicit "grammar of music" and to understand its properties.

Vijayakrishnan argues in detail, on grounds that often parallel recent linguistic conclusions, that the most suitable framework for characterizing the grammar of music is Optimality Theory (OT). OT is a non-derivational theory: it relies on constraints that apply in parallel, not on rules that apply in sequence. Its simple key tenets are that constraints are ranked and violable, and that violations are minimized. One of the attractions of OT is that it provides a precise reconstruction of concepts such as preference rules and relative complexity that have long figured in musical analysis, as well as an explicit account of how competition between preferences is negotiated within a constraint system.

Vijayakrishnan also adopts some (but not all) of the specific assumptions about the nature of grammar that come from Optimality-Theoretic work on language. He posits two main types of constraints: Markedness constraints and faithfulness constraints. Markedness constraints, assumed to be psychoacoustically grounded, function to assess the intrinsic complexity of various configurations. For example, the basic twelve tones of the scale are less complex (less "marked") than their various modifications. Faithfulness constraints assess the distance between a musical form and a set of input structures constituting the musical "lexicon" that defines a raga. Vijayakrishnan shows how the complex formal patterns seen in musical practice emerge from the competition between appropriately ranked simple constraints of these two types. A particularly interesting observation here is that context-sensitive distributional restrictions on marked tones can be explained as due to their avoidance in salient positions.

The proposed constraint system is a parallel interpretive system which maps pitch values into musical representations. It shares many substantive features with those assumed in recent linguistics, as the author duly points out. Familar themes whose musical aspects are dealt with in the book include the emergence of the unmarked, the tension between modular organization and parallel evaluation, and between bottom-up parsing and top-town effects, a predictive factorial typology, and the principled ranking of special constraints over general constraints (e.g. context-sensitive constraints trump context-free ones, and raga-specific constraints trump general ones). In these respects the analysis offers support for the OT model in a domain for which it was originally not designed.

Yet this theory is no slavish adaptation of ready-made linguistics. It reveals fundamental formal differences between music and language. The most striking of these is that Carnatic music has no analog to syntax. It requires only a few levels of representation, all of which have counterparts in phonology. Vijayakrishnan cautiously restricts his claim to Carnatic music, noting that Western music might have additional levels of organization, including even "syntactic" ones. Such radical differences between two musical traditions would be quite surprising, so the issue Vijayakrishnan has raised here is a crucial one. The case is by no means clear-cut; while it is true that phenomena such as phrasing and grouping into hierarchical melodic constituents have led researchers to posit a quasi-syntactic organization for music, they can arguably also be modeled with the enriched representations that have come out of prosodic phonology; let us also note that the traditional notion of syntax as the sole site of creativity is challenged by constraint-based models of language of the sort that this book adopts.

Creativity is perhaps the central problem of art. This study distinguishes between several levels of creativity. There is Chomskyan creativity, the "everyday miracle" of the productive use of the linguistic system (or in this case the musical system) to generate novel discourses or performances, which has long been the focus of linguistic research. Above it, and of special interest for esthetics, is "Humboldtian" creativity, the kind which renews the very system in which it is manifested. Here Vijayakrishnan introduces an illuminating distinction between scalar and idiomatic ragas and uses it to define two levels of Humboldtian creativity. Scalar ragas are defined by a unique scale which is decomposable into smaller units that resemble other scales. Musicians may form new scalar ragas by analogically combining elements of existing scalar ragas, as easily as they may introduce stylistic novelties into the tradition. Idiomatic ragas, on the other hand, are not just scales, but sets of raga-specific tonal and melodic constraints, which are handed down from teacher to student through traditional compositions. The invention of new idiomatic ragas, given to a only a few individuals of genius (Tyagaraja and Veena Dhanam are cited) instantiates the very highest form of creativity, an awesome mystery that eludes scientific study at least at present.

On the basis of his distinction between scalar and idiomatic ragas, Vijayakrishnan proposes a well-reasoned reform of music instruction, modeled on the proven techniques of second language teaching. The leading idea is that the student should be led from simple to complex melodic forms without ever being taught ungrammatical renderings in the name of simplification.

Here is an exciting new take on the formal analysis of Carnatic music. If all goes well, this treatment will provoke many others, and it may one day be surpassed by new ideas that we cannot even begin to imagine yet. But it will always retain the distinction as a pioneering document of the field, and if a Universal Musicology eventually does take shape, it will be thanks to works like this.

Paul Kiparsky

Foreword by Aruna Sairam

It gives me great pleasure to write about Sri K. G. Vijayakrishnan's book "The Grammar of Carnatic Music" for several reasons. Firstly, he sets out to describe current practices objectively without attributing any value judgments to any particular style, though he lets it be known, in no uncertain terms, where his heart is. Secondly, in my opinion, he clears many cobwebs about orthodoxy and authenticity in current practices. He is very persuasive in his arguments in support of the system being a language-like system which implies change across time and across users. Finally, his project especially touched me as I have, in my own way, gradually evolved a performance style on the foundation of my early training, in my concerts in India as well as in my 'concerts-in-dialogue' with French and German singers of medieval music. He describes very eloquently in chapter 9 the theoretical basis of such processes of transformation.

As he correctly says, time and again, this is only a model for a grammar of Carnatic music-a prototype, that can be adopted for describing the actual practices of performers across different schools of music. If used as a teaching device, it can inculcate a scientific approach to the teaching, learning and appreciation of Carnatic music. In addition, it can also be used as a research tool to evaluate different music systems to arrive at Universal values of pitch and rhythm.

I wish his book every success.

Aruna Sairam

Chapter 1
Introduction

There are innumerable references to music and extensive and detailed descriptions of musical practice in both the Sanskrit and Tamil traditions. Entire treatises on music have also been produced from time to time by renowned scholars, poets and musicians. The major works in this rich musicological tradition are Matanga Muni's Brihaddeesi (circa 9th century[1]), Saarngadeevaa's 13th century classic Sangiitaratnaakaraa, Raamamaatyaa's Swarameeḷakalaanidhi three centuries later and Goovinda Diikshitar's Sangiitasudhaa in the middle of the 16th century. Although the descriptive details are confusingly varied, when it comes to the core issue of the microtonal nature of Indian music, following Brihaddeesi, Sangiitaratnaakaraa traces the origin of the idea of 22 ʃrutis (microtones) within an octave to Bharataa (I will have more to say on the microtonal nature of Carnatic music in chapters 4 and 5). Goovinda Diikshitar's son Veenkaṭamakhi is the first land mark classic that still has a bearing on contemporary Carnatic music. His "Caturdaṇḍi Prakaasikaa" (1660) is relevant today mainly for the classification of the Carnatic raagam system, although his actual descriptions of raagas prevalent in his time are only of historical interest now. As Veenkaṭamakhi says, quoted from (Ranga Ramanuja) Ayyangar (1972: 159),

> "Saarngadeevaa (my spelling) claims to have described two hundred and sixty four raagas (my spelling). They have all disappeared. My venerable preceptor laid down the lakṣaṇaa (my spelling) for fifty raagas."

Many of the raagas described by Veenkaṭamakhi met the same fate as Saarngadeevaa's. The point that I wish to make is that Carnatic music as we know of it today is very different from the music that was described in all these treatises. The raagas that Veenkaṭamakhi 'described' (not more than nineteen, according to Ayyangar (1972: 158)) fared no better than the two hundred and sixty-four described in Saarngadeevaa. But what has survived, for better or for worse (see Ayyangar's critique of Caturdaṇḍi Prakaasikaa chapter 17, 155–174) is Veenkaṭamakhi's schema which created the logical 72 full scales 'Meeḷakartaas' given the 16 tone scale with four tones with dual functions (see chapter 4 for details).

There is no denying the fact that Indian music as we know it today has had a long, perhaps, continuous tradition enriched by several centuries of practice. But the systems the treatises mentioned above describe and the types of compositions they set forth are only remotely, if at all, connected with current practice. It seems almost like reading the grammar of a language we do not know. What we get from the texts is a vague feeling for the strange language and, at times, an intriguing sense of something tantalizingly similar to the language we know. Continuing the language analogy, going through the treatises on music is like reading the grammar of Sanskrit and telling oneself that so many of the sounds, affixes, words, syntactic patterns and word order peculiarities of Sanskrit find echoes in modern Indo-Aryan vernaculars. In fact, it may not be too far off the mark to say that the earlier varieties of music described in the treatises are as much related to contemporary Carnatic music as Sanskrit is to modern, Indo-Aryan languages.[2]

Carnatic music, as we know it today, can at best be traced to the early or middle of the eighteenth century. One of the most important reasons being the unbroken lines of guru–siʃya (teacher–disciple) that have come down to the present day bringing with them compositions and musical practices of distinct traditions. It is really remarkable that though the great Indian music tradition has remained oral down the ages, and is largely oral even today, ignoring a few small islands of literacy, only the practices of the last two and half centuries have survived without much damage. The question to ask is "what are the factors which contributed to the survival of Carnatic music from the mid eighteenth century?" Notice that whereas in the three centuries between Saarngadeevaa's classic Sangiitaratnaakaraa and Veenkaṭamạkhi's Caturdaṇḍi Prakaasikaa, everything had been lost, but so much has survived in the following three centuries. Obviously one cannot attribute both the facts to the oral tradition.

If one can hazard a guess, one may attribute the survival of musical practices from the mid eighteenth century to two factors, namely the unbroken lines of teacher–disciples and the bhajana tradition which was an offshoot of the bhakti movement in the south of India (approximately thirteenth century onwards). While the singing of religious verse in temple communities by singers called ooduvaars (literarily meaning 'one who chants') has survived in small pockets from this time (or earlier as claimed by some), the musical practice of group singing must have caught on much later. Whereas the former was restricted to individuals and families, the latter enjoyed community participation. Like many Indian traditions which were guarded 'family secrets', these practices were more likely to get weakened/lost rapidly than those which found community participation. Therefore my hypothesis is that, rudimentary (working) knowledge of music was inculcated by the bhajana tradition and this widespread knowledge of music helped in preserving Carnatic music in the last three centuries.

Thus for the first time, Carnatic music not being the family heirloom of isolated families, but rooted in the community spawned a lot of talent, largely people who could participate in group singing and, of equal importance, several generations of composers, all in and around the cultural centre of south India – Tanjaavuur (anglicized as Tanjore). My central thesis is that Carnatic music, like language, cannot thrive in isolated, minuscule groups. As long as the music fraternity remains small, below the critical mass, it will remain esoteric and will inevitably disappear.

The analogy that comes readily to mind, specially to a linguist by training, is that of secret languages that children the world over love to invent. Its very universality points in the direction of the faculty being innate. Yet these secret languages never develop beyond a point and their very practitioners tend to forget them as they grow up. Attempts to elicit complex data to construct the grammars of these secret languages from adult informants (who were once practitioners) often prove futile. For example, when several Tamil speaking adults were interviewed for data pertaining to the Tamil secret language ka-baaṣai, it turned out that the data set was non-unanimous, and ambiguous between speakers. I am told that several versions of the secret language are extent among Telugu children (and interestingly, sometimes the intended Telugu words are not uniquely recoverable from the secret language data). The point that I wish to make is that as long as a language or a language-like system remains esoteric, its cultural transmission to posterity cannot be ensured. Indian music before the early/mid eighteenth century must have been confined to small pockets of users lacking a large enough following to ensure cultural continuity.

In this context, if we consider the musical ambience in the cultural centre of Tamil Nadu – in and around Tanjaavuur in the times of the great composers, several factors point in the direction of the Carnatic music fraternity being fairly large and also a fair amount of musical sophistication can be attributed to them. The bhajana tradition had exposed the common people to a lot of music. For instance, consider the practice of unjavrutti (going along the streets singing and collecting food for the day) that, unarguably, the greatest composer of Carnatic music – Tyaagaraajaa – is supposed to have unfailingly followed all his life. It meant that the community in which he lived was exposed to his music every day of their lives. Not only did they listen to the great man singing his compositions, they may have even joined him and sung along with him several divyanaama and utsavasampradaaya kiirtanaas (compositions in praise of God and those sung during special occasions/festivals respectively). Let us take a brief look at some of the divyanaama and utsavasampradaaya kiirtanaas of Tyaagaraajaa. The musical ground that these compositions cover is truly remarkable. The sheer range of raagas and taaḷas they cover points to a fair degree of sophistication of the 'lay', i.e. untrained group of singers.

Table 1. Tyaagaraajaa's Divyanaama Kiitrnaas[3]

Beginning	Raagam	T
Hariyanuvaari	Tooḍi	A
Sriraamadaasa	Dhanyaasi	MC
Nammakanee	Asaaveeri	R
Paahikalyaaṇa	Punnaagavaraaḷi	MC
Naatha broovavee	Bhairavi	A
Indukaa ii Tanuvu	Mukhaari	MC
Raama raama	Huseeni	R
Siitaanaayaka	Riitigauḷa	MC
Shoobhaanee	Pantuvaraaḷi	R

And this amazing range attested in a small village twelve kilometers from Tanjaavuur.

(1) Musical demonstration
  a. Hariyanuvaari [⊙ 1.1][4]
  b. Paahikalyaaṇa [⊙ 1.2]
  c. Naatha broovavee [⊙ 1.3]
  d. Nammakanee [⊙ 1.4]
  e. Shoobhaanee [⊙ 1.5]

The sheer range of raagas and taaḷas of these 'simple' divyanaama compositions with their repetitive structure must have taught the people around the great composer the essence of Carnatic music.

I cannot help an aside here. Just imagine how a 'modern' gathering of 'bhaktas' (devotees) would react to so much Carnatic music. In contrast to the common people of Tyaagaraajaa's days, devotees now demand 'simple/filmy tunes' to display their devotion.[5] The teaching practices of the Carnatic music fraternity have, in a large measure, been responsible for alienating the general public, pushing them away from Carnatic music to more popular modes. One must not underestimate the importance of the music fraternity for maintaining the health of the Carnatic music system. It must be remembered that Carnatic music, unlike many other systems of music, is not an art form that is purely a performing art.[6] It is a 'cognitive art' like language and requires the same conditions for its nurturing, namely a robust community of performers and listeners. In this connection it is pertinent to say that, as of today, there seem to be more performers (whatever their quality) than listeners (if we go by attendance in many concert halls). This is surely not desirable. If the alienation of the general public continues along present lines, the music reviews/discussions of today, and why even this book, may seem like the earlier treatises to future generations – mostly incomprehensible.

As I said earlier, the robust health of the Carnatic music fraternity made the 'golden age' of Carnatic music possible. There must have been more interaction between performers and listeners and between performers too. This is the only explanation for the fact that though the great group of composers lived within a small radius of one another, very importantly, chose to compose in distinct styles. The pattern of composition has never been so varied after their times. The model of Pallavi Goopalayyar, a senior contemporary of Tyaagaraajaa is quite different from the latter, and Tyaagaraajaa's is quite distinct from Muttuswaami Diikshitar's and Shyaamaa Shaastri's. Not only with respect to the overall approach to composition, even in their musical phrasing, they seem to have been intensely aware of each other. As N.S. Srinivasan demonstrates (see (2) on the next page), the opening phrase of the compositions 'Raamakathaa' and 'Paalintsukaamaakṣi' of Tyaagaraajaa and Shyaamaa Shaastri respectively are distinct arguing for the two composers being aware of each other's compositions.[7]

Perhaps it is difficult to sustain such a degree of intensity over a period of time. But there can be no doubt that the 'miracle' of the golden age of Carnatic music became possible because of the interaction in the music community, the 'core' musical knowledge that the composers could take for granted and the intense awareness of the tremendous musical activity by the composers.

Carnatic music, a fortunate by-product of the Indian music system, is like language in yet another way. A language requires a speech community and, importantly, it must fulfill the community's communicative needs to be a living language. Carnatic music too waited for the music community to grow to a reasonable size to blossom as a full fledged 'living' system, and I advance the view that its 'communicational' needs were realized for the first time when musical compositions of amazing range and complexity emerged with the great compositions of the Carnatic music 'trinity', i.e. Tyaagaraajaa, Muttuswaami Diikshitar and Shyaamaa Shaastri, and their contemporaries.

(2) Musical demonstration

a. Raamakathaa Madhyamaavati [⊙ 1.6]
Tyaagaraajaa Aadi
// ; sa, - ni sa ri sa / ri,
ra: ma ka tha:

b. Paalintsukaamaakṣi Madhyamaavati [⊙ 1.7]
Shyaamaa Shaastri Aadi
// ; sa ni pa, - , ni sa ri, sa, /
pa: lin su

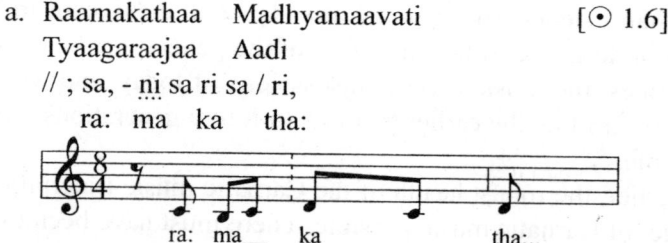

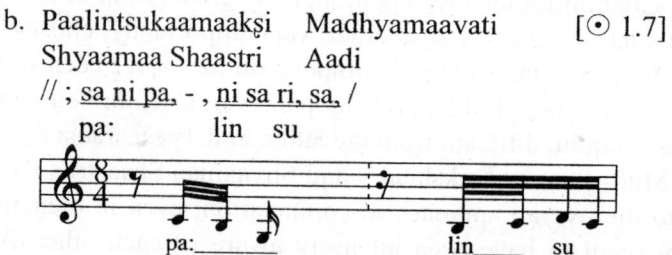

Before we take up the role of compositions in the health and development of Carnatic music, let us consider the importance of the communicative aspect of language for its survival. In India, we only have to look at our minority languages to see how quickly languages can die. In many cases, though the speech community is not really extinct, its language becomes extinct if the communicational needs of the community are not met by its first language but by some other 'dominant' language in the neighbourhood.[8] Thus for a language to survive, it is essential that it serves the communicational needs of the community. In the case of Carnatic music, what, could we say, is the equivalent of a communicational need? I am convinced that it is the composition which satisfies this need. Till the mid eighteenth century, by and large, music was clearly subservient to the language text. Either great poetry was set to music[9] (of a repetitive kind) (the case of the hymns of the bhakti movement), or devotional texts or merely a string of names of Gods and Goddesses set to music to attract the devotees. In either case, music was merely a vehicle to convey religious ideas.

However, with the advent of the great compositions of the trinity and composition types like the varṇams[10], the music took on a life of its own. The musical exuberance of viribooṇi, the Bhairavi raaga varṇam in Aṭa taaḷam by Paccimiriam Aadiappayyer or the great sangatis[11] of Cakkaniraaja of Tyaagaraajaa in raagam Karaharapriyaa are enough to prove the point.

(3) Musical demonstration [⊙ 1.8]
Pallavi and anupallavi of Viribooṇi, Bhairavi varṇam, Aṭa taaḷam performed in the first and second tempo by Sanjay Subrahmanyan
Musical demonstration [⊙ 1.9]
Pallavi of Cakkaniraaja in Karaharapriyaa (on the veena by the author)

Music had come of age and the language text was clearly subservient to the music. The range of musical and rhythmic ideas explored, emotions hinted at, were the 'communicative meanings' that Carnatic music had to convey. And this communicative need grew from strength to strength in more and more elaborate venues for its exploration. Once again, the germs of the ideas were in the compositions. For instance, the rules for kalpana swaram[12] (rhythmic improvisation) were already set out in the varṇams and the great pancaratna kritis of Tyaagaraajaa[13], the seeds for niraval (rhythmic variations on a line of the composition) in the sangatis, etc.

The logical extension of the freedom of the performer to communicate his/her musical ideas was the freedom allowed in rendering compositions. The so-called 'fixed' compositions were no longer all that fixed; the only boundary was that of the communicative expectation of the listeners. The rendering of a composition will not be acceptable to the listeners if it crosses a certain threshold of acceptability. So, as in language, what restricts the speaker/performer is the shared 'grammar' of the community, nothing else. Therefore, logically, there is nothing like copyright in Carnatic music (as in day to day language). There cannot be. Once a composer has finished composing, the thing composed is no longer in his/her hands. The performer has the right to 'interpret' it, meaning, change the musical lines ever so slightly, add sangatis, add ciʈʈaswarams[14] and so on. I demonstrate below two extent versions of a kriti of Tyaagaraajaa to illustrate the point that at times, renderings of the same musical composition can become unrecognizably different. The composition in question is Paripuurɳa kaamaa in the raagam Puurvikalyaaɳi set to Ruupaka taaɭam.

(4) Musical demonstration

a. Paripuurɳa kaamaa raagam Puurvikalyaaɳi
Ruupakam Tyaagaraajaa
Version 1 [⊙ 1.10]
// pa, pa mi / ; gu, - , ra; // sa
pa ri pu:r na ka:...

b. Paripuurɳa kaamaa raagam Puurvikalyaaɳi
Ruupakam Tyaagaraajaa
Version 2 [⊙ 1.11]
// ; sa, / ra, gu, - ra, gu mi // pa
pa ri pu:r na ka:...

c. Paralooka saadhanamee raagam Puurvikalyaaɳi
Aadi Tyaagaraajaa [⊙ 1.12]
// ; ; - ; pa, / pa mi, gu - , ra; // sa
pa ra lo: ka sa:...

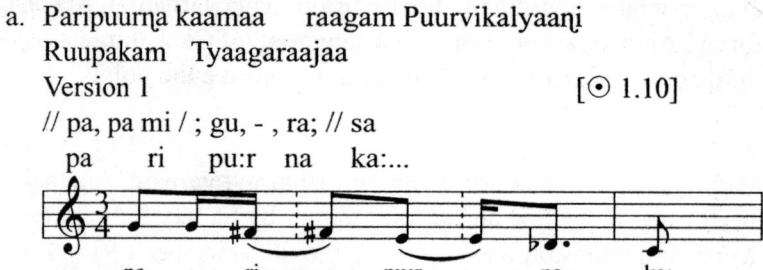

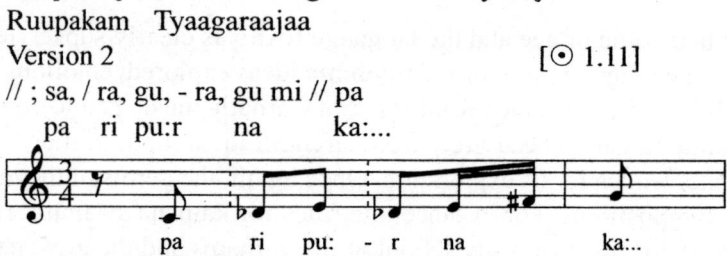

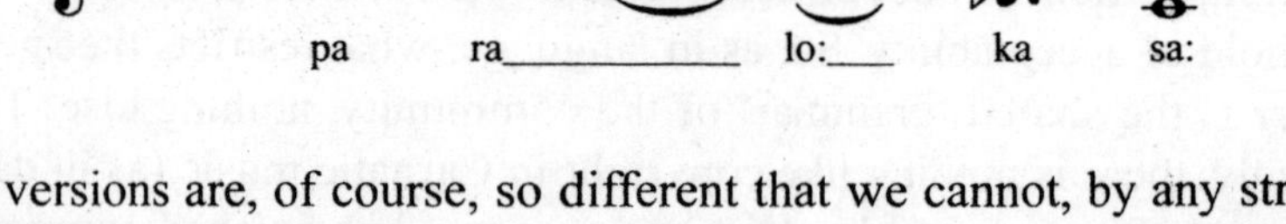

The two versions are, of course, so different that we cannot, by any stretch of imagination, call them the same composition. The interesting twist to the issue of 'authenticity' of a rendering of a composition (as composed by the composer) is that there is yet another Tyaagaraajaa kriti in the same raagam, namely Paralooka saadhanamee (4c) which begins exactly like version 1 above. I leave it to the judgment of the reader to decide which of the two versions is likely to be closer to the original keeping in mind the fact that this composer never repeated his own melodies nor of other composers' he was aware of.

For a learner, the only way to learn the idioms and phrases that define the 'grammar' of the major raagas of Carnatic music is through learning the great compositions in these raagas (see chapter 8 on the task of constructing the lexicon of Carnatic music). Thus for beginners, specially, early attempts at improvisation (the equivalent of spontaneous speech), usually means repeating idioms and phrases from compositions that they have learnt or render sequences allowed by the scale. On acquiring greater sophistication, a performer learns to avoid 'quotations' from compositions or give them a slight twist and use them to display irony, wit, etc. (see chapter 7, pp. 207–214 for a full discussion). So, unlike language, where one learns the language without the help of 'fixed' texts, in Carnatic music, fixed texts are used to create the 'lexicon' of Carnatic music and the 'grammar' of particular raagas. Once the process of learning is at an advanced stage, the initially internalized compositions are de-composed into a set of well-formedness requirements (see chapter 8 for details). However, performers (and listeners to some extent) have access to both the lexicons, namely the lexicon of compositions as well as the more cognitive 'de-composed' lexicon as performers have to render compositions without the help of any written prop in Carnatic music performances. Suffice it to say for the present that the repertoire of Carnatic music is used to build the lexicons of individual raagas extracting the finer points of each raagam thereby creating the vocabulary to enable free flowing musical discourse.

The point I am about to make now is the first lesson that we – linguists – learn: that there is no such thing as an inferior language and by implication an inferior variety/dialect. All languages and all dialects are equally adequate, efficient and there is no such thing as one language/dialect being superior to another. By implication, it means that there is no such thing as a standard dialect, from the language-internal point of view. A particular variety is elevated to the level of a standard purely for political and socio-economic reasons. Thus a 'naïve' view like 'standard British English' is better than other varieties of English is nothing but prejudice. The state of affairs is rather worse in languages in India than in English. In the Indian context, there has been a systematic drive to deny the dialects their rights and so we come across language 'pundits' holding forth on the child not knowing her/his first language even when she/he does speak the language perfectly.

Similarly, in Carnatic music too, there is no such thing as a 'pure' variety or a superior 'school' of music. Just as in language, variations in the practice of Carnatic music arise out of varying social, cultural and aesthetic considerations and certain varieties acquire prestige, once again, for extra-musical reasons (see chapter 9 for a discussion on styles in Carnatic music).[15]

Going back to variation and language, the philosophy of learning to respect language variation ties in rather well with the now firmly established doctrine of bio-diversity in organic systems. We now know that diversity is not only interesting (from a theoretical point of view) but essential for the survival of organic systems. Language displays all the properties of organic systems like change, self-organization, evolution, breaking up into distinct, related systems etc. It could be argued that suppression of diversity in a language will result in language entropy just as in organic systems.

I believe that the argument can be extended to Carnatic music also. Firstly, the earlier varieties of Indian music ('avataars' "incarnations") did not survive precisely because the community of practitioners was sub-optimal, perhaps, not allowing enough room for diversity. Secondly, perhaps, the communicational function of music was also severely limited. If we look at the contemporary scene, we find that the various, distinct types of south Indian music systems have benefited from each other over the years. For instance, the use of 'simplified' Carnatic music in film music has brought in fresh blood into the sphere of Carnatic music, more listeners/performers into the Carnatic fold; the influence of Carnatic music has enabled composers of film music to re-define the grammar of film music radically and so on. Finally, if we take a dispassionate look at the Carnatic music scene, we will agree that each variety/style of Carnatic music acquires its value in the context of other styles and the value of a style itself undergoes radical changes over the decades, giving rise to re-evaluation of earlier styles etc. In short, the existence of distinct styles makes for enlarging the Carnatic music community, bringing fresh ideas to bear on the shaping of the grammar of Carnatic music and, not least, adding to the health of the music system as a whole.

Given the view that Carnatic music is comparable to language, the notion of grammar itself must undergo a radical change. The view in modern linguistics is that the main function of a grammar is to 'describe' the practices attested in a homogenous speech community. In the case of language, the basic assumption is the postulation of a homogenous speech community. This is a necessary abstraction, as speech communities are never all that homogenous.

Individuals who make up the speech community, quite often, display degrees of variation even within the so-called 'same dialect'. Take for instance, the first and second pronunciations listed in many English dictionaries. But the abstraction is, nevertheless, necessary to construct a coherent grammar of the group of users. Therefore, in linguistics, an ideal speaker-listener (most often the author herself/himself) is postulated and her/his language is taken to be the object of analysis. In attempting a constraint-based grammar of Carnatic music, I shall take on the role of the ideal performer-listener as I have unlimited access only to my own practice and intuitive judgements. Of course, when I compare two styles I will be comparing my style with that of a specific practitioner.

I am aware that in the case of Carnatic music, unlike language, not every member of the 'community' is at the same level of proficiency. But the assumption I am making is that, given enough time, motivation, etc., every member of the Carnatic music community can, in principle, arrive at the grammar I am postulating on the basis of my own proficiency (ignoring the style bias). In reality, of course, as the communicational pressure to go the whole way in acquiring the system is much, much less in Carnatic music than in language, many members may never acquire the grammar of Carnatic music completely. Therefore, much more than in language, (but perhaps, as much in second language varieties), the inequalities in the level of mastery in a community is a real as well as a theoretical problem in Carnatic music. I shall largely ignore this problem, assuming that the object being described is applicable to all 'competent' performers and to most 'intelligent' listeners of Carnatic music whom I will call the Carnatic music fraternity[16]. However, I shall address the question of the progress from the composition learning stage to the stage of de-composing the Carnatic music lexicon in chapter 8 clearly hinting that not all learners/listeners may make it to the advanced stage.

However, to the general public, the word 'grammar' conjures nightmarish pictures of punishment/negative marking etc. Grammar, to them, implies prescription and judgement. Prescriptive grammars may have a limited function to perform in the process of learning at best, but they are of no interest to theoreticians. Whatever the merits and demerits of using grammar in language teaching, certainly grammar plays no role whatsoever in the acquisition of the first language by children or even in the learning of the second language in contexts other than the classroom. It is language use which facilitates the learning of a language. Thus, the focus in linguistic circles is on descriptive grammars which are analytical tools for various theoretical purposes. Coming as I do from this generative linguistic tradition, I have attempted a descriptive grammar of Carnatic music. Clearly it is not meant to set down 'prescriptions' for improving the standard of performers, methods of teaching or in analyzing the drawbacks of the music setup, etc.

Once again to make it amply clear to the reader, the primary objective of this book is to outline a descriptive grammar of contemporary Carnatic music applying the principles of generative linguistic theory. If this objective is satisfactorily met, then it becomes possible to compare the cognitive principles which are at work in language and Carnatic music. Thus, the subject matter of the book is narrowly confined to the melodic system of Carnatic music (with a brief look at some principles of rhythmic organization). I have nothing to say about the history of the system, the philosophical, religious or stylistic merits of the language texts of the musical compositions, the literary merits of the language texts, the evaluation of different composers and types of compositions, the intricacies of rhythm in Carnatic music etc. The reader is advised to go elsewhere for a discussion on these topics.

As the book is addressed to a mixed audience of lovers of music, lovers of Carnatic music and language theorists, certain sections may be too rudimentary for some readers. So the readers are requested to judiciously skip chapters which are likely to go over material already familiar to them. For instance, the first half of chapter 2 comparing the design features of language and music may be skipped by language theorists and musicians who are already convinced that language and music share many properties in common. Similarly, large parts of chapter 4 which explain the scalar tables of Carnatic music will be well-known to most lovers of Carnatic music and hence may be skipped.

The plan of the book is as follows. Chapter 2 lays out the similarities between language and music in general and variation in language and Carnatic music in particular claiming that the architectures of the grammar of language and Carnatic music are similar. Chapter 3 briefly outlines one of the current models of linguistics, namely a constraint based approach to grammar. Chapters 4 and 5 argue that, like the grammar of language which requires 'Phonetic Form' or rule mechanism for interpreting sounds into abstract elements, Carnatic music too requires rules to interpret the pitch values and pitch ranges as notes or 'swaras' and determine musical phrase and musical line boundaries. Chapters 6 and 7 take up the contentious issue of grammaticality and meaning respectively and try to show how the notion 'meaning' in language is very different form what constitutes 'meaning' in Carnatic music. The chapters show what types of rules could be postulated for the construal of meaning in Carnatic music. Chapter 8 dealing with the central issue of the 'Lexicon' in Carnatic music, shows how the lexicon is organized and constructed from lines, phrases and idioms and how, at advanced levels of learning/listening, it passes through stages of de-composition into more abstract principles. Finally, in chapter 9, I take on the reality of distinct styles in Carnatic music and show how different styles can arise from differences in the lexicon, differences in the ranking of constraints and differences in performing criteria.

Chapter 2
Language and (Carnatic) music

2.1. Introduction

In this chapter I will show in what ways music and language are similar and in what ways they differ from one another. I will also compare these systems with other symbolic systems. For instance, bird songs and the dance of the bees are also symbolic systems used for communication and so are logic and mathematics. But language is unique among these symbolic systems in displaying ten design features first identified by Hockett (1960). I shall review the ten design features proposed by Hockett for language and show which ones are evidenced in which communicative systems other than language, including music.

Having established the 'language'-like design features of music in general, I will go on to discuss the particular properties evidenced in the Carnatic music system which make it even more language-like, and propose the architecture of the grammar of Carnatic music. I will show in subsequent chapters 4 and 5 (the 'tone' interpretive system) and 6 and 7 (the 'meaning' interpretive system) when I motivate the interpretive mechanisms in the architecture of the grammar of Carnatic music, that the grammar of Carnatic music and the grammar of language are strikingly similar, though the particulars that make up the two grammars are obviously different.

2.2. Design features

In this section, I will take the reader through the ten design features of language proposed by Hockett showing how music, to the exclusion of other symbolic systems, shares nine of the ten design features with language.

2.2.1. Species specificity

A symbolic system is species specific if it is unique to a species. For instance, take the case of the baring of the teeth to communicate anger. Humans do it, the big and small cats do it, so do gorillas and dogs. Thus this communicational gesture is not species specific. However, the dance of the bees, bird songs, language, mathematics and music (covering at least an entire octave) are species specific, the last three to humans.

2.2.2. Cultural transmission

Though the type of bird song may be species specific, bird songs have to be learnt. A song bird raised in isolation will not sing like other birds of its species. Perhaps this is true of bees as well. Similarly, though humans have the innate capacity to use language, mathematics and music, these systems have to be learnt.

2.2.3. Specialization

The physical organs used by the system were not primarily meant for communicative purposes. It is true that the oral cavity, the tongue and the larynx were not designed primarily for speech, nor the fingers and the hands for sign language. Similarly, our ability to perceive differences in pitch is not primarily meant for either language or music. This ability is necessary for survival in the physical world. This feature is, of course, trivially true of all communication systems.

However, it is also true that our speech organs need not have been so fine tuned if they were meant only to serve the primary purpose, i.e. breathing and eating. The increase in the oral space with the lowering of the larynx has made speech possible by some quirk of evolution (compare the 'oral' space of gorillas, infants and older humans). Similarly, our ability to perceive and produce nearly two octaves of pitch (or even more) even by untrained people may not serve any purpose other than music. Therefore, perhaps, this feature should be reinterpreted to mean special evolution of biological organs enabling the appearance of particular symbolic systems in humans. (See Lieberman (1984) for a detailed discussion.)

2.2.4. Medium of transmission

Turning to medium of communication, once again, it is trivially true that all communication systems use either the aural or the visual medium and it is also true that all human symbolic systems have the ability to transfer the message from one medium to the other if there is a felt need. Languages can be written down, even Carnatic music can be notated, in principle, and so on. I have nothing more to say about this feature.

2.2.5. Arbitrariness

There is no inherent connection between the sign and the thing signified. For instance, honey bees indicate the direction of the source of honey by the angle of their tail and the copiousness of the source by the swiftness of their tail wagging. It is not necessary that they should have indicated the direction with the angle of their tail, for instance. They could have faced the source of honey to indicate the direction of the source. Similarly, there is no inherent connection between the word 'tiger' and the reference to the striped, big cat. In fact, different languages use different sound sequences to signal this object. It is this feature of arbitrariness that makes languages mutually unintelligible as they do not share their lexicons.

At this point, an astute reader may ask, "But what about onomatopoeia?". It is true, all languages have a minuscule vocabulary of onomatopoeic words. But even these words are bound by language-specific conventions. For instance, English expresses disgust/unreliability etc. by the use of the sound 's' as in words like 'slimy', 'slithering', 'slippery', 'slip shod', 'seedy', 'sickening', 'sloppy', etc. If we try and find near-equivalent words for these English words in our languages, we will see that though some of the words do belong to the onomatopoeic part of the lexicon of our language, the convention used would be very different. For example the near-equivalent for 'slimy' in Tamil would be 'koza̤ koza̤' or 'vaza̤ vaza̤'. Thus we see that even onomatopoeia is bound by the conventions of the language.

Now turning to mathematics and logic, there is nothing arbitrary about numbers and about functions like addition, multiplication, 'is a set of', etc. Thus logic and mathematics lack the design feature of arbitrariness.

What about music, and Carnatic music in particular? Definitely, it may be reasonable to think that the relation of the first, fifth and the eighth note in an octave (sa pa Sa, i.e. C, G and higher C respectively of the Western system) is not arbitrary but governed by mathematical laws of frequency of sound. But the frequencies defined in the even tempered scale of Western music did not prevail earlier and is not matched in other systems, e.g. Carnatic music. The only mathematical reality is that of the eighth. For example, the frequency of the eighth note in a scale is double the frequency of the first. But, other tone boundaries are set differently in Western music and Carnatic music. (More of this in chapter 4.) Further, specifically in Carnatic music, other combinatorial properties of the scale are quite arbitrary. For instance, for Bhairavi raagam in the ascending scale, one uses the second daivatam (A) but in the descending scale the first daivatam (A flat) is used. However, we don't have another raagam which is exactly like Bhairavi except for the fact that the daivatams are switched with the first daivatam in the ascending scale and the second daivatam in the descending scale (i.e., the choice of the daivatams is reversed, call it anti-Bhairavi or Bhairavi'). Thus, I would not be wrong to assume that the Carnatic music system is arbitrary in principle, even though some features may be conditioned by mathematical laws.

(1) Musical demonstration
a. Bhairavi [⊙ 2.13]
sa ri gi ma pa di ni Sa/ Sa ni da pa ma gi ri sa
b. *anti-Bhairavi [⊙ 2.14]
sa ri gi ma pa da ni Sa/ Sa ni di pa ma gi ri sa

However, I will return to the problem of the non-existence of an *anti-Bhairavi and make an attempt at an explanation in the context of the organization of the Carnatic music lexicon in chapter 8 p. 258.

I will show later on that the only law of mathematics that Carnatic music adheres to is the law of doubling the frequency of the fundamental for the octave. All other notes/pitch boundaries are arbitrary/performer dependent. It will be obvious even to the uninformed that the Western F sharp is generally lower than the prati madhyamam 'mi' very often used in Carnatic music, and similarly, the Western B is lower than the kaakali niṣaadam 'nu' of Carnatic music. Thus we see that pitch boundaries are arbitrarily assigned in cultural traditions.

In another sense also the Carnatic music system exhibits arbitrariness. For instance, while the raagam Aanandabhairavi admits anyaswaras (foreign notes) the raagam Riitigauḷa does not. While both raagas select the notes 'sa ri gi ma pa di and ni', only the former also allows the infrequent use of the note 'da' and the 'anyaswaram' 'gu' and 'nu' to be rendered rarely in the entire discourse. This arbitrary inclusion of notes in a raagam is still a matter of dispute for some orthodox musicians. I have nothing more to say on this matter.

2.2.6. Discreteness

This feature relates to the function between the symbol and the thing signified. In language, the symbols used are discrete and not continuous. For instance, no language in the world expresses multiple occurrence of an object by repeating the sign for the object that many times, e.g. a single book as 'book', two books as 'bookbook' and three books as 'bookbookbook', in other words, no language displays 'continuous' interpretation of the symbol. On the other hand, the honey bee's wagging of the tail is a continuous symbol with the vibrations per second correlating with the richness of the source of honey. Thus the symbolic system of language is a discrete system. A sound is perceived categorically as /p/ or /b/ but never as 25% p, 45% p, 25% b, etc. Take the sounds [p] and [b], for instance. The signal is perceived as [p] or [b] because of the time lag between the release of the closure for the labial stop and the following voiced vowel (to simplify matters for ease of presentation). One finds that if one manipulates the time lag for the setting on of the voice for the following vowel (artificially), within a single language speech community, one will find that around specifiable ranges speakers will increasingly perceive the sound categorically. In other words, starting from 0 till a certain point of time, speakers will perceive the sound as /p/ and then once again after a certain point of time they will perceive it as /b/. At no time will any speaker say that the sound is 45% like /p/ and 55% like /b/. Perception is always categorical in language. It is another matter that perception can vary with the context. But more of this later.

As for Carnatic music, or any music for that matter, though the frequencies are a continuum, notes are marked by frequency boundaries which are arbitrary. In fact, in Western music, we find notes being redefined, e.g. the difference between the Baroque scale and the even tempered scale later on. Similarly, in Carnatic music we find discussions of a Varaaḷi madhyamam (at a pitch range higher than F sharp) and the normal prati madhyamam (F sharp). The point that needs to be made is that tone boundaries are, in principle, arbitrary (not mathematically defined) allowing cultural systems to redefine them in many ways. The logical consequence of this fact is that the perception of a 'note' in a musical system is always categorical, never gradient. In other words, a pitch frequency will always be perceived as a distinct note rather than as an ambiguous interpretation between adjacent notes. Thus it would be reasonable to assume that music also exhibits discontinuity. I will have more to say on the interpretation of 'notes' in context in Carnatic music in chapters 4 and 5 where I argue for the need for an interpretive component comparable to Phonetic Form for Language. Suffice it to say for the present that music (and Carnatic music to a greater extent) does exhibit the property of arbitrariness.

2.2.7. Open ended

A symbolic system like language is open ended in the sense that certain lexical categories can not, in principle, be fully listed in any dictionary. Take nouns in English, for example. As the need arises, new names are coined, names which never existed before, e.g. xerox, astronaut, mouse (of a computer), laptop, blog, etc. In principle, nouns in all human languages are open ended (i.e., if the language does not wish to become extinct/redundant). It is another matter that in English nouns, verbs (e.g. outsource) and even adjectives (e.g. air-conditioned) can be freely, newly coined. However, the characteristic of being open ended is a fact of language. Now, this is not true of any other symbolic system except music. One cannot create new numbers nor can the bee devise a new gesture.

In Carnatic music, one can create new raagas (not just tunes) which have never been thought of before. In that sense, raagas are open ended in Carnatic music. This point is worth explaining in some detail. Let us begin with the names of notes in the Carnatic and the Western systems.

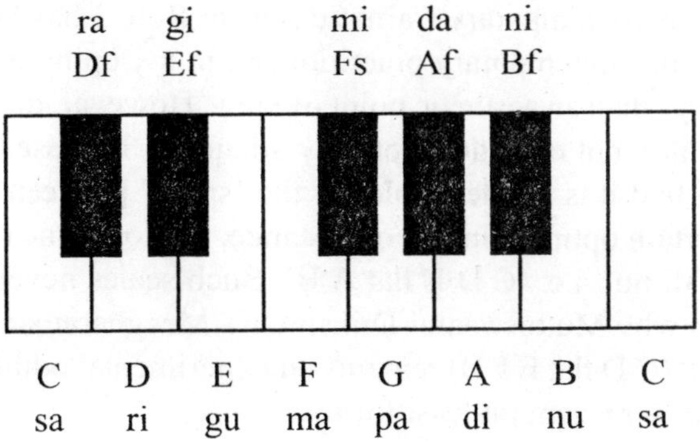

Figure 1.

(2) Labels of Notes in Carnatic music[17]
sa ra ri gi gu ma mi pa da di ni nu Sa
C Dflat D Eflat E F Fsharp G Aflat A Bflat B C

Taking the twelve notes in the octave (i.e., on the keyboard) and devising the following 'combinatorial rules' (like principles of word combinations in sentence grammar), one can illustrate the open endedness of the system.

(3) Combinatorial principles for scale formation in Carnatic music

Rule 1: sa (C) is obligatory for all scales. (obligatory)
Rule 2: any note may be missing in the ascending or descending scale.
Rule 3: a scale must have a minimum of five notes. (obligatory; see below)
Rule 4a: a minimum of one note to be selected between sa (C) and ma (F) or mi (F sharp). (obligatory; but see below)
Rule 4b: a minimum of one note to be selected between pa (G) upper Sa (C). (obligatory)
Rule 5: the choice is between ma (F) and mi (F sharp) if selected. (optional)
Rule 6: the set of notes that make up a scale is, in principle, not ordered in a sequence (but governed by the general principle that every raagam must be distinctive from every other raagam) (see chapters 6, 7 and 8 for a full discussion).[18] (optional)
Rule 7: in vakra (literally 'crooked') non-linear scales, certain sequences of notes are prohibited. The same note may occur more than once in a scale but will be counted only once. (interpretative)

These are not hypothetical rules but real principles which govern the creation of new raagas in contemporary Carnatic music. Rule 3 has been called into question by some contemporary practitioners, in my opinion, more from an 'academic' rather than an aesthetic point of view. However, there is a problem with rule 4 as it is not even descriptively adequate. It misses the functional generalization that it is not desirable for the 'space' between adjacent notes to exceed a certain optimal limit. For instance, it allows one to construct the scale 'sa ri gi di nu', i.e. 'C D E flat A B'. Such scales never quite become raagas. This is why Muttuswaami Diikshitar's Meegharanjani with its scale 'sa ra gu ma nu' (C D flat E F B) remains an experimental oddity and does not quite make it as a raagam (at least for me).

(4) Musical demonstration

a. Newly constructed scale which does not quite make it as a raagam [⊙ 2.15]
sa ri gi di nu Sa
Sa nu di gi ri sa

b. Experimental scale created by Muttuswaami Diikshitar:
Meegharanjani [⊙ 2.16]
sa ra gu ma nu Sa
Sa nu ma gu ra sa

On the other hand, one can think of a raagam which has successfully flouted rule 4, e.g. Kuntalavaraaḷi with the aaroohaṇam 'sa ma pa ni di Sa'. Unlike some of the raagas derived from folk music, which do not admit a full octave and which are performed at madhyama ʃruti, i.e. taking 'ma' (F) as the fundamental pitch, e.g. Naadanaamakriyaa or Punnaagavaraaḷi, Kuntalavaraaḷi, like other 'full octave' raagas, allows one to descend below the 'sa' and go above the higher 'Sa' and is thus a true exception to rule 4 requiring a jump from 'sa' to 'ma' without selecting any note in between. What is to be noted is that this notion of optimal distance between notes does not function blindly between notes. If we ask ourselves why is it that while Kuntalavaraaḷi succeeds, the scale I mentioned does not, the answer is that the former jumps from one good anchor/pivotal note, i.e. 'sa' to another accepted anchor, i.e. 'ma', while the latter jumps from 'gi' to 'di' neither of which is an accepted anchor/pivotal note.

(5) Musical demonstration
a. Naadanaamakriyaa [⊙ 2.17]
gu ma mi di ni Sa Ra
Sa ni di mi ma gu ma
Notated and sung as
nu sa ra gu ma pa da
pa ma gu ra sa nu sa
b. Punnaagavaraaḷi [⊙ 2.18]
gi ma pa da ni Sa ra
Sa ni pa da, mi ma gi ma mi ma
Notated and sung as
ni Sa ri gi ma pa da
pa ma gi ra sa ni sa ra sa
c. Kuntalavaraaḷi [⊙ 2.19]
Sa ma pa ni di Sa Ma
Ma Gu Sa ni di pa ma gu Sa (ni di) sa ma ma pa

This situation is quite similar to language and its rules. For instance, in English, the sound ['sh'] (as in shoe) occurs only with the consonant 'r' as in words like 'shrink', 'shrew' etc. in the core vocabulary of the language. But because of borrowings, we now do come across words like 'schnapps' 'schmuck' etc. In fact, the marginality of the consonant cluster with [sh] reinforces the rule in the language '[s] can occur with any consonant other than [r] to form a cluster, but [sh] can occur only with [r] in a cluster'.[19]

Setting aside the actual formalization of the principles of scale formation, it must be clear that the scales that one can create are infinite, in principle. Therefore the scale system in Carnatic music is truly open-ended. In practice, however, every scale does not become a raagam. The elevation of a scale to a raagam is achieved not by a fiat or ordinance but by general consensus among practitioners and composers; and it must be acceptable to the listeners as well in the long run. The situation is no different in language. A newly coined word must find wide currency to get listed in the next edition of the dictionary.

2.2.8. Creativity

By 'creativity' I mean the ability to send novel messages with the help of a finite set of rules. For instance, the honey bee is capable of sending a message never sent before regarding the direction and richness of the source of honey. Language – even everyday language – is the pre-eminent vehicle of creativity. We are able to send and receive messages never coded before. For instance, imagine a household where they store vegetables in steel cupboards and jewelry in the fridge; a member of this household can come up with the sentence "Darling, I have put the jewelry in the fridge and the vegetables in the cupboard as usual." This surely is a sentence which is perfectly comprehensible given the context, but not a sentence any of us would have actually encountered in real life. Or take this sentence my wife came up with while watching the Tyaagaraaja aaraadhanai (an annual celebration of the death anniversary of the composer) on television.

(6)	"adoo	saxophone	paaḍraaree"
	look,	saxophone	singing (honorific)

What she meant was that even the saxophone player was singing. Surely this is truly an example of creativity of everyday language use (and examples like this prove the impossibility of machine translation).

Now, in Carnatic music too, we come across new sequences never ever encountered in established raagas. Take the example of the Beegaḍaa raagam. Some of the well-known phrases in the raagam are:

(7) Musical demonstration
Beegaḍaa I [⊙ 2.20]
pa di pa Sa
pa Ri
pa Sa Gu

(The convention I will follow is to use the lower case for notes in the middle octave, upper case for the upper octave and under-dotting for the lower octave.)

In the composition 'vaa murugaa vaa' by the contemporary composer R. Venugopal, we have the following phrase in the anupallavi:

di pa Gu Gu

This unexpected, new sequence is comparable to the sentence in English given above as an example of the creativity of language. Therefore, Carnatic music admits of creativity in well-established raagas just like language.

This kind of creativity well-known in linguistic circles – called rule-governed creativity – is quite different from 'poetic license' which is often associated with the word 'creativity' by the general public. The latter is normally associated with literature and poetry, e.g.

(8) Creativity in poetry
"Day creeps down. The moon is creeping up."
Wallace Stevens: 'The Man On The Dump';
The Collected Poems of Wallace Stevens (1974: 201)

The moon creeping up is fine, every day language. But the day creeping down is not. In the context of this poem it is just right. This is what I would say poetic license is all about.

In Carnatic music too I find examples of 'poetic license', i.e. sequences which are contrary to the definition of the raagam as per the scale (and grammar) and yet found in great compositions/great renderings (by general consensus).

(9) Musical demonstration
Sahaanaa scale I [⊙ 2.21]
Aaroohaɳam: ascending scale
sa ri gu ma pa ma di ni Sa
avaroohaɳam: descending scale
Sa (di) ni; di pa ma gu ma ri gu ri sa

In the avaroohaɳam only the niʃaadam (ni) is generally prolonged and never the daivatam (da). Yet in one of the greatest compositions in the raagam 'giripai nelakonna' by Tyaagaraajaa, the first line that announces the composition is as follows:

(10) Musical demonstration
Giripai I [⊙ 2.22]
// ; ni sa - ri, gu sa, / ni , nisa - , ni di ,
gi ri pai ne la

Notice that the lower 'di' is prolonged, contrary to the scale. Similarly the last half line of the pallavi is as follows:

(11) Musical demonstration
Giripai II [⊙ 2.23]
// Gu Gu, Ma Gu Ri Ri, GuRi - Sa, ni ni, Sa ni
/ di, di ni di pa, - gu gu, ma gu ri ri, ri, gi ri // sa,

Another fact of the raagam is that in the descent, from Sa, the practice is to render the prolonged niʃaadam as a quick glide from 'di'. But once again, contrary to common practice, in the phrase given above, the niʃaadam is rendered in a plain fashion on the note itself, of course for reasons of symmetry.

As in literature where one has to justify the act of poetic license, in music also one must find justification for the license. Here is my interpretation offered as justification for the 'transgression'. The composer begins the composition on a quiet phrase – just four notes used – but dramatic statement 'having seen Raamaa ON THE HILL' (the focused phrase in caps is the opening musical phrase of the composition) and ends the section on a half line which spans one and a half octaves conveying jubilation (at least for me).

As is the practice in literature, rules of language are bent/relaxed/violated for creating a 'literary' effect, i.e., for a stylistic purpose. The fact that these 'variants' are accepted and appreciated in poetry does not mean that one will find the occurrence of these variants in normal language use. Thus if I were to say "well, the day is creeping down, we'd better wind up." people will look strangely (or perhaps indulgently) at me. Similarly, in Carnatic music too, I find that these two instances of poetic license still remain on the periphery of the grammar of Sahaanaa raagam, in spite of their great beauty, as I would not (nor do many performers I have listened to) use these phrases or highlight them in creative, free renderings of the raagam – i.e., in aalaapanai (arhythmic exploration), taanam (semi-rhythmic exploration), niraval (rhythmic variations on a line of a composition) or kalpanaa swaram (rhythmic exploration tagged on to a line of a composition). Of course, the success or failure of instances of 'poetic license' is a matter of aesthetics and, perhaps, personal preference.

2.2.9. Duality of structure[20]

In language, sounds combine to form words and words combine to form phrases and phrases combine to form sentences and so on. Similarly, in mathematics and logic also we find bracketing conventions which decide the order in which symbols should be combined and interpreted. But, the communication system of bees lacks this structuring. We can argue for duality of structure in music in general. In music too, notes combine to form phrases which in turn combine to be interpreted as musical lines (see chapters 6 and 7 for details). But the actual number of levels of hierarchical structuring may be different in different musical systems. While in Western classical music and systems related to it, there seems to be a need for a number of levels of structuring (comparable to syntax in linguistics), in Carnatic music we require only three levels comparable to the level of the mora, the phonological word and intonational phrase. Perhaps in certain styles of Carnatic music there could be arguments to include a level of representation between the phrase and the line. But while the Carnatic music representation requires only a three (or at most four) levels of flat structuring (i.e., with no internal hierarchical structure), theorists of Western music have argued for the need for an enriched structure. Thus, while Carnatic music seems to be satisfied with the limited structuring at the phonological/phonetic levels, Western Classical music seems to work from the syntactic end. Whether this is the result of a bias (syntactic/phonological) or a genuine issue in Universal musicology remains to be actively debated.

I will illustrate the importance of phrasing in Carnatic Music once again with an example from phrasing in Sahaanaa raagam.

(12) Musical demonstration
Sahaanaa II [⊙ 2.24]
aaroohaṇam ascending scale
ni sa ri gu ma pa di ni Sa
Phrasing A: [ni sa] [ri gu ma pa][di ni Sa]
Phrasing B: ni *[sa ri gu ma][pa di ni Sa]

Whereas phrasing A is grammatical, phrasing B with sa and pa initiating musical phrases is not.[21] Phrasal left boundaries are signaled by 'prominent' rendering of a note. For instance, when rendered on the veena, the plucking for 'sa' , if any, would be lighter than that for 'ri' signaling the beginning of a phrase boundary. Thus we see that structuring is imposed on notes at least at two levels, vindicating our stand that music admits duality of structure.

A logical consequence of a system having duality of structure is the trait 'structure dependence'. In informal terms, an element 'x' is interpreted depending on its occurrence as part of a larger structure. It is a well-known fact that in language some elements are variably interpreted depending on their occurrence in the larger structure. For example the pronoun 'he' is interpreted differently in the following sentences.

(13) a. Ram$_i$ promised his father that he$_i$ would not marry Siita.
b. Ram explained to Mohan$_i$ why he$_i$ should not marry Siita.

Whereas in (13a) 'he' cannot refer to its nearest preceding Noun Phrase 'his father' but only to the Noun Phrase 'Ram', in (13b) 'he' may, in fact, refer to the nearest Noun Phrase 'Mohan'.[22]

This characteristic structure dependence is exemplified in Carnatic music too. I demonstrate in chapter 5 how the same pitch value, say x, is interpreted as note 'a' in one structure and as note 'b' in another structure where the structures are comparable, i.e. minimally distinct. In the sequences [a t x T..] and [b t x T..], the distinct initiating pitch value 'a' in one case and 'b' in the other case, forces the variable reading of 'x' in the musical phrase. This is surely an instance of structure dependence. (see p. 144, chapter 5).

2.2.10. Displacement

This misleading title merely implies that one can use language to talk about events other than the present and objects other than real. In short, I can tell a story, talk about history, imagine a future world scenario or tell plain lies. Displacement is possible in neither mathematics nor logic. Nor is it evidenced in child language, for instance. Babies cannot even refer to objects which are not present in their physical vicinity and cannot talk about events in the past (Vihman 1996). It is not found in music either.[23] The reason is that music is not referential. It does not refer to objects/events in the real world. It could be argued that one can paint 'tone pictures' using music and mimic the outside world at times. However, since music is not referential and is not bound by truth conditions, there is no question of music exhibiting the feature of displacement (see Mukherjee for a discussion of 'reference' in music and see chapter 6 p. 144–145 for further discussion). I summarize below my assumptions regarding design features in the form of a tableau illustrating the features that language and music share to the exclusion of other communication systems. Thus we see that music (like child language) differs from language only in lacking one feature, i.e., displacement. We saw how this difference stems from the fact that, unlike language, music (like child language) is not referential. The design features that language shares with music is, perhaps, true for all systems of music.

Table 1. Summary of features shared by music with other symbolic systems

Features	Language	Music	Maths	Bee
Species Specificity	✓	✓	✓	✓
Cultural Transmission	✓	✓	✓	✓
Specialization	?	?	?	✓
Medium of Transmission	A & V	A & V?	A & V	V
Arbitrariness	✓	✓ (Carnatic music in particular)	*	✓
Discreteness	✓	✓	✓	*
Open ended	✓	✓	*	*
Creativity	✓	✓	*	!
Duality of Structure	✓	✓	✓	*
Displacement	✓	*	*	*

2.3. Other language-like features of Carnatic music

However, unlike the design features which may be shared by all systems of music, there are certain language-like characteristics of Carnatic Music which may not be attested in all systems of music. I am far from dogmatic about this language-like characteristic of Carnatic music being unique to it. It may very well turn out that other musical systems may also attest these properties, at least partially. Having shown which design features (Carnatic) music shares with language, I turn to another feature of language which is characteristic of Carnatic music, namely change/variation in the course of time and variation across users. An undeniable fact of language is variation over a period of time (diachronic) as well as a point of time (synchronic). Unquestionably, the language of an earlier time is quite different from the language we use today and the difference could be due to change/loss of a sound, how words are constructed and how sentences are constructed. I will stick to simple examples of diachronic sound change. Old English had the sound 'x' (pronounced like the last sound of the German word 'Bach'; a voiceless, velar fricative; informally, a voiceless sound with friction pronounced at the back of the mouth) in a word like 'night' literally pronounced 'nixt' this sound was lost in Middle English and the last sound in words like 'garage', 'rouge' did not exist in English but was 'imported' into the language around Chaucer's time from French. So it is clear, that sounds can be lost or added across time in a language.

In Carnatic music too, I find instances of loss and addition/creation. Raagas like Balahamsaa and Ghaṇṭa which were in vogue in the time of Tyaagaraajaa and Muttuswaami Diikshitar who had composed in these raagas are no longer in vogue today and as for the latter, even well-read musicians[24] of today are not sure how it should be rendered. The converse of loss is addition. For instance, popular raagas of today like Kalyaaṇi and Karaharapriyaa did not exist in the sixteenth century, at the time of Veenkaṭamakhi. As I mentioned in passing earlier, many composers have created new scales which have been accepted as raagas by musicians generally. Here are few examples of successful raagas along with the names of the composers who created them.

(14) Musical demonstration

a. Bahudaari Tyaagaraajaa [⊙ 2.25]

sa gu ma pa di ni Sa

Sa ni pa ma gu sa

b. Rudrapriyaa Muttuswaami Diikshitar [⊙ 2.26]
sa ri gi ma pa di ni Sa
Sa ni pa ma gi ri sa

c. Cintaamaɳi Shyaamaa Shaastri [⊙ 2.27]
sa gi mi pa di ni Sa
Sa ni, da pa mi gi ri gi sa

d. Kadanakuduuhalam Paʈɳam Subramaɳya Ayyar (1845–1902) [⊙ 2.28]
sa ri ma di nu gu pa Sa
Sa nu di pa ma gu ri sa

The list above is not comprehensive either with respect to the sheer number of new raagas created or the composers who created them.

Another possibility is for a word to change its pronunciation, ever so slightly, across time. In the time of Chaucer, the last syllable in the word 'divine' would have rhymed with the word 'seen' (as it is pronounced today); but in Modern English it rhymes not with 'seen' but with 'fine'. Similarly, raagas also change over time. Kaapi raagam did not admit the use of the note 'gu' (E) for Tyaagaraajaa and Muttuswaami Diikshitar. But a very popular twentieth century composition in this raagam begins on that very note. The composition is 'enna tavam seidanai' by Paapanaasam Shivan.

(15) Musical demonstration
'enna tavam seidanai' [⊙ 2.29]
by Paapanaasam Shivan.

// ; , gu - , ma pa, / ma gi gi,, sa - ri; nu //
en na ta vam sei da
sa,; - ; sa, / ri gi ri gi - sa ri;
nai ya shoo daa

Another example of a raagam which has changed, rather dramatically, over time, is Gauɭipantu. It was once a janya of Maayaamaaɭavagauɭa with suddha madhyamam (F); but now, for many performers it is a janya of Pantuvaraaɭi with a prati madhayam (F sharp). The dialect boundaries of the two varieties of Gauɭipantu raagam are pretty fuzzy with the same performer rendering it as a janya of Maayaamaaɭavagauɭa for rendering compositions of Muttuswaami Diikshitar and Ksheetragnya but as a janya of Pantuvaraaɭi for rendering compositions of Tyaagaraajaa. Perhaps, in a few decades from now, one of them will win over the other.

(16) Musical demonstration
Gauḷipantu I [⊙ 2.30]
as a janya of Maayaamaaḷavagauḷa
sa ra ma pa nu Sa
Sa nu pa da ma gu ra sa
For Muttuswaami Diikshitar and Ksheetragnya
Gauḷipantu II [⊙ 2.31]
as a janya of Pantuvaraaḷi
Sa ra pa mi pa nu Sa Ra Sa
Sa nu pa da mi gu ra sa
For Tyaagaraajaa

So, we see that raagas can be lost, created or may change over time. I now turn to variation at a point of time. It is a well accepted fact that languages admit of variation across geographical regions, social groups and the degree of formality of the occasion. While the first two types of variations are called dialects, the last one is called 'register'. I will illustrate all the types of variation with examples from English. All of us are aware that standard British and standard American English sound different, don't we? Similarly, all of us know that people of different social strata speak differently from one another. Closer home, we all know that every region has its own variety of the language and, in India, we can identify the caste of the speaker from her/his language. Finally, the language we use on formal occasions like radio talk/lecture is quite different from the language we use among friends, at home etc. For instance, we are more likely to use the phrase 'old man' for 'Prime Minister' in the latter context rather than the former.

The central point that I wish to make in this book is that, Carnatic music too admits, synchronic dialectal variation just like language. Let us use the broad term 'South Indian Music' to subsume all the varieties/styles of Carnatic music and classical based film music, represented below schematically.

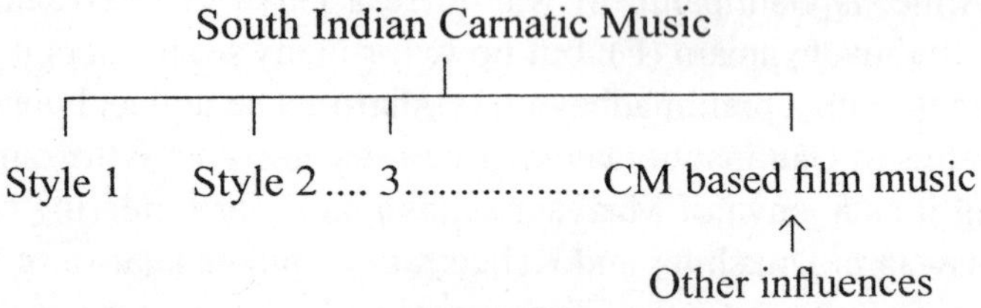

Figure 2.

All of us who are familiar with Carnatic music will agree that there are distinct styles of music, e.g. Veena Dhanam, G.N. Balasubramanian, Ariyakkudi Ramanuja Ayyangar, Musiri Subramanya Iyer, Maharajapuram Vishwanatha Iyer, T.R. Mahalingam, T.N. Rajaratnam Pillay, M.D. Ramanathan, Ramnad Krishnan, Madurai Mani Iyer, T. Brinda, M.S. Subbulakshmi, D.K. Pattamal and I can go on. In the line drawing above, I do not intend any linear precedence between styles meaning style 1 is closer to the 'standard' and style N is closer to film music, etc.

I argue that differences in styles arise from the interaction of two families of well-formedness requirements, one internal to the grammar of Carnatic Music and the other external to the grammar and governed by performance factors. The well-formedness requirement type internal to the grammar is composed of two constraint schemas mutually contradictory implying that either one set of constraints can be satisfied at the cost of the other. Thus differences in the grammars of different styles/dialects of Carnatic music arise from different interactions between two, contradictory well-formedness requirements, namely 'Be Faithful to the Lexicon' (FAITHLEX for short) where musical lines, musical phrases and pitch realizations of notes of raagas are listed like words in a mental dictionary and the performer is required to be faithful to the entry in the lexicon and 'Render as Scale' (RENSCALE for short) which is a markedness requirement which says that 'gamakkas' – the use of inter-tonal frequencies called 'microtones' 'ʃruti' is best avoided (as they are more difficult to render/perceive).

Be Faithful to the Lexicon henceforth FAITHLEX places a great burden on faithfulness to received texts. Rendering of any type of composition – be it free rendering or the rendering of a set piece is strictly governed by the phrases and idioms set down in the lexicon of that particular raagam. The extreme case is that of a well-known musician of yester years who said in an interview that she/he would get the permission of her/his 'guru' even to add a sangati to a composition. Surely this is an extreme view most performers of Carnatic music would not subscribe to. However, even in this case, in actual practice, it is far from clear how exactly similar his/her rendering was to that of his/her guru. As in language, in Carnatic music too, no two renderings can be exactly the same in principle. They can at best be close approximations to an idealized norm. For instance, if we do an instrumental analysis of the vowel /i/ pronounced twice, we will see that there are ever so many minor differences (many of which are not even perceptible to the naked ear) between the two renderings. This applies to all acts of repetition, in principle. It is in the nature of all organic elements in nature to be incapable of rendering exact (xerox) copies. In fact, it is this inability to make exact copies that constitutes the core of evolution and change in all things organic. Leaving aside this issue as technical quibbling, let us assume that FAITHLEX is, in fact, a desire to replicate, which is a kind of orthodoxy which ensures that a tradition is preserved, kept alive in a 'pure and unchanging' manner. Now that it is clear that FAITHLEX is a principle of orthodoxy, we can deduce that it naturally restricts the freedom of the individual. So many possibilities are denied as they are not sanctioned by the Lexicon. It is not unreasonable to assume that the requirement to be faithful requires more effort.

Let me illustrate the point with an analogy. Assume there is a faithfulness requirement in the lexicon of orthodox practices requiring the use of the right hand for serving food to oneself and others (this may not come as a surprise to many Indian readers). Then, while one is eating, in the Indian context with the fingers rather than a spoon or fork and knife etc., if one wants to take a second helping, one would have to stop eating, wash one's hand, take a second helping with the right hand and then resume eating. However, given the fact that all of us would like to expend as little energy as possible, the easiest way to take a second helping would be to use the left hand, violating the faithfulness requirement (and take a snipe at orthodoxy). Thus, in principle, faithfulness requirements are energy intensive and therefore, undesirable.

On the other hand, the well-formedness requirement RENSCALE requires that one avoid microtonal frequencies as they are more effortful, since microtonal targets require greater precision in order to avoid either under achievement or over shooting the target. RENSCALE frees one from cultural baggage, allowing one to render any sequence of notes that scalar definitions allow. Listen to the demonstration below:

(17) Musical demonstration
Moohanam scalar and microtonal [⊙ 4.56][25]
The phrase pa di Sa di pa
a. Scalar rendering
b. Microtonal rendering

It should be obvious to all listeners of Carnatic music that neither version is to be condemned nor does one find one of them to the exclusion of the other in any style of Carnatic music. In fact, both types will be attested in most styles of rendering. It is fairly obvious that (17a) requires less effort than (17b). This is because, in the former, the peak target 'Sa' is well defined and easy to render. In the latter, it is attempted as a pitch curve from 'di' coming back to 'di' with the target 'Sa' never being attempted as a static pitch value. I am sure all beginners of Carnatic Music will agree with this observation as, at that stage, they are conscious of the effort that they put in for rendering a musical phrase long before specific practices are internalized when they cease to appear to be effortful.

Styles in Carnatic music are differentiated normally not by the absence of any one type but by the frequency of usage of a particular type in a musical discourse. If the RenScale type is predominant then the style is characterized as a 'light' style and if the pitch curve type is predominant then the style may be considered 'heavy', 'orthodox' or 'ultra orthodox'.

I said that the two sets of constraints, namely FAITHLEX and RENSCALE are internal to the grammar of Carnatic Music. By 'internal' I meant forces which shape the grammar. Let me illustrate the point with Deevamanoohari raagam.

(18) Musical demonstration
Deevamanoohari [⊙ 2.32]
Aaroohaṇam: sa ri ma pa di **ni** Sa
Avaroohaṇam: Sa ni di ni pa ma ri sa
FAITHLEX: In the ascent ni (the bold ni) is rendered as a pitch wave with di as the starting point and the target a little higher than ni as peak and coming back to di
Rendering of a musical line:
// ri, ri, ma, ma, **ni, ni,** Ri Ri, // Sa ni di ni pa ma ri sa //

The 'ni' in bold in the musical line is rendered as RenScale violating FAITHLEX in one style of singing. In fact, RenScale rendering of 'ni' in the Aaroohaṇam is quite contrary to the grammar of the raagam, though RenScale ni is allowed in the Avaroohaṇam.[26] Thus we see that RENSCALE violations crucially determine grammaticality and is therefore grammar-internal. But if one assumes that I meant the musical line to be ungrammatical, one has not really understood the point. It is ungrammatical for me. But, apparently, for the musician who rendered this line it is perfectly grammatical. The point I am trying to make is that variation in styles create different grammars. Each style is legitimate if it has a following (a set of practitioners and listeners) and therefore there is no question of any super-ordinate authority judging it to be *ungrammatical as Carnatic music*. It must now be clear why I claim that these two sets of constraints are internal to the grammar. They are critical in shaping the grammar of a raagam.

As opposed to these two sets of constraints which are grammar-internal, we also have two sets of constraints which are performance oriented and hence external to the grammar of Carnatic Music. I talk about them here briefly as they play a role in defining styles of music. Moreover, I do not deny the possibility of these constraints defining the ranking of the two sets of grammar-internal constraints as I will show below how the external constraints can sometimes determine the ranking of the internal constraints.

To begin with, the two sets of constraints I have in mind are Performance Style henceforth PERFSTYLE and Suit the Music to the Medium henceforth MUSMED[27]. The former set of constraints, i.e. PERFSTYLE, encompasses all aspects of music that concern the image of the performer. For example, if a performer would like to address a large audience, he/she would have to suit his/her style accordingly. The various, by no means, exhaustive constraints that one can envisage are constraints like BEFASTPACED, BEFLUENT, BEMETICULOUS, BEORTHODOX, BEACADEMIC (!), etc. Almost independent of what one would like to be there is another factor which determines music style. That is the innate capacity of the musician and his/her medium, namely voice or instrument. The second set of performance constraints, i.e. MUSMED, deals with this issue. If one has an intractable voice, if one cannot render fast passages, if one's voice/instrumental technique does not allow for indulgence in gamakkam, if one cannot hold the breath long enough to render long musical passages etc. then one's style will be shaped by these constraints related to the medium. Music being a performing art, it is natural that performance factors should mould grammar-internal considerations. In language, the grammar of no variety seems to be determined by performance factors, e.g. the length of a sentence, the quality of voice, the degree of nervousness of the speaker, etc. Thus in Carnatic Music we see that a style is determined by two sets of internal and two sets of external constraints, which are not, perhaps, mutually totally independent. This configuration may be schematically represented as shown below:

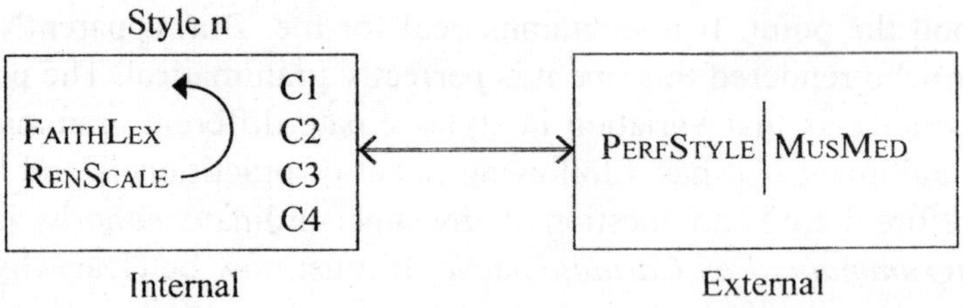

Figure 3.

I assume that the internal set is responsible for directly shaping the grammar and the other, namely the external set may influence the internal set and also be shaped by the grammar-internal set. This is perhaps a major departure from the architecture of the grammar of language where performance factors are not supposed to determine grammar-internal factors to this extent.

However, even in linguistics, the picture has changed considerably in recent years where functional/pragmatic factors have been shown to influence language structure in significant ways.[28] For instance, allowing markedness constraints to shape the grammar is, in effect, being shaped by performance factors like ease of articulation/perception etc. Thus, whereas in standard linguistics of the eighties functional/pragmatic factors did not seem to directly influence the grammar, in newer models of linguistics, specially Optimality Theory developed in the nineties, the thinking has changed radically and the model we have proposed for styles in Carnatic music may not be so very different from some current models of phonology for instance.[29]

Turning to the content of the grammar, once again we see that the grammar of language and the grammar of Carnatic music may not be all that different either. In fact, the claim in one of the current models of linguistics, namely Optimality Theory mentioned above is that the grammar is made up of the family of faithfulness constraints and the family of markedness constraints and the function of the grammar of a language is to determine the ranking of these family of constraints (but more of this in the following chapter). The question that needs to be asked now is:

"If Carnatic music and language are very similar symbolic systems with similarity in approach as well as content, is the architecture of the grammar of Carnatic music similar to that of language?"

I provide a simple, straightforward answer to this question: "Yes, the architecture of the grammar of Carnatic music is no different from that of language."

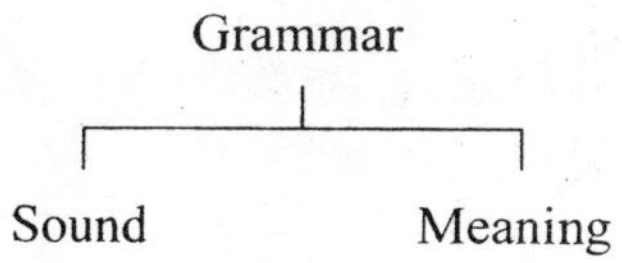

Figure 4.

The basic assumption in linguistics is that it is the function of the grammar of a language to mediate between 'sound' on the one hand and 'meaning' on the other and explain the way speakers/listeners relate the two in systematic ways. The diagram above schematizes this assumption.

Notice that this model is neutral to production and perception of the symbolic system. I show in chapters 4–7 that the grammar of Carnatic music too requires 'sound' and 'meaning' to be interpreted as in language and thus the architecture of both systems is comparable. I have just shown that it is possible to characterize the sets of output Wellformedness requirements for Carnatic music into types of constraints that have been motivated for language, namely faithfulness constraints and markedness constraints and that like the grammar of language, the only function of the grammar of Carnatic music is to rank the requirements in order of priority to account for variation across styles.

However, the only difference between the grammar of language and the grammar of Carnatic music lies in the specific Wellformedness requirements that go into the grammars. This is hardly surprising since the 'primitives' of the two systems are so widely different. Whereas language uses consonants, vowels, prefixes, stems, suffixes, verbs, nouns, etc. as its substantives, (Carnatic) music uses tones (pure, complex and tonal ranges) along with loudness as one of the parameters for phrasing/rhythm as its substantives. Thus while the overall architecture of both systems are the same, the objects that are under consideration in the two systems are different. This is by no means stating the obvious, as we will see in chapters 4, 5 and 6, 7 respectively, the need for interpretation of sound and the issue of meaning are both contentious with respect to (Carnatic) music.

In chapter 3 I give a brief outline of the specific model of linguistic theory that I employ in my description of the grammar of Carnatic music.

Chapter 3
Issues in modeling the grammar: Language and Carnatic music

3.1. Introduction

The word 'grammar' invokes, for most people, terrifying rules which are difficult to remember and which if violated would set off the wrath of the teacher with a scale or a cane or at least a threatening red pencil ready at hand. I will, in this, section outline three major options which have been adopted by linguists to explain the regularities that are observed in languages. This discussion on the grammar of language and the preferred model that explains language behaviour leads to issues in modeling the grammar of Carnatic music.

Let me start with a brief discussion of two types of 'grammars' and which one linguists prefer. There are broadly two types of grammars, prescriptive and descriptive. While the former 'dictates' what the user should and should not do and is used primarily in learning/teaching situations (their use has been called into question by theories of pedagogy and language learning), the latter is mainly the concern of linguists. While the former lays down rules the user should follow, usually from the perspective of the standard variety of the language, e.g. 'do not split the infinitive': *'to immediately go...', descriptive grammar says, contrary to popular opinion, people do split their infinitives very often and thus we find instances of 'to immediately go' along with 'immediately to go' and 'to go immediately'. The former is judgemental taking as its data only the usage attested by 'established users', the latter merely describes the usage that is attested by consensus in a more or less homogenous speech community. Only the latter is of interest to linguists.

As generative linguistics is a part of the cognitive paradigm, it tries to explain the mental constructs which explain language behaviour, i.e. speech and perception. It is interested not in language pedagogy but in the language faculty in humans (see Chomsky (1993))[30]. The ultimate question that linguists would like to answer is:

"How is it that children the world over manage to learn their first language so efficiently and in so short a span of time given minimal and impoverished language input?"

All of us would agree that parents and child minders provide meager language data and pay too little attention to language data while raising children and yet children the world over manage to master their first language very efficiently in the first few years of their life. Parents pay very little attention to language errors, unlike teachers, as they are more preoccupied with the child's social and behavioural traits than with language errors. Yet, every normal child succeeds in picking up all the rudimentary facts of her/his language by the time she/he is three years old.[31] This indeed is a miracle. Linguists claim that this miracle is made possible by the neural wiring of the child. They claim that the human child is programmed to acquire language because of what they call the 'Language Acquisition Device' (LAD of Chomsky). They claim that the child does not, in fact, require lots of data to fix a particular trait of a language. For instance, a few sentences from the adult is enough to fix the word order parameter, e.g. whether the order in a verb phrase is [noun phrase – verb] as in most Indian languages, e.g. [pustaham paḍiccẽẽ] 'book read (1st singular)'] or [verb – noun phrase] as in English, e.g. 'read a book' Children, they claim, look out for minimal, positive evidence for fixing the details of the grammar of their language.[32] To take another example, children look out for words like 'split', 'spring' to fix the consonantal beginning of syllables in English, i.e. words can start with 's [voiceless stop] l/r' but not *'s [voiced stop] l/r' producing a sequence like *sbring etc. It is another matter that they actually manage to pronounce full phrases and these three consonantal clusters only much later. Their performance lags far behind their knowledge, i.e. their competence. Recent research in the perception of speech sounds by infants support the claim that perception is far ahead of performance.[33] Therefore the empirically provable claim in modern linguistics is that children do manage to acquire the mental representation of their language (be it segments, words or word order etc.) with minimal, positive evidence and this is enabled by their mental pre-wiring for language. This being the case, the main concern of modern linguistics is to discover the principles that are at work universally in all languages which is what the neural wiring is all about. The thinking in modern linguistic circles is that languages differ widely one from the other mainly because of the differences in their vocabularies and that, in fact, vocabulary excluded, languages tend to have a lot in common and do not differ from one another that widely.

The corollary to this statement is that languages have a fairly limited set of options to choose from. For instance, all languages must have nouns and verbs though the other categories may be missing in many languages. At the phonetic end, given the articulatory apparatus, the possible sounds that a human can produce is a constant across the human species.[34] The function of the grammar of a language is to make a selection from this limited inventory of options. Take vowels, for instance. The two options available to humans is to use the front of the tongue or the part behind this section of the tongue called the 'back of the tongue' to produce vowels.[35] Once again, while using these two parts of the tongue, there are two options, namely either to advance the tongue root or not to advance it. In typical native speaker styles of English, while pronouncing the vowels in the words 'beat' and 'boot', the tongue root is advanced, such an advancement of the tongue root is not evidenced in the pronunciation of the vowels in the words 'bit' and 'put'. Assuming that the tongue is raised maximally towards the roof of the mouth in producing the former set of words and it is lowered maximally in words like 'cat' and 'cart', we have, in a rough and ready fashion, defined the maximal vowel space that is available for exploitation in languages. All the vowels produced in all the languages must lie within this vowel space. That is not the end of the story. We need to explain how languages construct an inventory from this universal set. A random theory of language variation would predict that languages are free to select any vowel from this universal set. But, a cursory look at different languages is enough to falsify this theory. For instance, it will not explain why all languages choose the vowels /i, a, u/ (or near equivalents of these). Random selection would predict that a simple five vowel system can be any of the three sets (i) i, e, a, o, u (possible/attested), (ii) i, ɪ, e, ɛ, æ (all front vowels: not attested) or (iii) u, ʊ, o, ɔ:, ɔ[36] (all back vowels: not attested). A theory which permits random selection of vowels from the vowel space cannot explain why (ii) and (iii) are unattested. I will take up further issues in the relation between Universal Grammar (UG) and individual grammars in the following sections. In other words, languages cannot vary as widely as the random theory of language variation would predict. Take the example of sentence formation. For example, while the sentence of English "The tense young man expected his wife to write to him." is perfectly fine, we do not expect to find a language like English whose word order is the mirror image of English, e.g. *"him to write to wife his expected man young tense the". Had variation been random across languages, there is no reason why we should not find a language with the word order as in the latter sentence.

The assumption in generative linguistic circles is that variation across language is strictly controlled by Universal Grammar (UG) which fixes languages in a limited number of ways. In spite of this strong assumption in modern linguistics, we have at least roughly three positions regarding language data and variation and how to deal with it. I shall outline the three positions in the following sections. I shall demonstrate the three positions, namely 'the rule based grammar approach' (3.2), 'the parameter setting approach' (3.3) and 'the ranked universal constraints approach' (3.4), and argue that the last is the best option to deal with language. Naturally, this is the model of grammar that inspires the model of grammar for describing Carnatic music in this book. Since the aim of this discussion is not to describe a full-fledged theory of language but to enable the lay reader to compare the broad outlines of the models of grammar of language and Carnatic music, I shall restrict the language data invoked in these sub-sections.

3.2. Rule based approach to grammar

All of us understand what is meant by 'rule based approach to grammar' as that is what we have been raised on – rules of grammar. Now, if grammars were just made up of rules – any set of rules – it is expected that languages could vary in unpredictable ways. Take the case of word order within the noun phrase. A rule based approach can, in principle, write a rule stipulating any word order within the noun phrase. But certain possibilities are systematically unexploited in human language.

(1) Word Order in the Noun Phrase
Determiner (Det), Adjective (Adj) and Noun (N)

a.	Det Adj N	'the pretty girl'	[English]
b.	Det N Adj		[French]
c.	N Adj Det		[Tangkhul Naga]
d.	*Adj Det N		
e.	*N Det Adj		

A rule based account of grammar, which is clearly stipulative, cannot rule out the non-occurring sequences in (1d) and (e) in a principled fashion.

Take the further example from phonology. Consider the vowel types and the languages in which they are attested in (2). While there are languages which select a basic five vowel inventory (2a) and there are languages which select a minimal three vowel inventory (2b), there is no language which selects an arbitrary three vowel inventory as in (2c–f) or any language which selects only the mid vowels (2c). Obviously the choice of vowels is not random but governed by some universal principle. Thus the rule based account of grammar makes the obviously wrong prediction about the ways in which languages can differ from one another.

(2) Segment Inventory

a.	i, e, a , o , u	Tamil, etc.
b.	i, a, u	Standard Arabic
c.	*e, o	
d.	*i, e , u	
e.	*u, o, a	
f.	*i, o, a	

Take yet another example of the wrongness of the rule based approach to grammar. Take the Sanskrit words [niveeda] ~ [naiveedya] 'offering to god'. One can write a rule as shown below:

(3) $\emptyset \rightarrow a$ / # C_0 _ i

and

(4) $\emptyset \rightarrow y$ / C_ a #

Informally, insert the vowel /a/ after the first consonant (if present or a consonant cluster if attested) and insert the glide /y/ after the last consonant in a word.

It is true that these two rules account for a lot of data in Sanskrit and are descriptively adequate. But the moment we write such rules, we must recognize that languages may admit rules which insert vowels and glides elsewhere within the word, not just before the first vowel and before the last vowel. But such rules have not been attested in any language. In other words, we do come across languages where a vowel is inserted precisely after the second consonant and a glide after the penult consonant in a word, though such rules are conceivable given the format of rules (3) and (4). This means that the rule writing system is too powerful in that it predicts language types which are never attested. Thus we see that the 'rule based account' of grammar is not really a very satisfactory system in that it predicts a random set of languages not attested till date. Be it the domain of word order, selection of segments or accounting for systematic derivation in languages, the rule based system allows systems which are not attested. This is the reason why modern linguistics has given up the notion of 'a rule of grammar'.

3.3. Parametric approach to grammar

Getting back to the question of the absence of languages which select only mid vowels as in (2c), one can predict the phenomenon provided one adds the notion of markedness to grammar. Markedness is a measure of complexity of a construct from the production and the perception[37] points of view. Informally speaking, producing the vowels /i, u, a/ is relatively easy because the tongue has to be raised or lowered to the maximum possible extent. Perceptually too, the difference in the acoustic patterns of the three vowels is the maximum (if you consider their spectrographic patterns). However, when we turn to the mid vowels, we find that they are not so easily definable as they may admit many possibilities, e.g. consider the difference in tongue height in the starting point of the vowels in the words 'get' and 'gate' for native speaker of English. Thus we can come to the conclusion that mid vowels are more marked than high or low vowels. Another measure of markedness is the frequency of occurrence across languages. While all languages select /i, a, u/ not all languages select /e, o/. Thus we see that the notion '*marked*' *is defined in terms of inherent complexity and it also has statistical backing.* We can now derive the theorem which is an implicational universal stated as shown below. This principle can be applied productively in predicting different phenomena in grammars. The examples below are from phonology.

(5) Implicational Universal and Markedness

$M_j \rightarrow M_i$ (where j >> i)
(The selection of a more marked element implies the selection of a less marked element (but not vice versa)).

a. Languages which select mid vowels also select the high and low vowels. [All systems which select /e, o/ also select /i, a, u/, but the converse of this is not true as there are languages which select /i, a, u/ but not /e, o/.]
b. Languages which select /b^h/ also select /p^h/, e.g. Sanskrit, Hindi (but never only /b^h/ and not /p^h/).
c. Languages which select /ɨ/, the unrounded, high back vowel also select /u/, the back rounded high vowel. [Tamil and Ao select both vowels but languages like Hindi and Malayalam select only the latter and not the former; and there is no language which selects only the former and not the latter.]

d. Languages which have closed syllables CVC also attest the open syllables CV, but not vice versa.

Similar implicational statements can be framed in the area of word formation, syntax etc. Armed with the notion of markedness and the derived statements of implicational universals we can, to a large extent, constrain the rule types that we allow in language. But markedness comes in two versions, namely context free and context sensitive versions. In other words, while certain elements are marked in themselves, certain elements are more marked in certain contexts than others. Let me illustrate the point with a few suitable examples. While context free markedness statements are of the type *X (an element X is marked), context sensitive markedness statements are of the type *%A-X (an element X is marked in the context of A (occurring either before or after; '%' standing for mirror image).

(6) Context free and context sensitive markedness

a. *Nasal Vowel
(Context free) [nasal vowels are difficult to produce]
b. *Nasal-Oral Vowel
(Context sensitive) [oral vowels are difficult to produce after nasal consonants]
c. *Obs.voice
(Context free) [producing a voiced obstruent (b, d, g, etc.) is more difficult than producing a voiceless obstruent (p, t, k. etc.)]
d. *V-Obs.voiceless-V
(Context sensitive) [producing a voiceless obstruent between vowels is more difficult than producing a voiced obstruent]
e. *Nasal-Obs.voiceless
(Context sensitive) [producing a voiceless obstruent after a nasal consonant is more difficult than producing a voiced one][38]

(7) Rule types

a. [obstruent] → [–voice] / __ #
Obstruents become voiceless at the end of words, e.g. Dutch, German

*b. [obstruent] → [+voice] / __ #
Obstruents become voiced word finally. This is contrary to the markedness principle, unattested in any language and hence not a possible rule of language.

c. [obstruent] → [+voice] / V __ V
Obstruents become voiced intervocalically, e.g. literary Tamil, Malayalam.

*d. [obstruent] → [–voice] / V __ V
Obstruents lose their voice between vowels. This is contrary to the markedness principle, not attested in any language and hence not a possible rule of language.

These markedness statements help us discard certain rule types as unattested and hence undesirable. Notice that the supposedly unattested cases do not rule out languages which allow both values of the feature in specific contexts. For instance, English allows voiced and voiceless obstruents at the end of a word, e.g. 'bag' and 'back'. Similarly, English allows both types of obstruents between vowels, e.g. 'repel' and 'rebel'. All this means is that English does not select rules (7a) and (c) and that the English speaking people have learnt to overcome the markedness factor with respect to obstruents through practice. But the fact remains that there is no language which selects rules like (7b) and (d) systematically selecting the more marked segment in specific contexts.[39]

A serious drawback for the rule based approach which incorporates markedness as an evaluative device is that the grammar may make wrong predictions. Though it may be able to rule out certain rules as contrary to principles of markedness, it will also rule out certain rules attested in natural languages as it does not have the power to do an overall evaluation of the phonotactics of the language output to allow for certain types of rules.

Consider the case of Tamil where the vowels /u/ and /ɨ/ are in complementary distribution,[40] while the former occurs in stressed, initial[41] syllables, the latter occurs elsewhere as the data in (8) show.

(8) Distribution of /u/ and /ɨ/ in Tamil

a.	i. kuḍɨ	'give'	ii. *kuḍu/*kɨḍu
b.	i. irɨ	'be'	ii. *iru
c.	i. vahɨ	'divide'	ii. *vahu
d.	i. kurɨḍɨ	'blind person'	ii. *kuruḍu
e.	i. mudɨhɨ	'back'	ii. *muduhu

We find that the unrounding rule affects the unstressed syllables (assuming that stress is on the first syllable in these words). We can write a rule to describe the phenomenon as shown below:

(9) Unrounding rule

$$[V, +back, +high] \rightarrow [-round] \,/\, [\underset{-stress}{\_\_\_\_}]$$

But, by itself the vowel /ɨ/ is more marked than /u/ as it is more difficult to pronounce high back vowels which are unrounded than their rounded counterparts and the general prediction on markedness in the theory is that unstressed vowels will change from a marked to an unmarked value. Thus a theory which uses markedness only to evaluate a rule will automatically rule out a process like the one captured in (9) above. But there are two major objections to such a theory.

Firstly, a theory which employs markedness to evaluate isolated rules will be unable to do its job effectively. For the evaluation to be done effectively, the grammar will have to examine this process in the context of the overall phonotactics of vowels in the language. In the context of Tamil, taking into consideration only non-stressed syllables, we find that the only vowels which are attested there are /i, ɨ and ə/, i.e. all the vowels are [–low], and all of them are [–round] and /i, ɨ/ differ along only one parameter, i.e. /back/. The reduction of perceptual salience in unstressed syllables is a totally welcome feature and therefore to be expected. But this kind of evaluation is possible only in a grammar which assigns a central role to markedness and that too to output wellformedness. In fact, the loss of perceptual salience in unstressed syllables in Tamil is entirely in keeping with the phonetics and phonology of the language vis-à-vis reduction/deletion of unstressed vowels in the language. Therefore we see that the phonology-phonetics of Tamil is really a continuum; the process of reduction of perceptual salience started by the phonology continues in the phonetics in reduction, and ultimately, deletion of unstressed vowels. The phonology starts out with the demand that stressed vowels and unstressed vowels be maximally differentiated in terms of quality and quantity and the phonology-phonetics of the language makes sure that featural salience and durational salience are preferably reduced/deleted in unstressed vowels. Thus we see that the grammar must make markedness a central concern of the grammar and not a peripheral, evaluating device.

Secondly, the parametric approach to markedness splits the options available to languages into two, namely an unmarked option and a marked option. And the parametric approach stipulates that each grammar will make a definitive choice with respect to the marked or the unmarked parameter once and for all, and once the choice is made, the language is expected to behave consistently. This assumption is simply unworkable with respect to any language as languages simply do not live up to this assumption.

Consider this case, once again from Tamil. It is true that Tamil normally prefers a vowel in the word final position. In other words, Tamil prefers an open syllable at the end of words (whatever its preference word medially). Thus, English loans like 'shirt', 'blouse', 'card' etc. invariably end in the epenthetic vowel /ɨ/. However, consider the words which end in a sonorant consonant in Tamil. While the words in (10a) tolerate a variant with a final epenthetic /ɨ/, the words in (10b) clearly do not tolerate epenthesis.

(10) Vowel epenthesis in Tamil

a. paal ~ paalɨ 'milk' tuuɳ ~ tuuɳɨ 'pillar'

b. muyal ~ *muyalɨ 'rabbit' paraɳ ~ *paraɳɨ 'loft'

The point I am labouring to make is that the 'parameter' of vowel finality is not selected by Tamil once and for all. It is sometimes enforced strictly, sometimes it is the preferred option and sometimes it is turned off completely – the parameter of vowel finality is sought to be enforced in Tamil (in the context of final sonorants) in monosyllables but not elsewhere. Thus we see that parameters can be switched on and off in the same language because of pressure form higher level concerns – in this case the enforcement of a disyllabic word minimum. I will take up this issue for further discussion in the next section. Thus we see that the rule based account which adds markedness concerns as an additional, peripheral function where 'setting a parameter' is supposed to explain parametric variation across languages fails to account for the facts of language and must therefore be discarded.

3.4. Constraint based approach to grammar

I now turn to the last approach (an approach I am sympathetic to) which has markedness as its central concern. And markedness in this approach is not a pedantic concern (which is an afterthought) but a real *output* well-formedness concern. In other words, markedness plays a central role in this type of grammar as it is the driving force of the grammar. A few words about this radical departure from modern, standard linguistics are in order. For the first time, the concern in linguistics has turned away from cognitive representation (which is begging the question actually) to a plausible mental representation arrived at deductively from the various, possible surface representations. This constraint based approach was first initiated by Prince and Smolensky (1993) and McCarthy and Prince (1993) called 'Optimality Theory' (OT henceforth). The ideas that lead to OT had been brewing for a long time, namely the observation that the driving force of rules was output well-formedness with concern for reducing the overall markedness of sequences and the concern for explaining the functional unity of rules in a system. For instance, if a language does not like consonant clusters word finally, it may attest rules to delete one of the consonants and also rules to insert a vowel finally. Both rules share the function of reducing the markedness of the output vis-à-vis final coda clusters.

In this framework, the function of the grammar of a language is to mediate between faithfulness, i.e. concern to preserve the lexical specification and markedness, i.e. to reduce the markedness values of output sequences. Naturally, both sets of constraints can not succeed as they have a conflict of interest. The revolutionary idea that the grammar of language is the playground where the conflict between faithfulness and markedness is resolved through constraint ranking is attributable to OT. The idea that OT explores is that a marked value does not cease to be marked just because a language chooses to select it and that it can be constrained by other considerations, namely constraint ranking. The central assumption in OT is that all languages contain the same set of markedness constraints but the prioritization of certain constraints reduce the power of markedness constraints, at times rendering them almost invisible. Take the example of aspirates in Sanskrit, Bangla and Tamil. While Sanskrit allows aspirates everywhere in a word namely the onset and the coda as in /b^{h}akti/ 'religious fervour' and /shub^h/ 'auspicious', standard colloquial Bangla allows aspirates only in onsets, e.g. /d^{h}up/ 'incense stick' but not in codas, e.g. '/bag ~ bag^{h}er/ 'tiger (nominative – genitive)' and Tamil does not allow them at all. Thus we see that the markedness constraint *ASPIRATION[42] is ranked very low in Sanskrit and so aspirates surface everywhere; in Bangla, however, the faithfulness constraint which requires syllable beginnings to be faithfully pronounced ranks above the markedness constraint *ASPIRATION which bans aspirates and so only the aspirates in onsets are pronounced. The ranking IDENTIOSYLLABLELEFT[43] >> *ASPIRATION makes sure that only syllable initial aspirates will be pronounced in Bangla. Finally, in Tamil, the context free markedness constraint prohibiting aspirates is high ranked and so aspirates are never allowed.[44] Thus markedness constraints are presumed to be present in all languages but their relative ranking allows them to be pronounced in all contexts in some languages, in some contexts in some languages or not at all in other languages.[45] Ironically, in OT, we see that because of its commitment to constraint ranking, constraints are not obeyed in all outputs. In other words, a constraint can be violated if there is a higher ranked constraint which demands something else (obviously incompatible with this constraint), as ranking is the ultimate arbiter.

I will demonstrate how ranking can affect the status of a markedness constraint in OT vis-à-vis the markedness constraint *NoCoda which prohibits codas in syllables. While Hawaiian ranks the markedness constraint *NoCoda very high in its constraint inventory prohibiting codas everywhere, even in loan words, English allows codas everywhere as words like 'tem.per', 'chap.ter' etc. illustrate (syllable boundary being indicated by dots). However, a language like contemporary, colloquial Tamil has a very ambivalent attitude to codas. I take up four distinct contexts where the grammar of Tamil[46] reacts differently with respect to the coda.

Firstly, in words in the contemporary variety which may be deemed to be non-derived and hence labeled monomorphemic, we do find codas in non-final syllables as the data in (11) illustrate.

(11) Codas in Tamil non-final syllables

a.	an.bɨ	'love'	b.	kaṣ.ṭam	'difficulty'
c.	nat.pɨ	'friendship'	d.	iḍ.li	'a steamed dish'
e.	al.pam	'trivial'	f.	gar.bam	'pregnant'
f.	kay.di	'prisoner'	g.	mau.nam	'silence'

We see that non-final codas can be obstruents, nasals, liquids or glides, in short, just about any non-syllabic segment. So medial codas are fully licensed in Tamil. The markedness constraint *NoCoda is turned off morpheme internally, by the high-ranking faithfulness constraint Morpheme Linearity which makes sure that the linear sequence of segments within a morpheme (IdentInputOutput[IO]MorphLin) is not disrupted by epenthesis or deletion.

(12) Ranking (first approximation)
IdentIOMorphLin >> IdentIOC, DepV, *NoCoda

(13) Tableau for nat.pɨ

		IdentIOMorphLin	IdentIOC, DepV, *NoCoda
a.	natɨpɨ	*!	*
b.	napɨ	*!	*
c.	natɨ	*!	*
d.	nat.pɨ		*

The ranking of IdentIOMorphLin >> *NoCoda, IdentIOC (consonants in the input must not be deleted), DepV (no vowel should be inserted in the output) is demonstrated by the optimal ouput natpɨ (candidate d) which turns out to be better than either a) natɨpɨ (violating DepV) or b) napɨ (violating IdentIOC) or c) natɨ as all of them violate IdentIOMorphLin. Even though the optimal output violates *NoCoda, it does not violate the higher ranked IdentIOMorphLin.

However, word-finally, only vowels and sonorant consonants (nasals, /l/ and /r/ and the glide /y/ are allowed). But when we look at (14), we realize that Tamil has strict restrictions on which segments can occur word finally. Tamil allows only the three vowels /i, a and ɨ/ and the sonorant consonants /m, n, ɳ, l, ɭ, r, ʐ, and y/. Significantly, no obstruent coda is allowed. So when Tamil encounters loan words which end in obstruents, it adopts the strategy of vowel epenthesis, epenthesizing the vowel /ɨ/ as the data in (15) illustrate.

(14) Final codas in Tamil

a. paɖi 'step' b. paɖɨ 'lie down'
c. pala 'many' d. maram 'tree'[47]
e. paraɳ 'loft' f. varan 'match (marriage)'
g. kural 'voice'[48] h. kuraɭ 'a two line verse'
i. paravay 'bird' j. tamiʐ 'Tamil'

(15) Loans in Tamil phonology

a. Rameesh [rameeshɨ] b. Edith [eɖitɨ]
c. carrot [kæraʈɨ] d. cake [keekɨ]
e. life [laifɨ]

At the edge of words we have a total ban on obstruent codas. This can be captured by a markedness constraint *WORDFINALOBSTRUENT or *FINALOBS. This constraint is higher ranked than the constraint which allows vowel epenthesis, DEPV, and the actual vowel inserted is driven by the markedness values of vowels – /ɨ/ being the least marked of Tamil vowels.[49] Thus the constraint ranking *FINALOBS >> DEPV accounts for the epenthesis facts in loans in Tamil. The ranking of these two constraints can be integrated with the previous ranking as in (16) below. As *FINALOBS does not allow IDENTIOC to be violated (the strategy adopted is no consonant deletion), *FINALOBS cannot be ranked with IDENTIOC but is ranked higher than DEPV allowing epenthesis. It must be pointed out at this stage that *FINALOBS is really a proper subset of *NOCODA as the former bans a small set of consonants (obstruents) as codas while the latter bans codas altogether. Ranking logic dictates that all part-whole set relation must have the subset >> set ranking for the smaller set to be visible in the output.

(16) Ranking (revised)
IDENTIOMORPHLIN >> IDENTIOC, *FINALOBS >> *NOCODA >> DEPV

So far, we have seen two contexts where Tamil displays an indecisiveness with respect to codas. Morpheme internally it wholeheartedly allows codas thereby setting the parameter 'coda' just like English. But word finally it allows only a small subset of consonants to occur as codas thus partially selecting *NoCoda. This is by no means the end of the story.

Consider next the verb + suffix combination in (17) below.

(17) Tamil verb morphophonology

	Root + future suffix	output	Gloss
a.	toɖ + v	[toɖɨv]	touch
b.	puh + v	[puhɨv]	enter
c.	peeʃ + v	[peeʃɨv]	speak
d.	ʃol + v	[ʃolv]	tell
e.	koɭ + v	[koɭv]	have
f.	kol + v	[kolv]	kill
g.	malar + v	[malarv]	blossom

It will be noticed that morphemes (verb roots in this case) cannot end in obstruent codas and so /ɨ/ is epenthesized between the verb root and the suffix just in case the verb ends in an obstruent. If the verb ends in a sonorant consonant, however, just as in the case of the word final position, sonorant codas are tolerated even in this context.

Of course, epenthesis is not attested when the suffix begins with a vowel, e.g. /toɖ + a/ 'infinite'. Therefore we might want to rephrase the constraint *FINALOBS as *MORPHEMEFINALCODAOBSTRUENTS. In the case of /to.ɖ + a/, the morpheme final obstruent is not the coda of that syllable and hence does not invoke any violation. Since morpheme edge and word edge are co-extensive, this newly suggested constraint can handle both cases. But a better solution is to suggest a general ban on obstruent codas and let it be dominated by IDENTIOMORPHLIN. Since morpheme internal obstruent codas cannot be saved an *OBSCODA violation because of high ranking IDENTIOMORPHLIN, only morpheme final obstruents if they are likely to surface as codas are prevented from doing so by epenthesis. Therefore, (16) can be revised as (18).

(18) Ranking (re-revised)
IDENTIOMORPHLIN, IDENTIOC >> *OBSCODA >> *NOCODA >> DEPV

Finally, consider now the data pertaining to optional epenthesis in Tamil presented earlier as (10).

(19) Optional epenthesis in sonorant final words

A	a.	paal	~	paalɨ	'milk'
	b.	tuuɳ	~	tuuɳɨ	'pillar'
B	a.	muyal	~	*muyalɨ	'rabbit'
	b.	paraɳ	~	*paraɳɨ	'loft'

It will be observed that while optional epenthesis is possible in set A, it is prohibited in set B. The significant difference between sets A and B is that whereas the former is monosyllabic, the latter is disyllabic. Further data like /araʃan[50] ~ *araʃanɨ/ 'king' clearly tell us that the difference between sets A and B is between monosyllables and the rest of the vocabulary of Tamil. While monosyllables optionally allow epenthesis changing the inputs to disyllabic outputs, epenthesis in sonorant final words is ruled out elsewhere in the grammar of Tamil. Epenthesis becomes a possible repair strategy only because of the presence of *NOCODA in the grammar of Tamil. The constraint set that accounts for the data in (19) is in (20).

(20) Ranking (final version)
(Disyllabic word minimum), IDENTIOMORPHLIN, FAITHIOC >>
*OBSCODA >> *NOCODA >> DEPV

Driven by the disyllabic word minimum, optionally, *NOCODA becomes a visible constraint in Tamil minimally triggering epenthesis. Thus we see that a grammar does not necessarily set a parameter one way or the other. In this case, *NOCODA has three options in Tamil, namely, firstly, totally suppressed morpheme medially; secondly, partially suppressed in allowing sonorant consonants morpheme/word finally; and thirdly, allowing no codas at the end of words because of its preference for disyllabic words. Thus we see that in a constraint based approach to grammar which has markedness concerns as its core, output wellformedness criterion, we find an explanation for the functional unity of all the processes and also an explanation for why only certain processes are attested in particular languages. A parametric approach which forces the grammar to choose between *NOCODA and its logical opposite will just not be able to account for the facts of Tamil. As we saw, in the Tamil case, the *NOCODA constraint is neither switched on or switched off all the time in the grammar of Tamil.[51] Thus OT allows us many subtle intermediate positions between a parameter being turned on or turned off in the grammar of a language. Its role can be precisely evaluated in the constraint hierarchy (CH) of the grammar in the OT model.

3.5 The model of grammar for language

As I have already stated, the model of grammar that I propose for Carnatic music is informed and inspired by the OT model for language. Let us begin by examining the architecture of the OT model for language in Figure 1 below. An input is taken from the lexicon (or several inputs strung together for sequences longer than the word) and subject to the 'Generator' or GEN which generates multiple candidate representations (possibly infinite) according to well-established structural principles in Universal Grammar (UG). These candidate representations are fed to the 'Evaluator' or EVAL which evaluates all the candidates at one go applying the Constraint Hierarchy (CH) determined by the grammar of the language to select a unique 'Optimal' candidate which least violates the constraints in the CH.

Let us begin with the notion of input. For language, it is reasonable to assume that the input pertaining to words (however the notion 'word' is defined) is taken from the lexicon (the mental dictionary). For instance, if the input is the Tamil verb /peesh ('speak') + v (future marker) + person number marker/ (which we will ignore for presentation purposes), Gen can generate candidates such as a) /peeʃv.../, b) /peeʃ.../, c) /peev.../ d) /peʃiv.../, e) /peeʃav.../ f) /peeʃɨv.../ and many more. All the candidates except the last one will turn out to violate higher ranked constraints in the CH given above in (20). While a) violates *ObsCoda, b) violates IdentIOMorphLin by deleting the future tense morpheme and c) and d) violate IdentIOMorphLin by deleting some element of the root. Candidate e) is suboptimal because it inserts a vowel other than the least marked of Tamil vowels and therefore g) turns out to be optimal. In this Tamil example, we see that the verb root, affixes (and also words) are supplied by the lexicon. For longer sequences like phrases and sentences, we could assume that 'words' supplied by the lexicon are strung together by universal principles of word combinations (syntax) with help from language specific syntactic constraints (like word order etc.).

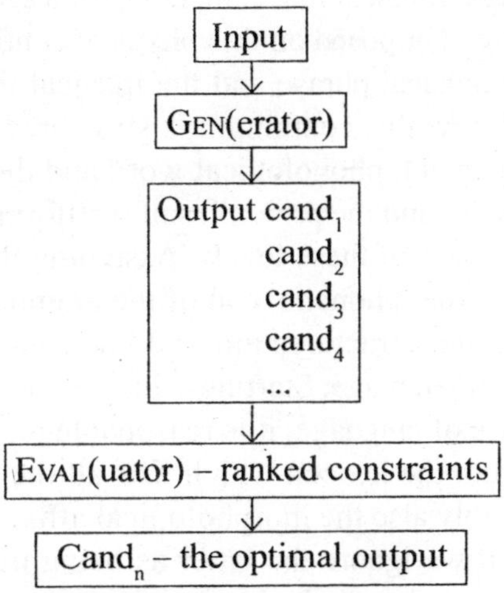

Figure 1. OT Model for Language

Having decided that the notion grammar (for language as well as Carnatic music) is best defined as a conflict resolution between faithfulness and markedness, the major concern now is to determine the nature of the constructs 'input', Gen and Eval in the context of Carnatic music. I assume that the grammar of Carnatic music, like the grammar of language, must explain the musical behaviour of a hypothetical ideal performer-listener of Carnatic music. The two major questions that need to be asked are:

"How would this ideal performer-listener check the grammaticality of an output?" (chapters 4 and 5) and
"How would this ideal performer listener evaluate the musical output for musical content?" (chapters 6 and 7).

I take up the issues of the Input, GEN and EVAL in the context of Carnatic music in the following sections (3.6 to 3.8) to show how and why the architecture of the grammar of Carnatic music is not identical with that of the grammar of language and that consequently the model proposed for Carnatic music, although inspired by OT, is quite distinct from the OT model for language.

3.6. The input and the lexicon of Carnatic music

I begin with the construct 'input' in Carnatic music. I assume here without discussion that the input musical line is made up of a sequence of pitch variations and that structure is imposed on this physical continuum at three levels, namely the note, the musical phrase and the musical line. I have discussed in detail in chapter 5 how this continuum is structured at these three levels (comparable to the segment, phonological word and the intonational phrase respectively in language) and the principles of wellformedness requirements for Carnatic music at each of these levels. Assuming that these interpretive mechanisms constitute the 'phonetic' end of the grammar of Carnatic music, we now come to the actual structured musical line which is the equivalent of the construct 'input' for language. Starting with the question where this input comes from in the case of language, it is reasonable to assume that the input is primarily drawn from the lexicon which lists all the lexical entries in the language and presumably also the morphological affixes and their grammatical properties. Even if we ignore the latter as being irrelevant for Carnatic music, we cannot assume that the lexicon of Carnatic music contains all the musical phrases which are the near equivalents of words in language. Words in language, although subject to change over time (across users), have a psychological permanence for the user that *all* musical phrases in a Carnatic music discourse may not have.

My assumption is that the lexicon of Carnatic music comprises at least the following constructs enumerated in (21) below.

For the phrases actually accessed from the lexicon we could assume that any deviation in interpretation (pitch values, sequential properties, prominence, boundary tones, etc.) would constitute IDENTIO violations. But the issue is far more complex than it seems at first blush. We will see that even a so-called lexically listed musical phrase may have to be subject to direct FAITHLEX constraints (distinct from IDENTIO constraints). However, assuming that not all musical phrases executed in a discourse are actually listed in the lexicon, it is reasonable to assume that those musical phrases which are not listed are put together by following the construals for tone, sequence, prototypes of phrases, construals pertaining to musical phrases like boundary tones, permissible prominent/emphatically prominent tones, etc. – all of which may be subsumed under FAITHLEX.

(21) The Contents of the Lexicon of Carnatic Music

a. Networked grammars of raagas (chapters 5 and 8)
b. Abstract prototypes for constructing musical phrases (chapter 5)
c. Components of the grammar of a raagam
   i. selected notes of the scale and the pitch interpretations of the notes (chapter 4)
   ii. specific phrase types, if selected (chapters 5, 8 and 9)
   iii. specific sequential constraints on notes (chapter 5)
   iv. choice of prominent/emphatic notes (chapter 5)
   v. choice of initial/final notes in phrases (chapter 5)
   vi. often used musical phrases (clichés or an inividual's favourites) (chapters 5, 7 and 9)
   vii. special phrases signalling the raagam (chapters 5, 7 and 9)
   viii. minor phrases, if any (chapters 6 and 8)

Recall the discussion in chapter 2 section 2.2.8 illustrating creativity in Carnatic music. I had illustrated the notion of creativity with phrases from the raagam Beegaḍaa music demonstration [2.20] given below as (22) for ease of reference.

(22) Music Demonstration: Beegaḍaa I [⊙ 2.20]

pa di pa Sa
pa Ri
pa Sa Gu

The raagam Beegaḍaa, a vakra (literally 'crooked') raagam, does not allow the sequence *[. di ni Sa..] The phrases given above would most certainly be listed in most performers' lexicons. Assuming that the phrase [pa di pa Sa] is taken from the lexicon, and in this case, all the notes would be rendered as almost steady pitches (which we term Rendered as Scale, RenScale for short). Therefore a pitch sequence of four steady pitch values with prominence on the intial pitch will receive the note interpretation [pa di pa Sa] (ignoring the presence of any pitch glides between notes). Now, we may assume that this output will be grammatical as it corresponds with the input taken from the lexicon.

However, now, assume another 'interpretation' of the same sequence of notes. As Carnatic music allows any sequence of two notes separated by a pitch interval of a tone (or a greater interval) to be rendered as a pitch curve, if the notes 'pa di' were to be rendered as a pitch curve on pa followed by steady pitch renderings on pa and Sa, the musical phrase as far as the 'notes' are concerned will be identical to the lexically listed phrase but its execution would have violated a tone construal in the lexicon of Beegaḍaa which requires that these notes be executed as steady pitch values and not pitch curves. The constraint prohibits pitch curve interpretations in two tone sequences like 'pa di', 'pa Sa', 'pa Ri' and so on in this raagam. As this constraint is part of the FAITHLEX set specific to this raagam, the faithfulness violation is perhaps not to the lexical entry but to this specific constraint. One can argue that repeated renderings of the phrase [pa di pa Sa] along with its optimal interpretation would have 'optimized' the former interpretation as the most probable lexical entry of this phrase and hence, one can maintain that the actual entry from the lexicon is the one that the output should correspond with.[52]

But as in language where one can coin new words, in Carnatic music too we can coin new phrases as the final phrase in the music demonstration of Beegaḍaa given below as (23) for ease of reference illustrates.

(23) Beegaḍaa I
[di pa Gu]

The phrase given above is not likely to be a sequence which would have been listed in any lexicon (prior to the popularity of the late twentieth century composition in which it is embedded) and so there can be no question of a corresponence between the input taken from the lexicon and the best output. faithfulness, in this context, has to be understood as the direct invoking of the FAITHLEX constraints specific to Beegaḍaa, specially the lexical entries listed in (22), namely [pa di pa Sa], [pa Sa], [pa Sa Gu], etc., and the constraint requiring steady pitch interpretations for tone sequences referred to in the discussion above. The actual phrase executed is a three tone sequence which is made up of a two-tone initial sequence that is sanctioned by the second and third notes of the first phrase listed in (22) and the third note is not prohibited by any starred sequence for the raagam Beegaḍaa I (e.g. *[di ni Sa]) and so not ungrammatical. And the steady pitch execution of all the three notes also does not violate the constraint requiring steady pitch interpretation for these notes in this raagam. Thus this novel sequence does not incur any serious violations and is therefore considered grammatical. Repeated rendering of this phrase, naturally, allows it to be listed in the lexicon for future access. This could be assumed to be the path that all lexically listed phrases take: the notes along with their precise pitch interpretation to be considered part of the lexical entry.

But not all phrases in a discourse are taken from the lexicon and several of the phrases need not even become so well-established as to warrant lexical listing. Therefore, the mechanism that was elaborated for the evaluation of the novel phrase [di pa Gu] in Beegaḍaa could be taken as the standard one involving FAITHLEX where a set of constraints specific to a raagam are involved in the evaluation of the input.

There is a further problem concerning the input in Carnatic music. Most notes in scales of raagas admit more than one pitch interpretation. Further, many raagas in Carnatic music have idiosyncratically specified pitch interpretations for specified notes of the scale (I classify these raagas as idiosyncratic raagas belonging to the Idiosyncratic Set (I Set) (see chapter 8 for a detailed discussion)). In many of these cases, multiple pitch interpretations are not only admissible, but of equal grammatical acceptability. The selection of a particular pitch interpretation for a note, even for a single performer may be random and not totally predictable. If entire discourses were to be analysed, with the help of a large body of data, it may be possible to predict the selection of particular pitch interpretations by particular artists using a probabilistic model. But at the level of the musical line, it is completely impossible to select a unique pitch interpretation as the optimal one. One solution is to assume that musical phrases may admit multiple listings in the lexicon, each of which could function as an input for evaluation in a musical line. But then, we end up merely augmenting the process of lexical listing without offering any explanation for the occurrence of such large scale 'free variation'. I will return to this problem in section 3.8 when we deal with the mode of evaluation best suited for the grammar of Carnatic music.

3.7 Generator and the grammar of Carnatic music

Recall that in an OT model the language input is subject to GEN – the Generator which generates possible candidate representations, possibly infinite, according to universal structural principles. The assumed universal structural principles in the case of language pertain to universal segment types, phonation types, universal syllabification and higher order structures, etc. For language, owing to a long history of investigation and research, one can assume quite a lot about possible representations. For instance, certain segment types are universally ruled out, e.g. labiodental stops; all languages must parse segments into syllables, universally, the nucleus of the syllables must be the most sonorous segment in the syllable, all syllables must be gathered into higher order structure which may be left or right headed (whatever that might mean to linguists) and the structure motivated by phonological criteria may not be isomorphic with that necessitated by syntax etc. Keeping these universally established guidelines, GEN can generate an infinite set of candidates for each input. For instance, take the English word 'grammar'. GEN can generate the following candidate representations and many more: [græmær], [gəræmær], [ˈgræˌmær], [ˌgræˈmær̥], [ˈgəræˌmær], [ˌgəræˈmær], [gəˈræˌmær] and many, many more. These candidate representations generated according to some universal principles turn out to be non-optimal for English for well-founded reasons. But the point is that if the candidate set generated by GEN is large enough it will always include a unique, optimal candidate as well. And the idea of generating a large candidate set is to systematically rule out all logical possibilities other than the one actually chosen by the language.

When we turn to Carnatic music, we already saw that more than one interpretation is possible for an input and that more than one output may be optimal as far as the grammar is concerned. But due to paucity of research in music in general and Carnatic music in particular, we do not know the guiding principles of structure building in music. For instance, while some types of music may require structure similar to that of sentences in language partitioning the line into a subject/predicate type of bifurcation (Lerdahl and Jackendoff (1983), Gilbers and Schreuder (2002) for Western music), Carnatic music seems to require structuring only at the levels of tone, phrase and line, resembling the phonological hierarchy of segment, phonological word and intonational group (see chapter 4 and 5 for details). Further, we do not know the range of attested behaviour in the realms of pitch realisations of notes, note boundaries, prominence in phrases, mapping rhythmic prominence to phrasal prominence, etc. in music (see discussion at the end of chapters 5 and 7). Therefore, as we have no idea of the universal structural principles of music, GEN cannot generate an infinite set of candidates for music and so we must be satisfied with a non-generative grammar of Carnatic music for the present.

But as we saw, even within the domain of Carnatic music we can, in fact, generate a fair number of candidate interpretations for every input musical line. Of these plausible candidates, our grammar can even explain the ungrammaticality of a large majority of the candidates. But because of the nature of the Carnatic music lexicon, the explanation could be attributed to one of two types of FAITHLEX violations, namely a raagam-specific one or a *AMBIGUITY type detected by the networked lexicon. As for the former, the constraint prohibiting pitch curve interpretations of two note sequences in the raagam Beegaḍaa is one such FAITHLEX constraint. Here is another example of a raagam-specific constraint pertaining to a prohibition on certain notes as boundary tones of musical phrases. The example is from the raagam Sahaanaa, the sample music demonstration in (12) in chapter 2 [2.24] given here as (24) below for ease of reference.

(24)   Musical demonstration
        Sahaanaa II   [☉ 2.24]
        Phrasing A: [ni̱ sa] [ri gu ma pa][di ni Sa]
        Phrasing B: ni *[sa ri gu ma][pa di ni Sa]

While phrasing A is grammatical, B is ungrammatical. Let us assume that the lexicon lists the information as a FAITHLEXSAHAANAA constraint given in (25).

(25)   FAITHLEXSAHAANAA
        FAITHLEXSAHAANAA[sa → *ma] (informally, an ascending phrase initiated by the note sa cannot have ma as the terminal note)
        When an input string {ni̱ sa ri gu ma...} is parsed as ...ni̱ [sa ri gu ma]... then FAITHLEXSAHAANAA is violated and the output is deemed to be ungrammatical though other parses like [ni̱ sa][ri gu ma], [ni̱ sa ri] [gu ma] and [ni̱ sa ri gu] ma and several others will not.

Turning to the second type of ungrammaticality, it is seen that it can be attributed to the constraint family *AMBIGUITY. Consider the instance of ungrammaticality, once again from a musical line in the raagam Beegaḍaa. The music demonstration [6.59] reproduces a musical line the author had come across in a live concert of a highly acclaimed artist. ((11–13) of chapter 6 and music demonstrations [6.59]–[6.62] reproduced below as (26); see chapter 6 for a detailed discussion).

(26) Musical demonstration
Beegaḍaa [⊙ 6.59]
Varṇam: Beegaḍaa: Aadi: Viiṇai Kuppayyer
The text: // pa, di pa - ma; pa / ; ma pa - di,...
           bha ga   va: ri
      *// pa di Sa, Ri Sa - ni di ni di pa, /; ...
           bo: da   na
Beegaḍaa [⊙ 6.60]
Di pa Sa
Sa Ni; di pa
Kaamboodi I [⊙ 6.61]
Pa di Sa
Sa Ni di pa
Varṇam II (contd.) [⊙ 6.62]
(?)// pa di Sa, Ri Sa - ni; di / pa

The reason for the ungrammaticality is that the musical line in the raagam Beegaḍaa smudges the raagam boundary between the raagam Beegaḍaa and another raagam, Kaamboodi. I assume that a major function of the Carnatic music lexicon is to create a network of raagas so that raagam identities are kept clear at all points of the discourse (see chapter 8 for a detailed discusssion). In other words, creating an entire musical line ambiguous between two raagas is not just a matter of bad taste, it is a matter of ungrammaticality. I term the constraint *AMBIGUITY (*AMB for short) as this a general constraint type which signals the smudging of raagam boundaries defined explicitly in the networked lexicon of Carnatic music (see chapters 5, 6, 7, and 8). In the case under discussion, the opening phrase in the rendering [pa di Sa, RiSa] will automatically signal *AMB for the raagam Kaamboodi and the situation gets worse with the next phrase with the short note ni in the descent which is not sanctioned for Beegaḍaa but only for Kaamboodi and the line earns a serious *AMB violation for the constraint *[Sa [*ni di] which is part of the FAITHLEX constraints specific to the raagam Beegaḍaa making the line ungrammatical.

The family of *AMB constraints, in addition to assigning a violation mark for a specific constraint in the set, identify network connections which trace the cause of the violation in the FAITHLEX constraint set of one raagam to another raagam/other raagas. In this case, the phrase Sa [ni di...] triggers a violation of the Beegaḍaa specific constraint *[Sa [*ni di... and the *AMB family of constraints trace the cause of the ungrammaticality to another raagam in the network. There is enough anecdotal evidence in Carnatic music circles of listeners actually identifying the raagas which have crept in inadvertently during the rendering of a raagam by less experienced performers. (See chapters 5, 6, 7, and 8 for discussions of *AMB constraints).

Getting back to our discussion of the role of GEN in the grammar of Carnatic music, though, in principle, every Carnatic musician of standing will be able to generate a fair number of plausible interpretations of a notated line of music constituting the input (if he/she can read music notation), we still do not have a clear idea of the limits of musical structure that should be considered for generating serious contenders for evaluation. This is the reason why the model of grammar that I propose for Carnatic music is not a 'generative' one as it lacks the component GEN. Therefore the model that I propose scans a musical line, assigns it structure and with the help of relevant FAITHLEX constraints evaluates it for a) grammaticality (chapters 4 and 5) and b) musical content (chapters 6 and 7).

However, the question of only one of the interpretations, i.e. a unique candidate representation being considered optimal, remains. As I said earlier, the ability to offer multiple interpretations for a line of music is an inherent characteristic of Carnatic music discourse (as the discourse is not meant to be a reproduction of a 'fixed' text but a spontaneous creation of musical ideas (see the last section of chapter 9)), I do not take on myself the task of parallel evaluation of multiple candidate representations at this stage of musical research. The model of grammar for Carnatic music is thus not quite an OT model as it is non-generative and it lacks the power to select a unique candidate as the optimal one from among a set of candidates.

3.8. EVAL and the grammar of Carnatic music

3.8.1. Introduction

I now turn to the component EVAL in an OT grammar. In a typical model of OT, the function EVAL comprises the ranked constraint set which is applied to all the candidate representations generated by GEN simultaneously. Constraint ranking is the ultimate arbiter selecting the optimal candidate output. Ranked constraints evaluate all the candidates in parallel and the candidate which minimally violates the constraint set emerges the winner. It must be emphasized that the winning candidate does not have to be free of violation (that is why the winning candidate is not called the best candidate), it is 'optimal' given the constraint ranking. As long as its violations are of lower ranked constraints than those of all other candidates, even if it were to incur ever so many violations of lower ranked constraints, it would still be considered optimal. In the standard model of OT, the only function of the grammar is to assign strict ranking to all the faithfulness and markedness constraints. While the latter is attributed to Universal Grammar (UG), the former is language specific. The markedness constraints are taken from UG along with their ranking (except for a few cases of indeterminate ranking) and the grammar of the language is free to rank its faithfulness constraints anywhere in the hierarchy with respect to the markedness constraints. It is against this background of strict ranking of constraints that I propose my version of EVAL necessary for the grammar of Carnatic music. I show in sections 3.8.2–3.8.4 how EVAL in the grammar of Carnatic music is distinct from EVAL elsewhere in OT in three ways, namely delimiting the constraint hierarchy, mode of constraint evaluation and constraint set prioritization.

3.8.2. Departure 1 from EVAL in standard OT: Delimiting the Constraint Hierarchy

In the abstract, a grammar of Carnatic music would have to put together a set of markedness constraints applicable to music in general and also propose markedness constraints specific to Carnatic music. As most of these ideas are contingent on extensive research in universal musicology (see the last section of chapters 5 and 7), I assume that there exist markedness constraints with respect to all the aspects of music making, listing them below (the list is by no means complete).

(27) Markedness Constraints Specific to Music

a. Markedness constraints pertaining to the twelve tones of the octave (chapter 4)

b. Markedness constraints specific to pitch realisations of a 'note' (chapter 5)
c. Markedness constraints characterising note sequences (chapter 5)
d. Markedness constraints defining prominence in phrases (chapter 5)
e. Markedness constraints defining emphatic prominence in a musical line (chapters 5 and 6)
f. Markedness constraints defining the alignment of musical prominence and rhythmic prominence (chapters 5, 6 and 7)
g. Markedness constraints defining the alignment of language text with musical text (chapter 7)

All these markedness constraints are traceable to universal properties of music (yet to be determined). Carnatic music being a distinct type of music, a large part of these constraints are ranked so low in the Constraint Hierarchy (CH) of Carnatic music to be almost invisible, but not quite. Take the case of the realisation of the notes gi (E flat), mi (F sharp) and ni (B flat) in Carnatic music. To begin with, these notes are not the least marked notes in the twelve tone scale, presumably, universally. Generally, in Carnatic music, the 'ideal targets' for these notes are achieved by deflecting the string on the preceding notes ri and di with the intention of achieving slightly lower targets for gi and ni respectively and deflecting the string on mi for the slightly higher target for this note (see chapters 4 and 5 for detailed discussion).[53] Let us assume that the markedness constraints *RENSCALEgi, *RENSCALEmi, *RENSCALEni are very high ranked in Carnatic music prohibiting their steady pitch values fixed by keyboard instruments in normal and slower tempos (see discussion below, however). These constraints then force the Carnatic musician to find alternate ways to render these notes. Obviously, the only type of constraints which can force markedness constraints to be violated are some type of faithfulness constraints. But as we will see in chapters 4 and 5, the constraints which prohibit steady pitch realisation of lower and higher targets for notes are even higher ranked than the *RENSCALE constraints (accounting for the fact these diminished and augmented targets are *never* realised with steady pitch values in Carnatic music see chapter 4 and 5 for discussion on micro-tone/ʃruti in Carnatic music). How then should these notes be attempted? Carnatic music answers this question by allowing the least marked, mild pitch wave realisation. The exact realisation of diminished and augmented targets of 'notes' is discussed in detail in chapters 4 and 5 along with algorithms for their realisation. Thus we see that the realisation of the notes gi, mi and ni in normal and slow tempos is controlled by the following CH:

(28) Constraint Hierarchy for the Realisation of the Notes gi, mi and ni
*RENSCALEreducedgi/ni/augmentedmi
>>
FAITHLEXMILDPITCHWAVEgi/mi/ni
>>
*RENSCALEgi/mi/ni.tempo.n (where 'n' is 1 or slower tempo)

Turning to other pitch realisations of notes in Carnatic music, I assume that the markedness constraint that prohibits pitch curve and pitch wave interpretations of a note of music formalised by the constraint *PITCHCURVE/WAVEN which may be undominated (hence inviolable) in many systems of music is so low ranked as to be almost invisible in the CH of many raagas in Carnatic music. However, even this low ranked constraint can help select a winning candidate if there are other higher ranked context sensitive constraints preventing pitch curve/wave interpretations on a note.

Let us take the concrete example of the note gi (E flat) in the raagam Tooḍi. In the case of the note gi (E flat) the markedness constraint in question is the requirement that a note be rendered as a steady pitch at the pitch value of the note, *RENSCALEgi. The fact that Tooḍi allows both a deep pitch curve and a pitch wave interpretation on the note gi (E flat) implies the following ranking:

(29) Partial Ranking for the note gi in the raagam Tooḍi
FAITHLEXPITCHCURVEgi, FAITHLEXPITCHWAVEgi
>>
*PITCHCURVEgi
>>
*PITCHWAVEgi
>>
*RENSCALEgi

However, notice that the requirement that a note be rendered as a scalar note with steady pitch is the least marked among the realisations of the note. We will see, by and by, that it can, in principle, never be totally banned in the lexicon of any raagam. It can only be banned in specified contexts. Continuing with the case of the raagam Tooḍi, RENSCALEgi (steady pitch E flat) is prohibited in a sequence like [sa ra gi ma] rendered in the normal tempo. Let us formalise this context sensitive markedness constraint as *RENSCALEgi [ra_ma]. In the normal tempo, let us call it tempo 1, the ranking FAITHLEX-PITCHCURVEgi, FAITHLEXPITCHWAVEgi >> *RENSCALEgi[ra_ma] accounts for the absence of RENSCALEgi in this context.

(30) Revised Constraint Ranking for the Pitch Values of the Note gi in Tooḍi

FAITHLEXPITCHCURVEgi, FAITHLEXPITCHWAVEgi
>>
*RENSCALEgi[ra_ma]
>>
*PITCHCURVEgi
>>
*PITCHWAVEgi
>>
*RENSCALEgi

The phrase [sa ra gi ma] ought to be grammatical with both pitch curve and pitch wave interpretations for gi given the fact that the raagam selects both pitch interpretations. Under one interpretation of FAITHLEX, assume there are two phrases listed in the lexicon one with the pitch curve gi and another with pitch wave gi. Whichever interpretation is the chosen input from the lexicon, both will be sanctioned by the CH because of the high ranking FAITHLEX constraints.

However, if we assume that there is only one listing for the phrase in the lexicon which leaves the pitch interpretation open to the performer (which seems reasonable to me), then the CH with only FAITHLEX constraints will not work, given the assumptions regarding EVAL in standard OT. In the absence of any lexical specification for gi, FAITHLEXgi will be inoperative and the higher markedness ranking of *PITCHCURVE will rule out pitch curve interpretation for gi in every input. The context-sensitive markedness constraint rescues the phrase from ungrammaticality allowing a pitch wave interpretation. Therefore, in principle, more marked pitch interpretations will never surface unless explicitly listed in the lexicon as part of the specific lexical entry.

I am committed to the view that

a) musical phrases are listed in the lexicon iff they are frozen expressions or clichés and these come with total specification for pitch etc.,

b) 'normal' musical phrases are constructed online using the prototypes and the FAITHLEX constraints,
c) for the evaluation to successfully characterise grammatical outputs, constraints below the context sensitive constraints are disregarded for evaluation,
d) free variability in the interpretation of musical phrases is solely governed by lexical FAITHLEX constraints specific to tones/sequences etc. Such free variation may be controlled by considerations of style.

These are the assumptions which underlie the exposition in the book. Particularly, c) above is a major deviation from standard assumptions regarding EVAL in OT. The assumption that works for Carnatic music is then the following:

(31) *Departure 1 from EVAL in Standard OT*
Evaluation of a musical line in the grammar of Carnatic music is undertaken by the Constraint Hierarchy which lists the relevant FAITHLEX constraints interspersed with markedness constraints upto the enumerated context sensitive markedness constraint(s). *The lower ranked context free markedness constraints play no role in the evaluation of a line of music.*

This kind of delimitation, while it works for the case just discussed above turns out to be problematic when it comes to the case I am about to examine and hence we will have to modify the delimitation condition suitably.

Just as in standard OT, in Carnatic music also we find that lower ranked constraints can emerge under constraint domination. Getting back to the case of the note gi in the raagam Tooḍi, consider now musical phrases in higher tempos. It must be noted that pitch manipulation on a note is easier when the tempo is slower (or the note is of longer duration) and hence the following two constraints are appropriate for capturing this generalisation.

(32) Markedness of Pitch Manipulations in Higher Tempos
*PITCHCURVEgi.tempo.2,
*PITCHWAVEgi.tempo.2.3

Informally, while pitch curves are difficult in tempo 2, even pitch waves are difficult at tempo 3. Integrating these constraints into the CH we have the following ranking.

(33) Constraint Ranking
*PITCHCURVEgi.tempo.2, *PITCHWAVEgi,tempo.2.3
>>
FAITHLEXPITCHCURVEgi, FAITHLEXPITCHWAVEgi
>>
*RENSCALEgi[ra_ma]
>>
*PITCHCURVEgi
>>
*PITCHWAVEgi
>>
RENSCALEgi

At tempo 2, since *PITCHCURVEgi.tempo.2 rules out pitch curves, an input which prespecifies a pitch curve on gi at tempo 2 will be non-optimal because of the high ranking constraint. However, under our assumption that the input could be assembled from lexical specifications, the optimal output will have a pitch wave manipulation on gi. At the even higher tempo, say tempo 3, since even pitch waves are over-ruled, we see the RenScale rendering emerging as the optimal output. Finally, in styles where *RENSCALEgi is ranked high, what emerges is the mild pitch wave rendering, given the integrated ranking in (34) below.

(34) Integrated Constraint Hierarchy for the Note gi
*RENSCALEreducedgi
>>
FAITHLEXMILDPITCHWAVEgi
>>
*PITCHCURVEgi.tempo2, *PITCHWAVEgi.tempo.3
>>
FAITHLEXPITCHCURVEgi, FAITHLEXPITCHWAVEgi
>>
*RENSCALEgi[ra_ma]
>>
*PITCHCURVEgi
>>
*PITCHWAVEgi
>>
RENSCALEgi

The presence of FAITHLEXMILDPITCHWAVEgi in more orthodox styles prevents the emergence of RENSCALEgi even in fast tempos. However, this does not imply that even these orthodox styles will ban RENSCALEgi altogether in the entire discourse. This least marked of pitch realisation does emerge in the absence of context sensitive FAITHLEX constraints in the lexicon of the raagam in question.

We are now in a position to modify the delimitation condition:

(35) *Departure 1 from EVAL in Standard OT (Final Version)*
Evaluation of a musical line in the grammar of Carnatic music is undertaken by the Constraint Hierarchy which lists the relevant FAITHLEX constraints interspersed with markedness constraints up to the enumerated context sensitive markedness constraint(s). *The lower ranked context free markedness constraints play no role in the evaluation of a line of music, unless the specific context free markedness constraint set is partially ranked higher in the constraint hierarchy.*

3.8.3. Departure 2 from EVAL in standard OT: Violation and value recognition

Taking up next the question of how to evaluate the musical input for musical content in chapters 6 and 7, I show that all the construals proposed in chapters 4 and 5 pertaining to tone, sequence, phrase, rhythm and line perform twin functions in the grammar of Carnatic music, namely determining grammaticality (chapters 4 and 5) and determining musical meaning/value (chapters 6 and 7). I have shown above how one can define grammaticality following the standard practice of requiring EVAL to display violation marks against constraints which are not obeyed in the CH (albeit a delimited one). Thus the line of music in (24) phrasing B (musical demo [2.24]) and the line of Beegaḍaa in (26) (musical demo [6.59]) are clearly assigned violation marks and are to be discarded as ungrammatical.

However, issues pertaining to musical content receive evaluation in different ways by the knowlegeable Carnatic music fraternity. And this must get reflected in the evaluation done by the grammar. There are two distinct functions that constraints perform while evaluating a line of music for musical content, namely style function and stylistic function. The former characterizes the style of a line of music. Let me give a few examples. In chapter 6, I show with specific examples how certain notes in certain raagas are invested with special emotive meanings. Evaluating the musical content of a musical line in such cases is not just a matter of registering the presence or absence of this feature. The grammar must evaluate the exact execution of the note to classify the style as restrained/classical, light, emotional etc. purely based on parameters like duration and the pitch execution of the note. This evaluation allows one to define the style of the musical discourse, maybe assign the symbol S_n 'n' standing for a specific style. Take another example, now from rhythm construal. There are distinct strategies for evaluating the occurrence of rhythmic pattern/formula in Carnatic music. Partitioning the Carnatic music discourse into a non-rhythm oriented part and a rhythm oriented part, the grammar has to evolve two different strategies for evaluating rhythmic pattern. In the former, the occurrence of a rhythmic pattern more than three times signals a flamboyant/flashy style. However, in the latter, it signals a deficiency bordering on ungrammaticality for which a specific value may have to be assigned. Take yet another example, of musical phrases in a musical line. If the musical line, specially as part of a spontaneous discourse (not based on any received text), contains clichés or quotations from well known texts, then the grammar has to evaluate it as an over used lexical entry or as an *AmbLine violation, a quotation taken from a text. Thus, altogether the style set assigns a descriptive value to a line of music and does not perform an evaluative function discarding any musical line.

Finally, turning to the stylistic set, the constraints in this set perform a range of functions beginning with checking for lexical listing to pattern recognition to checking for specific stylistic devices. Taking up each one of these functions, let us begin with checking for lexical listing. To repeat what I stated earlier, I assume that "musical phrases are listed in the lexicon iff they are frozen expressions or clichés and these come with total specification for pitch etc.". While the former could be special phrases signalling a school of music or an individual, the latter is a stock of phrases that are widely used (repeatedly in musical discourses). When such phrases are encountered in a musical line, the constraints performing a stylistic function assign phrases which are listed in the lexicon an *AmbPhrase violation. However, when novel phrases such as the phrase in Beegaḍaa in (23) above (musical demo [2.22]) are encountered which do not match any phrase in the lexicon then the constraints specific to phrase construal assign a '☞' sign signalling a novel phrase. Similarly, construals which examine a musical line for patterns assign a '☞' sign signalling a novel/interesting pattern (say, of specific number of note sequences satisfying one of several functions like symmetry, balance etc.).

Finally, construals which examine a musical line for specific stylistic devices like spatial imagery or specific devices like 'swara bheedam' (modal shift) assign a '☞' sign to signal the occurrence of a special stylistic convention.

The issue that we are now faced with is that of the overall evaluation statement that the complex CH comprising the grammaticality set, the style set and the stylistic set makes of a line of music. While the grammaticality set indicates violations if any, the style set classifies the style and the stylistic set recognises merit. The evaluation done by the three distinct sets of constraints can be summarized as in (36) below.

(36) Different Evaluation Procedures for Constraint Sets

Constraint Sets in the Grammar of Carnatic Music

a) Grammaticality	b) Style	c) Stylistic
*	S_n	☞

We need to determine how the evaluation done by the three distinct sets is put together as an overall statement of evaluation of a line of Carnatic music. First of all, let us take up the set pertaining to Style. Clearly the function this set performs is to characterise the style of the musical input and it is therefore non-evaluative. As it merely provides additional information about the line of music, we can assume that this set is the lowest ranked among the constraint sets.

Under normal circumstances, one would assume that considerations of grammaticality should receive higher priority than stylistic considerations as the former is a basic requirement which must be satisfied before one can even start looking for stylistic values in a line of music. Thus the 'normal' ranking would be set determining grammaticality >> set determining stylistic worth. The latter then merely adds stylistic value to a line lacking any grammatical violation marks. However, under certain circumstances, this ranking can be partially or totally reversed as we will see in the following subsection.

3.8.4. Departure 3 from Eval in standard OT: Set prioritization

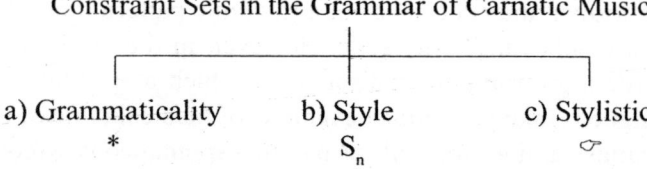

I show in chapter 7 while establishing the ranking of the constraints in the grammar of Carnatic music how under two special conditions, constraints pertaining to issues of grammaticality can be assigned lower priority over certain stylistic constraints and actually get turned off because of their lower ranking. The first type pertains to the style of certain estabished artists where violations of constraints pertaining to grammaticality can be over-looked because of 'merit' assigned to the artist. A crude example that I give now is that of an artist of the early-middle twentieth century. This artist had a problem aligning his voice with the fundamental pitch (like many others). His fundamental pitch would drop a full semi tone in the middle of a discourse lasting one or more musical lines. Now if this happenes in a raagam like Tooḍi for instance, the upper eighth would sound like a 'nu' or B which is not the selected note of this raagam at all. Thus the output would violate all the grammaticality constraints pertaining to tone construal, sequence construal, etc. It cannot be argued that the listener lowers the fundamental by a semitone as the accompanying violin would be at the original fundamental pitch. The listeners clearly overlook the grammaticality violations patiently looking for and finding many stylistic gems to appreciate. This is by no means an isolated example in the Carnatic music fraternity. In chapter 7, I give another example of an artist deliberately assigning lower priority to constraints pertaining to tone and sequence construals as a style statement, sometimes with telling effect.

The second instance of re-prioritization occurs in the stylistic device known as ʃruti bheedam (modal shift) where in the middle of a musical discourse (usually raagam aalaapanai), the fundamental note shifts from sa (C) of the selected scale to another note in the scale. Here again the constraint set specific to a raagam are re-prioritized in the middle of the discourse to get lower ranked (below the delimitated mark) than the constraints of a newly constructed scale from the old one. I shall elaborate on this point also in chapter 7. I mention this fact only to point out that the last of the departures in the grammar of Carnatic music from EVAL in standard OT is this possibility of re-ranking right in the middle of a discourse.

3.9. Conclusion

In this chapter, I outlined the architecture of OT grammar and showed how the grammar of Carnatic music, though inspired by OT, is significantly different from the grammar of language with respect to all the components of an OT grammar namely GEN, the Lexicon and EVAL. GEN is untapped in this model because of the absence of established universal musical structural principles. The notion of the lexicon is also different with the 'input' being a listed entry or a sequence put together online with the help of the FAITHLEX constraints listed in the lexicon. Finally EVAL is different in three ways, namely, it designates an active part of the constraint set which evaluates the input for grammaticality, there are three different ways of evaluation, and stylistic devices allow re-prioritization of the grammaticality set in the middle of the discourse. In the following two chapters I outline an approach that allows us to construct a notated musical line from a stream of pitch variations assigning them note values and attributing structure to the stream at three levels, namely note, phrase, and line, and determine its grammaticality.

Chapter 4
Conversion of pitch values to notes

4.1. Introduction

At the end of chapter 2 I had claimed that the architecture of the grammar of Carnatic music was like that of language in requiring, what is called, the PF component and I had argued at the end of the previous chapter that the evaluation process of a line of Carnatic music could begin if and only if the raw pitch values are interpreted as notes of music and assigned appropriate structure. Chapters 4 and 5 take up the task of establishing the need for the mechanism of interpreting pitch values as 'notes' of music and assigning the note sequence musical structure at least at three levels, namely the level of the mora, musical phrase and musical line. In particular, I argue that the grammar of music and particularly, Carnatic music, requires a mechanism for relating tones and tonal ranges as abstract 'notes'.[54, 55] In this chapter, I show how the interpretive mechanism is necessary for any musical system and particularly Carnatic music which has re-interpreted the twelve tone system as a sixteen tone system creating potential ambiguity in the tone-note interpretation which has to be sorted out in the musical discourse. Finally, I take up the further issue of Carnatic music systematically exploiting intertonal pitch frequencies which in Carnatic music theory has been claimed to necessitate a further re-interpretation of the twelve tones as twenty two 'ʃrutis'. I also attempt at resolving the conflicting claims between the twelve note theory and the twenty two 'ʃruti' to an octave theory, in principle, in this chapter. In the following chapter, I undertake a description of the pitch profiles that are typically used in Carnatic music, the system of abstract time and musical structure which are necessary for determining the grammaticality and stylistic values of a line of Carnatic music.

To begin with language, the PF (for phonetic form) component or its equivalent mechanism is required for language for a) interpreting the speech continuum as abstract elements of language and b) converting the abstract elements of language into speech sounds. For language, it is correctly assumed that the component deriving the sentence patterns mediates between 'sound' on the one hand and 'meaning' on the other. The need for a PF component for language is not quite self-evident, though. First of all, speech, either produced or perceived, is a continuum and the segmentation of the speech signal into segments, words and phrases is a process of abstraction which is a necessary step away from the physical reality and towards the abstraction that is grammar. When we speak or listen to speech, for instance, we will notice that what we recognize as 'words' do not invariably occur with recognizable 'pauses'. (Pause – the equivalent of 'space' between words in writing is not always present in speech.)

Starting with sounds, a little introspection will suffice to make us realize that the number of sounds that we produce/hear is actually quite a lot more than the number that we store as relevant 'sound tokens' of our language. Consider the example of an English consonant and its pronunciations. What we would normally represent orthographically as 't' is pronounced quite differently in different contexts, in different dialects. To make the presentation more dramatic, I take up the examples from General American English.

(1)
a. tea [t^h]
b. stop [t]
c. pot [t¬]
d. writer [D]

The 't' in the first word is pronounced with a strong puff of air, technically called aspiration. The 't' in (1b) lacks this additional, articulatory gesture. The final 't' in (1c) is normally not released in casual speech. Finally, the 't' in (1d) is voiced and 'flapped', i.e. the tip of the tongue is quickly flapped against the bump behind the upper teeth, known as the alveolar ridge (similar to the consonant which occurs between vowels in the Hindi pronunciation of the word 'saree'). And strangely enough, both 't' and 'd' are pronounced alike in words like 'writer' and 'rider' in American English. Though we pronounce and perceive different sounds, we store the sound as one, idealized, abstract sound 't', in the case of the words in (1) above, called a *phoneme*. And the variants in (1) are called *allophones*. In other words, we interpret what we hear/produce in the context of other speech sounds and extract the abstract information which may not even be really present in that part of the speech event. In the case of words like 'writer' and 'rider', the consonant between the two vowels is pronounced exactly alike, with voice and yet it is encoded as a voiceless 't' in the former and a voiced 'd' in the latter. The interpretation is dependent on the speech signal preceding this sound. In most dialects of American and Canadian English, the preceding vowel is distinctly longer when the following sound is basically voiced than when it is, to start with, voiceless.[56] In other words, in American and Canadian English while 'writer' is pronounced [raiDər], 'rider' is pronounced [ra:iDər]. It is this difference in perceived vowel length that signals one flap as 't' and the other as 'd'. In the case of (1a–c), 't', we see that different sounds are interpreted as the same token. But we also saw that, sometimes, the same speech signal may be interpreted as different tokens as in the case of the flapped consonant. This situation is by no means unique to English. For most speakers of Tamil, the symbols in boldface, standing for different sounds are interpreted as the same token (phoneme) in one case (2a) but as different 'phonemes' in the case of (2b).

(2) a. m**a**r**õ** 'tree'
b. shoo**r**ɨ 'rice' moo**r**ɨ 'buttermilk'

In the first word, the first vowel is a low vowel, i.e. the body of the tongue is kept low and the oral cavity is open and the second vowel (ignoring the fact that it is nasalized) is rounded and the body of the tongue is distinctly higher than it is for the first vowel. The two sounds are 'perceptibly' different and yet speakers would have no hesitation in saying that they represent the same token, i.e. the phoneme /a/. In the second case, for most speakers (of colloquial Tamil), the 'r's are pronounced alike in casual speech and yet most speakers would have no hesitation in claiming that the sounds represent different tokens, i.e. phonemes.[57]

We can represent this situation graphically as in (3) below:

(3) Speech sound – language token interpretation

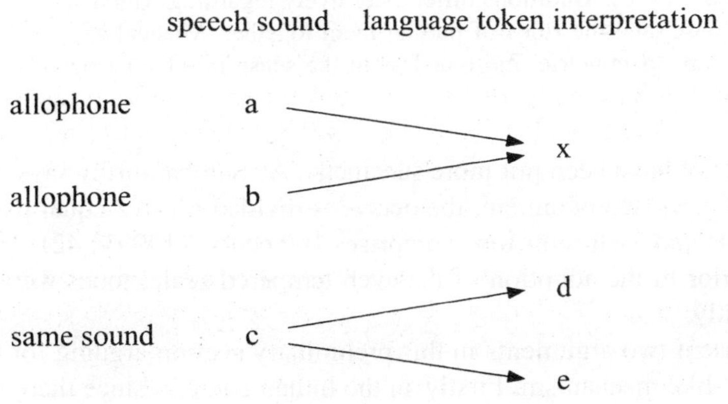

Without the PF component, or its equivalent, interpretation of speech sounds or converting the abstract tokens of the language into speech sounds would be impossible. The need for the PF component can be demonstrated in areas other than segments (consonants and vowels) too. Take the case of (4b) as a response to the question in (4a) below.

(4) a. Did you come by the **8** 'o' clock train?
b. *No, I came by the 9 'o' clock **train.**

The word in boldface represents the most important word in the utterance, normally signaled in speech by a different pitch pattern. The response in (4b) is inappropriate for the question in (4a). The ungrammaticality of (4b) can be determined only when we know how to interpret the pitch information present in the speech signal.

4.2. Interpretation of tone: Take 1

The question before us now is whether the grammar of music, Carnatic music in particular, requires a mechanism equivalent to the PF component in the grammar of language. Contrary to Lerdahl and Jackendoff (1983) (see Footnote 53 of Mukherjee (2000: 120)), music and Carnatic music in particular, definitely requires a module analogous to the PF component for language. Speaking up for music, Mukherjee correctly says

> "Conception of pitch-boundaries and their relations with each other subtly changes across periods and traditions and there is nothing like 'fixed' pitches (McLain 1976). Traditions differ extensively regarding which set of pitches to choose, and the rules of putting them together. Musical systems in that sense are 'parametric' more or less in the sense in which languages are..." (2000: 111)

It could not have been put more succinctly. As Sambamurthy says, "(i)n the scale of equal temperament, the octave is divided into 12 equal parts of cyclic cents and each semi-tone comprises 100 cents."(1999V: 42). And in the West, prior to the adoption of the even tempered scale, tones were defined differently.

I present two arguments in this preliminary section arguing for the need for a PF-like mechanism. Firstly, in the Indian context, since there is no 'absolute' value attached to any tone, the task of discovering the fundamental pitch – the first tone of the octave – requires an interpretive mechanism[58]. Secondly, the ingenuity of the Carnatic music system has re-interpreted the 12 tone system as a 16 tone system with D, E flat, A and B flat performing overlapping functions (owing to the ingenuity of the musicologist Veenkaṭamakhi*)* given below in Figure 1. In the re-interpreted scheme, the tonal equivalents of 'D', 'E flat', 'A' and 'B flat' perform dual roles as 'reduced E', 'augmented D', 'reduced B' and 'augmented A' respectively. Since a scale is allowed to choose only one tone to represent 'D', 'E' , 'A' and 'B' and since Carnatic music allows a scale to choose combinations of tones such as 2 and 3, 3 and 4, 9 and 10 and 10 and 11 of the Western numbering system, such a re-interpretation is necessitated.

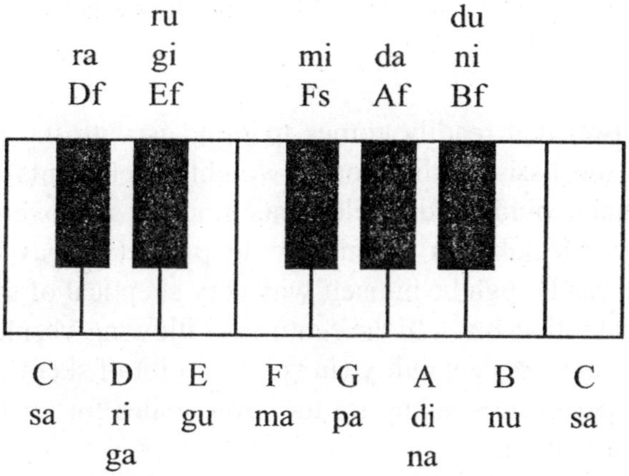

Figure 1. The Carnatic 16 tone system

This is the phenomenon I have termed as dual representation of tones as notes since 'D' can be interpreted as either 'ri' or 'ga' , 'E flat'can be interpreted as either 'ru' or 'gi', 'A' can be interpreted as either 'na' or 'di' and 'B flat' can be interpreted as either 'du' or 'ni'. Only the context can disambiguate the tones as notes of Carnatic music.

These overlapping functions are *interpretable only in context.* Thus if 'ri' is selected after 'ra', it performs the function of a Gaandhaaram, now newly termed 'ga'. Similarly, after 'sa', if 'gi' is selected before a 'gu', then the former is re-interpreted as 'ru'; after 'pa' and 'da', if 'di' is selected it is re-interpreted as 'na' and if after 'pa' and 'ni', 'nu' is selected, 'ni' is re-interpreted as 'du'. Thus there are in addition to a unique 'sa' and 'pa' and two Madhyamams, three Riʃabhams, three Gaandhaarams, three Daivatams and three Niʃaadams with the octave containing sixteen 'notes' and not twelve as in the Western system. Thus, for Veenkaʈamakhi, if every full scale has to have seven notes with the 'sa' and 'pa' fixed and the choice is between 'ma' and 'mi', by permutation and combination, we arrive at 72 full scales, called Meeɭakartaa. (i.e. in the first half and second half of the octave twice two sets of three notes; 6 × 6 = 36 × 2 (ma or mi) = 72).

To quote Ayyangar's (1972) quotation from Veenkaʈamakhi:

> "The 72 Meeɭakartaas I have suggested are doubtless the product of my creative urge. That is not their sole criterion. If it were so it is a waste of ingenuity. Nor do I claim that the scheme as a whole is practicable here and now. True, it covers only a few raagas in circulation at present. I have designed it as a honeycomb cabinet to provide a niche for all raagas past, present and future." (p. 159–160)

The comparison that readily comes to mind is with the periodic table constructed on the basis of the atomic weight of elements developed by Mendeleev which could predict elements not yet discovered. Similarly, Veenkaʈamakhi's Meeɭakartaa schema could predict raagas like Kalyaaɳi and Karaharapriyaa though he himself was very skeptical of the former (his schema was greater than him). In the centuries following Veenkaʈamakhi, his schema found general acceptability (in spite of a lot of skeptics) with many composers and performers taking up the rarer scales for creating compositions and for elaboration.

Further possibilities of 'full' scales are explored in Sambamurthy (1999) with scales selecting one or more different notes in the ascending and descending scale. Therefore, the actual list of possible 'full' scales is a very large number (of course not fully exploited till now).

Now, with the schema in place, if we allow scales that are not full (with a minimum of five (four?) per ascending or descending scale and scales that may be called 'non-linear' (known as vakra raagaa, literally 'crooked') scales which prohibit certain tone sequences[59], then we have the best example of creativity in Carnatic music as we can create new scales and, in principle, the set of possible scales is infinite. Therefore, in principle, new raagas can be *invented/created* by the Carnatic music fraternity (it is another matter for the new raagas to find acceptance among the fraternity).

Keeping all these possibilities in mind, if we consider the function of interpreting tones in a musical phrase/line, the inescapable conclusion is that interpretation is not always a simple '*local*' phenomenon but may involve non-adjacent tones in long sequences of tones.

(5) Musical demonstration [⊙ 4.33] & [⊙ 4.34]

Local interpretation

Sa ra 'gi' ma	interpreted as 'gaandhaaram' as E flat
Sa 'gi' gu ma	interpreted as 'riʃabham' – augmented D

Non-local interpretation

Sa gu ma .. ..

And much later

ma gi sa	where 'gi' interpreted as 'riʃabham', as an augmented D if and only if 'ra' and 'ri' are never attested anywhere in the entire musical discourse.

Therefore, the role of the PF-like component is unquestionably necessary in the context of the grammar of Carnatic music.

4.3. Interpretation of tone: Take 2

We now take a closer look at the issue of tone boundary and the systematic exploitation of 'inter-tone' boundaries in Carnatic music. It is generally claimed that the notes were supposedly derived mathematically as cycles of fifths and cycles of fourths from a fundamental note (see Sambamurthy 1999, V for a fuller discussion).

In other words, tuning for the fifth note proceeded from a fundamental, then taking the fifth as the fundamental the subsequent fifth was arrived at and so on. The derived notes were then transposed to the lower octave (if necessary) and the other notes in the octave were determined. Similarly, from a fundamental the fourth was derived, keeping the fourth as the fundamental the next fourth was arrived at and if the notes went beyond the octave they were transposed to the lower octave. By these two operations, the twelve notes in an octave were mathematically arrived at (supposedly).

Table 1. Hypothesized pitch values in cents of the Indian scale and the even tempered scale[60]

Tone label	Western	Indian
1. Df ra – suddha riʃabham	100	112
2. D ri – caturʃruti riʃabham	200	204
3. Ef gi – saadhaaraṇa gaandhaaram	300	316
4. E gu – antara gaandhaaram	400	386
5. F ma – suddha madhyamam	500	498
6. Fs mi – prati madhyamam	600	588 (590)
7. G pa – pancamam	700	700 (702)
8. Af da – suddha dhaivatam	800	814
9. A di – caturʃruti dhaivatam	900	906
10. Bf ni – kaisiki niʃaadam	1000	1018
11. B nu – kaakali niʃaadam	1100	1088

The values for the 12 Indian 'notes' and their related note in the even tempered scale are given above, along with the labels for the notes in both the systems.[61] But notice, that because of the different modes of derivation in the Indian and the Western scales, we see that the cent values of the Indian scale and Western scale do not match. However, notice that the 'notes' of the major scale, i.e. 'ri', 'ma' and 'di' differ minimally from the notes of the Western major scale in their cent values but 'gu' and 'ni' deviate quite a bit from the even tempered Western scale.

Now consider the real pitch values of the twelve tones in my veena tuned to 'E' on the pitch pipe, given in Figure 2. These frequencies translated to cent values presented below for comparison with the Western system and Indian theory are given below. The differences in cent values are quite bewilderingly different from any of the other values. Consider the differences in Table 2 on the following page.

The major point worth noting is that the Western even tempered cent values, the supposedly mathematically derived cent values in Indian music theory and the real values from my veena do not match (with the real frequencies in my veena converted to cent values). Not only do the values on my veena not match either value, they are far off the mark for even the major landmark like 'pa'. Thus we see that we have practical proof of Indian music theory being just that – 'theory'. It must be mentioned that the entire demonstration was done with this tuning on my veena which is attested in the demonstration MP3 collection. I have listened to my recording and so has the recordist and we found the note values 'tolerable'. Since these are the stable values of the twelve notes on my veena, we do not even have the excuse of saying that they are idiosyncratic points on the Indian scale.

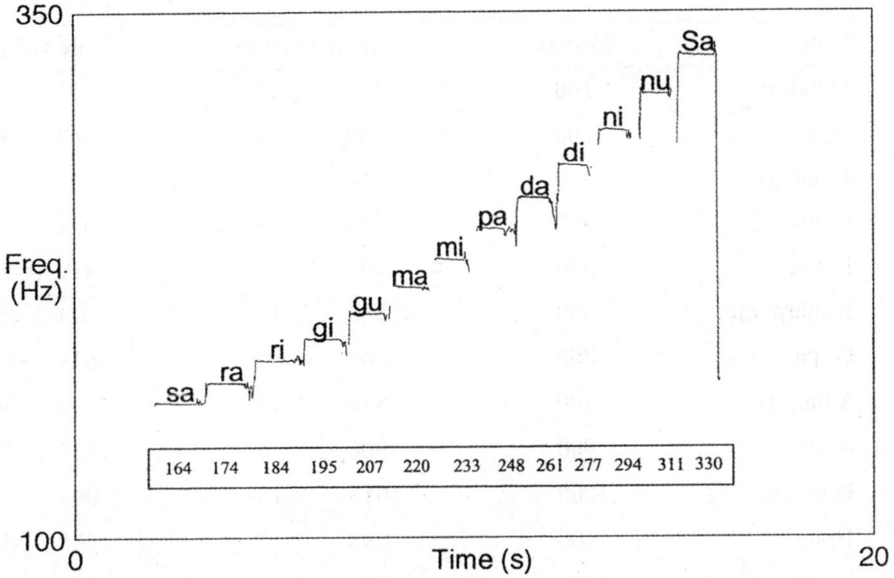

Figure 2. Frequency values on my veena set at E

I have no option but to say that the musical reality of the Carnatic scale has nothing to do with the Indian 'mathematical' values. The analogy is once again language. In language, when languages make use of pitch variation either for intonational or lexical purposes, they typically do not aim at 'absolute' values. Firstly, the pitch range of the speaker is age-sex dependent: younger people and women have higher pitch ranges and secondly, for the same speaker, depending on the emotion/expressive nature of the output the pitch range can vary rather widely. Thus what constitutes a 'high' pitch for one speaker may constitute a 'mid' pitch for another and what constitutes a 'high' pitch in one style for one speaker may constitute a 'low' pitch for the same speaker in another style. Thus in language, pitch labels like 'high', 'mid' and 'low' make no sense in isolation or in absolute terms as they vary with the speaker and with the register. To labour the same point, the same speaker when excited or when speaking to a child is likely to use an extended pitch range where the 'high', 'mid' and 'low' would be exaggeratedly far apart.

Table 2. The values of notes in cents in the Western, even-tempered scale, the Indian theoretical system and my veena[62]

Note	Western	Indian Theory		my veena	
D flat; ra	100	112	+12	98	–2
D; ri	200	204	+4	163	–37
E flat; gi	300	316	+16	241	–59
E; gu	400	386	–14	327	–73
F; ma	500	498	–2	419	–81
F sharp; mi	600	588	–12	511	–89
G; pa	700	700	±0	618	–82
A flat; da	800	814	+14	710	–90
A; di	900	906	+6	824	–76
B flat; ni	1000	1018	+18	944	–56
B; nu	1100	1088	–12	1065	–35
C upper; Sa	1200	1200		1200	

Unlike language, the only mathematical reality given to a Carnatic musician is the value of the octave (approximately). Everything else is culture-bound. The conclusion that I wish to draw is *not* that a cent value difference of, say, 37 between my veena and the Western absolute scale or a cent value of 41 between my veena and that of the Indian mathematical tradition is really imperceptible to the Indian ear. *I would like to maintain that 'absolute' values are really irrelevant to the Carnatic music system.* What the Carnatic music system deals with is pitch relations – as long as, perceptible boundaries are defined with respect to the twelve 'static' tones. And we will see in the next chapter that the Carnatic music fraternity can perceive differences as low as 20 cent values and make fine distinctions between different types of pitch movements. But more of this later.[63]

While the cycle of the fifths gives us a fairly close approximation to cent values in the Western major scale, i.e. the notes 'sa' C, 'ri' D, 'gu' E, 'ma' F, 'pa' G, 'di' A and 'nu' B in the Indian theoretical scale, it is quite likely that the hypothesized cycle of the fourths which is supposed to give us the 'minor' tones, i.e. 'ra' D flat, 'gi' E flat, 'mi' F sharp, 'da' A flat and 'ni' B flat are just that – a theoretical hypothesis worked out mathematically. But the cent value of my veena and the twelve tones is a real eye-opener. The entire exercise is only a theoretical justification of sorts, the actual reality cannot be determined mathematically or by any cycle of the fifths or the fourths. Like the setting of the pitch values of tones in language, the distinct twelve tones are perceptual landmarks in the octave which guide further minute pitch variations in a number of grammatically determined ways.

As is obvious by now, no instrument maker in India ever tunes all the twelve notes using the cycles of the fifths and fourths as theorized. The large part of the setting is done just by ear (and sometimes re-adjusted when there is disagreement between the tuner and the musician). Therefore, it is clear that the theory of the cycle of the fifths and the fourths is just that – theory. But an elegant one nevertheless. Notice that some of the differences in tones between the Western and the Carnatic systems are fairly large and, I think, perceptible to the musically trained ear. This difference is easily demonstrated comparing the scales rendered on a veena and any keyboard instrument. Therefore, since this is a major instance of re-interpreting pitch values which is culture bound, we definitely need the tone interpreting mechanism.

4.4. Interpretation of tone: Take 3

But Indian theorizing did not stop with this. They took the 'experiment' to its logical end and seemingly ended up finding more frequencies than they bargained for. The frequencies between the first and the eighth note of an octave is a fairly large number – precisely double the frequency of the first note and the Indian system is supposed to have mathematically derived 22 ſrutis or microtones or quarter tones (ignoring two more derivative tones which do not match the first–fifth note requirement) in an octave computing with cycles of fifths and fourths from a fixed fundamental. If one proceeds with the 'experiment' of the cycles of the fifths and the fourths then, one ends up with twenty two microtones or quarter tones. Of course, other possibilities also do exist. For instance, the third is also a possible candidate for such computing. We could then, theoretically, arrive at many more 'tones' combining the cycle of the fifth, fourth and the third. And many more possibilities exist in 'theory' only constrained by the human ear's ability to perceive smaller and smaller differences in frequencies.

But once again, the elegant part of all this supposedly 'mathematical' proof is that the magical number of twenty two gives us invariant 'sa' and 'pa' and two variants of each of the other ten notes, of sometimes higher, sometimes lower frequency. I suspect that this supposedly mathematical experiment is really an afterthought, a justification of what was already in practice. It is quite possible that the Indian musical system had started exploiting the inter-tonal frequencies and the so-called proof was really after the fact. However, whatever my conjecture, we cannot fail to admire the ingenuity of the entire enterprise. Whether sanctioned by theory or justified by it later, the fact that Carnatic music systematically exploits inter-tonal frequencies is a reality that we have to come to terms with. The fact that Indian music theory sanctioned it with a sophisticated, elegant mathematical argument is proof of the Indian genius.

The question of paramount importance now is whether we should recognize 12 tone boundaries or 22 '*significant*', '*perceptually salient*', tones in an octave, as claimed by many scholars in the Indian tradition. The crucial words here are 'significant' and 'perceptually salient'. Therefore what is at stake for Carnatic music is not, perhaps, the actual number values in cents[64] of the 12 fixed tones (at least in the fretted musical instruments) but the issue of the 22 distinct ʃrutis in the octave. The Indian tradition hypothesizes that, apart from the two fixed tones 'sa' and 'pa' (first and fifth respectively), all the other tones admit a lower or a higher variant. The list of the 22 *ʃrutis*, their labels and their hypothesized cent values are given below (adapted from Sambamurthy (1999, V: 41). While there are reduced versions of ra, ri, gi, di and ni, there are augmented versions of gu, ma, mi and nu. The reduced (henceforth red) are played on the preceding fret and the augmented (henceforth aug) versions are generally played on the same fret by deflecting the string of the veena. The cent values worked out from the cycles of the fifths and fourths in the Indian system may require 'imaginative' adjustments in 'real' values. For purposes of presentation, I will assume that actual number of ʃrutis and their real values could range between the mid value in the tempered scale or slightly less or more (depending on whether the quarter tone is reduced or augmented respectively) than the hypothesized Indian value. As we know from previous discussion, tone (semi and quarter) boundaries are not precise frequencies in real life in Carnatic music. They are a range of frequencies perceived to be 'the same' by convention in the music community and they even vary quite a bit from performer to performer in Carnatic music (see Krishnaswamy 2003a, b for details). We will see shortly that these reduced and augmented micro tones are 'notes' only in theory and that in practice it is something very different. The renderings are always a range of pitch frequencies which are interpretable as 'different' notes – specific to raagas.

Table 3. The 22 ʃruti microtonal system which Carnatic music systematically exploits

Carnatic labels		Temp.		Veena
1. ʃaɖjam (sa)	0	C	0	0
2. gauɭa riʃabham (red. ra)	90			
3. suddha riʃabnam (ra)	112	D flat	100	92
4. triʃruti riʃabhan (red. ri)	182			
5. caturʃruti riʃabhan (ri)	204	D	200	163
6. bhairavi gaandhaaram (red. gi)	294			
7. saadhaaraɳa gaandhaaram (gi)	316	E flat	300	241
8. antara gaandhaaram (gu)	386	E	400	327
9. cyuutagaandhaaram (aug. gu)	408			
10. suddha madhyamam (ma)	498	F	500	419
11. beegaɖaa madhyamam (aug. ma)	520			
12. pratı madhyamam (mi)	590	F sharp	600	511
13. cyuuta pancamam (aug. mi)	612			
14. pancamam (pa)	700	G	700	618
15. eeka ʃruti daivatam (red. da)	792			
16. suddha daivatam (da)	814	A flat	800	710
17. triʃruti daivatam (red. di)	884			
18. caturʃruti daivatam (di)	906	A	900	824
19. bhairavi niʃaadam (red. ni)	996			
20. kaisiki niʃaadam (ni)	1018	B flat	1000	944
21. kaakali niʃaadam (nu)	1088	B	1100	1065
22. cyuuta ʃaɖjam (aug. nu)	1100*[65]			

The point worth noting is that the reduced and augmented notes and their associated pitch ranges are quite distinct from other pitch range possibilities that Carnatic music systematically exploits (which I will examine in the next chapter).

I assume that the exploitation of inter-tonal frequencies must have struck the theoreticians as bizarre but the theory rose to the occasion to justify the practice offering an elegant mathematical proof of the fact.

We must recognize that there are two distinct claims implicit in this mathematical 'proof' of 'quarter tones/ʃrutis' in Carnatic music. *The first claim* is that frequencies much less than 50 cents are perceptible to the (south) Indian ear. On the one hand, it is doubtful that the adequately trained Carnatic fraternity can perceive tones as close as 12 cents. Notice that while the majority of reduced and augmented tones have a tonal distance of 22 cents, the tonal difference between kaakali niʃaadam and cyuuta ʃaɖjam is only 12 cents. Intuitively, this seems quite incorrect. The 'cyuuta ʃaɖjam' must be actually higher than the cent value of 'B' but it is not. I take it that there has been a miscalculation here and leave it at that. On the other hand, the general idea is that reduced/augmented versions of semi tones are in the range of 20 cents – an intuitively sound idea. In other words, the reduced/augmented versions of the semi tones are 'minor' deviations from the semi tone pitch frequency. Intuitively, it must have been the case that the 'note' in Carnatic music did not quite 'come up to' the frequency of the semi tone (in the case of the red tones) or went a 'little beyond' the semi tone (in the case of the aug tones) and the intuition is that the frequency is not half way between the semi tones (not 50 cents) but 'minor' deviations (of the range of 20–22 cents). The 'perceived' effect then receives theoretical support from the mathematical argument. But still, the first claim has two subparts to it. Firstly, the reduced/augmented tones are perceivable as static tones in different contexts and secondly, they are perceivable in strict context. I assume that while the former claim is not true, the latter is. Let me explain the difference in interpretation to the two sub claims. While the distinction between 'ra ma' and 'ri ma' is obvious enough to any music lover, as 'ra' and 'ri' are perceivable in a *broad context*, the difference between a static 'red.ra ma' and 'ra ma' may not be perceivable to the Carnatic music fraternity. However, what the Carnatic music fraternity can and does perceive is the distinction between a 20 cents reduced value of 'gi' from a twenty cents augmented value of 'gi' in context, i.e. when the anchors and the targets are well defined. In other words, perception of smaller cent values improves in context of relational pitch values in the musical phrase. Therefore, in one sense the Carnatic music fraternity is sensitive to minute pitch variations, i.e. distinctions in the range of twenty cents or even less, but only in *narrow contexts*, i.e., the musical phrase in which the pitch value is embedded.[66] But more of this in the next chapter.

The second claim implicit in the 'mathematical' proof is that Indian (Carnatic) music employs *22 static pitch* specifications instead of 12 static pitch specifications. *The two claims are distinct and not interdependent.* While we could easily demonstrate the incorrectness of the second claim, it would be unwise to dismiss the first claim off hand. The objective of the rest of this chapter is to show that while the first claim is 'psychologically' valid for Carnatic music, the second is valid neither psychologically nor in real pitch values and must be abandoned as a valueless 'theoretical' construct of a by gone era.

Questioning the second claim in traditional Indian musicology, Krishnaswamy (2002a, b) has shown conclusively with the pitch graphs of sample music clips (excerpted from musicians of 'standing') that there are, in fact, no more than 12 *static* pitches in Carnatic music. He has demonstrated visually that the supposedly lower tones, namely the riʃabham in Saaveeri raagam (Gauḷa riʃabham (red ra)) or the gaandhaaram in Tooḍi raagam (Bhairavi gaandharam (red gi)) are not static notes with lower pitch boundaries than 'ra' and 'gi' respectively. He says quite correctly,

> "We did not find any quarter tones… Rather we found a total of 12 clearly distinguishable intervals among the constant-pitch notes, and their values were also close to the 12 semitones used in Western music." (2002a:V-559)

These notes which are rendered from a lower note are, in fact, pitch spikes moving from the lower note to almost the next semitone for a very brief period of time. He adds that

> "(i)f we calculated the average value (in cents) of these spikes, we would end up roughly in the quarter tonal range or less. It is clear by simple visual inspection, that neither the peak heights nor the average values of these spikes are in any sense consistent with the interval values stated in (Sambamurthy (1999; V)) … Quartertones (constant pitch intervals bisecting the semitones) are not used in Carnatic music, and it is possible that they may even sound strange or unmusical to many Carnatic musicians." (2002b: 3)

Actually, one does not even need a pitch graph to tell a person trained in Carnatic music that the 'alleged' quarter tones are not static tones. All practitioners/connoisseurs of Carnatic music know that while the riʃabham in the raagam Reevati admits a static, long 'ra', i.e. one can prolong the note as a steady pitch, the riʃabham of the raagam Gauḷa (if prolonged) does not, i.e. it is a gentle pitch oscillation. While the former is a steady pitch, the latter is not. It is clearly a pitch variation which is determined precisely by the grammar of Carnatic music (we will see instances of pitch graphs and their interpretations in the following chapter). Further, had musical practice been fairly undisturbed across centuries (a rather questionable assumption, no doubt), then it must have been physically evident to our forefathers as well. That certain tones were held static at a frequency and others were rendered as pitch oscillations must have been obvious to early theorists as well. *Still they chose to posit 'abstract, steady microtones'. Why?*

Thus, Arvindh Krishnaswamy's observations are irrefutably true as far as the physical reality of the phenomenon is concerned. However, when we construct a grammar, our prime concern is the '*cognitive reality*' (psychological reality) of the constructs and the interpretation of the theoretical constructs as physical events is another matter altogether (of course, the theoretical construct must find adequate internal justification). Whereas the cognitive reality is a theoretical construct, the physical reality is the acoustic evidence. Neither can challenge the other directly. Let me illustrate the point with a few examples from linguistics before taking up the issue of the 22 *ʃrutis*.

If one were to take a high speed film of the lips pronouncing the word 'coast',[67] one would observe that the maximal lip rounding occurs not during the end of the vowel but during the articulation of 's'. But no one in his/her right mind would want to attribute rounding to the sound 's' in English as we 'know' that English does not employ labialization on consonants (rounding) unlike some languages which do. Thus, while constructing the grammar of English, we transcribe the 's' without any rounding and attribute the rounding to the preceding segment.

Of course, a researcher trying to synthesize the word 'coast' would be led astray if she/he were to follow the abstract grammar and allow rounding to coincide with the vowel. The issue of microtones at hand is a similar case. What Krishnaswamy is attempting is a *performance model* and its ultimate aim is to be able to feed, perfectly laudable, 'utilitarian' projects like 'automatic transcription' and 'music synthesis'. So the perspective is very different and, naturally, the conclusions would be different too. But his argument that "(quarter tones) may even sound strange or unmusical to many Carnatic musicians" is actually a non-argument. Of course it would be rejected as ungrammatical exactly as the substitution of one allophone for another would be in language. For example, pronouncing the words 'top' and 'stop' with the allophones of /t/ interchanged would not be acceptable to the native speaker. Nor would the voiceless 'allophone' of 'p' be acceptable after a nasal as in a Tamil word like [paampɨ] 'snake' as the pronunciation of the word is, irrefutably, [paambɨ] for all speakers of Tamil.

To take yet another example, while doing 'cognitive' linguistics, it is necessary to posit segment level constructs and principles of higher order organization like the onset, the rhyme and the mora as constituents of the syllable shown below with the syllabification of the word 'octave'.

There is ample theory-internal as well as external evidence for the constructs 'syllable', the optional 'onset', the obligatory 'rhyme' and the unit of abstract timing – the 'mora'. To begin with internal evidence, the constraints on initial consonant clusters are best stated on the construct 'onset' rather than on linear sequences of consonants. For example, English does not allow /p/ to occur before /s/ in a cluster – as an onset, e.g. in the word 'psychology' the 'p' is not pronounced in English but it is in French. But that does not prevent a word like 'upset' from being considered grammatical where the /p/ and the /s/ belong to different syllables.

(6) The syllable and its constituents

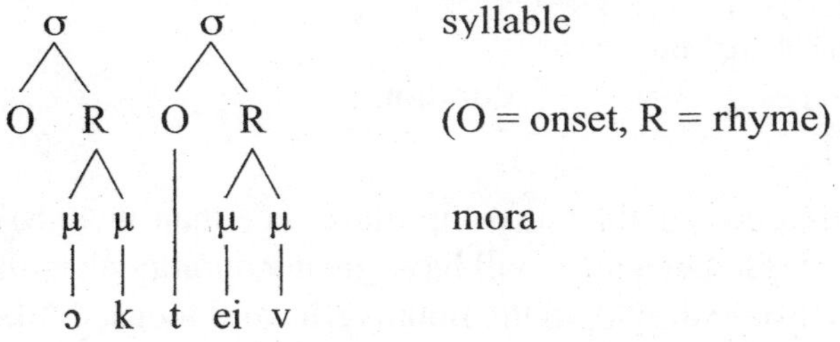

The constituent 'rhyme' is the domain in which combinatorial constraints are expressed. For example, in English, in monosyllabic, non-derived words, one finds only consonants pronounced with the tip and blade of the tongue (known as 'coronals') after the vowel /au/, e.g. 'loud', 'blouse' etc. but *'bloup', *'blouk'. But proper names like 'Mowbray' and the famous fictional name 'Mowgli' are perfectly fine. This is because the vowel /au/ occurs in one syllable and the offending consonant is the onset of the following syllable. Similarly, the abstract timing element called 'mora' allows us to capture many linguistically valid generalizations. For example, we can explain why consonant clusters are allowed after short vowels but generally prohibited after long vowels in monosyllabic, non-derived words, e.g. 'help', 'lisp' but *'heilp', *'leasp' etc.[68] Short vowels occupy one mora and hence there is enough 'time' for two consonants; but long vowels (and vowel glide combinations called diphthongs) occupy two moras and there is 'time' only for one consonant. The timing unit is clearly an abstract notion of time and 'real' timing is quite another issue, as can be easily demonstrated visually in a spectrogram. Moreover, this abstract timing unit pertains only to the theoretical construct 'rhyme', it must be obvious that consonants which are in the onset also do take up some time but are not accounted for by this timing construct. Even within the rhyme, vowels and consonants in different positions of the word tend to take up different timing spans which this 'abstract' theory of linguistic timing has nothing to say about.

(7) Abstract timing and duration mismatch

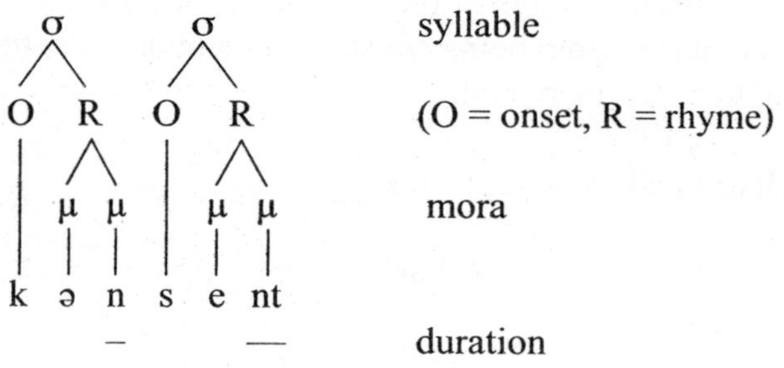

In English, as stressed syllables take up more time than unstressed syllables, the codas in stressed syllables will have greater duration than those in unstressed syllables. For example, in the noun-verb word 'consent' the duration of the nasal in the final syllable will be demonstrably longer than that of the nasal in the first syllable since the final syllable is stressed (irrespective of whether it is a verb or a noun) in native varieties of English.

As (7) graphically illustrates, though the nasal in the first syllable has a mora all to itself unlike the nasal in the second syllable which has to share it with the final 't', the actual duration of the nasal in the second syllable may be greater than that of the first nasal.

Turning to external evidence, the constructs onset and rhyme are the ones involved in 'slip of the tongue errors' where one onset may be switched for another (not just one consonant for another), e.g. 'bread and jam' may become #'jed and bram' but never *#'jred and bam' with just the first consonant being interchanged. And of course, the construct rhyme takes its name from the notion rhyme in poetry where identity is defined in terms of the segments in the rhyme.

Thus the syllable and its constituents are well motivated in linguistic theory and do not need any further justification. However, for purposes of speech synthesis etc., it is totally inadequate. First of all, segment sized elements are simply unmanageable in speech synthesis (and of course, segments do not exist in the speech continuum). For purposes of speech synthesis what may work better is a construct called the demi-syllable where the sequences CV and VC define possible combinations taking into account the fact that the consonants are defined with respect to the vowel in its vicinity and do not have *independent, constant identities*. For example, in the word 'pap', the two /p/s have distinct acoustic realizations in the vowel and similarly, the /p/s in /pip/ are different and so on. Thus, in reality, there are twice as many incarnations of a consonant as there are vowels in a language.[69] Therefore, for purposes of speech synthesis, the linguistic syllables CVC 'pap' ought to be segmented as demi-syllable CV 'pa' and demi-syllable VC 'ap' and the values of the two 'p's defined clearly in acoustic terms and the two demi-syllables put together or merged along the central steady state realization of the vowel 'a' keeping in mind the real timing of the monosyllable.

The point I am labouring to make is that the cognitive reality does not deny the physical reality nor does the physical reality challenge the hypothesized cognitive structure. Both are valid (equally valid) constructs and one can develop algorithms to map one onto the other and vice versa. The grammar one constructs to explain the cognitive process that is language does not undermine in any way the algorithms one constructs from the speech continuum for purposes of speech synthesis or vice versa. But one must remember that neither can directly falsify the other.

Another example from linguistics, more relevant for Carnatic music, is the representation of pitch. In reality, we employ a range of frequencies in speech. An utterance exploits some pitch perturbation *intentionally* to convey grammatical meaning; but there are many 'minor' perturbations which are caused by consonantal effects and are therefore *not intentional*. If the grammar were to consider all the pitch variations on a par, the grammar that would get written would be very uneconomical and inelegant (criteria of quite some importance in science).

Let us consider the possible pitch values on the first syllable of the words 'naalɨ' ('four') and 'pattɨ' ('ten') pronounced in distinct contexts by speakers of Chennai Brahmin Tamil.

(8) Neutral and Contrastive Focus in Chennai Brahmin Tamil

a. i. eppo vandɛ̃ɛ̃?
When came (you)
'When did you come?'

a. ii. naalɨ maɳikkɨ vandɛ̃ɛ̃
four hour-DAT came
'Came at four o'clock'

a. iii. pattɨ maɳikkɨ vandɛ̃ɛ̃
ten hour came
'Came at ten o'clock'

b. i. aarɨ maɳikkɨ vandiyaa?
Six hour came?
'Did you come at six o clock?'

b. ii. illɛ// naalɨ maɳikkɨ vandɛ̃ɛ̃
No; four hour came.
'No; I came at four o'clock.'

b. iii. illɛ// pattɨ maɳikkɨ vandɛ̃ɛ̃
no; ten hour came
'No; I came at ten o'clock.'

From the linguistic point of view, the relevant generalization is that neutral focus (the answer to the question "when did you come?") is realized as a low pitch on the first vowel and a rise on the following vowel and that contrastive focus (the answer in the negative to the question "did you come at six o clock?") is realized as a high pitch on the fist vowel and a low pitch on the following vowel is necessary and sufficient. However, in terms of actual physical reality one would see that the initial sounds /n/ and /p/ have their own influence on the pitch of the following vowel and the fact that the vowel is long in one case and short in the other would also affect the implementation of the 'low' and 'high' pitch ideal. But for 'linguistic', or rather, cognitive purposes, we ignore these physical perturbations as they are predictable performance factors. For linguistic purposes we would consider the former first syllable to be low pitched and the latter first syllable to be high pitched, not withstanding the initial pitch flutter due to the preceding sound and the duration of the steady state because of the length of the vowel. In other words, cognitively, what one sizes up as 'high' or 'low' may have different, variant physical realization in language.

Similarly, in Carnatic music, the acoustic proof that Krishnaswamy establishes does not necessarily deny the theoretical construct of 22 ʃrutis if we can show that this idea of microtonal music allows us to explain the cognitive reality of Carnatic music. The criteria I will be invoking to claim the need for the 22 ʃrutis in Carnatic music are:

(9) Criteria for establishing the validity of 22 ʃrutis
   a. the 'psychological reality' of ʃrutis or microtones (henceforth m.tones) which may be supported by perception experiments and
   b. the distinct nature of microtones which defines raagas.

I take up the issue in (9a) first. Given the fact that Indian music, and Carnatic music in particular, does employ frequency ranges in between the recognized semi-tones, the questions to ask are:
1. Can all these tonal boundaries (22 according to Indian theories) be perceived by trained/semi-trained listeners?
2. Does the Carnatic musical system exploit the *static* m.tone boundaries as independent 'notes' for musical purposes?

At the outset let me say that my answer to the first question is a "yes, most probably" and a definite "no" to the second. A positive response to the first question implies the "psychological reality" of at least 22 ʃrutis (or a slightly modified version) in an octave for the adequately trained performer/listener. The 22 perceived tonal boundaries would be some kind of abstract or 'cognitive landmarks' for the performer/listener which the grammar manipulates in different ways. The first question can be answered (positively or negatively) if and only if we can show with the help of perception experiments which can be replicated that trained performers/listeners can/cannot, in fact, perceive 22 tones in an octave (the boundary question to be determined either by the law of the average or according to the average of the Indian measurements).

The outline of a sample experimental setup is described here. As a baseline assumption, I take it that all humans can, with or without training, perceive the twelve tonal boundaries (this may be a questionable assumption, specially, regarding non-trained or inadequately trained listeners/performers[70]). The working hypothesis is that trained performers/listeners of Carnatic music can perceive m.tones, i.e. the intermediate 'fixed' frequencies (approximately fixed in the range of 20 to 40 cents around the tone with which it is related in the red or aug relationship). The data presented should be synthesized pure tones and, perception experiments must be tested on fairly large, homogenous groups for the result to be robust. For the test to be meaningful, we should select at least a 30 member, fairly homogenous group of the Carnatic music fraternity (in three random groups) who should be presented with carefully constructed tests (10 sets each level) of successively higher levels of 'cognitive' material. The question asked should be restricted to "Are the tones/tonal sequences heard the same or different?"

(10) Step 1: Test material: 'sa'; 'reduced ra' and 'ra' in normal tempo (the second and third notes in random order).
Question to ask: Are the second and third tones the same or are they different?

Step 2: Test Material in slow to moderately slow tempo:
Set 1: sa, reduced ra, ma
Set 2: sa, ra, ma
Question to ask: Are the second notes in the sequences the same or different?

Step 3 More complex sequences...
e.g. sa, reduced ra/gi or gu
sa, ra/gi or gu
Question to ask: Are the second notes in the sequences the same or different?

If the overall response to questions in steps 1 and 2 is positive (significance computed statistically), then we have sufficient evidence to establish beyond reasonable doubt the 'psychological reality' of m.tones in the Carnatic music system that is the foundation of the Indian tradition. The result obtained for red.tone can be then replicated for aug.tones as well. Pending experimental verification, I assume the 'psychological reality' of the m.tones in my grammar of Carnatic music. I thus assume the Indian tradition is, by and large, correct regarding the necessity of postulating m.tones as theoretical constructs.[71]

The claim that the grammar of Carnatic music may refer to 22 (or even 23) ʃrutis and not just 12 tones is, in fact, the corner stone of the theory that I propose here. I now need to demonstrate the 'distinct' nature of some of the m.tones to prove beyond reasonable doubt the distinctive nature of m.tones in the raagam system. As in linguistics, we are agreed that an element is 'distinctive' if and only if it occurs in an environment where its presence/ substitution with another note would make a difference. We are all agreed that the selection of one of the 12 semi-tones and the change in any one tone may signal a distinct scale, rendering all the 12 *distinctive* in the grammar of Carnatic music. The crucial word here is the word 'distinctive' meaning capable of creating a distinction. As in the case of language, the substitution of 'p' for 'b' in the word 'bee' can create a new lexical item, a substitution of one semi-tone for another can create another scale and that is how we prove the distinctive nature of 12 tones. For instance, in the scale /sa ri gi ma pa di ni Sa/ if we replace any one 'note', say 'nu for 'ni' the scale changes from Karaharapriyaa to Gaurimanoohari. This is why it is amply clear that the twelve 'notes' are distinct entities in Carnatic music and the substitution of one by another can bring about a change of scale.

The proof for the distinctive nature of the additional 10 tones is a little more complex. Recall that our answer to the second question

2. "Does the Carnatic musical system exploit the *fixed* m.tone boundaries as independent 'notes' for musical purposes?"

is a definite 'No'. As the instrumental evidence in Arvindh Krishnaswamy irrefutably demonstrates, Carnatic musicians do not, in fact, render approximations of more than 12 static tones as static reference points. In other words, there is an undominated context-free markedness constraint prohibiting the static realization of the reduced and augmented tones (the additional 10) which we label **Red/AugRenScaleTone*. This explains why there are no more than 12 static frequency reference points in an octave which are the least marked renderings of the 'notes' of Carnatic music henceforth referred to as *RenScale* rendering. Further, the constraint label also makes it clear that not only can the reduced/augmented tones not be realized as *static* targets, they cannot be specified as *targets* either, i.e. recognized pitch values to be achieved. To render a reduced/augmented tone, perforce, one would have to have an initiating anchor tone to start with, a target tone to be the maximum pitch value and a final anchor tone to which the glide must approach which are distinct, and which have to be one of the 12 semitones. This explains why these reduced/augmented tones always get realized as a glide from an 'anchor' tone to a 'target' tone satisfying the grammar's specification of a reduced/augmented tone by traversing the reduced/augmented tone by passing through these frequencies. Further, these reduced/augmented tones are always paired with their appropriate semi tone which could be the same or different from the target tone (more of this by and by). The distinct realizations of several reduced and augmented tones will be dealt with in detail subsequently.

Having outlined the issue of the execution of reduced/augmented tones (referred to as m.tones henceforth), I now demonstrate the distinctive nature of m.tones in Carnatic music. I show a few examples where, other things being equal, some raagas idiosyncratically select for an m.tone where others do not (but since the related semi tone is the least marked tone of that category, no raagam can avoid selecting the least marked semi tones). The distinctive nature of m.tones will be established if and only if we can show that in two or more sequences with (more or less) the same tonal sequence, while some select an m.tone others do not (as in the case of sounds in language). I give two sets of raagas below which help us establish the distinctive nature of m.tones in Carnatic music.

(11) Proof of the distinctive nature of reduced/augmented tones in Carnatic music.

a1. i. Maayaamaaḻavagauḻa [⊙ 4.36]
ii. Gauḻa
both raagas select 'sa ra gu…' and also select for reduced 'ra'.
iii. Saaveeri [⊙ 4.37]
selects sa ra ma…' and also reduced 'ra'.

a2. i. Bauḻi [⊙ 4.38]
selects 'sa ra gu…' but not reduced 'ra'
ii. Reevati [⊙ 4.39]
selects 'sa ra ma..' but not reduced 'ra'.
It is not even the case that the m.tone in question is not selected by the raagas in a2 because 'ra' cannot be rendered as a prolonged note because the 'ra' can be long but still must not be 'red.ra' for these raagas.

b1. i. Harikaamboodi [⊙ 4.40]
selects 'sa ri gu ma…' and also reduced ma.

b2. i. Ravichandrikaa[72]
selects 'sa ri gu ma…' but not reduced ma.

Thus we see that the reduced/augmented tones are really distinctive in nature and their presence/absence help us distinguish one raagam from another.

However, I am not sure all ten of them are equally 'distinctive'. While red. ri and red.di are of questionable standing (see chapter 5 for details), certain other notes if selected, automatically also select the m.tones associated with them, e.g. 'mi' and 'nu'. All raagas which select these notes also admit their respective aug.m.tones also. Similarly, all raagas which select 'gi' and 'ni' also select slightly lower values for these notes which I re-label as red.gi and red.ni respectively (not sanctioned by Indian music theory).[73] Thus clearly, certain m.tones are distinctive and certain others are not. So I conclude that the grammar of Carnatic music does indeed refer to m.tones, some of which are invoked selectively in some raagas and not others arguing for their cognitive reality for the Carnatic music fraternity. We will see later that in addition to the 22 ʃrutis, Carnatic music has several other devices like distinct patterns of pitch glides, fleeting tones etc. for distinguishing one set of raagas from another etc.

What I have tried to show is that Carnatic music not only sanctions m.tones (10 or 11 as the case may be) but also allows certain raagas to select them randomly and not others. The random selection of m.tones by raagas is irrefutable proof of the distinctive nature of m.tones in Carnatic music. This fact supports the often reiterated generalization that the system of gamakkam (pitch oscillations) is not a mere matter of ornamentation but the very essence of Carnatic music, often crucial for determining issues pertaining to grammaticality (more of this in chapters 6 and 7). However, as I said earlier, not all m.tones are distinctive as the choice of a note may necessitate the obligatory selection of its corresponding m.tone as well, to varying degrees. This is the reason why notes like 'gi' and 'ni' must always sanction their corresponding reduced m.tones but 'mi' and 'nu' may not. The difference lies in the nature of the rendering. While the non-selection of the corresponding m.tones in the case of 'mi' and 'nu' can be masked to a certain extent by rendering these notes as 'fleeting' notes or chaayaa swaram, the non-selection of the m.tones corresponding to the notes 'gi' and 'ni' cannot be masked as the following note is usually at least a semi-tone away and therefore 'gi' and 'ni' cannot be rendered as fleeting notes. However, when the following note is 'gu' or 'nu' (where 'gi' and 'ni' are interpreted as 'ru' and 'du' respectively, it is a matter of style whether these notes can be rendered as RenScale notes only or as reduced m.tones). Thus we see that while the m.tones of 'ra', 'gu', 'ma' and 'da' are totally distinctive, i.e. idiosyncratically selected by raagas, the m.tones of 'gi', 'ni' on the one hand and 'mi'and 'nu' on the other may not be distinctive but style-oriented, signaling differences across styles of Carnatic music. Another point worth noting is that while the reduced m.tones of 'gi' and 'ni', I claim, are selected by all raagas of Carnatic music, these notes admit an augmented m.tone each as well which are idiosyncratically selected by raagas of Carnatic music. But more of this in the next chapter.

Thus I argued in this chapter that Carnatic music definitely requires a tone interpretation mechanism and that while the twenty two ʃruti theory of the octave may be a cognitive reality for the Carnatic music fraternity, quarter tones are not realized as static targets because of a high ranking markedness constraint *RED/AUGRENSCALETONE, which prohibit these tones to function as stable anchors/targets.

4.5. Interpretation of tone: Take 4

In this section, I take a still closer look at some of the constraints that help us define the relative markedness of tones and their sequencing in Carnatic music. Once again, before addressing this issue, I shall go back to linguistics. Informally speaking, it is well-known that one produces 'voice' by the vibration of the vocal cords. But in reality, it is rather difficult to turn the vibration of the vocal cords on and off in a matter of milliseconds. Firstly, the effort required to vibrate the vocal cords is much less when air escapes without obstruction or friction through the oral tract or the nose (for the set of sounds called 'sonorant', i.e. vowels, nasal sounds and /l/ and /r/ type sounds (the last two types are known as liquids)) than it is for sounds during the production of which there is either complete block or friction in the oral tract (as it is for consonants called 'obstruents' comprising stops and fricatives), e.g. b, d, g, d͡ʒ (as in 'Jew'), v, ð (as in 'they' (this is a fricative, i.e. a continuous sound in native styles of speech), z (as in Zen), ʒ (as in 'rouge'). Therefore, generally, it is easier to pronounce voiced vowels, nasals and liquids and voiceless stops and voiceless fricatives. This fact is also reflected in the selection of sounds across languages. Whereas all languages select sounds freely from the easy, unmarked sets (called context-free unmarked), not many languages select any from the marked sets (called context-free marked). Thus, there are languages which select voiced vowels, nasals, liquids but only voiceless stops and fricatives (closer home, the only fricatives the south Indian languages select are voiceless ones) but there are no languages which select exclusively from the marked sets. There are no languages which select only voiceless vowels, or only voiceless nasals or voiced fricatives or voiced stops. By implication, if a language has a voiceless vowel, it must also have a voiced vowel; if it has a voiced stop it must also have a voiceless stop, etc.

Secondly, since it is difficult to control the vocal cords quickly, to turn voicing on and off on command, it depends on where the voicing occurs, whether it is preceded/followed by silence, a voiceless segment or a voiced segment. Thus one finds asymmetries like the following (referred to as context-sensitive markedness):

a) It is easier to pronounce voiceless stops at the beginning of a word as in 'peace' as there is enough time to adjust for voicing for the vowel later.

b) By implication, it is more difficult to pronounce a voiced stop at the beginning of a word as in 'bee' when the vocal cords are to be set in motion from a state of rest (silence)

c) The same situation obtains word finally where the vocal cords tend to prepare for rest in anticipation of the final silence. So, it is easier to pronounce the word 'rip' than the word 'rib'.

d) The time lag between the opening of the oral cavity and the vibration of the vocal cords that we are referring to is rooted in our physiology. But the way the time lag (technically called voice onset time (VOT for short) is exploited is language dependent. For instance, although initial voicing in obstruents is universally difficult (marked), English and French learn to cope with it in distinct ways. While English takes the easier route by suppressing the vibration of the vocal cords during and even a little after the release of the oral closure (for the stop /b/), French initiates the vibration of the vocal cords a little before the release stage (and it is quite possible many Indian languages may start the vibration well before the release stage, almost coinciding with the closure stage).

So, in effect what we call a 'voiced' consonant in the English word 'bee' has no voicing at all during the closure and the release stages clearly. And this causes no confusion to English speakers as what matters is the distinction between 'bee' and 'pea' which is maintained because of the extended VOT in the case of the latter (known as aspiration). In other words, in the latter word, the vocal cords start vibrating much, much later than the release of the closure and the start of the vowel resulting in a part of the vowel being voiceless which is what we call aspiration. Since French does not choose to delay VOT which would result in the production of a voiceless vowel, it opts for the marked early voice onset. And in many Indian languages there could be an increase in markedness as the contrast required is a four way one (/p, p^h, b and b^h/) rather than a simple two way distinction as in English and French.

Both from the point of view of distinctiveness and adult perception, it is amply clear that voicing and voicelessness are categorical and no language systematically distinguishes words on the basis of voiced, semi-voiced and totally voiceless segments. But the physical reality is very different across languages.[74] Thus the interaction of vocal fold vibration, context-free (general) markedness, context-sensitive markedness and the salient distinctions in a language is complex giving rise to a large set of possibilities across languages. We should bear in mind that we have considered only one feature namely [voice] till now. There are other features like the tension of the glottis [slack vocal cords] and [stiff vocal cords], and the state of the vocal cords whether they are [constricted] or [spread] which also affect the vocal cords' ability to vibrate and produce voice/affect the voice quality of the sound. Thus the eventual interaction gets more and more complex across languages. But the entire gamut of variation in 'voicing' effects can be adequately captured using the limited feature set mentioned above, rather than in terms of degrees of voicing.

The 22 ʃrutis and the different types of glides executed in Carnatic music can be tackled along lines analogous to 'voicing' effects across languages. As in language, we should be able to describe all the tonal effects evidenced in Carnatic music with the help of a small set of specific constraints which could be ranked with respect to each other in different ways to account for the variety of glide effects that are encountered in Carnatic music. As we have already seen, the execution of m.tones is strictly controlled by the undominated (hence inviolable) context-free markedness constraint *RED/AUG-TARGETTONE which ensures that m.tones are never specified as stable anchors or targets of execution and that they require an initiating anchor and a target semi-tone to be bounded in a glide for their 'fleeting' realization.

As a first approximation, I illustrate below the possible execution of some of the m.tones along with the specification of their anchor and target tones. Of course, I draw heavily on my practice while describing the execution of m.tones. I am aware that there could be (minor) variations in their execution across performers/styles. Once the mechanism for the execution of m.tones is in place, we can go on to examine the pitch realization of a note in several raagas to further refine the mechanism in the following chapter.

(12) Execution of some Reduced/Augmented tones

a. Reduced ra
   Anc.sa-Red.ra-Target.ri
   Informally, reduced 'ra' is rendered as a glide from 'sa' almost or up to 'ri'.

b. Reduced gi
   Anc.ra or ri-Red.gi-Target.gi
   Informally, reduced 'gi' is rendered as a glide from the preceding semitone selected by the raagam (sa or ra or ri) and the following semitone as the target (the preceding semitone is dependent on the raagam).

c. Augmented gu
   Anc.gu-Aug.gu-Target.ma

d. Augmented ma[75]
   Anc.gu-Aug.ma-Target.mi or even pa

e. Augmented mi
   Anc.pa-Aug.mi-Target.pa

f. Reduced da
   Anc.pa-Red.da-Target.di

g. Reduced ni
   Anc.pa, da or di-Red.ni-Target.ni

h. Augmented nu
   Anc.Sa-Aug.nu-Target.Sa

The details in (12) above capture the normal playing style of these m.tones on the veena (basically my style). Three major observations are in order pertaining to the execution of m.tones. As I said earlier, firstly, being a veena player, I hardly find much evidence for reduced 'ri' played on 'ra' or a reduced 'di' played on 'da'. This was the reason why I am a little skeptical about the postulation of triʃruti riʃabham and triʃrutidaivatam respectively in Indian music theory. Secondly, Aug.mi and Aug.nu, though played on 'mi' and 'nu' respectively, have a higher starting pitch, perhaps 'pa' and 'Sa' respectively and, as I mentioned earlier, all raagas which select these notes also select the related m.tones.. Finally, Red.gi, Aug.ma and Red.ni admit greater variation specifc to styles/raagas (more of this later).

Apart from the rendering of Aug.mi and Aug.nu, the generalization that one can extract from the formalization in (12) above is that a reduced m.tone is a glide from the immediately preceding (semi-)tone (selected by the raagam) to a higher goal and the augmented m.tone is a downward glide from a higher, immediately following semi-tone to the RenScale note ‘mi’ or ‘nu’ as the case may be via the aug. m.tone and back to the anchor. And while targets can be more than one semi-tone higher than the specified m.tone, in general, they can be particularly higher for red.gi, red.ni and aug.ma. Finally, the anchor of aug.mi and aug.nu are ‘pa’ and ‘Sa’ respectively rather than ‘mi’ and ‘nu’ respectively – the lower tone as in the other cases. These can be formalized as the constraints in (13) below:

(13) Constraints on anchors, goals

a. Markedness of Red.ri and Red.di
   *Red.ri,*Red.di
b. Execution of Reduced Tone (ERT)
   $[T_A\ T_{Red/Aug}\ T_G]$ Glide
   Informally, a glide is initiated from an anchor tone, passes through the reduced tone and has a higher goal.
c. Anchor of Augmented Tone I (AAT-I)
   $T_A\ T_{Aug.Ti} = T_{Ti}\ T_{Aug.Ti}$
   Informally, the anchor of the glide is the note which is to be augmented.
d. Anchor Augmented Tone II (AAT-II)
   (specific to Aug.mi and Aug.nu)
   $T_A\ T_{Aug.Ti} = T_{Ti+1}\ T_{Aug.Ti}$
   Informally, the anchor of the glide is the semi-tone higher than the tone to be augmented.
e. Execution of Target Tone (ETT)
   $\ldots T_{Red/Aug.Ti}\ T = T_{Red/Aug.Ti}\ T_{Red/Aug.Ti+n}$
   where n is at least a semi-tone or at most the next full tone.

In this section we took up the problem of the execution of reduced/augmented tones in Carnatic music and demonstrated how best we could reconcile traditional wisdom with modern, (acoustic) instrumental findings regarding the microtonal nature of Carnatic music.

The claim that grammar of music, in general, and that of Carnatic music in particular, requires a mechanism to interpret tones as notes of music is supported by several arguments. I showed how pitch boundaries are not universally, mathematically defined and that across cultures/performers boundaries could vary. I also explained how Carnatic music has re-interpreted the twelve tone scale as a potential sixteen tone scale giving rise to ambiguity in the interpretation of tones in isolation. Further, since Carnatic music systematically exploits inter-tonal pitch ranges, the mechanism to interpret tones and tonal ranges as notes of music is all the more important. Finally, an attempt was made to formalize the relative markedness of the additional reduced and augmented tones and formalize their rules of interpretation/realization.

Chapter 5
Representation of the musical line

5.1. Introduction

In the previous chapter I argued for the need for an interpretive mechanism which can work on the tone-pitch range to note relationship[76] in Carnatic music. I argued that since Carnatic music has a sixteen tone scale system and a twenty two (or twenty three) m.tone system the need for an interpretive mechanism cannot be questioned. I had shown how a tone in Carnatic music is interpreted from the perspective of a fundamental which is arbitrarily fixed by the performer, and disambiguation is necessitated by the fact that the tones 'ri', 'gi', 'di' and 'ni' are subject to dual interpretation solely on the basis of the context (sometimes not even local) and the practice of exploiting the inter-tonal frequency required Carnatic music to set up a fairly elaborate mechanism for the interpretation of pitch graphs as notes of music in the domain of the musical phrase.

In this chapter, I go on to demonstrate the major realizations of one of the three notes, namely 'gi' from the set 'gi', 'ma' and 'ni' which admit a range of pitch interpretations with a view to establish the characteristics of such a range of pitch interpretations and to account for the range of variation in the theory (abstracting away incidental, predictable or style dependent details). The summary of this discussion leads to a characterization of the types of pitch graphs attested in Carnatic music. Then I go on to further issues in the representation of notes in musical phrases and the musical line to include issues like the representation of phrasal prominence and extra prominence in a musical line. Thus the interpretive mechanism which is in place now for the Grammar of Carnatic Music has the responsibility of assigning 'note' status to tones and pitch ranges, assigning phrasal boundaries and phrasal prominence, assigning musical line boundaries and determining extra prominence at the level of the musical line for an input (perceived or intended). Thus we see that the tone interpretive mechanism (analogous to the PF component in language) performs the functions of assigning a 'note' value to a physical entity, assigns structure to the sequence at three levels, i.e. the level of the mora, the level of the phrase and the line and assigns prominence values to notes in the sequence. In short, this interpretive mechanism supplies the annotated input that the grammar can evaluate. In the last part of the chapter I take a cursory look at the south Indian system and ask questions which will, hopefully, determine the paradigm for future research in issues in Universal Musicology.[77]

5.2. Pitch range interpretation

I now go on to take a still closer look at some more constraints in the tonal grammar of Carnatic music. I will present below an outline of my theory of 'gamakkam' – the exploitation of inter-tonal frequency – in Carnatic music. As I pointed out earlier in chapter 4 and as Krishnaswamy (2003 a, b) correctly observes, gamakkam in Carnatic music cannot be translated as 'ornamentation' which would imply that it is an optional addition in the rendering which is not the case at all. Gamakkam is obligatory and the lack of it could very well render a phrase ungrammatical in many cases. As we saw earlier, m.tones are idiosyncratically associated with raagas and their execution becomes obligatory, not mere ornamentation.

To begin with, I assume, without much discussion, that of the twelve semitones, apart from 'ra' (D flat), 'mi' (F sharp) and 'da' (A flat), all the other tones are of equal context-free markedness. One could argue that the remaining tones are the ones found in the major scale with two additions namely 'gi' (E flat) and 'di' (B flat) from the scale derived from the four note signature of Saama Veedam.[78] Or one could look for more sophisticated mathematical proof etc. I advance two arguments in favour of my intuition regarding the relative markedness of 'ra' (D flat), 'mi' (F sharp) and 'da' (A flat) below.[79]

Firstly, these three tones seem to be fairly unstable anchors and 'pivotal' notes in a musical phrase. In other words, they rarely occur as the resting tone in a musical phrase (note: I did not say 'never'). And if they do, they are coupled with some, adjacent appropriate prominent tones as 'shadow' tones. I demonstrate this point with a few sample phrases from raagas Tooḍi and Kalyaaṇi.

(1) Musical demonstration
raagam Tooḍi [⊙ 4.42]
gi ra, gi ma
Here, 'ra' is a passing note and not a pivot (even though it is long).

gi ra ra ni da da
The second 'ra' and 'da' are rendered as split notes 'sa ra' and 'pa da' respectively where 'sa' and 'pa' are stable pivots.

raagam Kalyaaṇi . [⊙ 4.43]
Sa nu di pa mi
The 'mi' is actually a shadow note parasitic on the pivotal 'pa'.

Secondly, these three tones, i.e. 'ra', 'da' and 'mi' are found to be difficult to execute for beginners.[80] I therefore conclude, without further argumentation, that the relative context-free markedness of the twelve tones is as shown below.

(2) Relative context-free markedness of the twelve tones
a. *ra, *mi, *da
>>
b. *ri, *gi, *gu, *ma, *pa, *di, *ni, *nu

Apart from beginning stages, this ranking never shows up (or almost never does) as faithfulness constraints ranked higher than these two constraints render them invisible.

I now turn to context-sensitive markedness values among the twelve tones. I assume the following types of context-sensitive markedness constraints.

(3) Context-sensitive markedness of the twelve tones
Case I: Problem of proximal tones
a. sa ✓ru gu ... gu ✓ru sa >> sa ru: gu ... gu ru: sa
Informally, it is more difficult to render 'ru' (i.e., gi) before or after gu if the 'marked' tone is not assigned a double duration (indicated by ':'). Similarly,
b. pa ✓du nu ... nu ✓du pa >> pa du: nu ... nu du: pa
Informally, it is more difficult to render 'du' ('ni' before or after 'nu' if the marked tone is not assigned a double duration.

Some singers of standing even resort to gliding from the adjacent, more stable 'ri', 'di' respectively.[81] Of course, not all sequences of proximal tones are of equal context-sensitive markedness. For instance, sa ra ga and pa da na may not be as marked as the sequences ma ✓ga ra or Sa ✓na da respectively.

The reason is that a tone's context-sensitive markedness status improves considerably in the vicinity of stable tones which function as pivots. If the pivot is adjacent to the 'difficult' sequence, then the markedness value decreases considerably as in the case of sa ra ga and pa da na as 'sa' and 'pa' are very stable pivots and so are 'ga' and 'na' which are really 'ri' and 'di' respectively. But in the case of ma ga ra, 'ra' is a marked note and so is 'da' in Sa na da. Hence the greater markedness of these sequences.

(4) Case II: Problem of the lack of pivotal anchor in the vicinity
a. ga ✓ra nu >> ga ra sa
b. na ✓da mi >> na ✓da ma >> na da pa

(5) Case III: Problem of tonal distance in the ascent
a. pa ✓nu >> pa ni
b. sa ✓mi >> sa ma

It may be observed that many established performers of repute render the sequences 'pa nu Sa' as in raagas like Naaṯai, Hamsadhvani and Hamsanaadam as 'pa (di) nu Sa'.[82] No scale, to my knowledge, employs the sequence 'sa mi..' and, I am sure all performers will readily agree with me on the extreme markedness of this sequence which is ruled out altogether in Carnatic music as an undominated constraint. The problem of tonal distance is pronounced in the ascent because one has to leave a pivotal tone and target a non-pivotal tone at a distance. On the descent, however, there is no problem because the final tone is a pivot which is always unmarked and easy to render.

Thus we see that among the 12 tones, though the majority of them have the same context-free markedness status, i.e. low ranked markedness constraints implying that they are not marked at all, there are, at least, three distinct cases of context-sensitive markedness among the twelve tones. However, in the case of performers who are well trained, all the constraints pertaining to the twelve tones are fairly low ranked becoming invisible and thus do not perform any function in their grammar. But for performers for whom these context sensitive markedness constraints are visible, these constraints will have to be higher ranked than the raagam specific constraints which stipulate the member notes of the raagam set to the extent that specific sequences are blocked by markedness allowing 'non-designated notes' to act as intermediate notes. Thus for some performers for whom the markedness constraints *pa nu Sa is higher ranked than the faith constraints which select the notes of the raagam, the grammar of these performers would include a high ranking markedness constraint prohibiting this specific sequence but allowing an intervening 'fleeting' 'di' to alleviate the marked sequence thus rendering the sequence that will be notated as 'pa nu Sa' but rendered as [pa (di) nu Sa]. Unlike orthodox grammarians, I do not brand such renderings as ungrammatical but merely note that this practice is sanctioned by a specific constraint in the grammar of these performers. Remember, there is no such thing as right and wrong when it comes to the practice of established performers/users of Carnatic music (as in language). The descriptive grammar of these performers are significantly different from that of other performers who overcome the specific markedness constraint noted above.[83]

5.3. Pitch manipulations

So far, I have examined the markedness constraints pertaining to the twelve tones and the absolute prohibition (undominated status) on rendering m.tones as targets in Carnatic music. I now venture to take a closer look at *gamakkam – the systematic exploitation of inter-tonal frequency in Carnatic music.* As I said earlier, gamakkam is not ornamentation or added decoration but an obligatory part of Carnatic music.

(6) The twenty two ʃrutis of Carnatic music[84]

1.	ʃaḍjam	(sa)	C
2.	Gauḷa riʃabham	(red. ra)	
3.	suddha riʃabham	(ra)	D flat
4.	*triʃruti riʃabhan*	(*red. ri*)	
5.	caturʃruti riʃabham	(ri)	D
6.	bhairavi gaandhaaram	(red. gi)	
7.	saadhaaraṇa gaandhaaram	(gi)	E flat
8.	antara gaandhaaram	(gu)	E
9.	cyuuta...gaandhaaram	(aug. gu)	
10.	suddha madhyamam	(ma)	F
11.	Beegaḍaa madhyamam	(aug. ma)	
12.	prati madhyamam	(mi)	F sharp
13.	cyuuta pancamam	(aug. mi)	
14.	pancamam	(pa)	G
15.	eekaʃruti daivatam	(red. da)	

16.	suddha daivaṭam	(da)	A flat
17.	*triʃruti daivatam*	(*red di*)	
18.	caturʃruti daivatam	(di)	A
19.	Bhairavi niʃaadam	(red ni)	
20.	kaisiki niʃaadam	(ni)	B flat
21.	kaakali niʃaadam	(nu)	B
22.	cyuuta ʃaɖjam	(aug nu)	

Once the m.tone was sanctioned by the theory (maybe in hindsight to justify the practice) and once its execution was effected as a glide from a lower anchor to a higher target executing the m.tone in passing, an entirely new approach to the exploitation of inter-tonal frequency was in place. And more possibilities became available, once again leaving theoretical justification lagging far behind. The point I wish to make now, is that the theory sanctioned only two interpretations for all the ten tones (leaving aside 'sa' and 'pa'). But in practice, while 'ra' and 'da', 'gu', 'mi' and 'nu' still have roughly only two possibilities and the m.tones associated with 'ri' and 'di' are not really exploited in contemporary practice, 'gi', 'ma' and 'ni' have found more incarnations in practice. I showcase the note 'gi' and its range of interpretation with a view to setting up a theory of inter-tonal variation in Carnatic music and advance a description that will successfully bridge the theory–practice divide. The characteristics that I establish for 'gi' are definitely valid for 'ni' and, may also be valid, with minor adjustments, for 'ma'. Due to lack of space I am not able to take up each one of these notes for detailed analysis.

I argue that each of these three 'expressive' notes admits two m.tones each, a reduced one and an augmented one thus bringing up the total of tones in an octave to 23 – a theoretically inelegant number.[85]

But before I venture into the world of pitch intricacies in Carnatic music, I wish to take a brief excursus into the exploitation of pitch. According to Yip (2002), as cited in Gussenhoven (2004), "more than half of the languages in the world are tone languages", i.e. languages which exploit pitch to signal different lexical entries. For example, in the language Mizo spoken in the north eastern state of Mizoram, India, though the words in (7) have the same segmental specification, their pitch specifications are different signaling different meanings:

	H	LH	L
(7)	/lei/ 'slanting'	/lei/ 'to buy'	/lei/ 'a bridge'

Roughly speaking, languages which exploit pitch in this manner are called tone languages. However, in all languages, i.e. both tone and non-tone languages, pitch is also employed to signal communicative meaning, often referred to as intonation. For instance, in most languages we employ a rise at the end of the utterance to indicate that we have not finished speaking yet. For example, the sentence below is normally pronounced with a rising pitch at the end of the first break and a fall at the end of the sentence.

(8) Rising pitch to signal incomplete utterance

When I was going to the shop,// I met my friend.//

Similarly, all languages employ distinct pitch to signal declarative and interrogative sentences. Thus languages employ pitch to signal lexical differences and convey sentential meaning. Since speakers may chose to use a narrow or a broad pitch range in their speaking style, for instance, one will normally use a narrow pitch range if one wants to convey a sense of calmness but a broad pitch range for conveying excitement/anger etc. But irrespective of the pitch range employed, one can characterize the pitch movements using just two *abstract* heights *High* and *Low*.[86] These abstract specifications of H and L are indirectly related to actual pitch heights employed.

Languages adopt various strategies for keeping track of the pitch specifications. They allow the pitch to come down if distinctions in the sequence are maintained, e.g. in many languages in a H L H sequence, the second H is realized at a lower pitch height, a phenomenon known as downstep. The two H's are the same from the point of view of the phonology but, phonetically they are realized differently. Another strategy that a language can adopt is to enhance the H after a H L sequence so that the difference between the L and the following H is striking. This phenomenon is known as upstep. In Carnatic music too we have a comparable phenomenon in pitch movement sequences. In one type which I have recorded, the pitch glides achieve higher targets in consecutive curves and the dip is also higher in consecutive glides. We could take this to be comparable to 'upstep' in language. In phrases which are in the ascent as well in the descent, we see that the same principles are applicable in Carnatic music, namely, consecutive targets are higher and consecutive dips are higher. In other words, in Carnatic music what we seem to have, irrespective of whether the musical phrase in which the pitch curve is embedded is in the ascending phrase or descending phrase, is for consecutive dips and targets to obey upstep with higher dips and higher targets. This is only a conjecture but it may very well turn out to be correct. A larger corpus of data across performers is needed to establish this claim that pitch curves/waves/spikes whether upward or downward oriented are always subject to upstep in Carnatic music. Needless to say, such an investigation is beyond the scope of this book. But what one does not find is either downstep, a lowering of an intended pitch after a lower pitch or a general lowering of all pitch values towards the end of a musical line (comparable to 'declination' – gradual lowering of pitch within an intonational phrase in language) in music. Such a sliding of pitch would result in ambiguity in music where pitch values are much more stable than in speech.

I illustrate below the wide variety of interpretations that the note 'gi' admits across raagas. But the general point that I wish to make is that while the theoretical justification for m.tones paved the way for the systematic exploitation of inter-tonal pitch movement between designated anchors and targets traversing the m.tones, the practice opened up further systematic pitch movements between notes. The designated anchors could be RenScale ones, or m.tones in non-initial anchors, or notes not designated by the raagam in question. I will illustrate each of the possibilities below. While the former two instantiations get covered in the discussion below, the last cited example requires to be handled here first.

Take the example of a raagam like Sriranjani with the scale /sa ri gi ma di ni Sa/. If practitioners introspect on the manner in which they would render a phrase like //ni di di,// in this raagam when they sing,[87] they will realize that they, in fact, do invoke, although fleetingly, a 'pa' in between the two instances of 'di'. I can answer the question readily, being a veena player: the second 'ni' has a shadow 'pa' as its anchor, though 'pa' is not a designated note of the raagam.[88] Thus we see that 'fleeting' anchors need not even be designated notes of a raagam. But they may need to be from the twelve tone set. Another point that requires to be discussed is the general issue of intertonal exploitation. The m.tone issue had allowed a certain range of possibilities and, my hunch is that once the 'Pandora's box' of inter-tonal frequencies was opened up, there was a range of possibilities which had to be dealt with. I will deal with these possibilities in some detail before I venture into pitch ranges in raagas.

If we take a look at the pitch graphs that are presented below, we will see that minute variations of pitch are distinctive to the Carnatic music fraternity. Take this concrete example of Fig. 1 below (p. 115) where the three occurrences of Tooḍi 'gi' are at 191, 198 and 200 Hertz. I am sure every sensitive Carnatic musician would realize that while the first pitch wave illustrates a red.gi the second and third are not all that reduced. Now, the perception of red.gi is a 'real' value of 4 Hertz below the target for 'ri', i.e. a mere 28 cent. Therefore my claim in the previous chapter about a range of 20 to 30 cent value difference being perceptible to the Carnatic fraternity is validated. The further point that needs to be noted is that the second and third iteration of the pitch wave evidences progressively higher targets – finally the target exceeding 'gi' which stands at 195 Hertz and the target of the final pitch wave is 200 Hertz which is a 37 cent augmented pitch.[89] It is quite clear that the mathematical proof of the Indian tradition has gone awry. To give them the benefit of doubt, I take it that the proof that was given was, perhaps, valid for the practice then current.[90] Clearly, for the Carnatic musician, perception of reduced and augmented tones has changed radically in contemporary Carnatic music practice and there is every need to address this changed situation.

We have sufficient research evidence to say that language does not remain static over centuries; nor can we expect Carnatic music to be strictly faithful to sixteenth and seventeenth century theoretical premises, being a language-like system specific to humans. I shall argue with the support of pitch graphs for the need to re-define the Carnatic music octave. I would like to maintain that the insight presented by Carnatic music theorists is basically not misplaced; though the earlier arguments are purely theoretical (not supported by any raw data, nor can the model be replicated). My hypothesis is that their vision of multiple versions of the notes of the scale, in fact, led to the great pitch revolution in Carnatic music.

A considerable part of this chapter is devoted to an analysis of the pitch movements of the 'note' 'gi' in Carnatic music across raagas. I had made out a case for the red.tones and aug.tones to be pitch graphs in the previous chapter. In this chapter I demonstrate that the 'ʃrutis' of Carnatic music and 'possible pitch movements' in contemporary Carnatic music need to be defined anew. Thus the objectives of a large part of this chapter are the following:

(9) Objectives: Interpretation of pitch movement

a. The octave needs to be re-defined in contemporary Carnatic music vis-à-vis m.tones which are there to stay,
b. the practice of pitch movements introduced to accommodate red.tones and aug.tones opened the way for more systematic exploitation of inter-tonal frequencies and
c. the pitch realization of pitch variation is a function of time indicated by the abstract timing unit – the mora μ.

The issues in (9) above are inter-related and hence cannot be taken up one after the other. Therefore, I will have to tackle the issues as a related set of ideas. My plan for this section of the chapter is to examine the pitch readings of the 'note' 'gi' which admits a great variety of pitch movements across raagas and arrive at a general conclusion about all the three issues listed in (9) above. The reason why I target the 'note' 'gi' is that it showcases the problem and allows us to arrive at an elegant solution.[91] If this detailed interpretation of 'gi' could set in place a new theory of microtonal Carnatic music, the other 'notes' with equally varied pitch variation or less varied pitch interpretations can easily be handled by a less sophisticated mechanism. As I said earlier, 'ra' and 'da' admit reduced varieties and 'gu', 'mi' and 'nu' admit augmented varieties, however, 'ri' and 'di', in contemporary Carnatic music, to the best of my playing/listening experience of forty six years, do not, contrary to Carnatic music theory. But 'gi', 'ma' and 'ni' seem to admit more than one m.tone. Therefore, when I take up the issue of redefining the m.tone map of contemporary Carnatic music, I will keep these observations in mind.

A minor digression on the interpretation of the notes 'ri' and 'di' in contemporary Carnatic music. As I said earlier, I cannot find any instance of reduced varieties of these two notes in any raagam in any sample of contemporary practice, contrary to Carnatic music theory which postulates a triʃruti riʃabham and a triʃruti daivatam. What I do construe across styles of Carnatic music practice is a mild pitch wave on 'ri and 'di' signaling an *augmented* 'ri' or a *reduced* 'gi' standing for a 'ru' and 'an augmented 'di' or a reduced 'ni' standing for a 'du' in raagas where they function as 'reduced ru' and 'reduced du' where the actual riʃabham and daivatam which are really reincarnations of 'gi' and 'di' respectively are played on 'ri' and 'di' with a slight deflection indicating an augmented m.tone.[92] Thus in these 'vivaadi' scales which select actual 'gi' and 'gu' labeling them as 'ru and 'gu' respectively, or scales which select 'ni' and 'nu' labeling them 'du' and 'nu' respectively, where the former notes are, at least in certain styles of Carnatic music, really augmented versions of 'gi' and 'ni' played on 'ri' and 'di' respectively as a pitch movement between 'ri'/'di' and the higher target notes 'gu' and 'nu' respectively. Thus, in addition to raagas like Tooḍi and Bhairavi which employ aug.gi, the vivaadi raagas which select 'ru gu' and 'du nu' actually require the 'ru' and 'du' to be rendered as aug.gi and aug.ni respectively in certain styles of Carnatic music. But all Carnatic music performers would agree with me when I say that though the m.tone employed is the same, i.e. aug.gi and aug.ni in both Tooḍi and vivaadi raagas which select 'ru and gu' and 'du and nu', the pitch rendering can be quite distinct. While in Tooḍi, aug.gi and aug.ni may be instantiated by deep pitch curves with targets as high as 'ma/pa' and 'nu/Sa', the aug.gi and aug.ni renderings for vivaadi meeḷakartaas can never be deep pitch curves but have to be mild, flat pitch movements with much lower targets. So, in addition to selecting m.tones distinctively in raagas, raagam types are constrained to employ distinct pitch movements though the selected m.tone is the same. The type of pitch movement selected will then signal a difference in the raagam type.[93] In fact this restriction on selecting only mild pitch wave for aug.gi (and aug.ni) may be attributed to the fact that these raagas select a note which is only a semi-tone away as their adjacent note, namely 'gu' and 'nu'. I will return to a discussion of the selection of pitch movement types as a consequence of the notes of the scale selected by the raagam.

The discussion on pitch manoeuvres in Carnatic music is illustrated with varieties of 'gi' as found in the raagas Tooḍi, Bhairavi and Hindooḷam.[94]

(10)	Musical demonstration		Types of 'gi'
	'gi' in Tooḍi		
	a.	gi_1, gi_2 ra (sa) ra	Fig. 1
	b.	sa ra gi_3 gi_4, ma	Fig. 2
	c.	gi_5 ma pa ma gi_6,	Fig. 3

Tooḍi is specially interesting as it attests at least five different executions of the note 'gi' given below in Fig. 1–3 below.

Notice that there are five pitch movements which signal Tooḍi 'gi' in this phrase starting at 186 which is just above 'ri' and the peaks begin at 191 – which is clearly lower than 'gi, with the successive peaks getting higher and higher at 198, 200 which is well above 'gi' – almost half way between 'gi and 'gu'. What do we make of this? I propose to interpret the five pitch movements in the following way (see Fig. 1).

I assume that the first two pitch movements, which are gentle pitch waves, are instances of red.gi which the raagam sanctions. I assume that the next three pitch movements are pitch curves which are instantiations of the m.tone aug.gi, which I presented earlier while discussing vivaadi raagas and the rendering of the note 'ru' as an augmented 'gi' sanctioned by these vivaadi raagas. Thus, raagas like Tooḍi as well as vivaadi raagas sanction aug.gi. How do we distinguish their usage? As I said earlier, the vivaadi raagas are constrained to select only the mild pitch movement as the adjacent note is only a semi-tone higher. But the following note in Tooḍi is 'ma' which is tone away and therefore the aug.gi in Tooḍi admits all manner of pitch movements, pitch wave, pitch curve and pitch spike, etc.

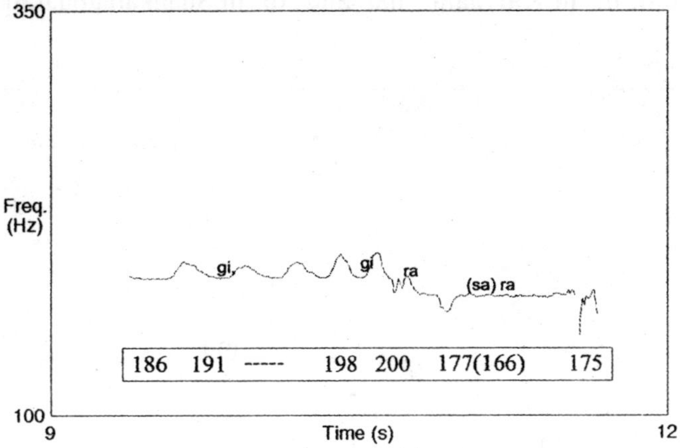

Figure 1.

Thus in this case, I suggest that two of the pitch waves out of the five of Tooḍi 'gi' which fall back on a lower note 'ra' are instantiations of red.gi and the following three of aug.gi. While red.gi has 'gi' as its target, aug.gi has 'gu' as its target, clearly showing us that targets and fleeting anchors need not be members of the scale of the raagam. However, stable anchors have to be sanctioned members of the scale of the raagam. Thus this first musical phrase illustrates the fact that red.gi and the aug.gi are selected by the raagam Tooḍi. It also shows how we have two different concepts of anchors – stable and fleeting; while the former must be a member of the scale of the raagam, the latter can be any appropriate 'tone' in the neighbourhood.

I next turn to a pitch analysis of the musical phrase "sa ra gi, ma". As in all things pertaining to Carnatic music, here too we have a considerable number of variations across iterations by the same performer but, more importantly, greater than usual, across performers signaling differences in style. I have heard performers who render the phrase shown above with 'pa' rather than 'ma' as the target. For want of a better label I shall refer to this style as 'ultra-orthodox' where phrases like "sa ra gi, ma" and "pa da ni, Sa" are rendered with distinctly higher targets, i.e. 'pa' and 'Sa' respectively.

I assume that a unique characteristic of this "ultra-orthodox" style is the selection of higher targets in pitch curves, perhaps uniformly. Typically, these higher targets occur in raagas of the idiosyncratic set (see chapter 8 for details) where the designated notes are at least a tone higher. So the same kind of exaggerated pitch curve (with higher target) is the practice for the notes 'gu' and 'di' in Kalyaaṇi, 'ma' and 'di' in Shankaraabharaṇam and so on.[95]

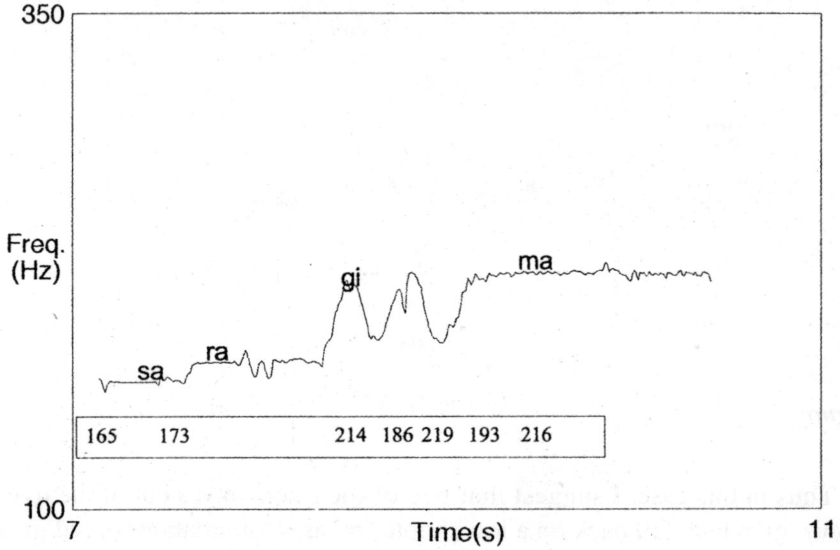

Figure 2.

Turning to the second phrase, we find the first 'gi from the anchor 'ra' going up to 214 which is almost 'ma' coming down to 186 which is slightly above 'ri' again shooting up to 219 which is a bit above 'ma' and gets back to 193 which is almost RenScale 'gi' for a fleeting moment. The two 'gi's are distinctly different. I take it that, generally, in consecutive pitch movements, the later pitch movements are always closer to the target than the earlier ones and that this incremental behaviour is really a performance factor which we find comparable to upstep in language. In the case of language and also in Carnatic music, cases of upstep should be deemed to be an implementational criterion and get on with our theoretical analysis. Further, in such cases while the initiating pitch movement has a lower anchor (in this case 'ra' – the designated note of the raagam) the second fleeting anchor is actually 'ri' which is not a designated note of the raagam. The generalization is that the second, fleeting anchor is always higher than the first anchor. I assume that, as far as the theory is concerned, the two pitch curves can be described as shown below and their actual pitch realization can be captured by the generalization below:

(11) Note–pitch relation generalization

a. In consecutive note pitch movements, the initiating anchor is a designated note of the raagam.
b. However, in pitch movements driven by aug.tones, the anchor need not be a designated note of the raagam.[96]
c. The anchor of the non-initial pitch movement is usually a fleeting anchor, a pitch value closer to the target by at least a semi tone/quarter tone.
d. In consecutive pitch movements, though the target remains stable, the achieved target pitch gets progressively higher (and closer to the target and sometimes, even overshooting the target).

Thus I take it that the two pitch curves are really theoretically the 'same', though their actual realizations are different. I term this type of pitch curve 'note pitch curve' to indicate that this type of pitch movement is possible between all designated notes in a raagam – in all raagas (idiosyncratic or scalar). In all raagas, note pitch curves are possible between the designated notes of the raagam provided the adjacent notes are at least a tone away from each other. In raagas like Kalyaaṇi, Tooḍi, Bhairavi, Karaharapriyaa, Beegaḍaa, Kaanaḍaa and so on, notes which are separated by an interval of a tone are allowed to interpret the lower note as a pitch curve from the lower note. Even in non-idosyncratic raagas like Hamsadhvani and Hamsanaadam etc., for instance, the 'ri' can be rendered as a note pitch curve. In the former its anchor would be 'ri' and target an appropriate higher note. It must be noted that for these scalar raagas, though pitch curves are admitted, the targets are never really the right adjacent note in the linear ordered scale. For instance, for Hamsadhvani, if one renders a pitch curve on 'pa', the target is never 'nu' but much lower (probably just 'di' which is not a designated note of the raagam). To sum up our discussion so far about Tooḍi, we take it that the raagam sanctions the pitch wave red.gi, the pitch wave and curve aug.gi, and the note pitch curve 'gi'.

Thus we see that the distinction between a pitch curve and a note pitch curve is that while the former happens when there is an aug.m.tone involved and its anchor may or may not be a sanctioned note of the raagam, the anchor of the note pitch curve, which is always between designated notes of a raagam provided they are at least a tone away from each other, is always a designated note of the raagam.

I next turn to the phrase "gi, ma pa, ma gi,, ra" and show that even this raagam does allow RenScale 'gi', in addition to all the other variations it sanctions: the first note is RenScale 'gi' in the musical phrase presented below:

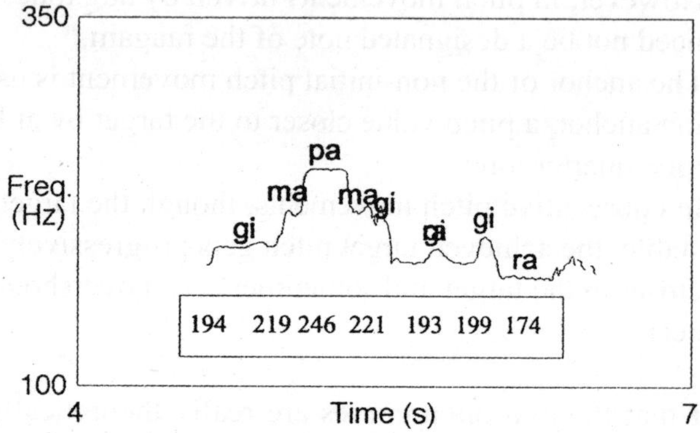

Figure 3.

In this phrase, we see that the first static 'gi' is a RenScale 'gi' at 194. The second 'gi' is once again a double pitch curve with 'gi' as target. I assume that the target is 'gi in both cases and that 'note' attempted is aug.gi. Thus we see that the pitch with the fleeting anchor 'ri' and progressively going higher with targeted 'gi' curves whether they occur as initiating notes or as phrase final sequences having the same properties I listed above in (11).

(12) The 'notes' of Tooḍi
Sa
red.ra ra
red.gi RenScale.gi aug.gi
pitch curve 'gi

(13) Renditions of 'gi' in Tooḍi
a. RenScale gi
b. Red.gi
This may have either 'ra' or 'ri' as anchors depending on whether the pitch wave/curve is an initiating one or a successive one.

c. Aug.gi
This could have 'gu' (or even 'ma' or 'pa') as its target depending on whether the pitch wave/curve is an initiating one or a successive one.

d. Like any other raagam, this raagam should also be allowed to execute a pitch curve between the selected 'notes' of the raagam which are at least a tone away from each other. The initiating anchor is unambiguously the lower note and succeeding anchors and targets are progressively higher 'gu' or 'ma' or even 'pa'.

These four stipulations above suffice to account for all the pitch range variations in Tooḍi. Thus we have a 'gentle' pitch wave from 'ra' to indicate the red.gi version, limited pitch wave to indicate aug.gi versions and extended note pitch curve to indicatc pitch curve between two selected 'notes' of a raagam. Thus we are able to account for all the variation in a uniform fashion.

However, this account has to deny the red. versions of 'ri' and 'di' and add two new m.tones to 'gi' and 'ni' respectively, and an additional red.m.tone for 'ma'. In addition to that, we still need to stipulate that
a) a red.m.tone can function as a fleeting anchor of a non-initial pitch movement and
b) 'gi', 'ni' and 'ma' have not just one but two associated m.tones each, and that 'ri' and 'di' do not have any m.tone associated with them.

In all, from the three phrases we see that the raagam Tooḍi admits widely different frequency interpretations for a single performer, even within the same phrase. The raagam has 'gi' around frequencies 190 which is like an augmented 'ri' or a reduced 'gi', 195 a proper 'gi', 198 which is an augmented 'gi' and a pitch curve which has 'ma' (or 'pa') as its target. Thus we see that the frequency range for Tooḍi 'gi' is between 190 (an augmented 'ri') to 219 (which is a target 'ma') or even higher for some performers. So the 'gi' arsenal of Tooḍi is fairly extensive and therefore, no wonder, it is such an expressive swaram 'note' spanning nearly 20 Hertz or more. If its execution is not entirely predictable even for a single performer, one can imagine what the situation would be across widely different styles of music.[97] It is now appropriate to formulate the constraints. I start with the flat rendering of 'gi', i.e. render the note as RenScale. Using the formula for pitch glides I had introduced earlier (chapter 4, (13), p. 102), I can now describe a composite pitch curve which is, in fact, made up of two halves, with the anchor and target reversed to form a composite curve. I modify the formula for augmented tone given in ((13c); chapter 4) as (14a and b).

(14) Constraints for Tooḍi ‘gi’

a. *RenScale gi*

b. *Ascending Glide for Tooḍi ‘gi’*

$T_{A.ra}\ T_{Aug.gi}\ T_{T.gu/ma/pa}$

c. *Descending Glide for Tooḍi ‘gi’*

$T_{A.gu/ma/pa}\ T_{Aug.gi}\ T_{T.ra}$

d. *Composite Pitch Curve for Tooḍi Aug.gi*

$T_{A.ra}\ T_{Aug.gi}\ T_{T.gu/ma/pa}\ /\%/\ T_{T.gu/ma/pa}\ T_{Aug.gi}\ T_{A.ra}$

The convention I follow is that ‘%’ indicates that the order of the two parts of the pitch glide can be reversed so that the composite pitch curve can be either an ascending or a descending curve. In the phrase [gi, ma pa] it is an upward pitch curve but in the phrase [ma gi, ma] it is an inverted one.

Keeping this formula in mind we can now actually state the constraints that derive the various pitch movements for Tooḍi ‘gi’ as shown below.

(15) The repertoire of Tooḍi ‘gi’

a. *RenScale gi* *steady pitch*

b. *Red.gi* *single or double pitch wave*

$T_{A.ra}\ T_{T.red.gi}\ T_{T\ gi}\ T_{A.ra/ri} \ldots T \ldots$

(if a single pitch wave then the second anchor is a ‘ra’; if a second pitch wave follows then the anchor is a fleeting ‘ri’ and the actual peak pitch gets progressively higher)

c. *Aug.gi* *single or double pitch wave*[98]

$T_{A.ra}\ T_{T\ aug.gi}\ T_{T\ gu/ma/pa}\ T_{A.\ ra/ri} \ldots T$

(if a single pitch wave then the second anchor is a ‘ra’; if a second pitch wave follows then the anchor is a fleeting ‘ri’ and the actual peak pitch gets progressively higher)

d. *Note pitch curve ‘gi’*

$T_{A.ra}\ T_{T\ ma/pa}\ T_{A.\ ra/ri} \ldots T$

(if a single pitch wave then the second anchor is a ‘ra’; if a second pitch wave follows then the anchor is a fleeting ‘ri’ and the actual peak pitch gets progressively higher)

I take it that the statements in (15) above are comparable to ‘phonological’, i.e. abstract generalizations and the comments in brackets are more or less like 'phonetic implementation' rules.[99] Just as in contemporary linguistic theory where we do not assign the phonological and phonetic issues to two separate modules, in Carnatic music too I wish to keep them integrated in a single set of constraints. However, more inputs are needed before a full blown theory of implementation is in place for Carnatic music. While the 'phonological' counterpart – the statements in (15) – are likely to be stable across musical events by and large (allowing slightly different anchors and targets in certain styles), the 'fine print' in brackets comparable to phonetic implementation is likely to vary across events and users.

Further, there is an inviolable, high ranked constraint which restricts the target to be the semi-tone closest to the m.tone when the glide is to be associated with a single mora or less. In other words, either when the 'gi' is to be rendered as a single mora or in a fast tempo (where more than one note is to be associated with a single mora), the distant target of 'ma'/'pa' are impossible and the 'gi' is rendered with a minimum of gamakkam. This is captured as a general constraint (16) given below.

(16) Prohibition on higher targets/lower anchors in fast tempo renderings

a. Ascending Glide

$*..T_{\text{Aug t}}\ T_{\text{T n}}(\text{if } n - t \geq 1)$

b. Descending Glide

$*..T_{\text{Aug. t}}\ T_{\text{T n}}(\text{if } t - n \geq 1)$

In plain language, we see that at faster tempo, pitch curves are prohibited (by markedness constraints specific to fast tempo rendition) and only mild pitch wave renditions of red.T and aug.T may be allowed. In certain styles even pitch waves could be prohibited making the notes in fast tempo pure RenScale or approximations to RenScale notes. (Recall discussion in chapter 3 pp. 64–68.)

We saw that the single note 'gi' in the raagam Tooḍi has as many as four different renditions and that the choice of a particular rendition of 'gi' was determined by i) idiosyncratic selection of the performer ii) the style of the performer and c) the time span mapped to the note in question. Between the three factors, it becomes almost impossible to predict when a certain pitch movement would be executed for the note 'gi' in the raagam Tooḍi. One would have to examine an enormous amount of data to be able to make a statistical prediction about the tendencies of certain patterns to occur in certain musical phrases and styles and so on. The moral of this is that synthesized

Carnatic music (just like synthesized language) still has a long, long way to go.[100] Further, unlike language where some head way has been made by decades of research, Carnatic music has yet to start detailed investigation of the intricacies of pitch movements, tendencies within a style / across styles, etc. Thus, even a recognition model for Carnatic music is a distant dream, leave alone a production model.

I now turn to the 'gi' in the raagam Bhairavi with a view to determine whether the execution of the note 'gi' in this raagam is very different from Tooḍi requiring different generalizations.

(17) Musical Demonstration
'gi' in Bhairavi

a.	gi, ri	Fig.6
b.	gi, ma	Fig.7
c.	ri, ri gi, ri	Fig.8

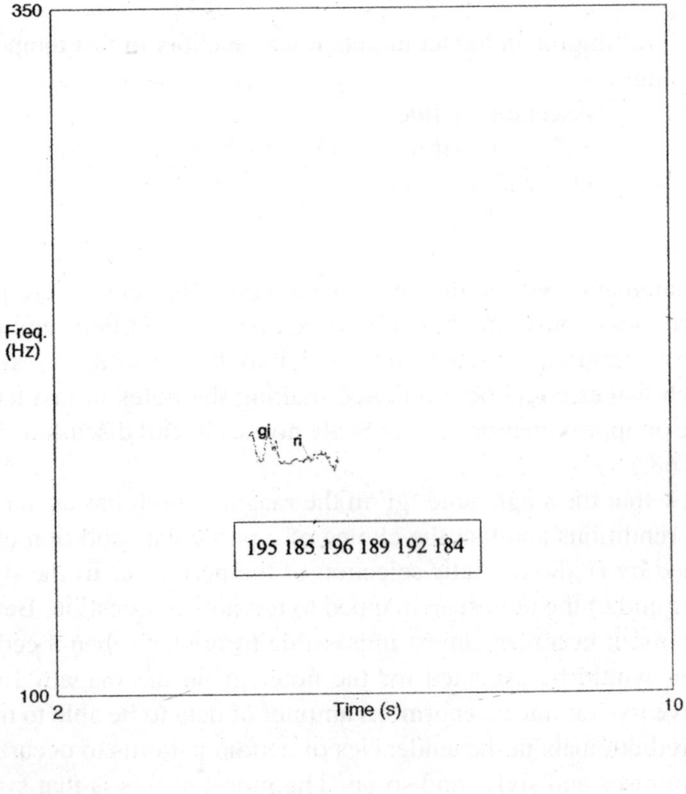

Figure 4.

What we have in Fig. 4 is a RenScale 'gi' at the beginning. The following two (or rather one and a half) pitch waves have RenScale 'gi' as anchor and then moves to red.gi at 189 and 192 Hertz before returning to RenScale 'ri' at 184. These are instances of inverted pitch curves for red.gi. The starting anchor is a RenScale 'gi' and the target is 'ri' traversing red.gi along the way. If we compare the red.gi of Tooḍi and the inverted red.gi for Bhairavi we do not see much of a difference in actual pitch values between the two. But we must keep in mind the fact that what we term a 'note' of Carnatic music is not really an isolated pitch value (static or otherwise). These notes of Carnatic music are composite pitch movements to be interpreted a) in the domain of a whole pitch movement and b) the musical phrase in which it is embedded. If interpreted in this spirit, what we have here is a pitch sequence denoting two notes of music 'gi' and 'ri' initiating the phrase. Thus there is no ambiguity in interpreting the red.gi here, and in Tooḍi earlier, as the context of the occurrence of the red.gi pitch wave is strikingly different in the two cases. While in Tooḍi the initial note 'ra' signals Tooḍi unambiguously, in the Bhairavi phrase, though the initiating note is RenScale 'gi', the target is unambiguously 'ri', a note signaling Bhairavi and not Tooḍi. But, nevertheless, from the theory point of view both are instances of red.gi, a single m.tone with specifiable pitch values.

In the next sample, the realization of 'gi' is as a note curve 'gi' as in Tooḍi.

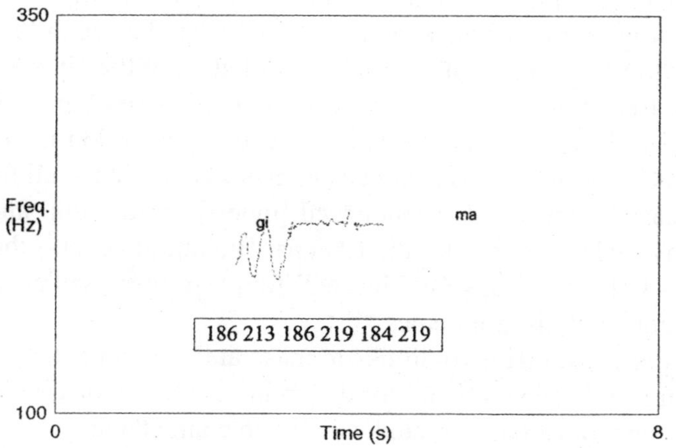

Figure 5.

If we compare the two occurrences of note curve 'gi' we find that, as is expected, the initiating anchor of the Tooḍi pitch curve is 'ra' at 173 Hertz but the Bhairavi initiating anchor is, naturally, 'ri' at 186 Hertz. The targets, significantly are not different as both touch peak frequencies of 186 and 219 indicating progressive incremental approximation to the target 'ma'. Once again, the proof is loud and clear: the 'gi' itself is not distinct but the disambiguation is in the different initial anchors, namely 'ra' in the case of Tooḍi and 'ri' in the case of Bhairavi.

Thus in both instances, several of my claims are justified. Firstly, pitch curves are executed as progressively higher peak values. Secondly, though the fleeting anchors in both cases are no different, i.e. at 186 Hertz, yet the theory interprets the pitch as 'ra' in the former and 'ri' in the latter. This shows that the fleeting anchor is just that, a fleeting approximation to a note and not to be taken as *significant*. I would hazard a guess saying that the fleeting anchors of Tooḍi and Bhairavi will be 'perceived' differently by the knowledgeable Carnatic music fraternity. They would perceive the former as 'ra' and the latter as 'ri' though their pitch values are identical. I do not see this as a problem for the theory I am trying to construct. In fact, it supports my hypothesis that *perception of pitch values is 'relative' in Carnatic music* (as in language and elsewhere for humans) and pitch values are converted to 'notes' in context by implementation rules. I conclude by saying that the abstract representation that the theory constructs and the double pitch curve that gets executed with their minute differences are all instances of pitch realization about which I will have more to say subsequently.

A small digression for the skeptics. Draw by hand a rough 's' like figure and show it in the context of a) numbers, b) letters of the alphabet, c) icons like moon, tree, owl, etc. and one will see that the same figure is interpreted differently in different contexts. This contextual perception is in the nature of human perception.[101] This is not an anomalous situation at all for linguists. Take the case of the words pronounced [mooɨ] 'buttermilk' and [sheviɨ] 'wall' in my dialect of Tamil – the Chennai Brahmin dialect – the 'r' is pronounced exactly alike but still 'educated' Tamil speakers will assign them to two different symbols/graphemes.[102]

The major point that I would like to make at this point is that

a) initiating anchors are crucial for determining grammaticality but
b) fleeting anchors are interpreted variably in context and
c) the target is realized in a gradient, incremental fashion.

The two anchors are interpreted differently depending on their context. While initiating anchors have to be sanctioned by the raagam, other pitch movements are interpreted 'relatively'. In the case of the fleeting anchor the same pitch value is interpreted as 'ra' in one case but as 'ri' in the other case. The point that I am making here is that the interpretation of apparently simple pitch facts is indeed a very complex affair. But we should not lose sight of the 'wood' of Carnatic music theory for the 'trees' of the pitch values and movements. This extended discussion is necessitated by mistaken attempts by some 'musicologists' in postulating distinctions where distinctions do not exist, proliferating classification without any real need.

What we have below are two further instances of 'gi'.

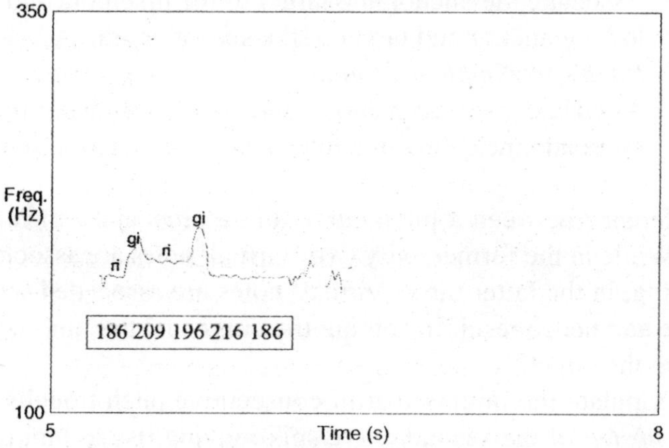

Figure 6.

The first pitch movement is a curve from the anchor 186, i.e. 'ri' to the peak of 209 which is 'gu' and this makes it an instance of aug.gi which the raagam sanctions. The second pitch movement is altogether different. First of all the pitch movement is a pitch spike (i.e., a pitch movement undertaken in a short span of time). While the target of the previous pitch curve was 'gu', the target this time could be 'ma' which is underachieved or 'gu' which is overshot. However, I advance the view that the imprecise realization of the target is a function of time. Due to lack of adequate time, the target is not achieved satisfactorily (from the perfectionist's point of view). The real pitch value, therefore, is a performance factor affecting the intended target 'gu' at 207 Hertz. Thus this may not be an instance of an aug.gi or 'ma'. Conversely, we could assume that pitch spikes have 'exaggerated targets which are underachieved and in this case, the target was really 'ma' which was undershot by the pitch spike. Whether the target is 'gu' which is not a designated note of the raagam or 'ma' which is a designated note of the raagam will remain a theoretical issue. The reality is that the real pitch peak of pitch spikes will always be imprecise given the timing factor and so I will leave this discussion at this rather inconclusive stage.

I now turn to the problem of characterizing a pitch wave and a pitch spike.

(18) Pitch value association to mora

a. *Pitch curve association to mora*
Associate the anchor and target to the first mora and the following anchor and target to the second mora.

b. *Pitch spike implementation*
Associate the anchor, target and following anchor to the first mora and the following note/target, if any, to the second mora.

The difference between a pitch curve and a pitch spike then is a matter of timing. While in the former, only two 'virtual' notes are associated with a unit of timing, in the latter three 'virtual' notes are associated with a single unit of time and hence result in spiking the curve and the 'imprecise' nature of achieving the target.

I also formulate the finding that in consecutive pitch troughs and peaks, there is an *upstep* of the second curve/spike giving rise to higher values of the second curve/spike. I will propose a total solution for the pitch variations towards the end of this section.

(19) Upstep in consecutive pitch curve/spike
In $[T_{Ai}\ T_{Ti}\ T_{Aii}\ T_{Tii}]_{curve/spike}$, A_{ii}, $T_{ii} > A_i\ T_i$

Informally, the successive pitch curves, the anchors and targets get higher.

The question to ask now is whether Tooḍi also allows pitch spike 'gi' like Bhairavi. And the answer is that it does.[103] So the entire range of 'gi's available to Tooḍi is also available to Bhairavi. Therefore, clearly the mechanism for disambiguation is at the level of the phrase and since the initiating anchor is different in the two cases in upward pitch movements and the targets in downward pitch movements, there is no ambiguity and hence no ungrammaticality.

I now turn to the third raagam which selects 'gi' in its scale, namely Hindooḷam.

(20) Musical demonstration
gi in Hindooḷam
sa gi, sa ga ma

In the raagam Hindooḷam we may safely say that there are only two possibilities for executing 'gi', namely a gentle pitch wave 'gi' which varies approximately between the value of 'ri' and 'gi' which we will now readily label m.tone red.gi (this is an m.tone which we have already added to the list of 22 ʃrutis (replacing red.ri) and RenScale gi.

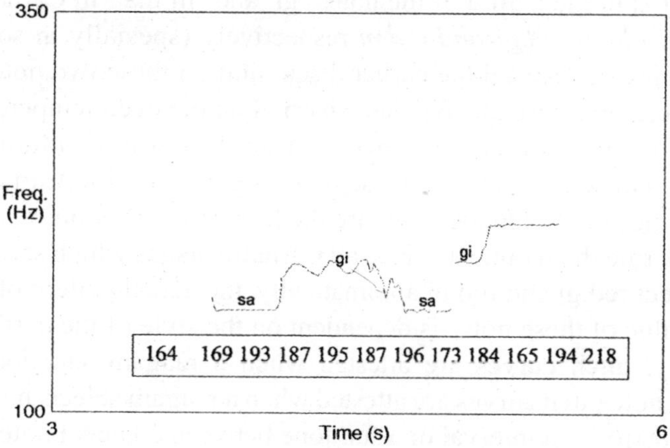

Figure 7.

The execution of the former red.gi is like that of any other red.tone, i.e. its anchor is the tone preceding it and its target is the next higher semi tone (gi). Unlike Tooḍi and Bhairavi, it does not allow higher targets. And, the only gamakkam allowed is the gentle wave type that we find in the picture.[104]

Note that in the case of Hindooḷam red.gi, the anchor is 'ri' which is not sanctioned by the raagam but notice that this anchor is a fleeting anchor as the static anchor is at 'sa' – 164 Hertz which initiates the phrase and hence the initiating anchor. Thus, our definition of 'fleeting anchor' also changes. A fleeting anchor is a pitch value which is not stable with respect to a range of time and in the case of Hindooḷam, the anchor 'ri' is not a designated note of the raagam and it is a fleeting note though it is the first anchor and not a succeeding anchor. This kind of phenomenon happens, specially, in raagas which skip certain notes and so 'surrogate anchors' are necessitated to execute pitch curves driven by m.tones. I have nothing further to say on this matter.

We saw how one note, namely 'gi', can be interpreted in quite distinct ways in different raagas. While Tooḍi and Bhairavi allow the same range of interpretations, ambiguity is avoided because of distinct anchors. However, raagas like Hindooḷam allow only a gentle pitch wave signaling red.gi (and red.ni) and the RenScale rendition of the note 'gi' (and 'ni'). Here too ambiguity is avoided by including the musical phrase as the point of reference.

Two further points for explication. Firstly, the fact that Hindooḷam selects red.gi (and red.ni) does not in any way imply that this raagam belongs to the 'idiosyncratic set' like Tooḍi or Bhairavi (for me and many other practitioners). It is in the nature of the notes 'gi' and 'ni that, in Carnatic music, they *always allow red.gi and red.ni* respectively (specially in some styles of Carnatic music). Recall the earlier discussion on these two notes where I said that these notes are always 'less sharp' than the even tempered scale or the scale of the Harmonium in Carnatic music. That was an informal way of saying that reduced versions of these notes are preferred in Carnatic music. However, since the RenScale notes are the least marked of notes, no raagam can actually rule them out. But since all Carnatic raagas which select 'gi' and 'ni' also select red.gi and red.ni automatically, the actual pattern of choice of the pitch value of these notes is dependent on the style of the performer.

Secondly, pitch curves are attested when a raagam sanctions an aug. m.tone and note pitch curves are attested when a raagam selects notes in such a way that there is an interval of a full tone between adjacent notes.

I had stated at the beginning that the mechanism meant for interpreting m.tones was extended to other pitch manipulations in a systematic manner in Carnatic music. What I had meant precisely was the extension of the aug. m.tone rendering as a pitch curve to any two notes separated by at least a tone for a note pitch curve rendering for all types of raagas. I had also noted that unlike aug.m.tone induced pitch curve which sanctions only notes selected by the scale as targets (in both upward and downward curve), note pitch curves are not constrained in this manner. This is the reason why
a) note pitch curves can select higher targets in idiosyncratic raagas like Tooḍi and Bhairavi (e.g., selection of 'pa' as the target in ultra-orthodox styles of note pitch cuvres on 'gi') and
b) note pitch curves can select notes not selected by the raagam at all even in scalar raagas, e.g. in Hamsadhvani which selectes only /sa, ri, gu, pa, nu, Sa/ a note pitch curve on 'pa' sanctions the target 'ni' rather than 'nu' or 'Sa' though this note is not selected by the raagam. One can test this claim recording the note pitch cuvre on 'pa' for raagas like Suddhasaaveeri which selects 'di', Madhyamaavati which selects 'ni' and Hamsadhvani which selects 'nu'.

Clearly in my style the pitch curve on 'pa' for all the three raagas is identical to my naked ear. Therefore I assume without further argument that the note pitch curve 'pa' may be characterized as selecting a target 'di' or 'ni' for the three raagas without any reference to the actual notes selected by the raagam in question (subject to instrumental verification).

This is what I call the 'extension of the execution of m.tone to scalar interpretations'. My strong hunch is that the theoretical construct of the m.tone set in motion a whole range of pitch movements which could not be contained any longer. Thus all raagas have to allow note pitch curves between notes which are at least a tone away from each other. In all other cases, pitch movements are strictly governed by the lexical class membership of the raagam and its idiosyncratic selection of tones. This makes eminent practical sense. Imagine a situation where pitch movements were allowed if and only if a raagam selected an m.tone. Then we would have two entirely different types of raagas in Carnatic music, one type allowing pitch curves and another allowing only RenScale notes. It is actually difficult to imagine such a state of affairs in contemporary Carnatic music. The extension of the note pitch curve mode of pitch movement to raagas which do not select any m.tones ensures that all raagas limit RenScale renditions, requiring "gamakkam" which is the hallmark of Carnatic music.

The detailed exposition of the range of possibilities that I illustrated for the note 'gi' can be demonstrated for the notes 'ma' and 'ni' – equally expressive notes. But for lack of space, I will assume that the postulation of a red. m.tone and an aug.m.tone may be allowed for the other two notes as well and the algorithm postulated for 'gi' can be extended to all the other notes in the scale, without further discussion.

To sum up, we now know that a raagam can select for the following:

(21) Selection of notes in Carnatic music
   a. Selection of RenScale value
   b. Selection of red.tone if sanctioned by the lexicon
   c. Selection of aug.tone if sanctioned by the lexicon
   d. Selection of note pitch curve if notes are farther apart than a semitone
   e. Pitch variation is a function of time.

Thus, in Carnatic music we find that the interpretation of a note of music is dependent on several factors, namely its preceding note, its preceding anchor, the abstract time factor, etc. Summing up my findings so far, we can say that Carnatic music systematically exploits inter-tonal pitch frequency in ways suggested below, namely:

(22) a. m.tones are specified in the lexicon of the raagam such that their execution is taken care of by the constraints pertaining to their implementation.

b. Note pitch curves are sanctioned for designated notes in any raagam which are at least a tone apart.

c. The actual pitch movement is a function of time: The longer the duration the greater the number of pitch movements.

d. The difference between a pitch wave on the one hand and pitch curve, note pitch curve and pitch spike on the other hand is purely a matter of the selection of pitch range.

e. There are only two kinds of pitch movements, namely a movement between an anchor-target (a wave/curve depending on the time allowed) and between anchor-target-anchor which generally denotes a pitch spike. While the former occurs when two pitch values are associated with a single unit of time, i.e. mora, the latter is selected when three pitch values are associated with a single mora. Thus, from the theory point of view the pitch curve, the pitch spike and the note pitch curve will receive similar interpretations. The difference lies in the implementation. We will see below how this is done.

Thus we see that we are now in a position to consider both the 'wood' and the 'trees' – reconcile Carnatic music theory and contemporary practice in a straightforward manner. Let us recall our earlier discussion on duality of structure and its consequent structure dependence. The interpretation of the non-initial anchor 'ra/ri' at 187 Hertz for both Tooḍi and Bhairavi is a good example of structure dependence. The interpretation of the raw pitch value is possible only in the context of the musical phrase; the identical pitch value will be analyzed as 'ra' in the former case but as 'ri' in the latter case because the total pitch movement specifies a 'ra' anchor for the former and a 'ri' anchor for the latter. Thus the interpretation of a pitch value is possible only in the context of the structure in which it is embedded – clearly a case of structure dependence.

I now turn to the question of representation. We have an abstract 'note' representation (like the phonemic representation in linguistics) and the pitch realization–implementation rules (like the rules of phonetic implementation in language). In the current model of linguistics which I adopt for describing Carnatic music, both types of phenomena are accommodated simultaneously as distinct sets of well-formedness requirements. Before I take up this issue in detail, a small digression is necessary. I have to demonstrate how this is done in linguistic theory. Take the simple example of the difference between a phonological representation and its related phonetic representation. Take the Tamil words [maradi] 'forgetfulness' and [marattɨ] 'become numb' in the sentences given below in (23).

(23) a. avanɨkkɨ kaal marattɨppooccɨ
for him leg numb became
"His leg became numb."
b. avanɨkkɨ romba maradi
for him very much forgetfulness
"He is very forgetful"

From the phonological point of view, the sound 't' is long (as represented above) and 'd' is not. However, in the sentential context where the preceding words are highlighted, it is quite likely that the sounds 't' and 'd' do not have significantly distinctive duration. If that is the case then the phonological and the phonetic representations of these two sounds could be as shown below.

(24) a. Phonological representation

b. Phonetic representation

It could turn out that durationally, the two sounds are not significantly different. However, with respect to voice onset they could still be distinct. While the former sanctions the voice immediately after the release of the sound 't', the latter could initiate voice even before the release of 'd'. Thus, while phonologically, the main difference between the two representations is durational (and also 'voice'), phonetically the durational effect is rendered null in this particular sentential context and the sole factor is the onset of the vibration of the vocal cords, just after release in the former and a little before the release in the latter. Thus we see that the phonological and the phonetic representations could be significantly different. The specific constraints that map one representation onto another are a little complicated and so I do not wish to go into the details here. But suffice it to say that each of these representations are eminently suitable to a) satisfy the wellformedness requirements of their level and b) they are amenable to 'adjustment constraints' which can translate one to the other and vice versa.

The case at hand in Carnatic music is no different. Below are the two representations namely the Note Representation (like the phonemic representation) and the Pitch Implementation Representation (like the phonetic representation).

The constraints I have set in place do the needful in converting 'note representation' to 'pitch implementation' and vice versa. All the generalizations made so far are encapsulated in the representations in (25) and (26). The generalizations that fleeting anchors are higher than initiating anchor, successive targets are progressively higher and that the only difference between a pitch curve and a pitch spike is in the difference in timing.

(25) Note Representation

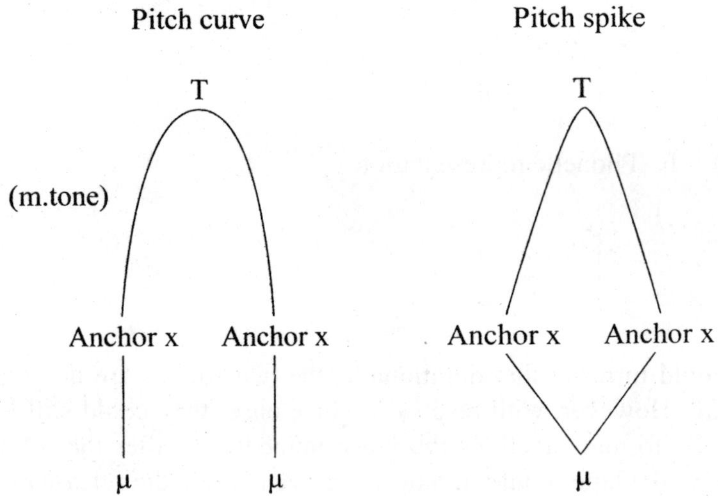

(26) Pitch Implementation

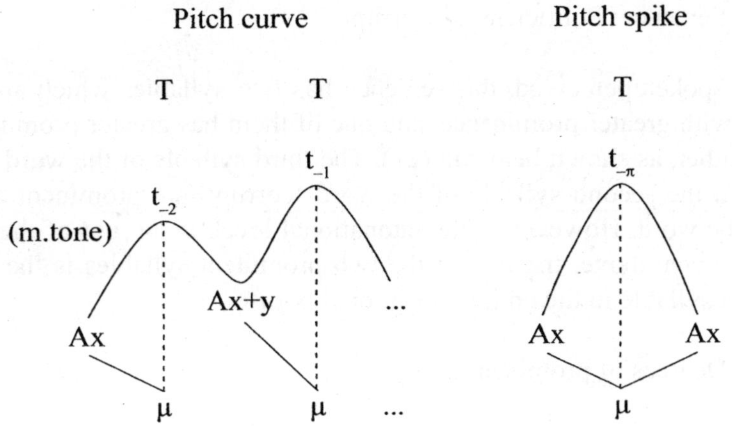

With this discussion we come to the end of the note–pitch implementation interface in Carnatic music. This is a major interpretation mechanism which has to be in place before the input can be evaluated for grammaticality and stylistic factors. But the actual implementation by different performers may admit further additional details. For instance, those who choose the 'ultra orthodox' pitch curve on, say, 'gi' in Tooḍi will choose a higher target, say, 'pa' and, perhaps, underachieve the target. This would be style dependent and listed in the lexicon of the performer. Hence the tone implementation constraints would have to select the appropriate targets from the lexicon of the performer and then set about the task of implementation. Further, in this case, the lexicon of the performer would have extra specification listed as permissible for the rendering of the note 'gi', some of the renderings not listed in the lexicons of other performers.

But the input representation that the grammar can access and evaluate requires further annotation. We see the details of this process in the following section.

5.4. Assigning structure

Before I take up the issue of duality of structure in Carnatic music, let me briefly introduce the notion of structure in language. In language we have structure at the level of the word, phrase and the intonational phrase. Let me illustrate these notions with concrete examples from English.

(27) Structure in language
Words: politicians, corrupt
Sentence: Politicians are corrupt.

When spoken/perceived, this sentence has two syllables which are pronounced with greater prominence, and one of them has greater prominence than the other, as shown below in (28). The third syllable of the word 'politician' and the second syllable of the word 'corrupt' are prominent at the level of the word. However, at the intonational level, in an 'out-of-the-blue' sentence given above, the first of the two prominent syllables is the most prominent syllable in the entire intonational phrase.

(28) Degrees of prominence

```
  *
  *         *
Poli'ticians are co'rrupt.
```

Thus we see that every word has a location for prominence and every intonational phrase has a unique placement of ultimate prominence in the intonational group in an utterance.

Just like language, Carnatic music too has structure at least at two levels (they will be motivated in chapter 6). Carnatic music needs to recognize the units musical phrase (comparable to the phonological word (see chapter 6 for a detailed discussion)) and the musical line (comparable to the intonational phrase). And in each of these structures, as in language, there are rules which determine prominence (just as in language, but more of this in chapter 6).

Thus, suffice it to say for now, that a sequence of notes are assigned structure, prominence and fully annotated before the line is subject to evaluation by the grammar of Carnatic music. One such annotated musical line is given below (36b) of chapter 6, p. 168).

The musical line has several musical phrases indicated by brackets, each phrase has a designated prominent note indicated by the symbol " ' " and the musical line contains two notes which receive extra prominence indicated by the symbol '*'. The rationale for this kind of annotation of the music input is given in chapter 6.

(29) Himaadrisutee: [⊙ 6.76]
Kalyaaṇi; Ruupakam: Shyaamaa Shaastri

*
// /['ri, gu]['ri - sa sa, nu] // ['ri; ri / ;] ['gu, - ; pa mi // pa;]
hi ma: dri su te: pa: hi ma:m

*
/ ;; - ['gu di pa mi] // ['gu; ri] / ['gu di pa mi] - ['gu,; // ri, sa,]
va ra de: pa ra de: va te:

The question that arises at this point is: "What physical evidence do we have for assigning this kind of structure to a sequence of pitch variations which constitutes a sequence of notes?"

Frankly, I do not have the entire range of physical correlates that signals phrasal/line boundaries. I can, however, suggest a few plausible candidates. Phrases could be initiated by 'attack', i.e., a fresh breath of air/strumming/fresh bowing etc. across various styles of Carnatic music. What we yet have to determine are the following:

a) What are the correlates of phrase/line initiation?
b) What are the correlates of phrasal/line prominence?

What I have set down here and also in chapter 6 is my impressionistic judgement on these issues. Let me say what my impressionistic views are on these matters. Firstly, I think the phrasal prominence is audible and may be interpreted as a fresh plucking/breath/greater intensity/attack etc. and the notion of extra prominence at the level of the musical line is a matter of extra prominence clearly signaled by greater emphasis (not just length). Once again, I show in chapter 6 with examples how phrasal sequencing is crucial to determining grammaticality and how placement of prominence can repair a borderline ungrammatical phrase thus showing the theoretical importance of these constructs. The evidence for the phrase boundary, phrasal prominence, musical line boundary and the extra prominence at the level of the musical line are interpreted from the raw physical input/output. Thus we see that the structure assigned to a sequence of pitch movements is based on purely physical signals like pause, phrase initiating 'attack', prominence, extra prominence, etc. that are contained in the pitch sequence.

We will see that the structure that we have assumed for Carnatic music is significantly different from the structure that has been proposed for Western Classical music by Lerdahl and Jackendoff (1983) and others in the next chapter. While the former has a three level, 'flat' structure, the latter seems to require a very articulate, hierarchical structure. The comparison that readily comes to mind, once again from language, is that the structure of the former is similar to the structure that the phonology–phonetics end of language requires while that of the latter is more comparable to the structure at the syntactic end.

5.5. Conclusion

In this chapter and the previous one we saw that there is definitely a need for a component like the Phonetic Implementation component in language in the grammar of Carnatic music. We saw that Carnatic music had added so much more to the standard twelve tone octave. With the addition of extra note interpretations, additional m.tones and an entirely new way of traversing the pitch space between tones the need for interpreting raw pitch values as notes of Carnatic music is indispensable. Further, an input also needs to be interpreted by assigning structure to it at the level of the musical phrase and the musical line and correctly interpreting phrasal prominence and emphatic prominence (if any) at the level of the musical line. Only when these annotating devices are in place can the grammar undertake the evaluation of a musical line for grammaticality and stylistic issues. Thus I assume that the grammar of Carnatic music takes up a sequence of raw pitch values, and assigns structure to it for the grammar to evaluate. The grammar of Carnatic music is then ready to evaluate the annotated line for judgements on grammaticality (based on style internal factors) and stylistic issues like 'creativity', 'avoidance of clichés', 'new ideas', 'imagery', 'wit', etc.

In this chapter I argued that the mechanism of interpretation, in addition to interpreting pitch values as notes of music also assigns appropriate structure to the pitch sequence based on purely physical signals like 'attack, prominence, duration, pause and extra prominence', etc.

I have so far been describing the system of one among innumerable systems of music. As I said earlier, the ultimate objective of Modern Linguistics (Generative Grammar) is to throw light on the cognitive faculty of humans. Analyzing languages, ultimately, allows us to look at the language faculty in humans which, in turn, throws light on the cognitive aspect of the language faculty. Research in linguistics has reached a certain stage of maturity such that it is possible to ask pertinent questions regarding human cognition and the language faculty in humans. For example, we do have reasonable answers to questions like "why does no language attest the word order Noun-Determiner-Adjective within a Noun Phrase?" and so on.

But in the field of music, since this kind of cognitive approach to music has not been attempted in a systematic manner, we do not have any answers to interesting questions like the ones below:

(30) Questions pertaining to Universal Music Theory

- Is the upper limit of steady tones within an octave 12 universally?
- What is the lower limit of steady tones in an octave? For instance, no musical system will select only two steady tones within an octave selecting the first and eighth.
- Is there a discernible pattern in evolving musical systems both historically and in acquisition? In other words, is there a progression from a three note scale to four and so forth and at what stage does the octave emerge? And when do musical systems expand beyond the octave?
- What are the other possibilities for exploiting inter-tonal frequencies? Which types of musical systems typically feel the need to exploit inter-tonal frequencies systematically?

Of course, I have answers to none of these questions at the moment. We have to await future research in 'Universal Musicology' along the lines that I have adopted for Carnatic music. It may not be the case that Carnatic music is the only system which exploits inter-tonal frequencies systematically. To say that the Carnatic music system is unique in the world music scenario because of its 'gamakkam' orientation with no empirical evidence is nothing but chauvinism. I am sure there are other musical systems which exploit distinct tonal ranges for distinct musical expressions. But what makes Carnatic music of considerable interest to a Theory of Universal Musicology is that the system allows us an insight into a language like, ever evolving system admitting several varieties in time and across time. This inherent typological characteristic allows us to define the outer limits of what constitutes the system of Carnatic music beyond which several characteristics of Carnatic music will cease to be operational.

Take for instance, experiments in orchestrating Carnatic music. When a group of melodic instruments are allowed to render the object 'orchestrated Carnatic music'[105], then the first casualty is the pitch curve. Since targets of pitch curves are variable in nature (such pitch variation is not quite amenable to precise manipulation), the first rule of orchestrated Carnatic music is the avoidance of pitch curves. I am stating this as a fact, with no value judgement attached to it. I merely note that this is a defining feature of orchestrated music that it strictly defines the pitch manipulation of performers so that a unique interpretation of a pitch rendering is made possible. The lexicon of this variety of Carnatic music automatically gets rewritten.

The theoretical point of interest for us will be to compare musical systems which give as much room to the individual melodic player as Carnatic music does or more and then compare the extent of inter tonal pitch exploitation of these systems with that of Carnatic music to define the universals of pitch boundaries:

(31)
- Is the upper limit 23 m.tones in an octave?
- Are there music systems which define prominence in musical phrases from the right edge (like right edge alignment of prominence in languages like English, Hindi etc., e.g. the last heavy syllable in the word 'eighˈteen' vs 'ˈeighty'.)
- Is the multi-layering of musical structure as in Western Classical music always motivated by concerns for simultaneous/linearly sequenced polyphonic/harmonic relations of notes/phrases/themes in a scale/musical line?[106]

Once again, I have no answers to any of these questions. But I will like to end this discussion on the interpretation of pitch manipulations in Carnatic music with the plea that this is just the beginning of a line of research which, according to me, will lead to a Theory of Universal Musicology which, in turn, will throw light on the music faculty in humans.

Chapter 6
Construing meaning in Carnatic music: Determining grammaticality

6.1. Introduction

I had claimed several times that the general architecture of the grammar of language and Carnatic music are similar in that both are concerned with capturing the systematic relation between sound and meaning.

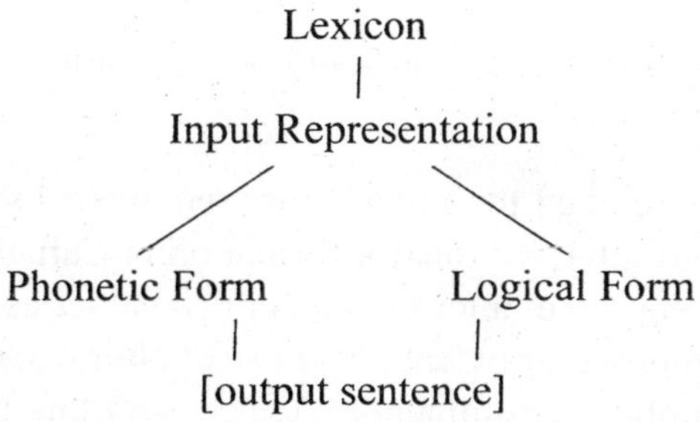

Figure 1. Architecture of the grammar of language

The implication is that 'meaning in language is derived from three distinct sources, namely a) the lexicon, b) syntax and c) Logical Form. While the lexicon gives the normative meaning of a lexical category, syntax adds a supportive syntactic relational meaning. Finally, the LF adds further details with respect to quantifiers/wh-words etc. Meaning in language is a composite factor and has to be compounded from, at least, three different sources. 'Meaning' in Carnatic music may have to be constructed from just the pitch form and the notated representation.

Further, both language and Carnatic music require mechanisms to interpret sound/pitch on the one hand and evaluate the interpreted sound sequence for grammaticality and meaning properties on the other hand. However, unlike language which is supposed to have the architecture as in Fig. 1 above, Carnatic music has the architecture as in Fig. 2.

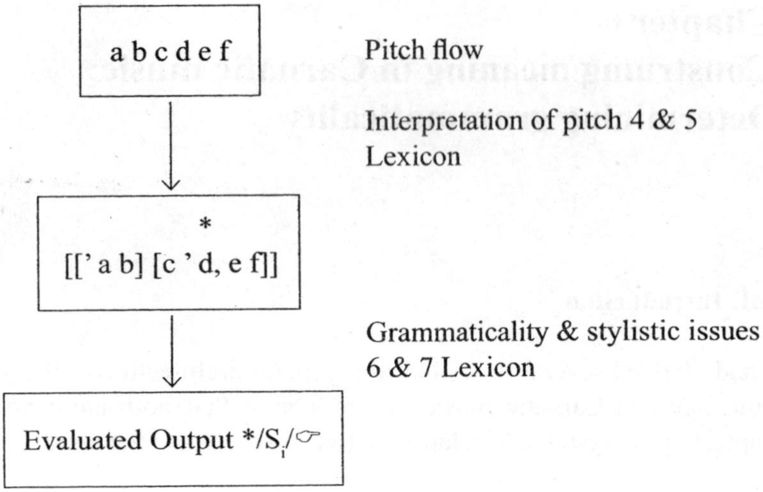

Figure 2. Architecture of the grammar of Carnatic Music

I had argued for the need for a mechanism equivalent to that of Phonetic Form for language to interpret tonal information in Carnatic music in chapters 4 and 5. This component interprets real pitch values as 'notes' of Carnatic music and also interprets raw data as musical phrase and line boundaries, prominence and emphatic prominence. Armed with this interpretation, the dynamic pitch input is converted into a structured notated musical line which is then subject to evaluation by the component equivalent to the one on the right, i.e. 'Logical Form' of language. I now take up the much more contentious issue of 'meaning' in music, particularly, Carnatic music.

6.2. The question of meaning in music

A grammar can be thought of as a box that mediates between 'sound' and 'meaning' allowing us to understand a sequence of sounds as a meaningful sentence and allowing us to express meaning as a sequence of sounds. I now turn to 'meaning' in language as, we will see, it turns out to be a difficult issue with regard to music.

How exactly do we construct the meaning of an utterance? Roughly, meaning, as we understand it, is constructed from three sources in a sentence as discussed below:

A) The lexicon
The lexicon is a repository of the meaning and usage of all the lexical entries in a language
B) Syntax
The syntax or sentence grammar lays out the sequencing principle of words in a language (and other things besides) and
C) Logical Form
The Logical Form component helps us interpret pronouns, negation and expressions like 'everyone', 'Wh' words, etc.

A and B are simple enough to understand. While the dictionary gives us meanings of words like 'men', 'love' and 'cars', it is B that spells out the relation between these words in a sentence. In other words, in the sentence 'Men love cars' because of the linear sequencing of words we know that 'men' is the agent/subject of 'love' and that the object of 'love' is 'cars'. Now, one might say that whatever the order of words, there can be no doubt about who loves what as the verb requires an animate agent to do the loving and cars, being inanimate cannot do it. Try substituting the word 'women' for 'cars' and you know how crucial word order is. Finally, coming to C, in a sentence like 'Everyone loves his mother', it is Logical Form which allows the sentence two meanings (the second meaning, if you have not got it yet, will become obvious – and the only meaning possible if you lay extra emphasis on 'his').

Let us now try to ask the question 'Does music require a meaning component like language?' Obviously not. Neither musical notes nor musical phrases are amenable to semantic interpretation unlike words in language. Therefore, the lexicon of Carnatic music, though it may list tones, phrases and idioms of particular raagas cannot list any meaning for each one of them as they may have none (as we understand the notion 'meaning'). Therefore, logically, music may be said to lack the constituent 'A' with respect to meaning (however, we will see that it is not as clear cut as it seems now and, more importantly, may require further refinement).

What about 'B'? What we called the sequencing principle of 'sentence grammar' revolves around the verb. In language, the phrases, informally speaking, that occur in a sentence are determined by the selection of the verb. For instance, consider the sentences of English given below where ungrammatical sentences are marked with an asterisk (please note that what is 'ungrammatical' is not determined by any grammarian but by the speaker/listener and arrived at by general consensus in a language community).

(1) a. The man disappeared.
b. *The man disappeared the forest.
c. The man disappeared into the forest.

(2) a. *The mother saw.
b. The mother saw a movie.

(3) a. *The father gave.
b. *The father gave a book.
c. The father gave a book to his daughter.
d. The father gave his daughter a book.

While (1a and c) are grammatical, (1b) is not. The verb 'disappear' does not take an object and hence the ungrammaticality of (1b). However, this verb can take an optional, oblique object (prepositional object) and hence the grammaticality of (1c). Whereas the verb 'see' requires one, obligatory object, hence the ungrammaticality of (2a), the verb 'give' requires two objects and hence the ungrammaticality of (3a and b). However, the two objects can occur in any order and hence the grammaticality of (3c and d). Whether a verb requires an object or two objects and whether the objects can occur in any order in the sentence are idiosyncratic properties of the verb listed in the lexicon. Compare the verb 'donate' with the verb 'give', for instance. Whereas the verb 'give' allows variation in the order of objects, 'donate' does not as the ungrammaticality of (4b) below illustrates.

(4) a. Ram donated his collection of books to the local library.
b. *Ram donated the local library his collection of books.

Similarly, the verb determines whether it requires a sentential object, and how it should be realized with two options; either to promote the subject of the clause to full subjecthood as in (5a) below or to force the entire clause to shift to the right as in (5b).

(5) a. [ ] appears [the man] to be a fool].
b. It appears that [the man is a fool].

I have by no means exhausted the subject of syntax. However, this brief discussion will suffice to illustrate the point that Carnatic music (and music in general) does not require syntax in the sense that languages do. Music crucially lacks grammatical categories like 'verb', 'noun', 'adjective' etc. Unlike language where the choice of a verb necessarily forces one to make several choices with regard to the type of words one can choose, in Carnatic music, the choice of a note no more forces you to select another note than some other note.[107] Therefore, as music lacks grammatical categories, it lacks syntax and hence the constituent 'B'. (However, like language, music too requires notes to be sequenced, I will take up this issue in a short while from now.) Finally, since music does not refer to the world of objects, since it has no equivalents of pronouns, Wh expressions etc., there is no question of the constituent 'C'. The crucial question is "Does the grammar of Carnatic music require a meaning construal component?"

It is indisputable that (Carnatic) music

(6) a. lacks grammatical categories
b. does not have predicate argument structure like language (i.e. verb, subject, object etc.)
c. has no syntax
d. is not referential
e. is not bound by truth conditions (being non-referential)

The questions to ask now are:

(7) a. "Does it mean that the concept of grammaticality is irrelevant in Carnatic music?"

and

b. "Does it mean that (Carnatic) music has no 'meaning' associated with it?

I will take up both the questions for detailed discussion below. I will examine issues pertaining to grammaticality in Carnatic music in this chapter and take up the issue of construing stylistic/aesthetic meaning in Carnatic music in the next chapter. Taking up the second question first, it should be obvious that since music is not referential, it can not refer to objects and events in the real world. However, several (rather vague) arguments have been advanced for the existence of 'meaning' in music. I summarize a few claims below and show how they are not quite appropriate.

Claim 1: *Tone pictures/visual association*
There are several successful attempts at 'painting' pictures with tones, e.g. Symphony VI of Beethoven and the tone poems of Debussy.

Rejoinder: It is difficult to assert that a *systematic* relation exists between music (individual tones) and the outside world. Indisputably, music can occasionally attempt at painting a picture, though music is not referential. E.g., thunderstorm in Beethoven's pastorale is quite transparent, as the association of drum roll with thunder is not far fetched by any account. However, drums do not always signal thunder in Beethoven/Western music. But Debussy's attempts at tone painting are not so transparent. Nor is the example from Carnatic music I give below. Consider a witty tone picture of a bounced ball in the Tamil padam (love song).

(8) Musical demonstration
Tiruvotriyuur Tyaagaraajan [⊙ 6.57]
'Tiruvotriyuur Tyaagaraajan'; Aṭaaṉaa, Ruupakam, Ganam Krishṇayyar.[108]

// ri, ma ri, / ma, pa ma - di, di,
pan da ḍi pa du
// Sa nu di, / Sa nu di, - ni di pa ma // pa,
po: le zhum bum

The glide from a lower note to a higher note and later from a higher note to a lower note translates into the spatial image of a ball bounced off the ground and later thrown up and caught on its way down (at least for me). But it must be admitted that the interpretation leans rather heavily on the language text. However, such attempts must be classified under imagery (and we will come across a few more examples of imagery in Carnatic music later) and it is quite clear that imagery works within traditions and is culture bound. But there is no question of associating individual sounds with specific referential properties. It must be pointed out that the interpretation is not raagam-dependent nor note-specific. It would have worked equally well in another raagam or from another set of notes.

Claim 2: *Magical meaning*
Some claim that Bauḷi raagam evokes sunrise and the picture of early morning.

(9) Musical demonstration
Bauḷi II [⊙ 6.58]

// sa ra gu, pa da pa, da pa pa gu, pa da pa da Sa, //
// Sa; nu da nu da, pa gu pa da, gu pa gu ra, sa //

It is true that this raagam invariably evokes a sense of sunrise/freshness etc. for the Carnatic music fraternity. But I feel that the response is due to regular association in the cultural context where this raagam is used for wake up songs (the meelukoo tradition) and with suprabhaatam which, once again, is a wake up slookaa addressed to specific deities in the Hindu pantheon. I am not denying the evocative quality of the raagam for the Carnatic music fraternity vis-à-vis this raagam. But what I am questioning is the reductionist consequence that this claim has on the raagam. It reduces a raagam to a specific emotion/scene denying other possibilities for the raagam. There are compositions in this raagam which have nothing to do with the early morning scene. In fact, one can even compose a fast paced tillaanaa (dance composition) in the raagam just to prove the point that the raagam is much more versatile than the associationists would admit. We will have more to say about such claims for associating raagas with specific emotions later on.

There is a strong tradition in India which asserts that 'sound' can influence the environment and that it has causative/curative properties vis-à-vis the magical properties of slookaas and the tradition of assigning raagas to different times of the season and the day. Each raagam is supposed to be associated with a deevataa/spirit which embodies the essence of the raagam and so on.

Counter-claim: Proving the general irrelevance of the seasonal/diurnal tie up with music, Carnatic music has, happily, abandoned this notion as unnecessary cultural baggage. The original association of raagas with specific times of the day etc. has been almost totally lost in contemporary Carnatic music and most performers may not even be aware of such associations now. Since most Carnatic concerts are scheduled in the evening, performers have got used to rendering any and every raagam in their concerts. However, I have nothing more to say about the 'magical' properties of music, in spite of recent claims to its curative/therapeutic properties.

Claim 3: *Emotive meaning*

There are claims that music can evoke emotions – the language of the heart.

Mukherjee (2000: 103) says,

> "...it is quite false that music primarily expresses emotions. If it did, then this property ought to be traceable to some aspects of the structure of musical expressions. Thus, even if some musical pieces, on the whole, evoke certain emotions like joy, sadness, chivalry, and the like, there is nothing in the musical passages or phrases or the individual notes to show how elements of emotions are attached to them."

First of all, I agree with Mukherjee in denying the claim that music *primarily* expresses emotions. I can show that emotions are only a part of the range of meanings music tries to convey. Carnatic music is an intellectual activity and a sizeable part of it is cerebral. And definitely in Carnatic music, a large part of it is sheer exploration of the tonal domain, stretching the limits defined by the grammar of a raagam; creating new ideas, creating complex mathematical combinations, etc. But getting back to music and emotion, the questions I try to answer are the following:

a) Is the correlation between the musical line and emotion constant across the music community?

b) If yes, where does the emotion reside? We will take up this issue when we examine certain notes in certain raagas being associated with certain emotions subject to criteria like 'emphatic prominence, tenor of the voice/instrument etc.'.

I argue that, contrary to Mukherjee, certain notes embedded in the musical line can and do convey specific emotions under some conditions.

So we come back to the question does music have 'meaning'? My own position on this issue is that since 'meaning' is internal to the system and as music is not referential, if a message with an emotion were intended, the most economical way to go about it would be to say it in so many words, using language. Contrary to Mukherjee, meaning is 'compositional' in music too the way it is in language. In language, the meaning of a sentence, for instance, "Ram loves his wife", can be arrived at from the meaning of the individual words, the meanings of 'Ram', 'wife' and 'love', the syntactic relations tells us the person who loves and the person who is being loved and the interpretation of the word 'his' from the sentential context and additional prominence (if present) etc. In Carnatic music too we need to interpret 'meaning' from the level of the tone, tonal sequence, musical phrase, the musical line and the musical content to arrive at a complete interpretation of a piece of music. I show in this chapter and the next that in Carnatic music too, as in language, interpretation starts from the smallest unit and moves up to include larger and larger units up to the musical discourse to construct a full interpretation. However, since I restrict myself to the level of the musical line (like sentence grammar), I do not have much to say about the interpretation of a piece of musical discourse, at this point.

6.3. 'Meaning' in Carnatic music

So, music lacks grammatical categories and syntax. If that is the case, how do we determine which sequence of notes is 'grammatical' and which 'ungrammatical' in Carnatic music? For surely, in Carnatic music, performers and keen listeners know when a piece of music has 'slipped'. As in language, speakers and listeners know when a chunk of language is of questionable grammaticality, where speakers do sometimes correct themselves, with or without any cue from the listener. For instance, consider the dialogue given below:

(10) A: What did you say when your wife accused you of over-spending?
B: Oh, I got around her saying her...
A: (A doubtful look from A)
B: I mean, telling her that it was a matter of over-billing.

This is a made up example to be sure, and perhaps not very convincing at that. But the example of musical ungrammaticality that I give now, is authentic (but for form's sake I will withhold the name of the performer – who was a highly acclaimed, extremely popular singer of the 70's and 80's). I give below the first two beats of the first line of the charaṉam – the final part of the varṉam (a two part composition rendered at the beginning of a concert) in Beegaḍaa composed by Viiṉai Kuppayyer.

(11) Musical demonstration
Beegaḍaa [⊙ 6.59]
Varṉam: Beegaḍaa: Aadi: Viiṉai Kuppayyer
The text: // pa, di pa - ma; pa / ; ma pa - di,...[109]
bha ga va: ri
*// pa di Sa, Ri Sa - ni di ni di pa, /; ...
bo: da na

If the performer had listened to the recording, perhaps, he/she may have frowned at the ungrammaticality of this phrasing. While Carnatic music allows a lot of liberty to performers to play around with musical texts, this rendition is clearly ungrammatical. The ungrammaticality arises from the phrasing leading one to interpret it as another raagam, namely Kaamboodi in this case. The ascent and descent of the two raagas in the upper half of the octave are distinctly different.

(12) Musical demonstration (continued)
Beegaḍaa [⊙ 6.60]
Di pa Sa[110]
Sa Ni; di pa
Kaamboodi I [⊙ 6.61]
Pa di Sa
Sa Ni di pa

Though the 'ascending' sequence 'pa di Sa' is not perhaps totally ungrammatical for Beegaḍaa, the ambiguity could have been considerably reduced had the 'ni' in the descent been lengthened, a marked feature of the raagam, and the phrase rendered as shown below. The grammaticality of the line will have improved considerably.

(13) Musical demonstration (continued)
Varṇam II (contd.) [⊙ 6.62]
(*)// pa di <u>Sa, Ri Sa</u> - ni; di / pa[111]

I wish to make two important points with this example. Firstly, extemporizing on musical texts is a tricky issue, not to be taken on lightly. Secondly, the repair strategy adopted here shifts the focus from the first half of the phrase, i.e. 'pa di <u>Sa, Ri Sa</u>' to the second phrase, i.e. 'ni , di pa' reducing the unintended interpretation as Kaamboodi considerably. In other words, just as in language where ambiguity can be resolved sometimes satisfactorily with the help of focus and intonational effects, in Carnatic music too, phrasing and focus (indicated by one of several strategies like emphasis, attack (plucking/bowing/breath) etc.) can be used to disambiguate musical sequences. However, unlike language, in Carnatic music ambiguity usually signals ungrammaticality/incompetence (unless of course undertaken as a 'joke') etc.

I will show, with suitable examples, that several mechanisms are involved in the work of extracting musical meaning from a musical line. I will list the mechanisms and also show how they work in the following sections. While some of the construals determine grammaticality, some define aesthetic issues which contribute to the construction of meaning in Carnatic music. I shall take up issues pertaining to grammaticality in this chapter and examine issues related to identification of style/aesthetic values in the next chapter.

6.4. Evaluating a line of music

Before I list the construals and their functions, let us consider the model of grammar of Carnatic music that I have outlined so far. As I said earlier, I assume that the mechanism of the grammar of Carnatic music is activated when a line of Carnatic music is presented to it as a physical, pitch reality. To begin with, the Tone Interpretive Mechanism 'interprets every tone and assigns it a note value, interpreting 'musical phrase' and 'musical line' boundaries and assigning phrasal prominence and determining emphatic prominence in the given line of music extracting the information present in the physical signal. We must remember that without the structure assigned by the Tone Interpretive Mechanism, the construals that I discuss here and in the next chapter cannot evaluate a line of music. The construals can evaluate only a structured representation of a line of music and not the raw data pertaining to a line of music. In short, the Tone Interpretive Mechanism assigns structure to the line of music and renders it interpretable by the grammaticality/style/stylistic construals. The construals have three functions to perform, namely a) determine grammaticality, b) determine style and c) evaluate the stylistic content of the musical line. As the functions of the construals are rather diverse, there is a need to assume that the mode of evaluation of the sets of construals is also varied depending on the function of the particular constraint in the construal set. I assume that the set which determines grammaticality assigns a violation mark '*' every time it encounters an ungrammatical note, sequence, phrase etc.; the set which evaluates a line for the style assigns a Style identification mark 'S_i' as a function, i.e. every feature that helps identify a particular style will be awarded a single Style mark which will eventually be interpreted collectively in the discourse. For instance, in a line of music three 'events' point to $Style_i$ and two to $Style_j$, then when the discourse is evaluated as a whole, the overall Style will be computed and evaluated for coherence etc. But as I do not discuss issues pertaining to the grammar of musical discourse, I have nothing more to add to this at this point.[112] Finally, the construals which evaluate a line for its stylistic content are of two types, namely positive construals and negative construals. Whereas the former assigns a '☞' to a line which attests the idea the construal formalizes, the latter assign a violation mark '*'. Thus we see that construals are evaluated in three different ways. I summarize the functions of the different components of the grammar in the schematic representation below.

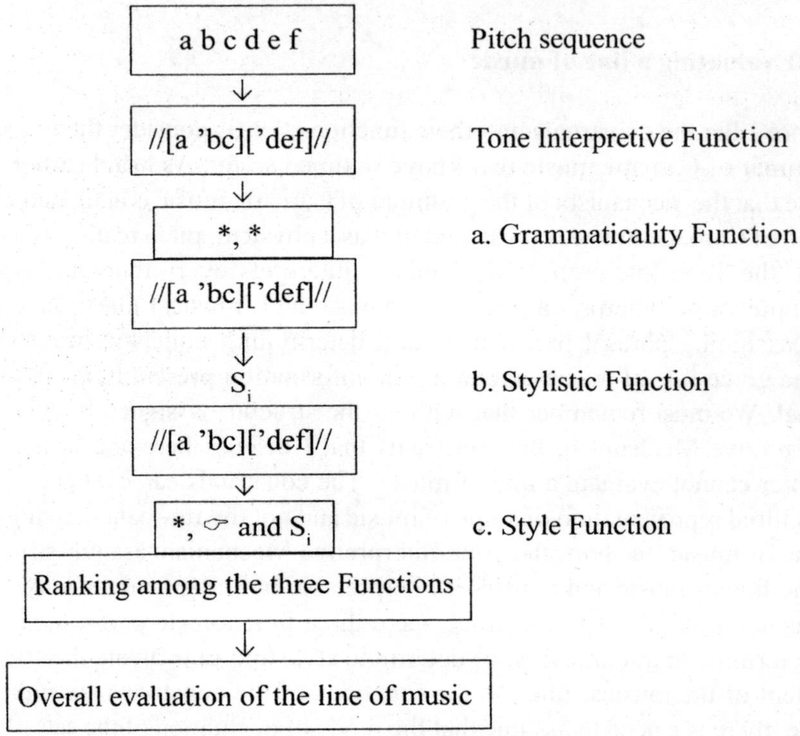

Figure 3.

I give below in (14) the set of construals which determine 'grammaticality and assign meaning' to a line of Carnatic music.

(14) Meaning construal mechanism in Carnatic music

a.	Tone Construal	(TC)
b.	Sequence Construal	(SC)
c.	Phrasal Construal	(PC)
d.	Line Construal	(LC)
e.	Rhythm Construal	(RC)
f.	Content Construal	(CC)

The construals (a–e) above perform three functions partly determining grammaticality, style and evaluating the stylistic merits of a line of music. The set of construals which determine grammaticality (14a–e) above (excluding (14f) which is responsible for evaluating the stylistic content of a musical line) evaluate an input and assign a violation mark '*' if a constraint belonging to this set is violated by the input.

6.5. Determining grammaticality: Tone Construal

I take up the content and role of Tone Construal (henceforth TC) first. As I discussed at length how tones are generated and interpreted as notes in the previous chapters, I will direct the attention to issues of grammaticality pertaining to tone in this section. TC has twin functions, local and global, both of which I will demonstrate below. The functions of TC are the following:

(15) Tone Construal (TC)
a. Checking for Grammaticality (Local Function)
b. Checking for *Ambiguity (Global Function)

To take up the local function of TC first, a tone, i.e. a specific pitch, pitch wave, pitch curve, note pitch curve or pitch spike which are the different realizations of a 'note' are, to begin with, checked with the lexicon of the raagam in question to see whether the executed/perceived entity is, in fact, sanctioned by the lexicon of that raagam. For instance, the double pitch curve execution of 'gi' from the anchor sa (demonstrated below) in the context of the raagam Hindoo|am will signal ungrammaticality as the lexicon of this raagam does not list this execution of the aug.gi m.tone.

(16.) Musical demonstration[113]
Hindoo|am and Dhanyaasi gi
sa gi, of Hindoo|am
sa gi, of Dhanyaasi

The reason is not far to seek. The undominated requirement in the networked raagam system of Carnatic music is that raagas should be different from one another at the level of the execution of the note[114] which we call *AMBIGUITYNOTE (*AMBNOTE).This family of constraints ensures that one raagam does not get mistaken for another raagam. Now, in this case, a pitch glide movement from sa which includes aug.gi is typical of another major raagam, namely Dhanyaasi and both raagas have the same first three notes in the aaroohaṇam – the ascending scale.

Thus we see that TC is crucial for determining grammaticality in a local domain and the explanation for the ungrammaticality lies in the global requirement *AmbNote. But the question to ask at this point is, "the specification for which raagam overrides the specification of which other raagam for satisfying *AmbNote" (vis-à-vis blocking in linguistics, e.g. the existence of the word 'children' blocks the regular plural *'childs'). The answer is rather clear cut in this case as only one of the raagas has the specification for the pitch curve for Aug.gi, in this case Dhanyaasi.[115]

But the case of 'gi' in Tooḍi and Bhairavi we discussed in the previous chapter is a good illustration of both raagas selecting aug.gi and yet ambiguity being avoided. We saw that this happened because of the initiating anchors which were 'ra' and 'ri' for Tooḍi and Bhairavi respectively.

However, in principle, since RenScale values are allowed for all raagas and some pitch specifications can be listed in the lexicons of several raagas (with partially overlapping scales), *AmbNote may be violated in some cases. Take the case of Moohanam which selects /sa ri gu pa di Sa/ and Naagasvaraaḷi which selects /sa gu ma pa di Sa/. Thus any musical phrase between 'pa' and 'Sa' with any interpretation of 'di' will result in an *AmbNote violation. Both raagas allow, in my style, RenScale 'di', gentle pitch wave 'di' and note pitch curve 'di'. Thus the lexical specifications are totally overlapping. In chapter 8 I show how, in such circumstances *Amb is held in suspension till the musical line at which level every line is expected to signal the raagam unambiguously by including a note which will disambiguate the two raagas in question. More of this later.

At least in the case of Moohanam and Naagasvaraḷi we could argue that both raagas are scalar raagas (or only marginally idiosyncratic). What about raagas like Harikaamboodi and Kaamboodi where both raagas are idiosyncratic with distinct lexical specifications? Here, in my opinion, the issue of grammaticality may have to be dealt with in a gradient fashion. The two raagas have many distinct lexical specifications for the note 'ma', e.g. while Kaamboodi lists aug.ma pitch curve Harikaamboodi does not. Yet both raagas allow RenScale 'ma', gentle pitch wave aug.ma. Therefore there is some scope for ambiguity. How is the issue resolved in practice? Since both raagas allow certain pitch renditions, the notion of grammaticality will have to be postponed to the next construal – the sequence or even the phrase. We will take up this issue later for carrying the discussion forward.[116]

We will see later that TC does not evaluate all notes with the same rigour while checking for *AMBNOTE when I take up the issue of prominence in musical phrase and the musical line. Some ambiguous renderings of notes are even tolerated. In other words, in the prioritized constraint set, some *AMBNOTE violations are actually ignored as the musical line is not trashed as ungrammatical. But more of this later.

6.6. Determining grammaticality: Sequence Construal

As the name implies, the main function of Sequence Construal is to check for the sequencing of notes.

(17) Sequence Construal (SC)
Checking for sequencing of notes

This function checks for grammaticality. Once again, like TC, the reason for the ungrammaticality of a sequence will be traced to an *AMB violation in the globally networked Carnatic music lexicon. The other two functions of SC which evaluate stylistic details will be taken up in the next chapter when I discuss constraints which belong to the stylistic set. Let us recall our earlier discussion of two types of scales in Carnatic Music in Rule 7 of (3), chapter 2, p. 20. I said that though we enumerate a scale as a sequence of notes, in principle, a scale is an unordered set of tones. Therefore in principle, for instance, though the scale of the raagam Kalyaaṇi is said to be 'sa ri gu mi pa di nu Sa', in principle, any note can precede or follow any other note as the scale is an unordered set of tones. However, in practice, not every logically possible combination is grammatical. The constraint on possible ordering is not imposed from within the grammar of a particular raagam but due to the high ranking constraint we have already referred to, namely *AMB. The particular constraint here is *AMBIGUITYSEQUENCE (*AMBSEQ for short). As I have already mentioned, the lexicons of raagas are networked and that *AMB is a global constraint looking for possible ambiguity to be starred as ungrammatical. Examine the musical demonstration in (18) below along with the explanations for the ungrammaticality of the starred sequences.

A shrewd reader would ask the question: "If raagas like Moohanam and Hamsadhvani have partially identical sequences in their scales, how will *AMBSEQ work in the case of these raagas?" I answer the question in chapter 8 where I classify raagas into two sets, namely the Idiomatic set and the

Scalar set and discuss how different strategies may be employed in these two sets of raagas to avoid ambiguity.

(18) Musical demonstration
Kalyaaṇi II [⊙ 6.65]

a. ri mi gu b. sa pa mi gu ri
c. gu nu di pa mi ri gu d. nu mi di nu pa
e. *ri gu pa Moohanam, Hamsadhvani
f. *sa ri mi pa Saraswati, Hamsanaadam
g. *sa gu Valaji, Amritavarshiṇi, Gambiira naaṭai etc.

In addition to *AMB deciding on the grammaticality of sequences of notes, as I have already mentioned earlier in chapter 2 (p. 20), there are certain scales called vakra raagas, which literally means 'crooked scales', which supposedly allow only a certain sequence of notes. Though in traditional classification these scales have a fixed non-linear progression of notes as illustrated below, in practice, it is taken to mean a strict prohibition on certain *linear* sequences. I illustrate this point below with the raagam Puurvikalyaaṇi.

(19) Musical demonstration
Puurvikalyaaṇi I [⊙ 6.66]

a. Scale: sa ra gu mi pa di pa Sa
Sa nu di pa mi gu ra sa
b. Practice: The sequence *di nu Sa is prohibited.
Permitted sequences: pa di nu di pa
mi di Sa
mi nu di Sa nu di ...
gu mi di nu (Ri) nu di pa mi[117]

Thus SC assigns grammaticality judgments to sequences checking the inputs for any violations of specific prohibitions in the lexicon of a particular raagam and also evaluating the grammaticality of sequences with the help of the global constraint *AMBSEQ to see whether there is any loss of identity with another raagam anywhere in the network and if there is ambiguity, to mark it as ungrammatical.

First of all, it is important to see how sequences are construed for evaluation. Let me illustrate the point, though I may be running ahead of myself in doing so. I just now said that the sequence 'ri gu pa' is disallowed for the raagam Kalyaaṇi. However, listen to the musical demonstration below of a structured sequence of notes in Kalyaaṇi raagam.

(20) Musical demonstration
Kalyaaṇi III [⊙ 6.67]
['ri gu,] [pa mi 'gu, ri sa]
['*pa nu* di,] ['pa mi gu,] ['*ri mi* gu,] ['ri sa ṇụ]
[pa 'nu, di pa mi]...
*['pa nu,]['Sa nu di,]...
*[pa 'nu, Sa]

Though 'gu' is followed by 'pa' in the sequence of notes, this musical line does not attract any *AMBSEQ violation. The reason for not attracting an *AMBSEQ violation is that while 'gu' belongs to the first musical phrase (enclosed in brackets), 'pa' belongs to another phrase (I will define the concept 'musical phrase' (enclosed by square brackets) and prominence in musical phrases (marked by a closing apostrophe) in the next section) and the domain of *AMBSEQ is the musical phrase. Sequencing of notes across phrases, however, is not checked by *AMBSEQ and so the grammaticality of the line above (we will see in the next chapter that sequencing beyond the musical phrase is taken care of by stylistic constraints checking for musical coherence).

Once again like TC, SC also does not evaluate all sequence violations alike. Just as TC ranks certain violations of tonal rendering higher than others (we will see shortly what the criterion is), SC also tolerates violations of certain notes/sequences in a musical phrase.

Clearly, *AMBSEQ does not blindly go by linear sequencing of the notes 'pa nu', even within phrases, but checks the overall use of notes. In the grammatical phrases, ambiguity is avoided by the use of the note 'di' within the musical phrase, though the note 'pa' is not followed by 'di'. Thus we see that *AMBSEQ is constrained to check for sequences within musical phrases and, crucially, partly ambiguous sequencing is tolerated provided the phrase contains clearly unambiguous notes to mitigate the potential violation.[118] In conclusion, normally the domain of the construal SC is the musical phrase. In addition, even within musical phrases, SC does not blindly check for linear sequencing of notes. If a note which is not allowed to be skipped (because of *AMBSEQ violation) is found to be absent at position 'n', checking continues within the musical phrase to confirm the presence of the skipped note in the musical phrase before evaluating the musical phrase for an

*AMBSEQ violation. In a sense, *AMBSEQ too may function as though notes in a phrase were unordered within the phrase and only absence signals a violation.

But this strategy of SC assuming that notes in a musical phrase are unordered will not work in the case of vakra raagas where what has to be scrutinized is the presence of a precise sequence *'$n_1n_2n_3$' which is banned. I assume that SC runs in two versions, namely SC (general) and SC (special). In the former, SC evaluates musical phrases under the assumption that notes are not linearly ordered and the checking only looks out for missing notes which may render the phrase ungrammatical. In the special version which is triggered only by 'vakra' raagas, the general assumption that notes are unordered is set aside. However, even in vakra raagas, strict linear ordering is assumed only for specifically targeted notes/sequences. For instance, in a raagam like Kaamboodi which disallows the linear sequences [di ni sa] and [gu ma pa di ni sa], checking for strictly linear sequencing within musical phrases is triggered by the presence of 'ni' in a musical phrase. Once the note sequence 'di ni' is located then the special version of SC goes into high alert making sure that it is never followed by 'Sa' immediately. Thus even the special version of SC does not have the impossible task of looking for unspecifiable violations.

Thus SC (general) checks for the presence or absence of a note in a musical phrase and then acts accordingly and SC (special) is triggered only for vakra raagas where specified notes require certain other specified notes not to follow this note which alone trigger a violation mark.

Let us get back to our earlier problem of two idiosyncratic raagas having partially overlapping lexical specifications with the specifc example of the raagas Harikaamboodi and Kaamboodi and the specifications for the note 'ma'. Since both raagas allow RenScale as well as gentle pitch wave aug.ma we need to know how *AMBTONE/*AMBSEQ operates here.

(21) Musical demonstration[119]
Harikaamboodi
Gentle Pitch Wave 'ma'
['ri gu] ['*ma* pa] ['di, ni di] ['pa ma gu *ma*,]
Kaamboodi
['*ma*, (di) pa ma gu] ['*ma* pa di ni] ['pa di,]

The dominant raagam in this pair being Kaamboodi, and Harikaamboodi being a 'poor relative', the former sets the terms for the use of the gentle pitch wave for aug.ma. The note in question, i.e. the gentle pitch wave aug. ma is in italics in the notation above. Note that while in Harikaamboodi the note in question initiates a phrase or is phrase final, in Kaamboodi it is phrase initial, long and prominent or phrase initial when the phrase includes notes till 'ni'. Finally, the gentle aug.ma pitchwave is allowed as a final pivot only for Harikaamboodi. Thus we see that there are subtle rules disambiguating raagas even when they select the same pitch values and these rules are encoded among the sequential constraints hence directly under *AMBSEQ.

6.7. Determining grammaticality: Phrasal Construal

In this section, I define the concept of the musical phrase and, importantly, the concept of prominence which is obligatory in the domain of the phrase. The functions of Phrasal Construal are the following:

(22) Phrasal Construal (PC)
   a. Checking Phrase Boundary
   b. Checking Phrasal Prominence

I had briefly invoked these concepts in chapter 5 where I had argued that the mechanism which interprets the physical reality of a pitch sequence must interpret this sequence assigning it note values and also assigning it structure at minimally three levels, namely the level of the abstract unit of timing - the mora, the musical phrase and the musical line. I had also claimed that the musical phrase and the musical line admit their own brand of prominence etc. I now motivate these constructs for Carnatic music.

Before I examine these functions, let us take a look at language. All lan guages have words and all of us would readily agree that we know intuitively what words are.[120] To begin with, let us start with the assumption that a musical phrase is something like a phonological word in language, a minimal, stand-alone unit (in speech, significantly not in writing).[121] Thus a musical phrase is a sequence of notes that is likely to be produced/perceived as a minimal musical unit. A musical phrase could be a simple sequence of random notes or it could be a structured sequence of notes which we will call a musical idiom. The musical idiom is a fairly small set of algorithms to combine notes to form musical phrases. To begin with, a musical phrase could be a random sequence of notes.

(23) Musical demonstration
Kalyaaṇi V [⊙ 6.68]
1. Random notes
['Sa nu] ['di pa mi] ['gu ri]

In this sequence of seven notes, there could be three musical phrases (each with initial prominence, indicated by ' before and above the note that is prominent). While teaching a student to perform, for example, this is the way the sequence of seven notes would be split; and while rendering it on the veena, there would clearly be three prominent notes if played at normal speed. I have a strong hunch that, irrespective of tempo, the sequence will always be rendered as three musical phrases governed by the need to assign prominence to the important notes of the raagam (the jiiva swaras). However, in ultra slow tempo, each note could be a musical phrase by itself, for example, in a kalpanaa swaram with six moras to a note.

(24) Musical demonstration
Kalyaaṇi VI [⊙ 6.69]
//['Sa,; - ;] ['nu, / ; ;] - ['di,; // ;] ['pa, - ; ;] / ['mi,; - ;] ['gu, // ; ;] - ['ri,; / ;]

The proof for each note being a separate musical phrase comes from a minimal rendering with each note receiving equal prominence (of course it is possible to add emphatic prominence to the 'Sa', 'di' and 'gu', but more of this later).

I next turn to the musical idiom. It is a formula for combining adjacent notes. Here are a few to illustrate the point.

(25) Demonstration
[where T is a note and numerical subscripts indicate the linear sequence of notes assuming an ordered scale]

a.	T_1, T_2 T_1	gu, ma gu
b.	T_1, T_2 T_1 T_1	gu, ma gu gu
c.	T_1 T_1, T_{-1}	Sa Sa, nu
d.	T_1 T_2, T_1	gu ma, gu
e.	T_2 T_1 T_1,	ma gu gu,

The idioms given above are not exhaustive. But what is of theoretical interest is that they open up an entirely new approach to the sequencing of notes. Many of them are of general applicability and some are specific to certain notes in certain raagas. For instance, while (25a) can be applied to any two adjacent notes in a scale, (25c) is restricted to certain notes a semi tone apart in certain raagas. For instance, whereas (25c) is possible for the notes 'ma' and 'gu' and 'ni' and 'di' in the raagam Suraṯṯi, it is disallowed in Keedaaragauḻa though both raagas select the same notes (in a manner of speaking).

(26) Musical demonstration
Suraṯṯi [⊙ 6.70]
ni ni, di ma ma, gu
Keedaaragauḻa
ni di ma gu

Actually, the combinatorial possibilities we have listed as musical idioms show that the interpretation of a note is rooted in abstract time where below a threshold unit of time a note is interpreted as a 'fleeting' note or a 'shadow'[122] note – chaayaa swaram of traditional parlance – the usage of which is, once again, regulated via the lexicon.

As I said earlier, a musical phrase is a sequence of notes which can be easily identified and extracted from a musical line, it can be a near random sequence of notes or a combination of notes and a musical idiom or a musical idiom by itself.

Since a musical phrase can also be made up of an idiom prefixed/suffixed with random notes, the construct which is more comparable in language with the musical phrase is the construct 'phonological word'. The phonological word, like the musical phrase, is made up of the morphological word (roughly uninflected words listed in the dictionary) and a few small elements (technically called inflections and 'clitics') before and after it, e.g. while 'book' is a morphological word, [the book] is a phonological word and so is [the book's] and the plural [the books]. And as in the musical phrase (see below), the phonological word also has a single prominence contained within the morphological word.

(27) Musical demonstration
Kalyaaṇi VII [⊙ 6.71]

prefixed	[mi pa ['di, nu di]]
suffixed	[['di, nu di] pa mi]
prefixed and suffixed	[mi pa ['di, nu di] pa mi]

Two observations on the nature of the musical phrase are in order. Firstly, I consider these forms to be single musical phrases because they can be rendered with a single prominent note (as indicated) (to be discussed below). And secondly, unlike language where, prefixed and suffixed forms always have binary structure at every stage of representation, e.g.

(28) Word structure

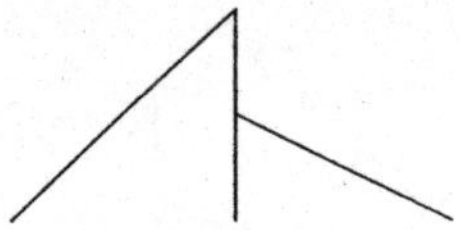

[$_3$ un [$_2$ [$_1$ character]$_1$ istic]$_2$]$_3$,

in musical phrases, I do not find any evidence for strict binarity; therefore a flat structure for the prefixed and suffixed form is quite adequate. I follow the convention of enclosing musical idioms and the musical phrase in brackets [...]. Assigning appropriate boundary and structure to musical sequences is the function of the constituent 'Checking for Musical Phrasing'.

(29) Musical phrase structure

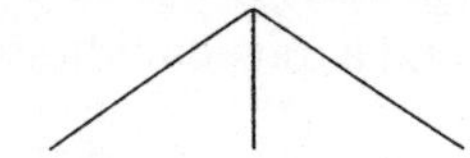

[mi pa ['di, nu di] pa mi]

At this point, suffice it to say that the musical phrase has no hierarchical structure unlike the morphological word or phonological word in language. We will see what the implications of this finding is when we compare the structured musical line proposed for Carnatic music with that proposed for Western Classical music in Lerdahl and Jackendoff (1983) and other literature.

Let us now see how checking for musical phrase boundary can evaluate musical inputs for grammaticality. Recall the earlier discussion in chapter 2 pertaining to duality of structure in language and Carnatic music (p. 26: (12), musical demonstration 2.24). I had given the example of the raagam Sahaanaa and given the musical phrases ['sa ri gu ma pa] and ['ri gu ma pa], stating that the note 'sa' cannot initiate a musical phrase which goes up to the note 'pa'. Consider the range of possibilities for musical phrases which begin on the note 'sa' for the raagam Sahaanaa.

(30) Musical demonstration
Sahaanaa IV [⊙ 6.72]
*['sa ri gu ma]
✓[sa ri 'gu ri ri,]
✓['sa ri sa ni sa,]
✓['sa, gu ri sa ni]
✓['sa, ma gu ri sa]

The generalization is that a musical phrase initiated by the note 'sa' cannot include the linear sequence 'ri gu ma'. This a case of a raagam-specific constraint which prohibits a musical phrase to begin with 'sa' and end in 'ma' *[sa ri gu ma..] for the raagam Sahaanaa. No student of Carnatic music is ever taught this negative constraint explicitly (to the best of my knowledge) and yet every 'good' performer 'knows' this and therefore avoids the offending phrase in his/her rendering of the raagam. However, though they avoid this phrasing, not many performers would be conscious of this knowledge. Of course, the reason for avoiding this sequence is *AmbSeq as the sequence in question would point to another raagam, namely Harikaamboodi or a Scalar raagam like Ravichandrikaa.

Instances of 'unconscious knowledge' like this are commonly encountered in language too. Facts of language form and use which are never explicitly taught or learnt are evidenced commonly in language output. For instance, given the nonsense words 'groump' and 'kround', every speaker of English would know that the former is not a possible English word whereas the latter is though no teacher or parent had ever told the learner that English does not allow labial consonants after the vowel 'au' in an uninflected monosyllable. Similarly, no one was ever explicitly taught that one cannot construct a word like, say " *inbelievable", though there was no *positive evidence* for the absence of this word in the input data that the child is exposed to. The point that I am trying to make is that while there is positive evidence for avoiding certain words/pitch realizations in language and music, there is no negative data to inform learners either in language or Carnatic music to inform learners of the finer points of grammaticality. Yet every child learning his/her mother tongue and every adequately knowledgeable lover of Carnatic music manages to acquire these subtle points of usage successfully. Children's ability to extract such minute points of usage from impoverished language data has prompted linguists to think of children as 'little linguists' who, like trained linguists, construct a grammar of maximal generality from the minimal data that she/he is exposed to. This trait has been attributed to the Language Acquisition Device (the famous LAD or the Black Box proposed by the founder of Generative Linguistics – Noam Chomsky) which is the genetically pre-wired neural network in the brain which explains the rapid and successful acquisition of the first language by the child in spite of impoverished data presented to the child. Since the learning experience of the first language and the successful learning of Carnatic music are, not obviously, comparable, I tentatively put forward the hypothesis that, as in language and the innate LAD, humans may have an innate Pitch Acquisition Device (PAD) which assumes that humans are pre-wired to perceive pitch patterns, musical phrase boundaries, emphatic renderings of tones, etc. The PAD hypothesis may not be too far fetched as children are known to perceive pitch patterns long before they perceive the sounds of language. The evidence for this claim comes from the well documented fact that children acquire the intonation patterns of their language (the tunes that go with statements, questions, incomplete utterances etc.) much before they acquire the segments and words of their mother tongue. However, more documentation is required before the implications of this hypothesis can be spelt out which can be empirically verified.[123]

But how do we explain the fact that all Carnatic music performers/listeners acquire the knowledge that the phrasing [sa ri gu ma] is ungrammatical for the raagam Sahaanaa though it was perhaps never taught explicitly to anyone? The postulation of the PAD explains how learners acquire the techniques of identifying musical phrasal edges and the phonetic correlates of phrasal prominence.[124] This in combination with the general notion that *AMB is a high ranking family of constraints in the Carnatic music lexicon informs the learner the ungrammaticality of this phrasing for the raagam Saahaanaa. Firstly, the offending phrase would never have been positively attested in the Sahaanaa input the learner is subjected to and secondly, when the learner is exposed to the raagam Harikaamboodi, she/he learns immediately that the phrase [sa ri gu ma] signals the latter raagam and not Sahaanaa.

Having defined a musical phrase, I now turn to the question of prominence within a musical phrase. As in language, every phrase must have a designated prominent note. When a sequence of syllables are put together in time, it would indeed be very monotonous for every syllable to be pronounced with equal prominence. In fact, it would sound like 'robotic' speech. Languages tend to favour either the left edge or the right edge of the word to select a syllable for prominence/stress. For instance, while French is said to have fixed final prominence, Tamil selects the left edge of the word for bestowing prominence. Once again, languages favour heavy syllables, i.e. syllables with two moras if present over light syllables, i.e. syllables with a single mora for prominence. With the edge orientation in place and syllable weight consideration noted, we can handle matters pertaining to word level prominence across languages. For example, whereas the Tamil word /'maradi/ 'forgetfulness' has initial prominence, /a'la:di/ 'strange' has prominence on the second syllable because the first syllable is light and the second is heavy – with a long vowel.[125]

Every musical phrase must also have a prominent note. We assume that musical phrases too have, like Tamil word stress, left edge orientation. While normally, the leftmost note is prominent, under three conditions this requirement can be suppressed. Firstly, the leftmost long note in a non-initial position is prominent (31a). Secondly, in the semi-rhythmic, free discourse called taanam any note can be prominent (long or short) (31c). Finally, in rhythmic passages, rhythmic formulae have to be highlighted, whether initial or not (31d). The convention we follow is to enclose musical phrases in square brackets, enclose the musical line with a double slash and add a stress (') mark above and before the note that is prominent.

(31) Musical demonstration
Kalyaaṇi VIII [⊙ 6.73]

a. Initial Prominence
   i. // ['mi pa di nu,] ['di pa pa,][126] — a sequence of notes
   ii. // ['di, [nu, <u>Sa nu</u>]] [<u>'di pa pa</u>,] // — a note + idiom + idiom

b. Non-initial Prominence because of a long note
   i. // [mi 'nu, di] [pa mi 'gu, ri] // — a sequence of notes
   ii. // [[mi '<u>pa, di pa, di</u>] ['pa mi]] [gu 'mi, ri] // — a note, an idiom and sequences of notes

c. Non-initial Prominence in taanam
   i. // [gu ri 'ri gu,] [ri 'ri gu,] — idioms in taanam

d. Non-initial Prominence in Rhythmic Phrases
   i. // [gu mi{'ni di pa mi gu} {'di pa mi gu ri} {'pa mi gu ri sa}] // — a sequence of notes + rhythmic idioms

Thus we see that every musical phrase has a designated prominent note just like every word has a designated prominent syllable in language. The conditions for the general placement of prominence in musical phrases, i.e. on the leftmost note/leftmost long note but never final is very reminiscent of stress systems in language where too we find leftmost/leftmost heavy syllable receiving stress but governed by non-finality. Having shown that prominence in Carnatic music phrases is similar to stress systems in many languages I go on to say that this information is provided and checked by the function 'Checking for Prominence in Musical Phrases'.

In a raagam, not every note is capable of receiving prominence in a phrase, unless it happens to be the only note in a phrase. Recall that in chapter 2 while discussing the notion of creativity in Carnatic music (chapter 2, p. 24: (9), musical demonstration 2.21), I had mentioned that in the raagam Sahaanaa, normally between the notes 'di' and 'ni', it is 'ni' that is the preferred note for receiving prominence in a musical phrase as the musical demonstration below illustrates. But the facts are a little more complex than that.

(32) Musical demonstration
Sahaanaa IV [⊙ 6.74]

a. i. [di 'ni, di pa ma]
ii. ['di ni di pa ma]
iii. [di 'ni , Sa ri] / ['di ni Sa Ri]
but iv. *['di, ni Sa Ri]
v. [di 'di] ['ni Sa Ri.]
vi. ['di,] ['ni, di pa ma]

b. i. [Ri Sa 'ni, di pa ma]
but ii. *['Ri Sa ni di pa ma]

c. ['ma di,] ['ni Ri,] [Sa 'ni, di pa ma]

d. ['ma di ni,] [Ri Sa 'ni, di pa ma]

e. i. ['ma di,] ['gu ma di,] ['pa ma di,]
['ma pa ma di,] ['ri gu ma pa ma di,]
but ii. *['ma di ni,] ['gu ma di ni,] ['pa ma di ni,]
['ma pa ma di ni,] ['ri gu ma pa ma di ni,]

Notice that it is not just a question of either prominence or length. While (32a.i–iii) are grammatical, (iv) is odd. It can be repaired, as it is in the varṇam with the phrasing [di 'di][127] ['ni Sa Ri..] where prominent 'di' belongs to a separate phrase and prominent 'ni' initiates another phrase (32a.v) or long 'di' and 'ni' may be equally long but belong to distinct phrases with equal prominence (actually, in most renderings, 'ni' will have additional prominence due to emphatic prominence in the musical line (see below)) as in (32a.vi). Clearly in the descent (32b), 'ni' has to be long where 'di' should not be long.[128] Another fact is that both 'di' and 'ni' can be long (32c and d). Finally, notice that 'ni' cannot be a phrase final 'pivotal' note in a series of musical phrases whereas the use of 'di' as a pivotal final note is grammatical (32d). Thus the grammar of prominence and length can be quite complex extending beyond the musical phrase to include the musical line in conjunction with another constraint checking for patterns across musical phrases. I summarize the findings regarding the notes 'di' and 'ni' in Sahaanaa in the constraints below in (33).

(33) Constraints specific to the notes di and ni in the raagam Sahaanaa

a. 'di' may be prominent in the context of 'ni' in the ascent if both notes are of the same length in the musical phrase.
b. 'ni' must be long in the descent.
c. long 'di' makes a good pivotal, final note in a series of musical phrases in the ascent; 'ni' does not.

Thus the function 'checking for prominence in musical phrases' has to assess the placement of prominence in a musical phrase keeping in mind constraints like those in (33a–c) and many more such constraints. Finally, evaluating grammaticality is a simultaneous function which takes in constraints pertaining to tones, tonal sequences, musical phrases and musical lines in tandem rather than in a bottom up, derivational fashion going from tone, to sequence, to musical phrase to musical line. Had it been a derivational model of grammar which works in a bottom-up fashion, one would have to undo the grammaticality/ungrammaticality marks earned at lower levels due to higher level considerations, unnecessarily complicating the grammar. The ranked-constraint based model that I adopt here allows us to elegantly capture the inter-relatedness of constraints at various levels evaluating a musical input simultaneously, at one go.[129]

6.8. Determining grammaticality: Line Construal

Before I try and define the construct 'musical line', let us look at the levels of organization higher than the phonological word in language. Take the English sentence and its Tamil equivalent given below and the possible ways it can be pronounced in English and Tamil.

(34) English

a. i. //[The young man loves a beautiful girl.//
ii. //The young man// //loves a beautiful girl//
iii. *//The young man loves// //a beautiful girl//

b. i. //orɨ iḻaiɲɲan orɨ aẓahaana peɳɳai kaadalikkiraan//
ii. //orɨ iḻaiɲɲan // orɨ aẓahaana peɳɳai kaadalikkiraan//
iii. //orɨ iḻaiɲɲan // orɨ aẓahaana peɳɳài // kaadalikkiraan//
iv. //orɨ iḻaiɲɲan orɨ aẓahaana peɳɳai // kaadalikkiraan//

In English, an intonational phrase (bounded by '//') can be either the entire sentence, or the subject noun phrase (NP) and the predicate verb phrase (VP); but the subject NP and the verb by itself cannot constitute an intonational phrase. Unlike English, in Tamil, all NPs and the verb can constitute independent intonational phrases, and any two adjacent NPs or the NP and the verb can constitute an intonational phrase. Notice that even the subject NP and the object NP which do not ever form a constituent in syntax may be taken together as a single intonational phrase.

In language, we find at least two higher levels of organization, i.e. the phrasal level, i.e. the noun phrase (NP) and the predicate/verb phrase (VP) and the intonational phrase (IP). Unlike language, in Carnatic music, if we equate the musical phrase with the phonological word, we find only one higher level of organization, namely the musical line, which is comparable to the intonational phrase. There is no level comparable to the 'phrasal level' of language.

There is yet another point of difference between language and Carnatic music. In language, every word has a designated syllable which is prominent, every phrase has a designated syllable which has the utmost prominence and every intonational phrase has an identifiable 'tonic', i.e. the most prominent syllable.[130] For instance, in English, while noun phrases normally have maximal prominence on the noun (the head of the phrase), the verb phrase has maximal prominence on the last object in the verb phrase (in out-of-the-blue statements). Therefore the pattern of prominence for English can be represented as shown in (35a) below. Unlike English, Tamil generally prefers initial prominence in noun phrases, and in intonational phrases the object immediately preceding the verb is the most prominent as in (35b).

(35) a. Levels of prominence in English

```
IP                              *
NP             *                *
W        *     *  *       *     *
     The young man loves a beautiful girl
```

b.

```
IP                  *
NP     *            *
W      *            *        *      *
     orɨ iḻaiɲɲan orɨ aẕahaana peṉṉai kaadalikiraan
```

While English systematically differentiates between compounds and adjective + noun sequences by assigning initial prominence to the former and final prominence to the latter as in ' 'blackboard' (found in a class room) but 'black 'board' (a board which happens to be painted black), Tamil does not differentiate between compounds and phrases using prominence. Thus both the compound ' 'maṉappeṉ' (bride) and ' 'nalla peṉ' (good girl) have initial prominence.[131]

Unlike language which has at least three levels of prominence, Carnatic music has only one obligatory level of prominence, i.e. the phrasal prominence that we have been discussing so far. Carnatic music does not seem to require a level comparable to the phrasal level of language and, unlike language, at the level of the musical line – the equivalent of the intonational level of language, Carnatic music does not require an obligatory super-ordinate prominence equivalent to the 'tonic' syllable at the intonational level in language. However, there could be an optional, emphatic prominence (or more) on any musical phrase(s) within the musical line for purely stylistic reasons. Before we go on to illustrate the finer points of difference between language and Carnatic music, let us first begin by defining the musical line and lay out the diverse functions of Line Construal.

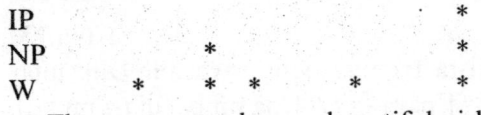

A musical line is that entity which can be repeated (in compositions) and that which is bounded by pause in free flowing renderings. I illustrate the musical line with examples from compositions (where it is indisputable). The renderings given below are typical of my style of playing (and it must be pointed out that other possibilities also do exist).

(36) Musical demonstration

a. Bhajaree: [⊙ 6.75]
Kalyaaṇi: Tisra Tripuṭai: Muttuswaaami Diikshitar
// ['gu; mi;] / ['pa,;] - ; ; // ['pa mi pa, di pa mi gu]
bha ja re: re:
/ ['gu ri, gu] - ['ri sa sa,]
ci tta
// ['sa , ri, gu ri sa,] / ['sa nu di nu - sa nu sa,]
ba: la: m
// ; [ri 'gu , ri] / ['gu, gu, mi gu - [['ri, gu ri] ri,]
bi kaa

b. Himaadrisutee: [⊙ 6.76]
Kalyaaṇi; Ruupakam: Shyaamaa Shaastri
*
// /['ri, gu]['ri - sa sa, nu] // ['ri; ri / ;] ['gu, - ; pa mi // pa;]
hi ma: dri su te: pa: hi ma:m
*
/; ; - ['gu di pa mi] // ['gu; ri] / ['gu di pa mi] - ['gu,; // ri, sa,]
va ra de: pa ra de: va te:

It will be noticed that in the musical line (36b) there are two occurrences of emphatic prominence at the level of the musical line while (36a) does not have even one. So, we find that 'emphatic prominence' in the musical line in Carnatic music – the equivalent of the 'tonic' in the intonational phrase in language – is optional and more than one occurrence of emphatic prominence is also welcome in a musical line. In (37) below, there is another example of a musical line without any emphatic prominence. The same line could be rendered with three emphatic prominences on the second 'di', fifth 'ri' and the ninth 'sa' phrase. Therefore, it is clear, this particular musical line has not one but may have three emphatically prominent tones.

(37) Musical demonstration
Daariṇi I: [⊙ 6.77]
Suddhasaaveeri: Aadi: Tyaagaraajaa
// ['Sa,] ['di,] - ['pa,] ['ma,] / ['ri,] ['sa,] - ['sa ri]
da: ri ṇi te lu su koṇ
['sa, ri sa sa di] // ['sa,;] - ;, [ri / 'ma, pa, - ['di Sa di Sa Ri,]
ṭi tri pu ra sun

Table 1. Levels of representation and representation of prominence

	Language	Carnatic music
1.	Phonological word obligatory 1	Musical phrase obligatory 1
2.	Phonologigal phrase obligatory 1	Missing
3.	Intonational phrase obligatory 1 or 2	Musical line optional 1 or more

The table above summarizes our discussion of the hierarchical levels and prominence pattern in language and Carnatic music.

However, in language, structure is necessitated not only by phonological requirements, namely layers of prominence at the word, phonological word, phonological phrase, the intonational phrase etc. but also by syntactic criteria. The implicit assumption that I have made through out the discussion in this chapter is that only the phonological end of structuring of language is relevant for Carnatic music. However, significantly, the assumption in the literature on applications of linguistics to Western music exemplified by Lerdahl and Jackendoff's (1983) classic and subsequent literature uniformly assume that Western music requires a many layered, structured representation more comparable to the syntactic representation. Compulsions of the tonic note, principles of harmony, thematic requirements, perhaps, make a musical line in Western classical music comparable to syntactic requirements in language in the sense that the choice of a tone/chord forces the artist to choose the following tone/chords etc. just as in language the choice of a verb forces the choice of certain types of subject, object, etc. Unlike Western music, in Carnatic music, such compulsions do not exist to the best of my experience both as a performer, listener and minor composer. The choice of a note or phrase does not in any way impinge on further choices in the musical line and further, there seems to be no need for any articulated, hierarchical structure within any level. Thus while the musical phrase has a flat structure as illustrated in (29) above, the comparable phonological word in language would have a binary structure motivated on internal grounds. Similarly, at the level of the sentence, language displays a richly articulated binary structure at all the intermediate levels unlike Carnatic music which once again has a 'flat' structure where all the constituent musical phrases in a musical line are at the same level multiply linked to the level of the line. Hierarchical structure in both language and Western music is motivated by internal considerations (of head-dependency etc.) which is totally lacking in Carnatic music.

Now that I have roughly defined the notion musical line, let me proceed to spell out the various functions of the construct Line Construal (LC). LC includes at least the following functions:

(38) Functions of Line Construal (LC)
a. Checking for boundaries
b. Checking for emphatic prominence

Clearly, musical lines have to be clearly defined (though, as in language, the length of a line is dependent on the performer/style of the performer etc.). Every tone in a musical line must be well parsed as a member of a musical phrase – avoiding dual membership to musical phrases/or parts of phrases (very much so as in language). The checking for emphatic prominence is usually also a checking for the grammaticality of note length as well as the appropriateness of emphasis on a particular note. As I have demonstrated earlier, not every note in a scale is amenable to length and/or emphatic prominence. Illustrating the optionality of emphatic prominence we have the rendering in [6.77] above and the one in [6.78] below. But the same line may be rendered with three instances of emphatic prominence on the second, fifth and the ninth phrase.[132] But the interpretation in [6.79] is ungrammatical as the important tones or jiiva swaras 'di' and 'ri' of Suddhasaaveeri are ignored and other tones are emphasized, in this case because of linguistic considerations, i.e. word prominence on the initial syllables of /'daariṇi/ and /'telusu/.

The point worth noting is that linguistic prominence (or stress) is totally irrelevant for musical reckoning. We will see shortly that the rhythmic beat (and the half beat) too can be disregarded in exactly the same manner in which linguistic prominence is ignored for placement of musical prominence in Carnatic music. In fact, words can even be split across musical phrases, musical lines in Carnatic music.[133]

(39) Musical demonstration

a. Daariṇi II: [⊙ 6.78]

// ['Sa,] ['di,] - ['pa,] ['ma,] / ['ri,] ['sa,] -
da: ri ṇi te lu su
['sa ri] ['sa, ri sa sa di] // ['sa,;]
koṇ ṭi

b. Daariṇi III: [⊙ 6.79][134]

*Ungrammatical

* *
// ['Sa,] ['di,] - ['pa,] ['ma,] / ['ri,] ['sa,] -
da: ri ṇi te lu su
['sa ri] ['sa, ri sa sa di] // ['sa,;]...
koṇ ṭi

A related point in question is the admissible length of specific tones being governed by the grammar of the raagam. I have already illustrated the complex factors governing prominence and length of the notes 'di' and 'ni' in the raagam Sahaanaa in [6.74] above. Here is another illustration of grammaticality and tonal length. For the composer Tyaagaraajaa, in Saaveeri, the note 'gu' is never lengthened beyond two pitch curves, occupying utmost four moras, in any musical phrase in the descent in the entire set of compositions in this raagam and when 'gu' occurs in an ascending musical phrase, length is altogether taboo.[135]

(40) Musical demonstration

a. Saaveeri II [⊙ 6.80]

According to Tyaagaraajaa
da pa ma gu, ra
*da pa ma gu;..ra

b. [⊙ 6.81]

sa ra gu ra
*sa ra gu, ra

Of course, in many contemporary renderings, both the starred phrases occur frequently. All I am saying is that the grammar of the raagam has changed considerably since Tyaagaraajaa and not that contemporary renderings are ungrammatical.[136] But without doubt, the function of checking for emphatic prominence is an important constituent of LC, one that can call into question the grammaticality of a musical line in a given style.

Nevertheless, in major raagas at least, though certain swaras may be designated to be the important notes – jiiva swaras – and naturally receive prominence and length in musical phrases and emphatic prominence in the musical line, the ingenuity of the composer/performer can force prominence, length, emphatic prominence on other notes as well provided satisfactory contexts are created. One such example that comes to my mind readily is the masterly musical line by the composer Shyaamaa Shaastri in the raagam Kalyaaṇi. As I have said before, the notes which are normally considered important in this raagam are ‘gu’ and ‘di’. Compositions like Tyaagaraajaa’s Eetaavunaraa and Nidhicaala sukhamaa begin on the note ‘gu’ and so does Diikshitar’s Bhajaree and Kamalaambaam bhajaree. But the Shyaamaa Shaastri compsition begins on an unlikely note – ‘ri’ and that too an extremely extended ‘ri’ at that. Listen to this marvelous line below.

(41) Musical demonstration
Talli ninnu: nera I: [⊙ 6.82]
Kalyaaṇi: Tisra Triupuṭai: Shyaamaa Shaastri (Kritimanimalai; IV; p 80)

```
                                              *       *
// ; ; [’ri, / ; ;] - [’ri sa sa; ; ni] //[’ri,;] [’ri, / ;] [’gu,] - [’gu,;]
        ta             lli                  ni    nnu      ne        ra

        *                                                         *
// ; ; [’pa, / ; ;] - [’pa, mi,] // [’mi, gu, gu, / ri,] [ri, - ’mi, gu,
        nam             mi            naa nu                vi    na
// gu, ri,]
   vee
```

Not only is the unlikely ‘ri’ made long and prominent, it is also made to bear emphatic prominence twice in a row in a grand display of confidence. Further, the emphatic prominence on ‘pa’ gives a sense of balance – ‘ri’ and ‘pa’ being the natural fourth. Finally, ‘mi’ is given emphatic prominence leaving no room for doubt about the identity of the raagam. And the note which is expected to receive prominence – ‘gu’ – never does at any point in the entire musical line. But it must be pointed out that this musical piece is a difficult one to execute with conviction. Most performers make slight changes, bringing in a shadow or a full fledged ‘gu’ and shifting the emphatic prominence onto ‘gu’ as shown below.[137]

(42) Musical demonstration
Talli ninnu nera II: [⊙ 6.83]
Kalyaaṇi: Tisra Triupuṭai: Shyaamaa Shaastri (Altered version)

```
            *                                       *          *
// ; ; [ri 'gu, / ; ; ] - ['ri sa sa; ; ni] // ['ri,;] ['ri, / ;] ['gu,] - ['gu,;]
       ta                   lli               ni      nnu        ne          ra
             *                                                       *
// ; ; ['gu, / ; , mi] - ['pa, mi,] // ['mi, gu, gu, / ri,] ['ri,] - ['gu, ri,
        nam                mi               naa      nu       vi          na
// ri sa, ri]
   vee
```

This version is, no doubt, a lot easier to render as length and emphatic prominence sit much more comfortably on 'gu' than 'ri'. But the 'fun' is missing (at least for me).

Thus we see that phrase and line construal checking for prominence and emphatic prominence respectively, primarily check for grammaticality, though it could be argued that the distinctions between versions [6.82] and [6.83] is really stylistic rather than grammatical. But assuming that the composer did, in fact, conceive of the line as in [6.82] (we have no evidence for being dogmatic about these issues, Carnatic music being orally transmitted and each performer doctoring the input according to his/her taste[138]), then what we have on our hands is a musical line of remarkable boldness questioning the basic tenets of musical orthodoxy.

Another point which needs to be made is that the distinction between grammaticality and stylistic consideration (which I take up in the following chapter) is not always clear cut. An instance of 'poetic license' if not acceptable to a performer becomes a point of grammaticality. Music being a 'constructed' language, it is not always possible to distinguish what is purely grammatical and what is purely aesthetic as, with practice, certain aesthetic preferences get entrenched as points of grammaticality.

6.9. Determining grammaticality: Rhythm Construal

As this book is primarily about the melodic aspects of Carnatic music, I will not dwell at length on rhythmic principles in Carnatic music. I will show that the super-ordinate constraint in this domain is a prohibition on phrasal prominence coinciding with 'too many' consecutive 'beats' of the rhythm.[139] And rhythm construal runs in two versions (like SC) with one version evaluating style in certain types of musical discourse and another looking out for violations of grammaticality in other types of musical discourse. While the former assigns and 'S_i' mark, the latter assigns the normal violation mark '*'.

Let me begin with a brief explanation of the notion of taaḷam which is a cycle of beats either of equal or unequal duration marked with the palm and fingers by vocalists and by the special strings meant for this purpose in the veena. Taaḷam is a matter of abstract timing. We illustrate below some of the taaḷas frequently encountered in performances.

(43) Common taaḷas in Carnatic music

a. Aadi taaḷam eight beat cycle.[140]

$//\ _{p}\mu\mu\ \ -\ _{lf}\mu\mu\ \ /\ _{rf}\mu\mu\ \ -\ _{mf}\mu\mu$

palm little finger ring finger middle finger

$//\ _{p}\mu\mu\ \ -\ _{up}\mu\mu$

palm upturned palm

$/\ _{p}\mu\mu\ \ -\ _{up}\mu\mu\ //$

palm upturned palm

'p' stands for the beat indicated by bringing down the palm
'lf' stands for the beat indicated with the little finger
'rf' stands for the beat indicated by the ring finger
'mf' stands for the beat indicated by the middle finger[141]

b. Ruupakam[142]

$//\ _{p}\mu\mu\ /\ _{lf}\mu\mu\ -\ _{up}\mu\mu\ //$

c. Tisra Tripuṭai (or Misra Caapu)[143]

$//\ _{p}\mu\mu\mu\ /\ _{p}\mu\mu\ -\ _{up}\mu\mu\ //$

d. Jampai (or Kaṇṭa Caapu)[144]

$//\ _{p}\mu\mu\ /\ _{p}\mu\ /\ _{p}\mu\mu$

For a detailed exposition of the classification of the system of taaḷam, the reader is advised to refer to Sambamurthy (1999), R. R. Ayyangar (1972 etc.) and other references cited there.

First of all, we must keep in mind the fact that 'prominence' in a musical phrase need not coincide with a beat of the rhythm in Carnatic music (and I have already mentioned that musical prominence need not coincide with linguistic prominence). Just as musical lines can split words with a part of a word in one musical line and the remaining part of the word in another line, the beat does not have to coincide with musical phrasal prominence or musical phrase boundaries. To simplify issues a little for ease of presentation, I classify rhythmic line style into two styles, namely the 'measured style' and the 'missed beat style'. In the measured style as in many of the compositions of the composer Muttuswaami Diikshitar we find that musical prominence and the beat do coincide either on the full beat or the half beat as shown in (44) below (the half beat indicated by " ' ").

(44) Musical demonstration
Measured style
Baalagoopaala I[145] [⊙ 6.84]
Bhairavi: Aadi: Muthuswaami Diikshitar
// ['sa ni] ' ['sa gi - ri,] ' ['gi ri]
baa la goo
/ ['gi ma] ' ['pa ma - pa,] ' ['da pa]
paa la
// ['pa,] ' ['di ni] - ['di ni, da ' da pa]
paa la ya
/ ['ma gi ma, ' pa, da pa] - ['pa ma gi, ' , ri ri sa]
aa shu maam

I indicate the beat with / or or // and a half beat with '. Noticc that not a single beat or half beat is ever mis-aligned with respect to musical prominence (though not all instances of musical prominence are aligned with the beat or the half beat). However, monotony is avoided by making the musical prominence align with the full beat or the half beat in a manner not totally predictable.

I now turn to the other style – the missed beat style where very often neither the beat nor the half beat coincide with musical prominence, creating a tension between melody and rhythm (which makes rhythm in Carnatic music what it is – subtle and complex). Here is an excerpt from Tyaagaraajaa's composition Cakkani Raaja in (45) below.

(45) Musical demonstration
Missed beat style
Cakkani raja (vocal): [⊙ 6.85]
Karaharapriyaa: Aadi: (8 moras to a beat): Tyaagaraajaa
// ; ; ' ; ['ri, - ; , gi ' ri ; ,] / ['sa , ; ' ; ;] - ['ni,; 'ni di di,]
ca kka ni raa ja
// ; ; ' ; ['ni , - ; sa ' ri ; ;] / ['ri, sa, 'ni, sa, - ;] ['sa sa ' ; ;
ma:r ga mu luṇ ḍa ga // ; ; ;[146]

In the missed beat style, musical prominence may be misaligned with the rhythmic beat and the half beat. It goes without saying, in this style too, linguistic prominence may occur just anywhere, irrespective of the musical or rhythmic prominence. I illustrate this point in the musical demonstration below where I highlight linguistic prominence in italics.

(46) Musical demonstration
Broovabaaramaa: [⊙ 6.86]
Bahudaari: Aadi: Tyaagaraajaa[147]

```
                      *
// ; ; - ; [pa di / 'ni, Sa;, ni - pa,] ['(ma) pa ma]
             broo      va       baa          ra
```

broo va baa ra

```
                                         *
// ['ma gu ma gu - ; , ] [ma / 'ni; pa pa,] - ; ['pa, di pa
     ma                         ra    ghu   raa       maa
// ma,; - ;]
```

ma *ra* ghu raa maa

Notice that the priority for aligning musical prominence with rhythmic prominence is much higher than the alignment of linguistic prominence. In the second example of the missed beat style we find that every alternate beat, i.e. a strong beat is aligned with rhythmic prominence. However, notice that in both the styles, what does not happen is for every beat/half beat to coincide with musical prominence. To state it formally, in a beat of say, x moras and n beat cycles, we do not find musical phrases of precisely x number of notes. If we did, we would find a musical line like the following which would be extremely odd in Carnatic music (bordering on ungrammaticality).

(47) Musical demonstration
Baalagoopaala II [⊙ 6.87]

```
a. *// ['sa ni sa,] - ['gi ri ri,] / ['gi ri gi ma] - ['pa ma pa,]
          ba:            la             go:              pa:...
```

Baalagoopaala III [⊙ 6.88]

```
b. *// [; 'sa ni - sa,] ['gi ri / ri,] ['gi ri - gi ma] ['pa ma // pa,]
            ba:              la              go:               pa:...
```

Whereas in (47a), every beat coincides with prominence on every musical phrase, in (47b), every half beat coincides with prominence on every musical phrase. Since we come across neither types in Carnatic music, we can safely conclude that both types are ungrammatical in Carnatic music. We can formulate this finding as a negative constraint given below.

(48) Negative Constraint on alignment of musical prominence and rhythm: Do not Align consecutive beats/half beats with musical/ rhythmic phrasal prominence. We will call it *ALIGNBEATPROMINENCE (*ALIGNBP for short)
* / or ' ['sa sa ..] / or ' ['sa sa ..]

The only occasion where this principle is systematically set aside is at the beginning of a percussion solo, where at least half the cycle of a taaḷam is regularly aligned to indicate clearly the measure of the beat. In all other occasions *ALIGNBP is adhered to more or less strictly. In most music performances, while rendering either niraval or kalpanaa swaram, musicians generally follow the missed beat style to make the interaction of the beat and prominence more and more complex. Therefore rhythmic groups of four moras are eschewed in beats with two or four moras.[148, 149] Thus we see that 'rhythm' in Carnatic music is an interesting conflict between musical prominence and rhythmic prominence and the conflict gets resolved, may be after several cycles of taaḷas, but the more delayed it is the greater the pleasure.[150] Here is one such 'delayed' align satisfaction in the rhythmic passage in (49). I enclose a rhythmic formula in { } to indicate the number of iterations of the formula clearly.

(49) Musical demonstration
Kalyaaṇi: Aadi [⊙ 6.89]

Taaḷam Cycle 1
// ; ; ; ; - ; ; ; ; / ; ; {['Gu, Ri Sa] - ['Ri, Sa nu Sa; ['Gu
// Ri, Sa nu Sa,] ['gu Ri - , Sa nu di] ['Ri Sa, nu
/ di pa] ['gu mi, pa di nu]}$_{\text{rhythmic cycle 1}}$
- {['Gu, Ri Sa] ['Ri, Sa nu

Taaḷam Cycle 2
// Sa;] ['Gu Ri, Sa nu - Sa,] ['Gu Ri, Sa nu di]
/ ['Ri Sa, nu di pa] ['gu mi - , pa di nu]}$_{\text{rhythmic cycle 2}}$ {['Gu, Ri Sa]
// ['Ri, Sa nu Sa; ['Gu - Ri, Sa nu Sa,] ['gu Ri
/ , Sa nu di] ['Ri Sa, nu
- di pa] ['gu mi, pa di nu]}$_{\text{rhythmic cycle 3}}$

This is a fairly simple formula of 26 moras and three rhythmic cycles of 78 moras covered in one cycle and five and a half beats of taaḷam. Longer rhythmic cycles with odd numbered units, to be adjusted to end at finishing points either before or after the start of a taaḷam can be encountered frequently in music performances (involving fractions at times). Therefore this is but the tip of the iceberg as far as rhythm in Carnatic music is concerned. It is not an exaggeration to say that the grammar of rhythm in Carnatic music is a book in itself.[151]

We saw that RC classifies a musical line in one of two styles of rhythm, namely the 'measured style' and the 'missed beat style'. While RC is irrelevant for non-rhythmic discourse like aalaapani and taanam (to a certain extent), it performs a classificatory function while evaluating a line of a composition marking it S_{ms} or S_{mb} (for the measured style and the missed beat style respectively). However, it performs a grammaticality function while evaluating a rhythmic passage such as kalpanaaswaram or niraval awarding a violation mark '*' for not observing the missed beat style in these discourses. Thus a performer who aligns rhythmic prominence unfailingly with the beat or the half beat will be severely looked down upon (considered ungrammatical). For instance, a performer who chooses a four mora rhythmic formula [ta ka di mi] either with the beat or the half beat is clearly not going to be appreciated much. It would be far more interesting to use a five mora rhythmic formula [ta din gi ṇa tom] for a four mora beat where one would have to start before the beat to end on the next beat or if one starts on the beat then the right edge of the formula will be properly aligned with a beat only on the fifth beat after the fourth iteration. But, as we will see later, in rhythmic passages, the number of iterations of a rhythmic formula is strictly laid down as three – neither more nor less (see chapter 7 p. 206). Therefore, to get the proper alignment at the end of the rhythmic passage one is required to start before or after the beat. The matter is further complicated when the line of the composition to which the rhythmic passage is attached either starts before or after the beat.

6.10. Conclusion

With the exception of Content Construal (CC), I have examined all the other construals pertaining to grammaticality in this chapter. Starting with the tone, the sequence, the phrase and the line, we examined each one of the functions of the construals determining grammaticality. We saw that in every domain, interpretation is complex subject to top-down considerations which are easily amenable in a non-derivational model of grammar that I have adopted. For instance, consideration of grammaticality of a note is over-ridden by the greater strength of prominent/emphatic notes over non-prominent notes; determining grammaticality of sequences is bound by the musical phrase (we will see that this function has to be modified depending on the nature of the raagam (see chapter 8, pp. 251–252)); and even within the musical phrase, emphatic prominence can overlook certain apparent anomalies in sequencing etc. We saw that checking musical phrase boundaries is not a trivial issue as it crucially involves notions of grammaticality. Certain notes may not be allowed to initiate musical phrases in raagas and certain notes may not occur as pivotal notes in phrase final position repeated in the musical line in certain raagas. We also saw that placement of prominence/emphatic prominence is once again a matter of grammaticality. But Carnatic music being an artificially created language-like system, stylistic considerations may be involved in certain violations being condoned. More of this in the next chapter. We saw that, unlike language where the placement of the tonic in the intonational phrase is obligatory, in Carnatic music, emphatic prominence is not obligatory at the level of the line and one may find more than one instance of emphatic prominence in a musical line. Finally, we saw that the alignment of linguistic prominence is of least importance and that consecutive occurrence of musical prominence may not be aligned with the rhythmic beat/half beat in any style of rhythm. In the next chapter, I go over the entire list of construals from the perspective of style/stylistic consideration which, I argue, is not external to the grammar of Carnatic music the way stylistic issues may be in language.

Chapter 7
Construing meaning in Carnatic music: Style/stylistic issues

7.1. Introduction

In the previous chapter I examined constraint sets which determine grammaticality under the heads Tone Construal (TC), Sequence Construal (SC), Phrasal Construal (PC), Line Construal (LC) and Rhythm Construal (RC). Of the proposed six construal sets only Content Construal (CC) was not dealt with as I explained that it dealt exclusively with stylistic matters. Of the three concerns of construal of meaning in Carnatic music, I dealt with issues pertaining to grammaticality judgements and marginally touched on a few issues pertaining to determining the style of a musical input in the previous chapter. Of the issues pertaining to style those which are evaluated at the level of the musical line were discussed at some length, e.g. RC. I take up issues pertaining to assigning stylistic meaning to a line of music in this chapter. What do I mean by 'meaning' in the context of music? Reiterating the point I made in the previous chapter, meaning in Carnatic music is defining grammaticality, style and determining the content which is partly emotive and partly intellectual. As music is not referential, meaning is purely internal to the grammar of Carnatic music and it is compositional. I show in this chapter how one could proceed with the construction of emotive and intellectual meaning in a musical line. Let us go over the entire set of construals proposed for Carnatic music.

(1) Meaning construal in Carnatic music

a.	Tone Construal	(TC)
b.	Sequence Construal	(SC)
c.	Phrasal Construal	(PC)
d.	Line Construal	(LC)
e.	Rhythm Construal	(RC)
f.	Content Construal	(CC)

To repeat, except (1f) all the construals have a grammatical part and a style/ stylistic part and the former, i.e. (1f) is entirely stylistic. In the following sections, I take up the style/ stylistic aspect of each one of them.

7.2. Style/stylistic issues: Tone Construal

Taking up TC first, I assume that at least the following two sets of construals are required for Carnatic music, while the former determines style and stylistic factors, the latter determines only the style of the music sample.

(2) Tone Construal
   a. Checking for emotive/aesthetic content
      (local function) (style and stylistic)
   b. Checking for pattern of usage
      (global function) (style)

Apart from the grammatical functions of TC, another function of TC is to give an emotional/aesthetic interpretation to a note which is part of the lexical information of the raagam in question. I give two sets of examples where the same note has different emotional colours in two raagas or a 'loaded', emotional interpretation in one raagam but not in the other.

In linguistics, for instance, if one wants to prove that two elements are distinctive/ contrastive, one looks for minimal pairs or, in the absence of minimal pairs, at least semi-minimal pairs. For instance, to prove that the dental sounds /t/, /t^h/, /d/ and /d^h/ are contrastive/ distinctive in Hindi, we can select the following minimal or semi-minimal pairs. The fact that /t/ and /d/ are contrastive/distinctive is proved by the minimal pairs /taal/ 'beat in rhythm', /daal/ 'a gruel made with lentil' where the substitution of one sound for another brings about a change in meaning, other segments being kept constant. For the other two sounds, in the absence of minimal pairs, we can consider the words /d^haan/ 'charity' and /t^haanaa/ 'police station' which are semi-minimal pairs as the other segments in the words are not completely identical (one word has an extra vowel). Using the same principle of semi-minimal pair, we can establish the four way contrast between these four sounds in Hindi as the left environment of the sounds, namely beginning of the word, and the right environment, namely the vowel /aa/, is identical. Thus we can prove that the four sounds /t/, /t^h/, /d/ and /d^h/ are contrastive/ distinctive in Hindi.

This principle of contrastive/complementary distribution can be applied in other areas of language too. For instance, the adjectival suffixes -al/-ar are not contrastive/distinctive as they predictably occur with nouns with different specification, e.g. /circle ~ circular; table ~tabular/ but /parent ~ parental; form ~ formal/. In other words, while the former attaches only to nouns which end in /l/, the latter attaches elsewhere and they perform the same function, i.e. converting a noun to an adjective. Therefore, the two suffixes -ar and -al are not distinctive/contrastive (i.e. they are the different realizations of the same adjectival suffix). On the other hand, the nominal suffixes -ation and -al are distinctive/contrastive as a) they attach to the same category of the word, namely verb, b) they output the same category, namely noun but c) if one substitutes one suffix with another, keeping the base constant (if possible), then one produces words which have a distinct meaning. For instance, 'recitation' recite+ation and 'recital' recite+al which have distinct meanings associated with them in the lexicon of English. Therefore the nominal suffixes -ation and -al are distinctive/contrastive in English.

Applying the same principle of contrastive distribution I show that the 'same' note in different raagas may have distinct emotional associations when embedded in minimally similar musical phrases proving the claim that specific notes in specific raagas may have emotional interpretation listed for them in the lexicon of Carnatic music.

(3) Musical demonstration

a. Shaamaa [⊙ 7.90]
// ['di Sa di pa] [ma '*gu*; ri ri...] //
shaanta/calmness etc. for gu
Deevagaandhaari [⊙ 7.91]
// ['di ni di pa, (ma)] [(gu) ma '*gu*; ri ri,] //
pleading/devotion etc. for gu

b. Hindooḷam 'ni' [⊙ 7.92]
// ['ma da ni Sa] ['*ni*; da] ['da; ma] //
no particular emotional colour for ni
Aahiri [⊙ 7.93]
// ['da ni Sa] ['*ni*; da da pa] //
supplication etc. for ni

Notice that the notes in italics are embedded in identical contexts in the sets of musical phrases. Also notice that the notes in question are identical with respect to phrasal prominence (indicated by a closing inverted comma) and comparable in length. As I said earlier, in linguistics, we would call such phrases 'semi-minimal pairs' and it would constitute proof of the distinctive character of the element in question. Whereas in (a) the same note has different emotional interpretation in the two raagas, in (b) while one note has no specific emotional interpretation, the other does receive an emotional interpretation. Clearly, Mukherjee is wrong in that emotions can be and are associated with certain notes, but idiosyncratically and hence specified in the lexicons of certain raagas. TC also gauges the extent of the emotional reading of the prolonged note equating over-length with cloyingly over-expressive emotion/sentimentality/wearing religiosity on one's sleeve etc. only in the raagas which admit this interpretation.[152] Of course, this emotional meaning is culture-bound but so is the meaning of a word. And the meaning of a word is no more derived from its sounds than the meaning of a note from its frequency. When Mukherjee (2000) says,

> "even if some musical pieces, on the whole, evoke certain emotions like joy, sadness, chivalry, and the like, there is nothing in the musical passages or phrases or the individual notes to show how elements of emotions are attached to them." (p. 103)

the problem with his argument is that he equates notes with words,[153] which is completely off the mark. If notes were words, then words in music would be limited to 12 in an octave or at best 23, if one accepts my claim. Not only is a note not equivalent to a word, all the realizations of a note do not have fixed meanings across raagas in Carnatic music. Each raagam is like a language with a unique history, lexicon and a life of its own.

While we are on the topic of emotional interpretation for specific notes in specific raagas, I would like to take up another claim regarding global association of raagas with emotion. As I said earlier (chapter 6, pp. 144–146), in the Indian music tradition there is a persistent claim that each raagam has a presiding deity (deevataa), a specific colour, the ability to invoke a specific mood/emotion and an appropiate time of the day/year when it should be rendered, etc. This belief system is still strongly entrenched in the north Indian classical music system. But in the south, while 'theorists' pay lip service to old beliefs in their treatises, performers have quietly buried the entire belief system (quite rightly too in my view).

For instance, this popular belief is endorsed even by the eminent musicologist Prof. Sambamurthy. He asserts that raagas are associated with specific emotions globally. In my view, this belief has done a lot of damage to the appreciation of raagas by the lay public. It creates a crude association, usually negative, between certain raagas and certain emotions, e.g. the raagam Mukhaari is supposed to evoke lamentation (notice that the Tamil word for lamentation 'oppaari' rhymes with the name of the raagam). In my view, this kind of glib talk merely creates a prejudice in the public mind. Let us examine one of Sambamurthy's claims with respect to a raagam. He is of the opinion that the raagam Keedaaragauḷa expresses bhakti (emotion?) (1999: 172). But consider the Arunaacala kavi composition 'viṭṭu viḍaḍaa siitayai'.

(4) Musical demonstration
Viṭṭuviḍaḍaa Siitayai [⊙ 7.94]
Keedaaragauḷaa Aadi: Aruṇaacala Kavi
// ; , ri - ; ma pa / pa, pa ma; - pa; ni di // pa,
vi ṭṭu vi ḍa ḍaa sii ta yai

The musical line clearly expresses anger/command/threat etc.[154] If a raagam can express emotions as diverse as 'bhakti' and 'anger', surely there is something wrong with the claim of global association of a raagam with a specific emotion. A raagam cannot be associated with as diverse emotions as bhakti and anger. My claim is much more modest; I claim that some notes in some raagas can have specific emotional interpretation under certain conditions (like emphatic length/over-length, a tremolo rendering, etc.). This leaves the majority of notes in the majority of raagas still open to interpretation. This is the reason why the majority of raagas admit a variety of emotional interpretation, depending on the melodic content and the language text.

Here is another example of a raagam expressing very different emotions. Among the many extraordinary compositions in the raagam Bhairavi, I present below a musical line which according to me is the best example of Carnatic music marrying emotion – intense supplication – with melody and extremely intricate rhythm spanning nearly two octaves; starting on a low pitch and soaring high (symbolizing, at least for me, total surrender – throwing up of one's hands) till the voice can go no higher. It is the second last musical line of the last caraṇam of Shyaamaa Shaastri swarajati 'Amba Kaamaakshi' in Misra Caapu. The second example is of pure joy, the composer is bubbling with enthusiasm to decorate the idol that is about to be worshipped, the composition 'Ceetulaara' by Tyaagaraajaa in Aadi Taaḷam.

(5) Musical demonstration
Abhimaanamuleedaa [⊙ 7.95]
Amba Kaamaakshi: Bhairavi: Tisra Tripuṭai: Shyaamaa Shaastri
(Kritimanimalai: IV: 13)[155]

*   *
// ['gi ri ri ni] // ['sa,; ; / ; ;] - ['pa; di pa ma] // ['pa,; ; / ; ['di, - ; ;]
a   bhi   ma: na   mu   le: da:

*   *   *
// ['ni,; ; / ;] ['Sa, - ; ;] // ['Ri,; ; / ;] ['Gi, - ; ;
na: pai   de: vi...

(6) Ceetulaara: Bhairavi: Aadi: Tyaagaraajaaa
(Kritimanimalai I: 414)[156, 157]

*   *
// - / ['pa, di ni] ['di, ni Sa] // ['ni Sa] ['pa, di ni] ['di ni] [pa 'pa / ,]
srin   gaa   ra   mu

*   *
[di pa 'ma, gi - ma,] ['di pa] ['pa ma] //
jee   si

*   *
['ma gi] ['gi ri] ['ri sa] ['ri,] - [ri sa 'ni, sa,;] / ; ;
ju   tu   noo

// - / - ['ri gi ma pa] ['di ni Sa Ri]
srin

*   *
/ [Sa 'Sa] ['pa, di ni - di ni] [pa 'pa] /
ga: ra   mu
['ma gi ri,] [da 'pa, ma - gi ri] [pa 'ma, gi ri sa]
je: si

*   *
// ['ma gi] ['gi ri] ['ri sa] ['ri,] - ['ri sa ni, sa,; / ; ; -
ju: tu   no:

The same raagam Bhairavi expresses the emotion of intense pleading in one case and great joy in the other. Thus raagas, in general, admit a variety of emotional expressions, with perhaps, some raagas leaning more to certain kinds of emotions than others. But, on the whole, it would be quite wrong to tie most raagas down to specific emotions, seasons, rasaa etc. in Carnatic music.

As I said earlier, originally, in Indian music, there must have been a strong tradition of associating raagas with the seasons of the year, time of the day and to specific rasaas (emotions). But the death of this tradition in the Carnatic music system is all the more strange when we see that it is the more conservative of the two major systems of music in India. Primarily, I believe that it is the strong influence of music composition in the south that has made this revolutionary idea of breaking away from traditional association of raagas with specific emotion/specific timing for their rendering possible in the largely conservative south. Considering the sheer range of compositions created in the majority of raagas by the major composers of the south since the middle of eighteenth century, it was no longer possible to equate a raagam with a specific emotion/time of the day or year. Each of the popular raagas attracted the attention of all the great composers since the music trinity to the present day with each composer adding his/her own emotional interpretation of the raagam thus laying to rest any vestige of specific association of emotions to raagas. The second important factor, a pragmatic one, in getting rid of this traditional associationist, reductive hypothesis of the raagam-emotion-diurnal tie-up was the fact that Carnatic music had to move out of temples and temple rituals to the local Prince's court and eventually to music halls/wedding receptions etc., where concerts were scheduled only in the evenings. With the result, Carnatic musicians have gradually given up on this traditional association between raagam and seasonal/diurnal/emotional association in general. Many contemporary musicians may not even know that whereas raagas like Dhanyaasi and Sri are morning/forenoon raagas, raagas like Tooḍi, Madhyamaavati, Bhairavi, Mukhaari are meant to be rendered in the evening or late at night. Similarly, contemporary musicians generally do not associate most raagas with specific rasaas or emotions. Thus most Carnatic musicians may not associate Varaaḷi with disgust just because one of Tyaagaraajaa's compositions expresses this emotion (Sambamurthy 1999: 173) or Suraṭṭi with vanity (emotion?) (Sambamurthy 1999: 175) since there are other compositions in these raagas which express a range of emotions.

Having established the point that not entire raagas but only certain notes in certain raagas can and do have specific emotional association set down in the lexicons of these raagas, we must now turn to the task of determining the evaluative function of TC "Checking for emotive/aesthetic content". Since determining the emotional message of a line of music is part of the meaning determining function that I call 'stylistic' function, TC should perform a stylistic function in the evaluation of a line of music. Whenever it encounters an appropriate note-emotion association endorsed by the lexicon of the raagam, it would assign a reward mark '☞'. However, the actual execution of the emotion reveals the style of the performer. For instance, a 'classical' style would attest the subdued/understated execution of emotional messages. It would severely restrict the exploitation of either duration or pitch variation on the note. But more overtly expressive styles ranging from the popular emotional to the frenetic religious styles would have more prominent execution of emotion in terms of duration, emphatic prominence and the pitch rendering of the note. Thus the same function performs two, not mutually contradictory, functions. It evaluates, at the level of the musical line, the presence of emotional interpretation and, at the level of the discourse, it additively sizes up the discourse classifying them in terms of distinct styles in a gradient fashion. I have nothing more to say about the latter function of TC.

We saw in the previous chapter that TC could evaluate a tone locally to determine grammaticality and it could also evaluate globally activating a network of raagas to diagnose the reason for the grammaticality violation. Both cases would have earned the musical representation a violation mark. We now consider another type of global computing which takes the entire musical discourse as its input to evaluate its style and assign the 'S_i' mark. Take a raagam like Tooḍi, for instance. We saw in chapter 5 pp. 114–119 that it employs at least five different executions of 'gi', namely RenScale 'gi', red.gi pitch wave, aug.gi pitch curve, note pitch curve 'gi' and pitch spike 'gi'. No two styles will have the same profile of the use of these four variants of the note 'gi' in the entire musical discourse. The predominance of, for example, RenScale 'gi' in the musical discourse will signal that the musical style is 'light' or one which avoids 'orthodox' gamakkam. Notice that it is not necessary to actually count the number of instances of each of the three types of execution. Assuming that the style in a musical discourse is constant, sampling a random portion of the discourse, say a 20 second bit will give us the information which type of execution predominates (not in actual numerical values but as a 'greater than' indicator).[158, 159] That is to say in a 20 second sampling if RenScale 'gi' is attested more than aug.gi pitch curve which is again more than note pitch curve 'gi', then we can conclude that the style is 'light'/unorthodox etc. I have nothing more to say on this kind of global computing of a section of the musical discourse as I limit myself to the grammar of Carnatic music up to the level of the musical line.

We saw in this section what functions the constraint set TC performs in construing style/stylistic 'meaning' in a musical discourse. However, notice that these construals of TC determine primarily the emotional 'content' of the music sample before going on to determine the style. Obviously, the set of constraints which actually evaluate notes for emphatic prominence, their duration, mode of rendering etc. will have to be worked in detail for TC (Style) to be able to classify music samples. The details of the specific constraints and their mode of evaluation will have to be worked out.

7.3. Style/stylistic issues: Sequence Construal

I take up the two stylistic functions of SC here.

(7) Sequence Construal (stylistic)
   a. Checking for new sequences (local function)
   b. Checking for iterations of 'minor' phrases (Global function at the discourse level)

In chapter 2 (pp. 22–25), while discussing 'creativity' in Carnatic music, I had mentioned that Carnatic music admits creativity just like every day language where phrases never heard before can be commonly encountered. The example I had given (musical demonstration 2.20) was from a contemporary composer in the raagam Beegaḍaa. The sequence I had mentioned was [di pa Gu] which is not prohibited in the raagam but not encountered in any of the extent compositions (and not commonly attested even in free renderings). Here I give another example of an unusual sequencing in a composition by the contemporary composer Tanjavur Shankara Iyer in the raagam Sindubhairavi (2001). The final phrase with the pivotal note ma and the phrases built around it are rather striking (at least for me).

(8) Musical demonstration (Adapted from Compositions of Tanjavur Shankara Iyer, 2001: 28)
   Manadirkkuhandadu [⊙ 7.96]
   Sindu bhairavi: Aadi: Tanajavur Shankara Iyer
   // ; ['da pa - ;] ['ma gi pa ma] / [gi 'ra ; - , sa sa,
   ma na dir ku han da du
   // ;] [sa 'gi - ,] ['sa gi ma pa ni da] / ['pa da] [ma 'pa - , ma ;]
   mu ru han ru: pam

Checking for new sequences, like SC in general, takes the musical phrase/line as its domain. It assigns a value '☞' whenever it comes across a new sequence in the musical input, i.e. a sequence not listed in the lexicon either as a phrase, idiom or even in the lexicon of compositions.[160]

Turning to the other stylistic function of SC, 'Checking for iterations of minor phrasing', let me begin by explaining what I mean by minor phrasing. While discussing a scale, I had said that, in principle, scales are unordered sequences of notes (enumerated as a sequence) and that certain logically possible sequences are considered ungrammatical either because they incur an *AmbSeq violation in the lexical network or they are explicitly prohibited by the grammar of a (vakra) raagam. While the sequence *[sa ri mi] is prohibited for Kalyaaṇi as it would incur an *AmbSeq violation because of the raagas Saraswati, Hamsanaadam etc. in the lexical network, the sequence [pa di ni Sa] is prohibited for Beegaḍaa as the grammar of this raagam explicitly prohibits this sequence. In addition to these two types of prohibition, there exists another type of sequence which is not prohibited entirely but is allowed only rarely in the discourse. More than one iteration of such sequences in the entire discourse may not result in ungrammaticality but will result in the discourse being branded as of questionable taste reflecting the lack of judgement on the part of the performer etc. But such phrases must be rendered at least once in the discourse for the discourse to be deemed to be complete. I call such sequences 'minor phrases'. These minor phrases are generally present in the lexicons of all performers/listeners, irrespective of style.[161] Here are a few examples of minor phrases in some raagas.

(9) Musical demonstration

a. [ma gu Sa] in the raagam Kaamboodi [⊙ 7.97]
b. [Sa, di pa] [gu ri, sa]
in the raagam Shankaraabharaṇam [⊙ 7.98]
c. [*gi*, ma pa, ma gi ri] with the italic gi as RenScale in the raagam Riitigauḷa [⊙ 7.99]
d. [ma *gu* ri *gu* ma pa, ma] and [Sa *nu* di *nu* Sa Ri, Sa] in the raagam Aanandabhairavi [⊙ 7.100]
e. [nu Sa *GU*, Ma Ri Sa] in the raagam Aṭaaṇaa [⊙ 7.101]

I will take up these phrases one by one. Although (9a) is sanctioned by a famous varṇam which begins with this phrase, it remains a minor phrase as it invokes an *AMBSEQ violation with raagas like Naaṭakuranji, Kamaas, etc. Similarly, (9b) is sanctioned by great compositions like Srikamalaambikaayaam, Akshayalingavibhoo, Dakshiṇaamuurtee of Muttuswaami Diikshitar. But once again, this sequence skipping the 'nu' and the 'ma' will bring the raagam to the brink of an *AMB violation and hence it may be called a minor phrase. Though I hasten to add that it only takes the musical line to the brink of an *AMBSEQ violation and not an actual violation as the pitch interpretations of 'di' and 'gu' are 'softened' adequately to contain in them hidden 'nu' and 'ma' respectively. Turning to (9c), the RenScale 'gi' rendering, sanctioned by the composition Dvaitamu sukhamaa of Tyaagaraajaa is an unusual phrase with a stark rendering of 'gi' which must be used sparingly. As I observed earlier (see chapters 4 and 5), normally, RenScale renderings of 'gi' and 'ni' in Carnatic music are always 'softer' with a lower value, executed as a pitch wave, than the keyboard notes E flat and A flat respectively.[162] This is the reason why this stark rendering of 'gi' in this phrase is a 'minor phrase' permissible just once in the discourse and not the regular interpretation of 'gi'. The rest of the phrases have accidental notes – in italics – which, once again, must occur just once or twice in the entire discourse. If they were to occur more often they would not be 'accidental' any more.

This brings us to yet another problematic issue in some well known raagas. What must have been an accidental note at one point of time has acquired a lot of importance being found in many phrases till it is difficult to assert which note is part of the scale and which note is an accidental note. Take the raagam Aṭaaṇaa, for instance. Take any composition at random and one would find both 'ni' and 'nu' in fairly equal measure. Which note belongs to the scale of the raagam and which one is an accidental note? One can dispute the parentage of this raagam forever and yet be no wiser. Take this notation adapted from Ayyangar (Kritimanimalai, III ii: 97) of the composition Tyaagaraajoo viraajatee by Muttuswaami Diikshitar in Ruupakam.

(10) Musical demonstration
Tyaagaraajoo viraajatee: [⊙ 7.102]
Aṭaaṇaa: Ruupakam: Muttuswaami Diikshitar (adapted from Kritimanimalai, III ii: 97)
// Sa *nu* <u>Sa; Ri</u> / Sa nu di, - di ni pa,
tyaa ga raa
// ma <u>pa ma, pa</u> ma ri / ri ma <u>pa ni pa</u>, - ni ni pa ma
joo vi raa ja

// pa Sa di, / , <u>ma; ni</u> - pa ma ri ma
tee ma haa
//ri sa pa ma / <u>ma; ni</u> papa di - , *nu* Sa Ri
raa ja raa ja sri

Except for the two occurrences of 'nu' in italics in the above musical line, the use of 'ni' and 'nu' is totally undisputable, fixed by usage. Which note belongs to the raagam and which note is accidental is hard to decide. Yet Ayyangar is not wrong in claiming that in this composition the raagam Aṭaaṇaa should be treated as a janyaa (derivative) of Shankaraabharaṇam – with 'nu' as its natural note and 'ni' as an accidental note, I think, on the basis of the original notation of the 'nu' in bold letter. But, setting aside the debatable issue of authenticity in the largely oral tradition of Carnatic music, it would not be considered ungrammatical or unacceptable to substitute 'ni' for the two occurrences of 'nu' in italics. But then would the raagam suddenly change its affiliation to Harikaamboodi? At best it is an academic issue.[163] But notice that once we accept the phrase [*nu* Sa Ri] for Aṭaaṇaa, the raagam does change ever so subtly, beginning to acquire more phrases where 'nu' replaces 'ni'. I will take up this issue at length in chapter 9 where I discuss the issue of intra-style musical phrasing. The point that I wish to make now is that many raagas have such minor phrases sanctioned by great compositions which are, however, rendered sparingly in the discourse. Global computing of the entire discourse is required for evaluating the use of minor phrases in these raagas. But, nevertheless, minor phrases belong to the domain of grammaticality since their minimal rendering in a discourse is obligatory for the evaluation of the grammaticality of a discourse.

7.4. Style/stylistic issues: Phrasal Construal

Having examined two functions of SC which evaluate sequences for stylistic meaning, I now take up Phrasal Construal.

(11) Phrasal Construal (stylistic)
a. Checking for clichés
b. Checking for iteration of phrasing/phrasal types

Consider the constituent 'Checking for clichés' first. A cliché is a musical phrase or a series of musical phrases which is/are proto-typical of a raagam.

(12) Clichés in musical phrasing
a. Tooḍi aalaapanai [⊙ 7.103]
['gi, gi ra ra,] ... ['ni, ni da da,]
b. Kalyaaṇi aalaapanai [⊙ 7.104]
['ri, gu ri sa sa,] ... ['di, nu di pa pa,]
c. Moohanam aalaapanai [⊙ 7.105]
['Sa Sa,] ['Sa Sa,] [Sa 'Ri, Sa di] ...
['pa pa,] ['pa pa,] [pa 'di, pa gu]

Interestingly, both in language and Carnatic music, beginners revel in clichés (and fixed expressions) and only at later stages of acquisition do they learn to avoid them (if at all) in their discourse.[164] Like clichés in language, clichés in Carnatic music too reflect a kind of mental inertia. Instead of thinking up new combinations of notes, it lifts an entire phrase from the lexicon.

It can be argued that cliché is, in fact, an *AMB violation at the level of the musical phrase; let us call it *AMBPHRASE for short. It too like other *AMB constraints looks for a match in the lexicon and when it does come up with a match stars it. The only difference between *AMBTONE and *AMBSEQ on the one hand and *AMBPHRASE on the other is that while the former set globally computes for identity across raagas from the raagam network, the latter set checks the lexicon of a particular raagam and finds an identity at the level of the musical phrase and whereas the former set determines grammaticality, the latter merely assigns a stylistic value to the input. It is worth noting that, while on the whole construals which determine stylistic values assign an award mark '☞', since 'checking for clichés' is, in fact, an *AMBPHRASE violation, like other *AMB family of construals, *AMBPHRASE too assigns a violation mark. We will see in the last section of the chapter how ranking of the constraints helps us in the holistic evaluation of the musical line and how the various marks, namely '*' violation mark, '$Style_i$' mark, and the stylistic award mark '☞' are computed by the grammar.

As in creative language use, in Carnatic music too, a discourse is not evaluated highly solely on the basis of avoidance of common words and phrases. A poem by Wordsworth is rated highly even though it uses simple words to telling effect. Similarly, in Carnatic music too, a familiar phrase may be used to create a special effect. On the one hand, common phrases make raagam recognition easier and hence more listener-friendly. Rare phrasing, on the other hand, may mislead the listener. Therefore, a performer may have to judiciously mix different types of phrasing to create a new discourse that is appreciated by the comparatively un-initiated as well as the keen listener.[165]

The last constituent of PC is 'Checking for iterations of phrases/types of phrases'. This constraint also belongs to the stylistic set like 'Checking for clichés' and not the set which determines grammaticality. Like *AMBPHRASE which assigns a violation mark (*) when it comes across a phrase which is listed as a cliché in the lexicon of the raagam, 'Checking for iterations of phrases' also assigns a negative value (*) every time it comes across a repeated phrasing/sequence in a discourse, i.e. at the next higher level of musical organization, namely the musical discourse. But since I restrict myself to the level of the musical line (comparable to sentence grammar), I have nothing more to say regarding this constituent.

7.5. Style/stylistic issues: Line Construal

I now examine the stylistic issues pertaining to Line Construal in Carnatic music.

(13) Line Construal (stylistic)
   a. Matching language text and musical phrasing
   b. Checking for link-ups between musical phrases
   c. Checking for type of phrases in the musical line

The stylistic function of matching language text and musical phrasing performs a stylistic function evaluating the placement of syllables of the language text in musical phrases. Consider two versions of the beginning of the Muttuswaami Diikshitar composition Maamava Paʈʈaabhiraamaa in Maɲirangu, Tisra Tripuʈai.

(14) Rendered in Madhayama ʃruti: Version I[166]
Maamava Paʈʈaabhiraamaa: Maɲirangu:
Tisra Tripuʈai: Muttuswaami Diikshitar
// ; ; sa, / sa; ni - sa,; // ri, ri,; / gi, ri, - ri, sa,
maa ma va pa ʈʈaa bhi...

(15) Rendered in Madhayama ʃruti: Version II
Maamava Paʈʈaabhiraamaa: Maɲirangu:
Tisra Tripuʈai: Muttuswaami Diikshitar

// sa, ri sa ni, / sa,; - ri,; // ri, sa ri; / gi, ri, - ri, sa,
maa ma va pa ʈʈaa bhi

Though musical prominence does not respect word level prominence in Carnatic music (as I have said several times), syllable weight considerations are generally respected in Carnatic music when aligning syllables with notes. It is odd, at least for me, that the first syllable with a long vowel (which is also the prominent syllable in the word) should be aligned with a note which is shorter than the following note which has a syllable with a short vowel in the first version. I think the second version is an improvement because it respects syllable weight while aligning syllables with notes. I would justify the longer note aligned with the first syllable of the second word (in the second rhythm cycle) arguing that as the first syllable is the most prominent syllable in the compound 'paʈʈaabhiraamaa', a longer phrase aligned with it is perfectly fine. Of course, it is not easy to arbitrate between different versions so easily all the time. Take the example of two versions of the Tyaagaraajaa composition Kaligiyuɳʈee in the raagam Kiiravaaɳi set to Aadi.

(16) Musical demonstration
Kaligiyuɳʈe Version I [⊙ 7.106]
Kiiravaaɳi: Aadi: Tyaagaraajaa.
// ; ; ; sa, - ra; gi ri sa sa, /ni, sa, ri,;
ka li gi yuɳʈee
Kaligiyuɳʈee Version II [⊙ 7.107]
Kiiravaaɳi: Aadi: Tyaagaraajaa.
// ; ; ra; gi ri sa sa, - ; sa, ni, sa, / ; ; ri,;
ka li gi yu ɳʈee

The first three syllables in the word 'kaligiyuɳʈee' are light and prominence is on the first syllable. Personally, I prefer version two with the phrases aligned with the first two syllables of equal weight. But the first version is clearly neither awkward nor ungrammatical.

Consider now the alignment of syllables with the musical line in the Purandara daasaa composition Dayamaaɖoo in Kalyaaɳi. Aadi.

(17) Musical demonstration
Purandaraviʈʈalana [⊙ 7.108]
// ; di Gu - , Ri sa nu / nu di pa mi - di, nu Sa
pu ran da ra vi ʈʈa la *na ra*

// Sa Sa nu, Ri Sa - Sa nu di, / pa mi gu, - mi di nu Ri // ;
ha ri saar va bau maa

First of all I would like to make it clear that this discussion is not a critique of the father of Carnatic music. While his texts have survived, his music to a large extent has not. Even when we do have a continuous line of disciples as in the case of the Carnatic music trinity we have so many different versions of their compositions,[167] in the case of the father of Carnatic music, who established the kriti pattern among other things, sadly, the music has not survived at all. In most cases the language text has been set to music by modern musicians based on slim or unclear authority.

Whatever way in which we re-distribute the syllables in italics, we get an alignment which is awkward by all standards. The musical line improves drastically if we substitute 'hari' for 'narahari'. Another example of mutilated language text for the sake of the musical line is from the Muttuswaami Diikshitar composition Sri Krishṇam bhaja in Tooḍi where he cuts short the language phrase 'vaṭapatra shayanam' meaning 'he who lies on the banyan leaf' to 'vaṭa shayanam' leaving out the word 'leaf' which is linguistically quite odd.[168] But, I am sure everyone will agree with me that the composition does not suffer because of this linguistic deviation. In fact, I take it as proof of the primacy of music in our compositions (where language, for all the piety and lip service that gets paid to the role of religion in Carnatic music, takes a back seat).

In fast tempo musical lines, of which Muttuswaami Diikshitar is the best exponent, language text and musical notes have to be aligned paying attention to syllable weight (with syllables with long vowels or short vowels in closed syllables, i.e. a vowel followed by at least two consonants one of which closes the preceding syllable counting it as heavy) considerations. Whereas heavy syllables have to be aligned with either a long note or a note sequence, light syllables are aligned with a single short note.[169] Consider this example from Muttuswaami Diikshitar's composition Bhajaree in Kalyaaṇi set to Tisra Tripuṭai (M.C).

(18) Musical demonstration
Bhaavaraaga [⊙ 7.109]
Bhajaree: Kalyaaṇi: Tisra Tripuṭai:
Muttuswaami Diikshitar
// sa nu sa ri, ri, / gu, gu mi - , pa di,
bhaa va raa ga taa ḷa moo diniim

// mi, pa, di, / nu, Sa Sa - , di nu Sa
bhaktaa bishṭap pra daa yi nim
// Sa nu Gu Ri Sa Nu / di, nu di - pa mi pa di
see va ka ja na paa li ta gu ru gu ha
// nu Ri, nu di nu / , di mi di - , mi gu mi // gu ri
ruu pa mud du ku maa ra ja na niim

One cannot fail to appreciate the perfect alignment of syllable weight with notes of music. This is why this composer is known for his great fast tempo lines in his compositions. Also notice that the alignment with the rhythmic beat subtly and unpredictably skips a few beats.

But there is another, perhaps, major tradition, of a composer prior to the trinity, who was scarcely known, whose compositions were revealed to the Carnatic music fraternity only in the latter half of the twentieth century – Uuttukkaaḍu Veenkaṭasubbayyar who had a very different idea of composition. He composed mainly in Tamil (and also in Sanskrit) where generally closed syllables do not count as heavy. Consider his musical line in the fast tempo.

(19) Musical demonstration
Paalvaḍiyum muham: [⊙ 7.110]
Naaṭakuranji: Aadi: Uuttukkaaḍu Veenkaṭasubbayyar
// [ma 'di, ni] - [Sa 'ni, Sa Sa,;] - [ni 'di, ni] // [pa 'di, ni ni,;]...
{KaaLinga} {shi ra tti lee} {ka di tta} {pa da tti lee}

Apparently, while closed syllables are always aligned with long notes or note sequences, syllables with long vowels are sometimes aligned with short notes and sometimes with long notes. However, the alignment is not as random as it may seem at first blush. Two observations are in order. Firstly, in this style of composition, primacy is given to rhythm (as it was predominantly a dance style closely related to the opera tradition). The primary concern being for the phrases to match rhythmically, long vowels may be articulated in a slightly shortened manner if necessary. The rhythmic line is the sequence of two rhythmic phrases {[##,#][##,##,]} with the second long note and a sequence final long note that has to be matched with a language text and so, the first syllable with a long vowel is aligned with a short note. Linguistically, this is quite odd as there are no languages where closed syllables count as heavy but long vowels may not. But it makes eminent sense musically (in Carnatic music and specially in dance music) for rhythmic consideration to take precedence over the language text. Secondly, notice that musical phrases and 'words' are perfectly aligned at both edges of musical phrases.

Consider a musical line by the same composer when he composes in Sanskrit, Bhajanaamrita, in Naaṭai, Aadi.

(20) Musical demonstration
Bhajanaamrita: [⊙ 7.111]
Naaṭai: Aadi: Uuttukkaaḍu Veenkaṭasubbayyar Charaṇam 8
// [ma, pa ma - ru,;] / [ma, pa ma] - [ru ru] [sa sa]
Krishṇa ka thaa kar ṇa na vita japa
//[sa ṇụ,] [sa - , pa pa ma] / [gu, pa ma] - [gu ma gu ma]
ta pas stroo trag va ni taarca na yoo ga
// pa, nu] [pa - pa, nu pa] / [ma pa nu pa - , nu] [pa ma
raasa ma hoo tsa va vibhava bhaa va para
// gu, pa ma] - [*sa, sa sa / sa sa*] [*pa, - pa pa pa pa*]
maatbuta *nar ta na va ra nrt tya ca tu ra*
// [Sa Sa Sa Ru] - [Sa; Ru] / [pa pa pa nu] - [pa; nu]
a ga ṇi ta raa ga na va vi da taa ḷa
// [ma gu] [pa ma] - [nu pa] [Sa nu] / [Sa, Ru Sa - Sa, Sa Sa]
kra ma la ya ga ti swa ra tan tri sa man vi ta
// [Sa, Sa, - Sa;] [Ma / Gu Ma] [Sa Gu] - [Sa Sa, Sa]
aa nan daa di sha ya su kha ni mag na
// Ru Sa, Sa] - [pa pa, pa] / [ru sa sa, - sa gu gu ma]
a nan ta mahaanta ca raṇaa ra vin da

Here we find that both long vowels and closed syllables are aligned with long notes or a sequence of notes, as is the standard practice in Carnatic music. But, as is the practice in the Tamil compositions, words are aligned with musical phrases at both edges, making it a distinct 'spoken/operatic style' of Carnatic music. Another characteristic feature of this style is its uninhibited repetition of the same note, for the entire word/phrase (indicated by italics).[170]

Contrast this operatic style with the 'standard' style of composition where words can be split by the intervention of a break (caesura) or even across musical lines. The musical demonstrations below illustrate both types. Notice that the word is split across musical phrases. Performers not aware of the word division (in the Telugu language text) will normally take a breath between the second musical phrase and the third making the language text irrecoverable. An improved rendering is one which retains the musical phrasing but shifts the prominence to the second note in the third phrase.

(21) Musical demonstration
Juutaamuraaree: [⊙ 7.112]
Aarabhi: Ruupakam: Tyaagaraajaa
// [pa,; ;] / [pa ma pa, - ;] [ma, // pa, di] / [pa ma; ; , gu] -
  [juu   taa   mu] [raa   ree]
[ri sa ri ma]

Consider next a musical line from the Tyaagaraajaa composition Chakkani raajaa in Karaharapriyaa set to aadi.

(22) Musical demonstration
Vaṇṭisri [⊙ 7.113]
Chakkaniraaja: Karaharapriyaa: Aadi: Tyaagaraajaa
// ; ; ; Ri, - ; Gi, Ri,; / Sa, Ri Sa ni,; - di, ni, di ni Sa,
  va   ṇṭisri   saa   kee
// ni Sa Ri, Sa ni <u>Sa, Ri Sa</u> - ; ni, di,;
  ta   raa   muni
/ pa, di pa ma, pa ma gi, gi ri ri,;
  bha   ktya   ne:
// ; ; ; {or // ; ni, Sa,}
  {i ṭu

In the above musical line, the line begins in the middle of the word 'iṭu*vaṇṭi*' (in italics) and generally many performers repeat the line from beginning to end a number of times rendering the language text total gibberish. A considerable improvement is achieved if the musical phrase in curly brackets is appended before the line is repeated. However, the point that I set out to make is that in the standard style, unlike that of the operatic style, words are clearly subordinate to the music and ru'es of musical phrasing, line break and tonal prominence have a higher priority than word structure etc.

Thus we see that in all styles, at normal tempo or slow tempo, syllable weight and prominence are totally irrelevant for aligning a syllable with a note – prominent or otherwise. But in fast tempo, we have two distinct styles, namely the syllabic style where closed syllables and syllables with long vowels have to be aligned with long notes or a sequence of notes, and the rhythmic style where closed syllables are preferably aligned with long notes or a note sequence but primarily the rhythm of the phrases in a line have to match even at the cost of aligning long vowels with short notes. In addition, in the latter style, words and musical phrases must be perfectly aligned at both the edges.

It must be obvious by now this construal 'matching language text and the musical phrasing' is operative only for assessing compositions (and that too not for the un-initiated). It is a construal that determines the style of the composition (I add two more to the two already discussed), i.e. whether a composition is in a measured style, mixed beat style, syllabic style or the rhythmic-operatic style, etc. Even while evaluating compositions it, perhaps, does not assign any violation marks but merely assigns a 'Style$_i$' mark to a line which has a less than desirable alignment of the language text with the musical line. Or we could assume that it is a style-internal matter where there is no question of awarding any kind of mark whatsoever but preferences are always clear cut and definitive. However, the criteria of this style dependent alignment are not always clear (at least to me). As in the case of the two versions of [7.106] and [7.107], the choice is not always logically determined but is arbitrated by popular decision. The clearly clumsy cases like [7.108] are easy to decide and one may even mark them as violations '*'. But the large majority of cases are really cases of style-internal decisions and within styles, of course, decisions are black or white; but the reasons for the choice are not always clear. So I assume that style dependent values are assigned to this construal a) only by the adequately initiated and b) only for reference purposes.

I next take up the issue of 'Checking for link ups between musical phrases'. Let me illustrate the point with a musical demonstration.

(23) Musical demonstration
konʈi I (the three last phrases of [6.76]) [⊙ 7.114]
['sa ri] ['sa, ri sa sa di] // ['sa,;]

koɳ ʈi

(24) Musical demonstration
konʈi II: [⊙ 7.115]
?['sa ri] ['sa, ri sa sa di] *// ['sa, ;]
koɳ ʈi

It will be observed that while there is hardly any linking up between the first two phrases, there is a clear glide which links the last note of the second phrase with the first note of the last phrase (7.114) indicated by the line underneath connecting the two phrases. If such a link is absent as in (7.115), it does not signal ungrammaticality but it would signal a clipped style (we could call it 'the keyboard style).

Can we predict when such link ups are desirable across musical phrases? As it is a matter of style, the answer is "no". The linking between musical phrases cannot be predicted and the strategies used for linking between phrases may even differ from style to style. I take it that 'linking' is really a matter of adding details to the musical line. Since I have unlimited access only to my own style, the following discussion of linking between phrases is specific to my style of Carnatic music which I call Chamber Music Style A in chapter 9 where an extended discussion of two distinct styles is taken up.

In my style, linking between phrases in a musical line takes place under certain conditions. Listen to the music demonstration [7.95]. The notation is repeated below for ease of reference as (25) but with underlining to indicate the notes which are linked in the rendering.

(25) Musical demonstration
Abhimaanamuleedaa [⊙ 7.95]
Amba Kaamaakshi: Bhairavi: Tisra Triputai: Shyaamaa Shaastri
(Kritimanimalai IV: 13)[171]

```
    *                                                      *
// ['gi ri ri ni] // ['sa,; ; / ; ;] - ['pa; di pa ma] // ['pa,; ; / ; ['di, - ; ;]
              ______         ____         ______
     a    bhi     ma:          na    mu        le:       da:

     *                 *          *
//['ni,; ; / ;] ['Sa, - ; ;] // ['Ri,; ; / ;] ['Gi, - ; ;
         ______
     na:          pai        de:         vi...
```

Notice that firstly, the two notes linked stand in a lower-upper relation in the octave and secondly, linking does not take place when the following note has emphatic prominence. On introspection, I find that linking is not always between a phrase final lower note to a phrase initial higher note within the line. I find that linking is also possible from a phrase final higher note to a phrase initial lower note as in the varnam in Kalyaani by Puucci Srinivaasa Ayyangaar which is notated below.[172]

(26) Musical demonstration
Varɳam in Kalyaaɳi by Puucci Srinivaasa Ayyangaar: Aadi
...['pa di nu] ['pa, di nu Sa]

Therefore, linking by gliding is not restricted to a lower–higher note relation across phrases. But linking is not possible between a non-prominent final note in the preceding phrase and an emphatically prominent initial note of the following phrase. The reason for such linking not being possible is also quite clear. As a phrase with an emphatic note always initiates its own domain of 'supra-phrasal' organization, the preceding phrase is beyond the purview of any linking.

As I said earlier, there exist other devices which link notes in and across phrases. Consider the musical line in (27) which is reproduced from chapter 6 (36b) for ease of reference but with additional 'linking' information (notes in parentheses).

(27) Himaadrisutee: [⊙ 6.75]
Kalyaaɳi; Ruupakam: Shyaamaa Shaastri

*
/// ['ri, *gu*] ['ri - sa sa, nu] // ['(*sa*) ri; ri / ;] ['gu, (*di*) - ; pa mi //
hi ma: dri su te: pa: hi
pa ;]
ma:m

*
/ ; ; - ['gu (*di*) pa mi] // ['gu; ri] / ['gu (*di*) pa mi] - ['gu,; // ri, sa,]
va ra de: pa ra de: va te:

The notes in italics are really notes of embellishment/shadow notes that are not to be played as full fledged notes. These could also be taken as a linking device which is employed both in the inter-phrasal and the intra-phrasal domain. Of course, the more such details, the more complex the musical line. If one assumes (as I do in chapter 9) that the hallmark of the concert hall style is an uncluttered musical line and the prerogative of a chamber music style is the detailed style which forces attention on minute details in the musical line, then, one can generalize that the more details there are in a musical line the more it veers towards the chamber music style. Thus we see that this construal is really a gradient construal evaluating style in Carnatic music. Of course, given a musical line, this construal can only attribute the acoustic properties present in a musical line to a distinct style. The evaluation of style in a musical discourse will of course be done in a gradient fashion with the additive style marks leading to a distinct style characterization. But as I take on the grammar of Carnatic music only up to the level of the musical line, I have nothing more to add on this issue.

Of course, as linking notes within and across musical phrases is a style based issue, it will certainly exhibit style based differences. It is quite likely that styles which have distinct preferences for more intra-phrasal linking may also require a level of structural organization between the musical phrase and the musical line, let us call it the musical supra-phrase. Such styles, it is quite likely, may exhibit some variation in the overall organization of the musical structuring. I capture the possible architecture of such styles as compared to other styles which lack this intermediate level of musical organization. I leave it to future research the minute details of the differences that may become necessary to describe such styles.

(28) Style: normal

Musical phrase	Obligatory prominence
Musical line	Multiple/optional emphatic prominence

Style: chamber music

Musical phrase	Obligatory prominence
Supra musical phrase	Multiple prominence
Musical line	Multiple/optional emphatic prominence

However, the new level is rather difficult to motivate as of now as the only criterion for its existence is the use of the linking devices between musical phrases. In language where the intermediate level, i.e. the phrasal level is motivated by additional prominence (phrasal prominence) and also grammatical criteria, e.g. [a ˈbook] and [a ˌbig ˈbook] (the primary and secondary prominence are indicated as upper and lower vertical bar). Unlike language, it is rather difficult to motivate such articulate hierarchical structure in Carnatic music as differences in degrees of prominence are not so obvious and hence difficult to motivate. Further as the only motivation for the supra-phrase in certain styles of Carnatic music is the intra-phrasal linking, I leave it to future research to sort out this issue with more robust acoustic backing.

Finally, the function of 'checking for type of execution of phrases in the musical line' has the following constituents:

(29) Checking for type of phrases in the musical line
a. Checking for musical coherence. (stylistic)
b. Checking the number of iterations of a pattern/musical phrase. (style and grammaticality)
c. Checking the mode of execution of phrases in a musical line. (stylistic)

I take up the constituent 'checking for musical coherence' first with the musical demonstration in (30) where, (30a) is clearly 'incoherent' but other choices such as (30b), (30c) or (30d) are equally plausible. In other words, determining 'coherence' does not in any way predict in what direction a musical line will go but, given a sample, it will be able to determine the relative coherence among possible candidates.

(30) Musical demonstration
Kalyaaṇi IX [⊙ 7.116]
a. // ['gu mi di,] ['mi di nu,] ?['pa Ri,] //
b. // ['gu mi di,] ['mi di nu,] ['di nu Ri,] //
c. // ['gu mi di,] ['ni di pa mi] ['di nu Ri,]//
d. // ['gu mi di,] ['mi di nu,] [di pa mi 'gu, ri] //

In (30a), the last phrase is neither ungrammatical nor aesthetically undesirable in itself, far from it. It is just that as a third phrase after the first two in that particular musical line it is less than pleasing. I repeat once again (as it is a point worth repeating), the progression of a musical line is no more predictable than the choice of lexical items in a sentence in language, though, the choice of the clause types, types of objects selected for, etc. are determinable to a great extent. Thus like language, in Carnatic music improvisation too, a musical line, in principle, is unpredictable as possibilities are infinite. But as in sentence grammar, so too in musical line parsing, many possibilities may turn out not to be ungrammatical but aesthetically not 'desirable'. As we see, aesthetic considerations in Carnatic music are more central than they are in everyday language (and that is to be expected music being an art form). The centrality of aesthetic considerations are reflected in the 'positive' evaluation of satisfied stylistic constraints.

The question to ask at this juncture is: "What are the elements which contribute to musical coherence?"

I identify a few below (there may be more):

(31) Checking for musical coherence
  a. Checking for pattern
  b. Checking for balance
  c. Checking for symmetry

Pattern, balance and symmetry are overlapping functions defined over several musical phrases. When we consider patterns of musical phrases, for example, we do not just look at the number of notes in a phrase etc. In the example above, if we examine the first phrase, we find that the first phrase with three notes with four moras has the fifth note – 'pa' – missing. And the second phrase also continues the pattern with a three note-four mora phrase avoiding the fifth. The musical line (30b) above satisfies the criterion 'pattern' with three similar phrases each of then avoiding either the fifth – 'pa' – or the eighth – 'Sa' – and is therefore considered coherent. If we consider (30c), we find the second phrase is comparable in length with the first with 4 moras but it does not follow the pattern set out by the first phrase. However, while the first phrase uses notes on the ascent, the second uses notes on the descent, satisfying the criterion 'balance'. Balance requires notes/idioms in the ascent to be matched with notes/idioms in the descent. Finally, the third phrase continues the pattern started by the first phrase, i.e. avoidance of the three most important anchors in an octave, namely the first, the fifth and the eighth – 'sa', 'pa' 'Sa' and picking up the pattern at a higher point in the octave satisfying the criterion 'symmetry' which requires that phrases/idioms in the lower part of the octave be matched with similar phrases/idioms in the upper half of the octave. And the musical line (30d) satisfies 'balance', once again, by matching the third phrase with the first two phrases taken together in both number of tones and satisfying the ascent-descent aspect of balance.[173]

It will be noticed that a musical line does not have to satisfy all the criteria of 'coherence' to be considered a coherent execution of a musical idea. All the three criteria are optional but at least one of them has to be satisfied to earn a mark – an award '☞' – for coherence. As this is a stylistic factor, musical lines which do not merit a positive mark for coherence can still escape being assigned a violation mark. But the absence of a mark for any of the construals of coherence renders the line an unremarkable line of music.

I now take up the issue of restrictions on the number of iterations of a pattern in a musical line. This principle has variable interpretation in non-rhythmic and rhythmic passages. Whereas in non-rhythmic discourse (meaning not pertaining to kalpanaa swaram etc.), it remains highly desirable to limit the iteration of a pattern to three, it is mandatory to render three iterations in rhythmic passages (no more no less); this point is illustrated with a sangati 'variation' of the musical line in (32).

(32) Musical demonstration
Daariṇi telusu konṭi II: [⊙ 7.117]
Suddhasaaveeri: Aadi: Tyaagaraajaa
// ['Sa Ri, Gu Ri] ['di Sa, Ri Sa] - ['pa Di, Sa di]
dha: ri ṇi
['ma pa di Sa] / ['di pa ma ri] ['sa,] - ...
te lu su
Daariṇi telusu konṭi III: [⊙ 7.118]
*// ['Sa Ri, Gu Ri] ['di Sa, Ri Sa] - ['pa Di, Sa di]
dha: ri ṇi
['ma pa, di pa] ...
te ...

We do not normally find more than three iterations of a type of musical phrase in a row in a musical line. However, if more get piled up, which does happen rarely, then it clearly signals a bravura passage meant for 'the gallery'.[174] Here is one such passage which is very popular. When compositions attest a violation of this restriction, then, as the construal performs a style function, the presence of three or more than three phrase types will elicit an S_i mark from the construal branding the style as 'popular', 'flamboyant' or 'playing to the gallery'.

(33) Musical demonstration
Ninuvina: [⊙ 7.119]
Navarasa kaanaḍaa: Ruupakam: Tyaagaraajaa[175]
1. // pa, pa, / Sa, Sa, - ni Sa; // Sa, Gu Ri / Gu,; - Ri Gu Ma,
ka nu la ko ni: so ga sen
// Gu,; / ; ; - ; ; // Ri,; / ; ; - ; ; // Sa,; / ; ; - ; ;
to:
// Gu,; / Ri,; - Sa,; //
X. // pa, pa, / Sa, Sa, - ni Sa; // Sa, Gu Ri / Gu,; - Ri Gu Ma,
ka nu la ko ni so ga sen
// Gu, Ma gu Gu, Ma gu / Gu, Ma gu Gu, Ma gu

- Gu, Ma gu Gu, Ma gu
// Ri, Gu Ri Ri, Gu Ri / Ri, Gu Ri Ri, Gu Ri
- Ri, Gu Ri Ri, Gu Ri
// Sa, Ri Sa Sa, Ri / Sa, Ri Sa Sa, Ri Sa
- Sa, Ri Sa Sa, Ri Sa
// Gu, Ma Gu Gu, Ma Gu / Ri, Gu Ri Ri, Gu Ri
- Sa, Ri Sa Sa, Ri Sa

This is a principle which is not totally inviolable in compositions, aalaapanai and tanam. Though it is not an inviolable principle, it surely signals a 'certain' style which may put off the orthodox Carnatic music fraternity.[176] But it is quite a different matter when it comes to rhythmic passages. A rhythmic formula, if repeated, should be iterated neither more nor less than three times in a rhythmic line. Consider the patterns in (34a–c) below. Clearly, this construal has a grammaticality function when checking rhythmic passages and will consequently award a violation mark '*' in case just two iterations or more than three iterations are encountered in a line. Thus this construal has varied interpretation in 'rhythmic; and 'non-rhythmic' passages.

(34) Iterations in a rhythmic line
  a. // [μμ:μμμ] [μμ:μμμ] [μμ:μμμ] μμ...//
  b. *// [μμ:μμμ] [μμ:μμμ]] μμ...//
  c. *// [μμ:μμμ] [μμ:μμμ] [μμ:μμμ] [μμ:μμμ] μμ...//

In other words, the constraint has different functions in different domains. While it has in non-rhythmic domains a mere 'style$_i$' function,, in rhythmic domains it has a grammaticality function. Thus the rhythmic construal has dual function; to determine grammaticality and also to determine style in different domains. I assume that the annotated input which is subjected to evaluation is partitioned into appropriate rhythmic and non-rhythmic portions prior to evaluation, presumably by the Tone Interpretative component (see chapter 5 pp. 133–136 for details). However, though we partition the constraints into the arhythmic and rhythmic sets, the partitioning of the constraints remains problematic. As style keeps varying even within the set [aalaapanai, niraval and kalpanaaswaran] and definitely between the so called 'manoodharma sangiitam' including aalaapanai, addition of sangatis, niraval and kalpanaaswaram, from performer to performer, we would have to do the partitioning on an individual basis.

I next consider the last function of 'Checking for type of execution of musical phrase', namely 'Checking the mode of execution of musical phrases in a musical line'. Consider the musical line in (35a and b) below where the difference lies in the execution of the same 'notation'.

(35) Musical demonstration
Kalyaaṇi X [⊙ 7.120]
a. // ['Sa, Ri Sa] ['nu, Sa nu] ['di, nu di pa mi] // (typing)
b. // ['Sa, Ri Sa] ['nu, Sa nu] ['di, nu di pa mi] //

In (35a), the beginning of all the phrases are executed exactly alike signaling a 'typing effect'/monotonous rendition etc. In (35b), however, the same musical phrase is executed in two different ways with the crisp rendering and the mellow rendering alternating to avoid monotony. Thus 'checking for execution of a musical line' evaluates musical lines looking for iteration, repetition, types of execution, namely crisp, mellow, slightly delayed renderings[177] etc. to assign a precise evaluation to the musical line. The avoidance of monotony is naturally awarded a positive value, i.e. '☞'. But the absence of a positive evaluation of a particular musical line does not damn the entire musical discourse. Far from it. A performer/listener is not expected to be at his/her creative best in every musical line. If 'Homer can nod', so can the Carnatic performer. The weightage given to a Carnatic music discourse is not strictly additive, assessment is not strictly musical line by musical line, but holistic. I have nothing more to say on this matter as I do not undertake to consider the grammar of Carnatic music discourse.

7.6. Style/stylistic issues: Content Construal

Finally, I come to the last set of construals that assign 'meaning' to a line of Carnatic music, namely Content Construal (CC). Unlike the other construals which have multiple functions, the CC performs only a stylistic function and has at least the following constituents (these are perhaps not exhaustive).

(36) Content Construal (stylistic)
a. Checking for quotation (awards a '*')
b. Checking for new ideas (awards a '☞')
c. Checking for imagery/wit (awards a '☞')

As is my usual practice, I will take up each one of these construals for discussion, beginning with 'Checking for quotation'. As I said in chapter 1, the equivalent of free flowing language which is a pre-requisite for language acquisition, is the 'fixed text' in Carnatic music, in other words well-known compositions by established composers. Just as frequent, repeated exposure to words and phrases help in building the child's mental lexicon, frequent, repeated exposure to these compositions help set up the lexicon of Carnatic music (I will have more to say on this matter in the next chapter). As Carnatic music performances require total recall of compositions without the aid of any physical prop,[178] all Carnatic performers have an online dictionary of compositions which can be accessed during performances. Thus, for the 'ideal' Carnatic music performer/listener, every experience of performing/listening to a raagam is inextricably linked to the musical lines of the compositions already known to the individual. So, when one encounters the following musical line in a Kalyaaṇi aalaapanai, it immediately sets the bell ringing and gives it the label 'Nidhicaala sukhamaa' of Tyaagaraajaa.

(37) Musical demonstration
Kalyaaṇi XI [⊙ 7.121]
// [gu 'di, pa, mi gu, ri] [sa nu 'ri; gu] ['ri sa sa,] //

Nidhicaala sukhamaa: [⊙ 7.122]
Kalyaaṇi: Tisra Trupuṭai: Tyaagaraajaa
// ; gu di; / pa,; - pa mi gu, // gu,; ri, / sa nu ri; gu] ['ri sa sa,]
ni dhi ca: la su kha ma: ...

With more exposure/experience, one slowly realizes that it may not be a very good idea to reproduce an entire line from a composition as part of an improvised sequence. More sophisticated performers take pleasure in changing the quotations in subtle ways to display their creativity (perhaps an act of over-coming a mental copyright violation) as shown in (38) below.

(38) Musical demonstration
Kalyaaṇi XII: [⊙ 7.123]
// ['gu di,] ['gu, pa, di pa pa, mi gu, ri sa] //

It is not a good idea to reproduce an entire line from a composition as part of an improvised sequence unless it is done intentionally to start a series of variations etc.

(39) Musical demonstration
Kalyaaṇi XIII: [⊙ 7.124]
// [gu 'di, pa, mi gu, ri] [sa 'mi, gu, ri sa, nu] //

It is a mark of mastery when one learns to disguise quotations in a free rendering.

Checking for quotation is actually a part of the *AMB family of constraints which search globally for matches. In this case, a musical line matches a line of a well known composition. Thus I conclude that checking for quotation is actually *AMBMUSICALLINE violation (*AMBLINE for short). An *AMBLINE violation can be evoked by a line of the aalaapanai, a line of a new composition etc. Here is an example of an *AMBLINE violation found in the opening line of a twentieth century composition by the composer Paapanaasam Sivan which copies the opening line of a Tyaagaraajaa composition.[179]

(40) Musical demonstration
iishanee inda: [⊙ 7.125]
Cakravaaham: Ruupakam: Paapanaasam Shivan
// ; pa, / di, ni di - pa ma pa di // pa, ...
ii shanee in da

(41) Musical demonstration
Suguṇamulee: [⊙ 7.126]
Cakravaaham: Ruupakam: Tyaagaraajaa
// ; pa di / , ni di, - pa ma pa di // ,
su gu ṇamu le:

Notice that we now have *AMB at every level of music starting from the tone, sequence, phrase and the line. Whereas *AMB violations at the levels of the tone and sequence indicate ungrammaticality because the identity of the raagam is at stake, at higher levels, namely the musical phrase and musical line, violation marks indicate lack of originality/mental laziness etc., and therefore belong to the stylistic set of constraints. It is nevertheless an *AMB violation because here it is the identity of the performer which is called into question.

I now turn to 'Checking for musical ideas'. This constraint is turned on *if and only if* the musical line in question has not been assigned any violation of *AMBPHRASE and *AMBLINE. Some of the constituent construals of this overall constraint are, to name a couple:

(42) Checking for musical ideas (stylistic)
a. Checking for varied phrasing
b. Checking for varied sequencing

Unlike the other constraints we have been examining so far, (42a) requires the musical discourse as its input (and not just the musical line).

(43) Musical demonstration
Shankaraabharaṇam II [⊙ 7.127]
The repeated, final musical phrase of several musical lines
[pa gu, ma ma ma, gu]

I recall a recording of the National Programme of Music, All India Radio where the singer rendering an aalaapanai of Shankaraabharaṇam ended several, consecutive musical lines with the phrase [pa gu,mama,gu] and even when he/she had switched over to variations of this phrase, the accompanying violinist insisted on holding on to the earlier phrase to the annoyance/amusement of the listener. This construal presumably awards a violation mark '*' to a phrase/sequence which is repeated several times in the course of the discourse. But since I restrict myself to the grammar up to the level of the musical line, I have nothing more to say about this constraint. Unlike (42a), (42b) works at the level of the musical phrase and the musical line. While discussing the concept of creativity in Carnatic music vis-à-vis everyday language use in chapter 2 (pp. 22–25 and music demonstration [2.20]) I emphasized the fact that as in everyday language use, so too in Carnatic music, 'novel' sequences, sequences never encountered before, can be and are encountered in new compositions, ongoing musical renditions, etc. Here is another example, once again from a twentieth century composition of the composer Paapanaasam Shivan in Bilahari, set to Aadi taaḷam.

(44) Musical demonstration
Bilahari [⊙ 7.127]
The sequence *di nu Sa is prohibited (among the other sequences not allowed in the ragam)
Cittam mahiẓ: Bilahari: Aadi: Paapanaasam Shivan

// - / - // pa di Nu; Ri - nu di, nu di pa
kaṉ ha ḷum kaṉ

This is indeed a new way of avoiding the prohibition *[di nu Sa] in the raagam Bilahari by by-passing Sa altogether. This constraint checks for such gems in musical lines and every time it encounters one it awards it a '☞' sign.

Finally, I consider 'Checking for imagery/wit'. Here, once again recall the musical demonstration [6.56] at the beginning of the previous chapter where the downward and upward movement in the tonal domain was transferred to the spatial domain creating an imagery. Here I give another example of an imagery – this time the beauty of the unpredictably slow or fast flowing river Cauvery in Tyaagaraajaa's kriti 'Kaaruvelpumu' in Kalyaaṇi and Aadi taaḷam.

(45) Musical demonstration
Kaaruvelpumu: [⊙ 7.128]
Kalyaaṇi: Aadi: Tyaagaraajaa
The first and the last sangatis of the pallavi
('Kritimanimalai' II: 614)

1. // Sa,; - nu di Sa nu / di pa mi pa - pa mi gu, gu,
ka: ru vel
// ri sa ri gu - , ri, gu ri sa sa, / , ri gu, mi pa, - di nu Sa Ri
pu lu ni: ku sa ri

7. // Ri Sa nu di pa mi gu ri - sa nu di pa di nu sa ri

/ gu mi pa din u di pa mi - Sa nu di Ri Sa gu Ri Sa

// di nu Sa nu ni di di pa - gu mi pa mi gu ri gu,

/ mi pa di pa Sa nu di pa - di nu Sa Gu Ri Ri,

Of course, imagery, specially in music, is a cultivated artifact and may not be obvious to one and all. Another example of imagery is a simple glide from the first to the eighth note in the great Tyaagaraajaa pancaratna (one of the five great compositions in the five gana raagas, namely Naaṭai, Gauḷa, Aarabhi, Sri and Varaaḷi) composition in the raagam Naaṭai.

(46) Musical demonstration
Oomkaara: [⊙ 7.129]
Jagadaanandakaaarkaa: Naaṭai: Aadi: Tyaagaraajaa
// sa; Sa - ; Sa,...
om ka: ra

In the Indian philosophical/religious tradition, the sound 'Om' is supposed to be the primordial sound filling the entire universe, ante-dating the birth of galaxies, the solar system, etc. And musically, the glide spanning the entire octave is the best way to capture the philosophical notion (in my view).

There are two more kinds of imagery which are exploited in Carnatic music. One is called 'swaraaksharam' where the syllables of the language text match the names of the notes when sung and the other is an elaborate system of 'yati' where the musical phrases are matched spatially to stylistically determined objects in the real world. I will give examples of both below.

(47) Musical demonstration
Swaraaksharam (partial)
Paashavalai: [⊙ 7.130]
(The underlined syllables in the language text constitute swaraaksharam)
Maamoohalaahiri: Kamaas: Raapakam: Anonymous
// [pa; ; ; pa / ni di] [pa; ; , - ; ; pa ni di pa]
pa: sha va lai pa: sha va lai
// ma; gu, ma gu; ma / ; pa, pa; ni - di; pa di pa ma,
ma ha: ma: yai pol la: da da ḍi

The underlined syllables of the language text constitute swaraaksharam. Another very beautiful example of swaraaksharam is the play on the note 'ni' and the language syllable 'ni' in the great Tyaagaraajaa composition in the raagam Naayaki.

(48) Musical demonstration
Swaraaksharam
Nii bhajana: [⊙ 7.131]
Naayaki: Aadi: Tyaagaraajaa
(Kritimanimalai I: 609)
// di,; - di; ni di, / di ni, di - di, di, // pa, di, - ; pa
ni: bhaja na ga: na

Although when notated the note 'ni' does not figure prominently, when the swaras (notes) are sung for the first three beats, it would be sung as 'ni' throughout. And the later sangatis go on to elaborate on the variations of 'ni' to great expressive effect.

Turning to the concept of 'yati', it is best described as a 'translation' of spatial imagery into a tonal one, taking real life objects which are stylistically set in fixed modes. Below in (49) we have what is known as 'ghoopuccchayati' i,e something shaped like the hair on the cow's tail.

(49) Musical demonstration
Ghoopucchayati: [⊙ 7.132]
(shaped like the hairy end of the cow's tail – narrow at both ends and swelling at the middle)
Kalyaaṇi swaram
2 moras: [nu Sa]
[di nu Sa] [pa di nu Sa] [mi pa di nu Sa]
[gu mi pa di nu Sa] 6 moras – the broad middle
[mi pa di nu Sa] [pa di nu Sa] [di nu Sa]
[nu Sa] 2 moras

Finally, I turn to the task of defining 'wit' in Carnatic music.[180] By wit I mean a novel turn of phrasing which results in building up of tension (arising from an expectation of an impending grammaticality slip) whose unexpected release may result in humour/a modified world view – requiring the lexicon to be re-defined – etc. Naturally, one does not encounter instances of wit very frequently as it requires a musician of extraordinary caliber to carry out the enterprise successfully (and success here also depends on how much sense of humour/flexibility the listener has). I give below two instances of 'wit' one from a musical line from a composition of the composer Muttuswaami Diikshitar[181] and another from a rendering of the great veena player – the legendary Veena Dhanam.

(50) Musical demonstration
Niilakaṇṭham: [⊙ 7.133]
Keedaaragauḷa: Ruupakam: Muttuswaami Diikshitar
$//_1$; , ma / ma,; - ma, gu ma gu sa
na ksha tre:
$//_2$ ri ri ma pa di ; , / , pa pa , - pa, di pa pa ma ;
sha she: kha ram

$//_3$; ma, / pa, Sa ni - <u>di; ni di pa</u>;
na:maru: pa
$//_4$; pa ni Sa, / ; Sa...
vi ci tra

In the first two cycles of the taaḷam it is like tight rope walking where every tone is sanctioned for the raagam but still uncomfortably close to the raagam Yadukulakaamboodi and therefore *AMBTONE, *AMBPHRASE are on high alert; but the composer sedately (remember he is the master of the measured style) goes on in the third cycle with his picture of Keedaaragauḷa and the listener's tension is released. That is not the end of the story. The composer has the last laugh as he includes the word 'vicitra' meaning 'strange' at this point and then finally at the end of the line he goes on to give the name of the raagam also. According to me, this is quintessential musical wit.[182]

The next example of wit is from a sangati rendered by one of the wittiest of Carnatic musicians – Veena Dhanammal. The last sangati of the pallavi of Tyaagaraajaa's composition 'Sri Naarada' in Raapakam is the one I have in mind.

(51) Musical demonstration
Sri Naarada: [⊙ 7.134]
Kaanaḍaa: Ruupakam: Tyaagaraajaa
// ; ; / ['ri gi] ['ma pa] - ['di ni] ['Sa Ri] // ni; di...
Kaanaḍaa: A vakra raagam [⊙ 7.135]
a. [ri gi ma pa]
b. [ri gi ma di]
c. [di ni Sa Ri]
d. [ma di ni Sa]
e. *[ri gi ma pa di ni.]

Kaanaḍaa is a vakra raagam and therefore the sequence in (51e) is disallowed, while allowing (51a–d). Therefore the former sequence will elicit an *AMBSEQ violation. Dhanam cleverly seems to argue that *AMBSEQ can consider only sequences within the musical phrase (specially in an I set Raagam (see chapter 8)) and each phrase is perfectly legitimate and if the witticism works for you (it does for me), she stops an *AMBSEQ violation on its tracks chuckling with glee (it seems to me).

7.7. Evaluation Procedure and the setting up of the Constraint Hierarchy

In chapters 4 to 7 I presented construals for tone, sequence, phrase, rhythm and line which postulate markedness constraints, both context sensitive and context free, for note implementation and faithfulness constraints at all the levels. I had argued in chapter 3 that, in a large majority of cases, the notion of input in Carnatic music is quite different from that of language. Though musical phrases are comparable to the phonological word, unlike words in language which are listed in the lexicon, a sizeable portion of the musical phrases in a Carnatic music discourse may not be listed but constructed on-line following specific templates listed in the Carnatic music lexicon, and therefore what one requires to be faithful to is not neccesarily any specific input entry in the lexicon but to the construals specific to raagas called FAITH-LEX constraints which capture the requirements of the raagaṃ. Thus a musical input will be judged ungrammatical if it incurs violation marks for these FAITHLEX constraints.

I had argued in chapter 3 how the evaluation procedure in the grammar of Carnatic music is significantly different from that of language in three ways. Firstly, the entire CH does not seem to be involved in the evaluation of a musical input all the time. I had showed how context free markedness constraints ranked below context sensitive markedness constraints must be inactive in evaluating a musical input. Many potential notes in the input admit more than one pitch interpretation, and all of them may be equally grammatical. Recall the example of the raagam Tooḍi and the note gi in chapter 3 (3.8.2 pp. 64–68). The lexicon of the raagam lists pitch curve and pitch wave interpretations for the note gi. But assuming that the ranking of the markedness constraints are *pitch curve >> *pitch wave reflecting the greater difficulty of the pitch curve interpretation, if the entire CH is active for the evaluation, the pitch curve interpretation will always emerge less than optimal when compared with the pitch wave interpretation. Therefore both the context-free markedness constraints must be rendered inactive to allow either of the interpretations to be considered grammatical. However, when a context free markedness is ranked high, then in order to allow the emergence of the unmarked, we need access to the entire CH. This had prompted me to formulate the delimitation condition for the CH in the grammar of Carnatic music ((35) of chapter 3), repeated below in (51) for ease of reference.

There is a further issue that needs to be attended to. We can offer any number of musical data arguing for a top-down and against a bottom-up model.

Take the instance of a phrase in the raagam Bhairavi as rendered by many established musicians. This phrase is the opening phrase of the Tyaagaraajaa composition Upacaaramu ceesee in Ruupaka Taaḷam, given in (52).

(52) Departure 1 from Eval in Standard OT (Final Version)
Evaluation of a musical line in the grammar of Carnatic music is undertaken by the Constraint Hierarchy which lists the relevant FaithLex constraints interspersed with markedness constraints upto the enumerated context sensitive markedness constraint(s). *The lower ranked context free markedness constraints play no role in the evaluation of a line of music, unless the specific context free markedness constraint set is partially ranked higher in the constraint hierarchy.*

(53) Musical Input[183]
[ri ma *ˈgi, ri]

As many established musicians render this phrase as I have notated, a descriptive grammar of Carnatic music must take it to be grammatical. However, when asked to notate the phrase these same musicians would (if they can notate music) notate the line as [gi ma *ˈgi, ri]. But I can vouch for it, the phrase initial note will be almost right on the pitch values of ri.[184] Also consider several variations of the phrase in (54) below all of which would be unhesitatingly considered ungrammatical by the Carnatic music fraternity.

(54) a. *[ri ma *ˈgi, ri]
b. *[ri (*)ˈma, gi ri]
c. *[ˈri ma gi ri]

All the variants in (54) are instances of unalloyed ungrammaticality. The raagam Bhairavi does not allow the sequence [ri ma] in normal tempo as it is listed for an allied raagam, namely Mukhaari. A bottom-up model cannot allow the phrase in (53) to be constructed in the first place. Even the fast tempo [ri ma] would be ungrammatical in other musical phrases where it is not immediately followed by an emphatic, long gi as illustrated by the ungrammaticality of phrases like *[ri ma pa], *[sa ri ma pa]. What saves the phrase is the fact that the intended note gi is the initial note of a fast phrase and is realised just a semitone lower. We need to formulate a higher ranked construal which allows us to ignore a mismatch of a semi tone note (the notes ri and gi are a semi tone apart) at higher tempos. The specific constraint could be formulated as given below in (55).

(55) Pitch-Note mismatch
Award a violation mark to the intended initial note of a phrase in the fast tempo if and only if
a) it is not a semi tone lower and
b) the achieved note is not of less markedness than the intended note.

The initial phrase <u>ri ma</u> will not incur a violation for this constraint as it is only a semi tone lower and the achieved note is less marked than the intended note. If we now combine this constraint with the sequential constraint Bhairavi *[ri ma] and rank the conjoined constraint higher in the CH, the conjoined constraint will incur a violation if and only if both the constituent constraints are violated. In this case, the pitch-note mismatch does not elicit a violation mark and therefore the constraint conjunction does not incur a violation mark and the input is saved. However, we still need to delimit the CH (or render the sequential constraint invisible). As it would have become clear by now, whatever device in the OT arsenal we might employ, my delimitation requirement is still required. Of course, I am aware that we need to do a lot more detailed analysis before we can precisely define the delimitation condition. The delimitation condition I have proposed thus remains a tentative one which needs to be examined in great detail before we can arrive at a better formulation.

Turning to the second departure from standard OT, the construals proposed in chapters 4 to 7 concern grammaticality requirements (chapters 4 and 5), as well as style and stylistic considerations as part of the exercise of extracting musical meaning from the input (chapters 6 and 7). These construals, however, have different methods of evaluation, unlike standard OT where there is only one value of evaluation, namely a violation mark. In the construal set that I have proposed, there are at least three different methods of evaluation. While the grammaticality set awards a violation mark (as in standard OT), the style set awards an S_n mark indicating an affiliation to a particular style (from an enumerable set) and the stylistic set awards a ☞ sign to inputs which attest some unusual feature in the input. The question that now arises is: "How do we constitute a composite CH for the grammar of Carnatic music with such disparate methods of evaluation?" The first pass of the answer to this question is to delimit the style set as it is primarily meant to identify the style of a performer, which is crucially dependent on the entire discourse. As my effort has been to lay the ground rules for a grammar of Carnatic music till the level of the musical line, any construal that considers the entire discourse (however we partition the construals) is certainly beyond the scope of this book. Thus the style construals can easily be set aside for this preliminary attempt undertaken in this book. Between the grammatical and stylistic constraints, the unmarked ordering is, of course, grammatical construals >> stylistic construals. But even within the grammatical construals we saw that a bottom-up prioritization will not work for Carnatic music. Therefore, a top-down grammaticality ranking for Carnatic music as in (56) below is appropriate.

(56) Constraint Ranking for Grammaticality construals

Construals for musical line
>>
Construals for musical phrase
>>
Construals for note sequencing
>>
Construals for tone interpretation

Thus we see that the prioritization is top-down, ranking higher levels above lower levels (and certain lower ranked pure markedness contruals delimited, turning invisible, so to speak). We will see in a little while how this CH is taken advantage of by the grammar of Carnatic music where stylistic issues are involved.

I now take up the third and final difference between the grammars of Carnatic music and language. Under normal circumstances, grammaticality considerations take precedence over stylistic considerations. However, since Carnatic music is an art form where each artist must strive to create her/his individual 'unique style of performance' which may be termed 'dialect of Carnatic music', we can understand why stylistic considerations are of prime importance. The crude example that I gave in chapter 3 was that of an extraordinary artist who had a handicap of falling a semi tone when he approached the upper Sa. Thus in a raagam like Tooḍi when his pitch fell a semi tone at the upper Sa, he was really at nu which is not a designated note of the raagam. The musical line with this re-designated upper Sa would therefore be a case of pure ungrammaticality. However, his admirers set aside this episode (though the violinist would still be at the original fundamental sa) as there were enough stylistic awards waiting for them.

But the examples that I will give now are more concrete, one from a style of a great performer and another from a stylistic device. I shall take up one particular example of style to illustrate the idea how style factors can be prioritized over grammaticality factors in the grammar of Carnatic music. The style I have in mind is that of an acclaimed, male vocalist of the last half of the twentyfirst century, who was much admired by fellow musicians and a few knowledgeable Carnatic music lovers. He had a resonant low, pitched voice. But the voice was not highly manoeuvrable as pitch manipulations and fast tempo passages were not easy to handle with this voice. Given this voice profile, the artist had to define his style by restricting pitch curves and pitch spikes and maintaining a steady, slow tempo. Had the artist merely done this, he would have achieved a sober, perhaps, careful style, nothing more. But what he did achieve was nothing short of a miracle ; he was an innovator and at the heart of his innovative approach was this simple idea of taking RenScale values of notes and exploring the relationships among steady pitch values of notes in scales of raagas. The central style statement of this artist was then 'Explore RenScale relations of notes in a scale'. When one is exploring the relations that hold between notes in a scale, the criteria that are put to work are the following:

(57) Style Set for RenScale Relations in Scales

a. explore steady pitch contrasts of non-linear notes
(Informally, consider notes which are not linear adjacent in the scale, e.g. sa di/ pa Gu ; sa gu pa/ ma di Sa, etc.)
b. look for symmetry
c. look for patterning
d. look for unusual sequences of notes

Let me explain briefly once again how these construals work in the grammar of Carnatic music. They are not unworkable, abstract concepts of art but concrete principles which are at the heart of the grammar of Carnatic music. Taking up construal (57a), if non-adjacent notes are sequenced in phrases, then what one looks for is the distance between notes on the scale. For instance, sa and di are five notes apart and so are pa and Gu. Construal (57b) pertains to notions of symmetry, a notion central to music (I return to the importance of the notion symmetry in the next chapter where I discuss the issue of raagam change). Dividing the scale into two parts sa-pa, pa-Sa or sa-ma and ma/mi-ni/nu one gets two easily accessible and definable measures of symmetry between notes in the lower and upper parts of the octave. For instance, in the raagam Tooḍi the notes ra and da are symmetrical and so are gi and ni. Further, the lexically specified pitch manipulations on the latter pair of notes are identical, another example of symmetry. Like symmetry, patterns are at the core of melody and rhythm in music. One can look for patterns by finding identical phrase making templates and/or finding the same distribution of short and long notes across phrases, e.g. [ta taa ta ta ta] is a frequently used six mora phrase with a long second note and so on. The patterns can and do get very complex with complex combinations of patterns employed very frequently. Finally, (57d), the last construal, is not really an undefinable concept at all. In the context of Carnatic music, keeping in mind that performers do not perform with notes in front of them, phrases culled over a life time, common and usually heard phrases are entered in the lexicon as input. Going over the listed phrases allows us to recognise novel sequences. It is not very different from speakers recognising new coinages or nonce words in spoken and written discourse.

One can list more specific strategies. But for our purposes, these would more than suffice. Armed with this style constraint set, the above-mentioned musician set out to explore the world of musical ideas in Carnatic music. The result was great music but certain issues of grammaticality were the casualty. The style set can and does override many constraints specific to the grammaticality set. I base this discussion of this artist on his rendering of aalaapanai and taanam in the raagam Shankaraabharaṇam.[185] Like other raagas belonging to the Idiosyncratic set (see chapter 8 for an extended discussion of the topic), Shankaraabharaṇam has several notes which admit complex pitch movements. For instance, the raagam selects the scale [sa ri gu ma pa di nu] (the major scale of Western music) and the notes ri, ma and di admit a range of pitch interpretations.[186] As in other raagas there are context sensitive *RENSCALE constraints specific to these notes prohibiting RenScale rendering of these notes in the lexicon of Shankaraabharaṇam. These grammaticality constraints are deliberately violated when the artist launches his RenScale explorations time and again in both the aalaapanai and taanam.[187]

As mentioned earlier, in addition to determining the grammaticality of notes in the scale there are grammaticality issues pertaining to note sequences governed by the overarching constraint *AMB that requires each raagam (specifically raagas belonging to the Idiosyncratic set) to be distinct from every other raagam at the level of the sequence, musical phrase.

Shakaraabharaṉam too has several such *AMBSEQ constraints (avoid ambiguous sequences of notes), e.g., avoid *[sa gu pa], *[gu pa nu] (as that would point to another raagam, namely Hamsadhvani) etc. because they will result in Shankaraabharaṉam being mistaken for some other raagam. The exploration of RenScale relation by the artist results in violations of constraints pertaining to *AMBSEQ. Thus we see that the constraint ranking pertinent for the artist has the set ranking as shown in (58). The higher ranked style set overrules violations at the lower levels of notes and sequences.

(58) Set Ranking for the Style
Set for RenScale Relations in Scales
a. explore steady pitch contrasts of non-linear notes
b. look for symmetry
c. look for patterning
d. look for unusual sequences of notes
Delimited set ——————————
>>
Context sensitive *RENSCALE constraints specific to several notes,
*AMBSEQ constraints specific to sequences and musical phrases

The question that arises is 'if all constraints which define the grammar of the raagam can be violated, how is the discourse perceived as Shankaraabharaṉam?' Naturally, irrespective of style, if *all* constraints defining grammaticality may be violated, there is no question of the discourse being perceived as Shankaraabharaṉam. It will not be Shankaraabharaṉam. For the discourse to be recognised as Shankaraabharaṉam it should be possible to partition the grammaticality constraints into a violable and an inviolable set with the latter working to maintain the identity of the raagam. One natural place to look for this partitioning is the note and sequence within the musical phrase in one set and the musical line in the other set. In fact, this seems to be the required partitioning that explains why each musical line is unambiguously assigned to Shankaraabharaṉam even though there are violations at lower levels which are tolerated. If every musical line is taken as the domain for evaluation, then we see that constraints at the level of the musical line like interpretation of emphatic prominence, checking to see that all the notes listed in the scale are satisfied, then the grammar of Shankaraabharaṉam is not really jeopardised. Thus the overall constraint ranking for the artist (for this discourse) is as captured below.

(59) Set Ranking for the Style
Grammaticality Set 1
Construals pertaining to the musical line :
Construals for emphatic prominence,
Checking for presence vs absence of notes in the scale
>>
Set for RenScale Relations in Scales
a. explore steady pitch contrasts of non-linear notes
b. look for symmetry
c. look for patterning
d. look for unusual sequences of notes
>>
Delimited Set ———————————
Grammaticality Set 2
Context sensitive *RENSCALE constraints specific to all notes,
*AMBSEQ constraints specific to sequences and musical phrases

Thus, specifically, the two major areas where violations are tolerated are with respect to individual notes and sequences in musical phrases. This results in a delayed satisfaction of grammaticality concerns, creating a kind of tension which is resolved at the level of the musical line. The two issues that this discussion leads to regarding this delay are in the satisfaction of grammaticality concerns and whether even higher order grammaticality concerns can be set aside, even temporarily. As for the first issue, I would like to submit that the delayed satisfaction of grammaticality concerns is a stylistic convention in Carnatic music which I call 'wit' in this chapter (and see discussion below). As for the second possibility, namely whether the entire set of grammaticality constraints can be set aside temporarily, we will see below how this is done when the stylistic convention called ʃruti bheedam (modal shift) is undertaken.

I next turn to stylistic factors in Carnatic music. To recapitulate the idea discussed earlier in this chapter, by stylistic factors I mean those conventions of musical discourse and musical meaning making that are at the disposal of the artist. For instance, devices like imagery, the matching of the language and the musical note, wit and ʃruti bheedam or modal shift are some that come to mind readily. Musical imagery is bound by the conventions of the system (like onomatopoeia being bound by the phonotactics of the language), e.g. the scale sa ra gu pa da Sa-Sa nu da pa gu ra sa of the raagam Bauḷi is considered to evoke sunrise for the Carnatic music fraternity (see Claim 2: Magical Meaning and the music demo [6.58], chapter 6 pp. 156–157). Further, imagery can be the transfer of spatial relations to that of pitch. For instance, to convey the concept of vastness of space the pitch glide may range over the entire octave (music demo [7.129] this chapter, p. 212). Imagery can also be highly stylised. The Sanskritic tradition has conventions for capturing the meandering of a river, the shape of the cow's tail etc. which are used fairly frequenly in Carnatic music (music demo [7.132] this chapter, p. 213). The matching of the syllables of language with the solfa notation is much appreciated in Carnatic music (music demos [7.130], [7.131] this chapter, p. 212). Turning next to wit, I had defined wit in Carnatic music as an instance of a musical discourse where the elaboration of the raagam leads to the brink of an *AMB violation but getting rescued just in time, sometimes barely so, but within the musical line. Some popular artists of the past were known to render a few phrases which were deliberately ambiguous between two raagas and after the violinist made bold to assume that it was one of the raagas, to go on to the other raagam to the discomfiture of the accompaying violinist. Of course, this is not a very good example of wit as it violates the basic convention to be followed in a public recital – the principle of mutual cooperation. However, there are good examples of wit in Carnatic music where composers have created this tension in the first few musical phrases of a musical line to go on to resolve the tension later on in the musical line (musical demos [7.133], [7.134], this chapter, pp. 213–214). It should now be clear why I had compared the style of the artist in the discussion above to the stylistic device 'wit'. The artist also revels in taking the raagam to the brink of *AMB violations at the levels of the note and the phrase, but rescuing it finally at the level of the musical line.

I turn next to the stylistic device ʃruti bheedam or modal shift. I will show that this device allows the artist to temporarily violate *all* the constraints pertaining to grammaticality. ʃruti bheedam is a device which shifts the fundamental from sa to any other note of the scale in the middle of a discourse without changing the designated notes of the original scale – only their relations are redefined. This results in the scale of a different raagam. For example, if one takes the scale of Shankaraabharaɳam – the major scale, sa, ri gu, ma, pa, di, nu, Sa, and shifts the fundamental to ri, then the relation that obtains is the scale sa, ri, gi, ma, pa, di, ni, Sa, the minor scale of Western music or the scale of the raagam Karaharapriyaa. If ʃruti bheedam is undertaken in a Carnatic music recital, it is usually done while rendering the aalaapanai of the main raagam, towards the end of the aalaapanai. Typically, when ʃruti bheedam is undertaken, then all the constraints defining the base raagam are set aside when the fundamental shifts to some other note of the scale. In the example quoted above, if an artist were to do ʃruti bheedam on Shankaraabharaɳam on ri then she/he has to set aside all the constraints for interpreting the notes, sequences, phrases of Shankarabharaɳam and replace them with those for Karaharapriyaa. There is no question of interpreting the discourse as Shankaraabharaɳam as long as the ʃruti bheedam is on (the vocalist signals the violinist to keep bowing the shifted fundamental). The ranking that would account for this stylistic convention then is as shown below:

(60) Ranking Convention for ʃruti Bheedam
Constraints specific to Raagam y at the level of note, phrase, line,
The fundamental note of Raagam y is a RenScale $note_n$ of Raagam x
\>>
Delimited ————————————
Constraints specific to Raagam x at the level of note, phrase, line,
Constraints specific to $note_n$ of Raagam x
The fundamental note C of Raagam x

The stylistic device of ʃruti bheedam sanctions this set prioritization. However, not all performers/theoreticians accept this type of ʃruti bheedam. Let me outline a more subtle approach to ʃruti bheedam which may be acceptable to more performers/theoreticians, in principle, though it is much more difficult to execute/perceive. This approach demands that all the lexical pitch specifications of the parent raagam be kept inviolable and RenScale pitch value be sanctioned for the selected note of the original raagam which is to be taken as the changed fundamental note of ʃruti bheedam. Thus, for example, the note ri would no longer be an appropriate note for undertaking ʃruti bheedam in the raagam Shankaraabharaɳam as this note has many FAITHLEX pitch specifications. More appropriate notes would be gu or pa. But the former note would be problematic as its third note pa (the gi of the new scale) would never admit any pitch manoevres at all resulting in a fixed gi which is only sparingly used in Carnatic music as a RenScale note. Under ʃruti bheedam, only the lexical pitch specifications/phrase requirements of the new raagam which match those of the original raagam are selected for rendering the new raagam. This approach requires partitioning the constraint sets of the original raagam ($Raagam_a$) and the new raagam ($Raagam_b$) such that there exist a partition ($Partition_{sx}$) of each raagam where there are no mututally conflicting pitch/phrasal requirements which are to be exclusively utilized under ʃruti bheedam.[188] The set prioritization required is then as in (61) below.

(61) Ranking Convention for ʃruti Bheedam (Revised)
$Partition_{sa/x}$ = $Partition_{sb/x}$, *$Partition_{-sb/y}$,
Fundamental $note_n$,
>>
Delimited ——————————
Fundamental $note_c$,
[$Partition_{-sa/y}$]

The overlapping constraint partition sets of the two raagas are exclusively to be used and are therefore inviolable. The residue partition set of the new raagam is negatively stipulated and the change in fundamental note is also ranked above the original fundamental note. This kind of ʃruti bheeedam is not only more difficult to render, it is also more difficult to perceive. However it is done, ʃruti bheedam as a stylistic device requires reprioritization of the constraint set defining grammaticality. The downgrading of the grammaticality set, even if only partial, is a major departure from the grammar of language. In language one cannot imagine a scenario where grammaticality issues would be set aside, unless one is thinking of constructing a CH for international intelligibility of a language. But then we are considering cross-dialectal intelligibility as the focus of our grammatical description. That would really be a move in the right direction where we write grammars for perception as well as production. Surely, an unforseen fallout of my preoccupation with Carnatic music.

7.8. Discussion

Reading chapters 4 to 7, it would have been clear that this book does not really sketch the grammar of Carnatic music but lays the ground rules for what a grammar of Carnatic music would be like if attempted. It is more an outline of a research programme on Carnatic music situating the system in universal musical values of pitch and rhythm.[189] The outlined ideas can lead to descriptive work as well as more fundamental, challenging work on the basis of human musical competence.

Armed with the construals outlined in the chapters here, work of a descriptive kind can now examine a single raagam handled by a single artist/composer or even across artists/composers, or even take up related raagas for similar explorations. Other systems of music may also be profitably analysed using these tools. Finally, this paradigm allows one to ask fundamental questions about the musical faculty in humans. A few sample questions (each one of which could be a research topic) are:

- When does the twelve note scale emerge in musical systems?
- Which kind of musical systems exploit inter-tonal pitch intervals?
- Prominence in language performs a phrasal parsing function allowing one to delimit either or both the edges of words; thus languages are known to have left edge orientation to prominence, e.g. Dravidian languages, or right edge orientation to prominence, e.g. French, Latin, Hindi, Punjabi, Arabic, or both edges, e.g. English and Bangla. Can musical systems exhibit such diversity in orienting prominence to one or both edges of musical phrases too?
- When does a musical system begin to evolve distinct, complex melodic systems as raagas in the Indian classical traditions?
- When does a musical system start ignoring performance factors like voice quality, production values and shift its focus to the musical content?

We do not have even partial answers to any of these questions at the moment. It is hoped that this research programme, if it takes off, will spawn a generation of research where a discipline called 'Universal Musicology' may become a reality.

I would like to end this chapter with a discussion on another issue that is at the heart of a system like Carnatic music. To begin with, we should situate it in the primarily oral tradition. But that does not explain all the characteristics of a system like Carnatic music. Traditionally Carnatic music discourse has been classified into a rendering of a fixed text, a composition attributed to a specific composer in most cases and a manoodharma part where the performer is 'composing' at the performing event, a concert. As we know by now, examples of the latter are aalaapanai, taanam, neraval and kalpana-aswaram. The latter types of spontaneous compositions are not meant to be rehearsed texts; but must flow spontaneously while performing. I have questioned the validity of keeping the two groups in water-tight compartments arguing that even the so-called fixed texts are not all that fixed (varying considerably across performers/schools of music etc.). Be that as it may, what I would now like to focus on is the nature of this spontaneous composition, what Amritavalli (1999) calls 'creative compositions'. We now know precisely how this spontaneous creativity becomes possible in Carnatic music. Performers de-compose the construals pertaining to tone, sequence, phrase etc. from extended listening, and also store templates for creating musical phrases (some of which could be raagam specific). Then this spontaneous creativity becomes possible because of the stored construals in the lexicons of the raagas, a large part of which are commonly shared among the Carnatic fraternity (hence the 'sameness'). But the issue that I would like to address is the nature of the Carnatic music event. As Amritavalli (1999: 12) correctly observes,

> "They do not result in 'objects' that become fixed texts. They exist only within the space of time within which they are being actively created."

As they do not have the permanence of objects, they have, strictly speaking, no value when reproduced/recorded and so there can be no copyright. Then the question is: "What is the status of a Carnatic music event?"

Is it to be evaluated as a performance? The rules of evaluation of a performance are not very dissimilar to those of printed matter and visual/audio productions. They are all subject to the same set of evaluative procedures. They are judged on their production values like good editing, sound production, absence of slips, etc. But a typical Carnatic musical event is not evaluated like that at all. The artist could slip, go off key at times, talk in between, fight with the accompanist, etc. No critic will include these intrusions while reviewing the recital, if the performer is considered an eminent artist. Though the one often repeated complaint about Carnatic music events is the intolerable level of the audio system. So, I would like to advance the view that a Carnatic music event is not really a performance and Carnatic music is not a performing art but that it is a cognitive art and it is judged as other cognition-based activities are evaluated. Like language, when people use language in every day life, they are not judged on the basis of the false starts, the slips they may produce. Their message is evaluated for its content (of course issues pertaining to style are always on high alert to judge the social status of the interlocuters). I would like to advance the view that a Carnatic music event is on a par with any language interaction which we may have with people known to us. Its worth is evaluated in direct proportion to the type of content one is looking out for. Just as people have different expectations from people they meet or even friends, the Carnatic music fraternity also has similar differing expectations. The musical event is a meeting of the fraternity where the performer happens to hold forth. It is not uncommon in a Carnatic music concert to hear listeners singing along (quite annoying though), producing loud noises of appreciation (equally annoying). I really do not know how to classify the performer in such a setting. Is she/he an actor performing an aside or a soliloquy? I don't think either of these terms do justice to the event. One should come up with a new term for this phenomenon – perhaps, the term 'intimate revelation' may capture the intention of the event. Whatever it is, it is not just a performance where production values are always in focus. Unfortunately, of late many Carnatic music events have been reduced to mere performances with duets where the artists plan every detail well before the event and performers concentrating more on performance factors like sound amplification, stage presence, performing with an eye to audience applause, etc. A perspective music critic remarked, correctly, that duets and group performances are contrary to the spirit of Carnatic music. But there is no stopping the tide of group dynamics. There is comfort in numbers.

In conclusion I would like to offer (with a lot of trepidation) that Carnatic music is not or should not be considered a performing art but a cognitive art on par with every day language use (which however does not get elevated to the status of art because of its possible banality and the lack of control on the part of any one interlocuter). The Carnatic performer is elevated to the status of an acclaimed artist on the basis of certain criteria that the audience decide. Just as every day language use is a miracle that we take for granted, Carnatic music events are also equally miraculous in that they are a window on the cognitive knowledge of the user and the human faculty which makes Carnatic music possible. The only difference is that while language use is universal, musical discourse is contigent on several factors like good training, public acceptance, and other factors.

Chapter 8
The lexicon of Carnatic music

8.1. Introduction

In this chapter the overall structure of the Carnatic music lexicon is examined assuming near-perfect competence in the ideal performer-listener. I argue that although the beginnings of the construction of the Carnatic music lexicon is just the filing of the compositions, line by musical line of the often heard/rendered compositions of Carnatic music which remains intact, ready for recall in every performance (as performers generally do not sing from written texts but from memory), at a critical stage in the listening/learning of Carnatic music the process of de-composition starts. I claim that it is this process of de-composition which is the active grammar making tool for every established performer which is my central concern. When I refer to the Carnatic music lexicon, unless otherwise stated, I refer to this de-composed phenomenon and its structure. The process of de-composition is an unconscious process like learning the grammar of a language where musical lines are broken down into smaller and smaller units and stored for later use in extempore renderings. Without the de-composed lexicon in place it will be impossible to undertake any of the creative (manoodharma) aspect of Carnatic music like aalaapanai, taanam, niraval or kalpanaa swaram. Even a convincing rendering of a composition will not be possible without this de-composed lexicon; by 'convincing' I mean a rendering which unmistakably signals a performer. It is this de-composed lexicon which guides the performer when she/he alters a line ever so slightly, when he/she adds a sangati or when she/he feels the need to reinterpret a line, all of which are legitimate activities in Carnatic music. It is this act of reinterpretation which makes the composition not the composer's sole intellectual property once it has been taken over for rendering by a performer. Although I assume this process of de-composition to be complete in the hypothesized ideal listener/performer, in reality, it may be that the Carnatic music lexicon is at different stages of de-composition for different members of the Carnatic music fraternity. Of course, it must be remembered that Carnatic music being inherently variationist oriented, even for established performers and seasoned listeners, the content of the lexicon may be distinct for each person. However, it may not be difficult to determine how successful or complete the process of de-composition is or at what stage it is on listening to a rendering of a performer. I have nothing more to say of the lexicon of the texts of Carnatic music as apart from its sheer enormity it has nothing of theoretical interest.

I argue for a specific structure of the de-composed Carnatic music lexicon. A new, binary classification of the raagas of Carnatic music is offered here with a view to a better explanation of the overall contemporary scene. In the following sections, I outline two experiments one of which can be easily replicated by adequately trained performers of Carnatic music.[190] The other one is more of a 'thought' experiment which, once again, argues for the bifurcation of the Carnatic music lexicon into two distinct sets. The objective of the experiments is to show the validity of my claim regarding the primary bifurcation of the Carnatic music lexicon into two sets of raagas, namely the *idiomatic set* (the I Set for short) and the *scalar set* (the S Set henceforth). While it is true that the large number of raagas of Carnatic music admit many possible types of classification,[191] I demonstrate the usefulness of my classification from several points of view. I believe that a classification is only as good as the work it does for us and that classification is not just a clever past time. Once the bipartite structure of the Carnatic music lexicon is in place, I show how it is possible to account for the following:

(1) Arguments for a bipartite structure of the Carnatic music lexicon
   a. Distinct strategies adopted for teaching/learning raagas from the I Set and the S Set, (4.)
   b. Distinct performance strategies available to performers, (5.)
   c. Distinct evaluation strategies of *AMBSEQ with respect to the two sets of raagas, (6.)
      and
   d) Predictability of the direction of change in the contemporary, synchronic grammar of Carnatic music. (7.)

Once again falling back on linguistics, take the example of speech sounds. It is possible to classify sounds at least in two ways, namely according to the *place of articulation* (in the oral tract) and according to the *articulator* that is used for producing the sound. A scientific approach will select that classification which serves the concerns of linguistics better, not the classification which, at first blush seems more fine-grained, more detailed. The classification based on place of articulation allows us to distinguish between bilabial sounds (also called stops since the air-flow through the mouth is blocked during the production of these sounds) /p/, /b/, and /m/ produced by the lips and labio-dental sounds produced by the upper teeth and the lower lip /f/, /v/ and /ɱ/ as in the word 'comfort'. However, as far as the stops are concerned (i.e. /p/, /b/, /m/), the distinction between bilabial and labio-dental is not distinctive in any language. The labio-dental nasal occurs only before the labio-dental fricative and is therefore not contrastive. Thus we do not require two classificatory labels, namely bilabial and labio-dental. A single classificatory label based on the active articulator with 'labial' as the only classification would suffice. As simple as that. Therefore, linguistic theory does not need a finer classification as the broader one, namely the articulator based classification (the articulator being the lips hence the term 'labial'), will suffice. The moral of this discussion is to ask the reader to judge the merit of the new classification of raagas proposed here on the basis of the explanatory load it carries in the grammar of Carnatic music set out in (1) above. However, I must add that this new classification that I propose is not meant to supersede earlier classificatory mechanisms. I merely argue that this new classification is 'psychologically real' for the ideal listener/performer as it performs all the functions that I laid out in (1) above.

In the last section of the chapter I take up the theoretical problem of raagas migrating from one parent raagam to another over a period of time. The issue is amenable to an explanation given our *Amb family of constraints and the network hypothesis in conjunction with my bipartite structure of the lexicon.

8.2. The experiment with the scalar set

The first of the two experiments described here can easily be replicated by any person who has had considerable training in Carnatic music by which I mean any one who has trained in Carnatic music up to the level when she/he can perform fairly competent renditions of improvisation, specially aalaapanai in raagas belonging to the I Set (I will specify the characteristics of raagas which belong to the I Set shortly).

Let the person select a meeḷakartaa raagam (full scale) which she/he has never heard before and in which she/he does not know any composition. Let the person introspect how she/he does an aalaapanai in that raagam. Let us make a random selection and select, say, raagam no. 50, namely meeḷakartaa, Naamanaaraayaṇi with sa ra gu mi pa da ni Sa.

(2) Musical demonstration
Meeḷakartaa no. 50: Naamanaaraayaṇi [⊙ 8.136]
sa ra gu mi pa da ni Sa; Sa ni da pa mi gu ra sa

What does one do with this scale? The first step is to de-compose this unfamiliar scale in terms of more familiar scales. The lower half of the octave with 'sa ra gu mi pa' reminds us of raagas like Pantuvaraaḷi (meeḷakartaa no. 51), Ramaamanoohari/Raamapriyaa, (meeḷakartaa no. 52) and Puurvikalyaaṇi (derivative of meeḷakartaa no. 53). Of these, though all of them allow RenScale 'gu', Pantuvaraaḷi does not allow RenScale 'gu' if the note is long where it selects pitch wave rendering of aug.gu (according to conservative schools of thinking) (see chapters 6 and 7, pp. 106–108 for a discussion). Of the two renderings of 'gu', RenScale is the unmarked variety (see chapter 6, p. 129 for a discussion of markedness among renderings of a note). Since the marked rendering is attributed to a raagam-specific constraint as in the case of Pantuvaraaḷi, the natural assumption is that this unfamiliar scale is unlikely to opt for the raagam-specific constraint. Therefore, the selected rendering will be RenScale gu. When it comes to the upper half of the octave, the resemblance is to Shaṇmukhapriyaa (meeḷakartaa no. 56) and also perhaps Riʃabhapriyaa (meeḷakartaa no. 62) but without the special wrinkles allowed in the former raagam.[192]

(3) Musical demonstration

Meeḷakartaa raagam no. 50 Naamanaaraayaṇi

Lower half of the octave /sa ra gu mi pa/ [⊙ 8.137, 138, 139]
Pantuvaraaḷi (meeḷakartaa no. 51) selects pitch wave 'gu' for a long note;
Ramaamanoohari/Raamapriyaa (meeḷakartaa no. 52) selects RenScale 'gu';
and Puurvikalyaaṇi (derivative of meeḷakartaa no. 53) with RenScale 'gu' and pitch curve 'gu' (between 'gu' and 'mi').
The least marked of the rendering is selected, i.e. RenScale 'gu' and, of course, note pitch curve gu.

Upper Half of the octave /mi pa da ni Sa/ [⊙ 8.140, 141, 142]
Shaṇmukhapriyaa (meeḷakartaa no. 56) selects RenScale 'ni', pitch wave 'ni' (and also pitch curve 'ni' for some musicians);
Meeḷakartaa Riʃabhapriyaa (no. 62) selects only RenScale 'ni' and pitch wave 'ni'.
Therefore, the selection is restricted to RenScale 'ni' and pitch wave 'ni' and also, perhaps, note pitch curve 'ni'.[193]

Having arrived at the decision that this scale is a composite of two, partially over-lapping sets, one sets out to adopt specific strategies to construct musical lines but more of this later. Whatever the strategies for constructing sequences of notes, the point I wish to make at this juncture is that an unfamiliar raagam is likely to be assumed to belong to the *S Set* and only the unmarked values of notes are selected.

Similar experiments can be carried out with other types of scales as well. Here is another 'constructed' scale which a similarly trained person can tackle as easily. Take the ordered sequence //'sa ri gu ma di ni Sa; Sa di pa gu ma ri sa'//:[194]

(4) Musical demonstration
Unlabeled new non-linear scale [⊙ 8.143]
//'sa ri gu ma di ni Sa; Sa di pa gu ma ri sa'//
Choice of tones for the notes:
RenScale gu, di
RenScale and Pitch wave ma and ni

Strategies for constructing musical phrases and musical lines
[⊙ 8.144]

a. @[gu ma di ni Sa Ri]
b. @[di pa gu ma di ni Sa]
c. @[pa gu ma ri]
d. @[di ni Sa di pa gu ma pa]
e. ? [ma di ni Sa] *AMB Maaḷavi
f. ? //[ni Sa,] [di ni Sa,] [ma di ni Sa]// *AMB Maaḷavi

[Sequences marked '@' are approved sequences and those marked '?' or '*' are not.]

Given this scale, a performer first decides that the tonal interpretation for all the notes will be the least marked ones. So, 'gu' and 'di' will have only the unmarked RenScale values and 'ma' and 'ni' will have the unmarked RenScale interpretation and in addition, in my style, since RenScale 'ni' is not preferred in the ascent, a pitch wave rendering of red.ni will be allowed (as I mentioned in chapter 5 p. 128). Then, a musician has to come to grips with the possibly tabooed sequences, and construct musical phrases like [gu ma di ni Sa ri], [di pa gu ma di ni Sa], [pa gu ma ri], [di ni Sa di pa gu ma pa] and so on. While constructing musical phrases one has to be aware of possible *AMBSEQ violations. For example, a musical phrase like ?[ma di ni Sa]] will trigger a high alert for an *AMBSEQ violation as it will be too close to Maaḷavi. And building on this idea if one were to construct a musical line //[ni Sa,] [di ni Sa,] [ma di ni Sa]// we will only aggravate the *AMB violation further.

A Carnatic musician is able to interpret new scales never heard before because of the following two guidelines:

(5) Interpretation of 'new' scales
  a. Notes receive the unmarked tonal interpretation, i.e. the RenScale interpretation and rarely the note pitch curve interpretation between adjacent notes which are a tone away if the note in question is long with the additional allowance of a red.tone pitch wave interpretation if the notes are 'gi' or 'ni', if at all necessitated by the sequence.
  b. The new scale is sought to be integrated with the lexical network of raagas and exploring the new scale is done keeping in mind possible *AMBSEQ violations.

The question to ask now is the following:

(6) Can we predict which pitch values a note will select in a scale belonging to the S Set?

I find on introspection (other Carnatic musicians can bear me out), that the choice of the pitch value is directly controlled by three factors, namely

(7) a. duration of the note,
  b. selection of the adjacent note in the scale
  and
  c. selection of a particular pitch value by a raagam in the I Set to the exclusion of another raagam in the I Set.

Let me elaborate all the three points with examples. Taking up case a) first, in the scales that we looked at, it will be noticed that all notes select the RenScale pitch value. I find that all notes are rendered as RenScale if linked to a single mora (or if two notes share a mora). However, when rendered as a long note linked to two or more moras, all notes do not uniformly select the RenScale value. I find that I prefer the red.tone pitch wave values for 'ra', 'gi', 'da', 'ni' when long. But S Set raagas do not allow the selection of red.tone at all. On introspection, I find that I adopt the following strategy to tackle this problem. In my rendering, rather than allowing a long RenScale ra or RenScale da I construct musical phrases which avoid long 'ra' and long 'da' in certain contexts. To take a concrete example, in the raagam Bauḷi, a phrase final 'ra' or 'da' must be RenScale only and never red.tone pitch wave as the raagam does not select this interpretation (see chapter 4 (11b1), music demonstration [4.40]). But since I do not like these phrase-final RenScale renditions as they sound too dramatic, the strategy that I adopt is avoidance. While not avoiding long 'ra' and 'da' altogether, I avoid absolute phrase final long 'ra' and long 'da' thus satisfying the grammar of the raagam and also satisfying the high ranked constraint in my style eschewing the dramatic effect. Thus, the lexicon of this raagam in my grammar is faithful to the orthodox requirement in banning red.tone values but at the same time the high ranking constraint *RenScaleRa:/da:] (avoid RenScale long, phrase final 'ra' and 'da' is also obeyed).[195]

Turning to the notes 'gi' and 'ni', as I have said several times earlier, when these notes are selected, in my style, automatically, red.tone is also selected so that 'gi' and 'ni' always allow pitch wave renderings in all I Set and S Set raagas. That is the reason why even S Set raagas like Subhapantuvaraaḷi with {sa ra gi mi pa da nu Sa}, Vasantabhairavi with {sa ra gu ma da ni Sa - Sa ni da ma pa ma gu ra sa} attest minimal RenScale values in my style when compared to other styles. Thus we see that the choice of a pitch rendering is controlled by duration and the context in which the note occurs.

Turning to the next criterion, namely the selection of the next note in the scale, take the case of the note 'gu', for instance. On introspection, I find that 'gu' admits only RenScale value if 'ma' is selected. This is why in S Set raagas, if 'gu' and 'ma' are selected, then 'gu' admits nothing but RenScale value. However, if an S Set raagam were to select either 'mi' or 'pa' as its next note, then in addition to RenScale value, note pitch rendering is also possible, e.g. S Set raagas like Bauḷi with {sa ra gu pa…} and Ramaamanoohari with {sa ra gu mi pa…}. Thus to reiterate a point made towards the end of chapter 5 p. 129 (21d), any note, irrespective of the affiliation of the raagam will allow a note pitch rendering of a note provided that the next note is at least a tone away.

Finally, as for case c), we have already come across a concrete example of case c) in operation, namely the existence of Pantuvaraaḷi with pitch wave aug.gu for a long note ruling out a pitch wave rendering for a raagam of the S Set.[196] Thus, in the ranked constraint-based approach that I adopt here, case c) >> case b) >> case a). As we saw in the previous chapter, raagam-specific constraints take precedence over general constraints, i.e. case c) >> case a, b) and finally, as we saw in chapter 5, context-sensitive constraints are higher ranked than context-free constraints, i.e. case b >> case a. Let us now formulate these findings as ranked constraints.

(8) Note specific constraints in the S Set

a. *RENSCALEra,]da,] {i.e. as a long note phrase finally},[197, 198]

b. *RENSCALEri/ru and di/du[199]

\>>

c. *NOTE[pitch wave for a note] in T_m T_n if 'n' is a tone away from 'm',

d. *NOTEma [pitch wave] if the scale does not select pa,

\>>

e. *RENSCALENOTE if note is linked to more than one mora[200]

\>>

f. RENSCALENOTE

Now, I proceed to demonstrate all the constraints with illustrations to back my findings.

(9) Musical demonstration

a. Illustration Bauḷi [⊙ 8.145]

? [gu pa da,] with da as RenScale

* [gu pa da,] with da as pitch wave

? [da Sa Ra,] with Ra as RenScale

* [da Sa Ra,] with Ra as pitch wave

b. Illustration Naaṭai [⊙ 8.146]

? [sa ru, gu, ma pa] with ru as RenScale

[sa ru, gu, ma pa] with ru as pitch wave glide from sa

? [pa du, nu Sa] with du as RenScale

[pa du, nu Sa] with du as pitch wave glide from pa

c. Illustration contrast ri in Karaharapriyaa and Harikaamboodi [⊙ 8.147]
  i. [sa ri, gi ma] with ri as RenScale
  ii. [sa ri, gu ma] with ri as pitch wave
d. Illustration ma in Karaharapriyaa and Sriranjani [⊙ 8.147]
  i. [ma, pa di ni di pa] with pitch wave for ma
  ii. [ma, di ni di ma,] with RenScale for ma
e. Illustration of Pantuvaraaḷi and Puurvikalyaaṇi [⊙ 8.148]
  i. [nu da pa mi gu,] with gu as pitch wave for Pantuvaraaḷi
  ii. [nu di pa mi gu,] with gu as RenScale for Puurvikalyaaṇi

The next, theoretically interesting question to ask is the following:

(10) "Will this 'new' scale trigger further *AMB considerations if new related scales are presented to the musician?"

First of all let us explore the implications of this question. If the answer is 'yes', it means that the new scale has been fully accepted as a genuine raagam and included in the network. If and only if it is accepted as a new raagam, will it trigger further *AMB considerations given slightly modified versions of this scale for testing. If the answer is 'no', the implication is that the new scale has not been accepted as a full fledged raagam but is merely taken as an experiment, a nonce raagam, to coin a new term.

The answer to the question can be arrived at by deduction given the nature of the raagam. Firstly, scalar raagas cannot *ever* trigger *AMBTONE violation as all of them have unmarked values for tonal rendering (as we have just demonstrated). Secondly, since they select only unmarked tonal values, there is no question of these type of raagas triggering any *AMB violation with the raagas of the I Set. Thus the only *AMB constraint set they can ever activate is the *AMB type. And we know that *AMBSEQ violation is triggered by two kinds of evaluation, namely
a) accessing the global, networked set which compares the sequence under scrutiny with other raagas in the network, and
b) checking locally for *sequences (in the so-called vakra raagas (i.e. non-linear scales).

Of the two types of checking for *AMBSEQ, new, full scales will access the global network exactly like other scales. However, we should keep in mind the fact that the new scale is made up of two overlapping sets which result in unavoidable ambiguity among members of the two sets. It is because of this that the S Set generates a new strategy to circumvent *AMB violations when constructing musical phrases and musical lines. But more of this later. However, the new scale is unlikely to trigger any *AMB violation, on its own, as it has no unique identity in either parts of the octave. As for the non-linear, new scale, it is highly unlikely to trigger *AMB violation on its own as *AMB violations are driven by the network and this raagam is yet to be integrated into the network. A new entrant is likely to become part of the network only after repeated use.

Thus we see that, in principle, a member of the S Set is a uniquely determinable scale which carries no historical baggage; will never invoke an *AMBTONE violation with respect to any other raagam; and is always de-composable into smaller groups of notes which resemble other scales. A member of the S Set acquires a composite identity through repeated use where the identities of its parts cease to stand off and it develops into a full-fledged raagam in its own right. Finally, through further extended use, we may not rule out the possibility of the S Set member acquiring idiosyncratic usage patterns shifting the member finally to the I Set. Historically, this must have been a distinct possibility. But in contemporary Carnatic music, for various reasons which are discussed in section 8, pp. 257–264, contemporary performers, by and large do not seem to invest in new tonal possibilities, forging new phrases etc. probably because of pressure from a conformist audience/critic ambience.

8.3. The experiment with the idiomatic set

As I said earlier, this experiment is rather difficult to set up and so replication is doubtful. This is primarily because of the nature of the member of the I Set and the fact that the learning process exposes the learner to most of the commonly encountered raagas in the I Set. This point is best explained with a musical demonstration. Consider the musical line in (11), the beginning of the fourth charaṇam of the Shyaamaa Shaastri masterpiece Amba Kaamaakshi in Bhairavi. If you listen carefully to this musical line, you will find that each occurrence of the note 'ma' in italics is rendered differently. While the first 'ma' is a RenScale 'ma', the second is pitch curve with 'gu' as anchor. The last three 'ma's are glides, each one slightly different from the other. And all of them are notated as 'ma'. While it is true that across performers and across performances there could be variation in the handling of this note, there is no doubt one cannot interpret this passage from notation if one has never heard any rendering of Bhairavi. Unlike a member of the S Set where all notes are interpretable given unmarked pitch values of notes, in a typical member of the I Set all notes may not be amenable to such interpretation.[201]

(11) Musical demonstration
Amba Kaamaakshi: Bhairavi: Tisra Tripuṭai: Shyaamaa Shaastri.
[⊙ 8.149]
// *ma*, ; pa, / pa, ni da ^- *ma*, ; // pa, da, pa, / *ma*; pa - gi, ri,
bhak ta ja na kal pa la ti ka: ka ru
// gi, ; *ma*, / pa, ; - gi, *ma* , // pa *ma* pa, ; / ; ; - ; ; //
ṇa: la ya sa da ya:

The experiment I am going to outline is more of a 'thought' experiment which any trained Carnatic musician can introspect on. Assume a student of Carnatic music who is capable of aalaapanai etc. of many members of the I Set but who is systematically not exposed to any one member of the I Set, say Madhyamaavati. Present this person with the musical line given below.

(12) Musical demonstration
Madhyamaavati [⊙ 8.150]
['pa *ni* ;] ['pa, *ni* Sa, *ni* pa,]

I am quite sure this person will render all the three occurrences of 'ni' as RenScale 'ni', with utmost a gentle pitch wave rendering thrown in once, or will render all of them as red.ni pitch waves (if the style happens to be like mine). But, all well trained Carnatic musicians would know that the first 'ni' admits a double pitch curve (with 'ni' as the anchor and Sa as the peak for some performers), the second 'ni' is a red.ni gentle, double wave from 'di' and the third is a RenScale 'ni'. The crucial word in the previous sentence is 'admits'; a performer is not forced to chose only this interpretation. Depending on her/his style, other interpretations are also possible. Whatever the actual interpretation, it is unlikely that all the three occurrences of 'ni' would be rendered in an identical way. It is this unpredictable interpretation of certain notes that characterizes a member of the I Set. First of all, a member of the I Set selects some marked pitch values for at least one note in the scale, if not more. Secondly, a member of the I Set acquires through usage a set of characteristic/typical phrases which signal a particular member raagam to the exclusion of all other member raagas of the set.

As the first point has already been amply illustrated, let me take up the second point for discussion now. Musical phrases, as I said in chapter 6 while explaining Musical Phrase/Prominence Construal (p. 155–163), can be a random set of notes or musical idioms with or without affixed random notes with a single prominent note. Samples of musical phrases in raagas of the I Set are derived mainly from often heard compositions which are handed down from a teacher to the taught establishing different schools of music. In fact, schools of music can sometimes be identified from the musical phrases.[202] Schools tend to have their own repertoire of compositions, distinct ways of rendering compositions and an over all approach to different types of improvisation. All this contribute to the fact that schools have non-overlapping or only partially over lapping sets of musical phrases in their lexicons. Of course, as in language, specially in a multilingual setting as in India where dialect switching is the norm rather than the exception, users have several lexicons, one for production and other(s) for perception, in Carnatic music too, we would not be wrong to assume that the Carnatic music fraternity too acquire several lexicons in the course of their musical life.

I will demonstrate below how musical phrases from compositions can mould the thinking of the performer/listener in crucial ways. Let us take up the raagam Bhairavi for illustrating this point about musical phrases being derived from compositions. Some of the commonly occurring phrases/phrasal sequences in aalaapanai are listed below and the fairly well-known compositions in which they occur are also identified.

(13) Musical demonstration
Bhairavi [⊙ 8.151]
a. ['sa, ri ni, ni di]
b. ['ni sa gi gi ri sa]
c. ['gi gi ri gi ma pa da]
d. [ri 'gi, ma pa da]
e. [ma 'pa, di ni Sa]
f. [Gi Ri (Sa) 'ni, di]
g. ['di ni da da,]
h. ['ni da ma ma,]
i. ['ma da pa da] ['ma pa gi ma pa,]
j. ['ni di ni] ['pa di ni] ['ma pa di ni]
[a–j] viribooɳi: varɳam: Aʈa

Paccimiriam Aadiappayyer
k. ['ni, da] [da 'pa, di]
l. ['ni Sa pa da ma pa]
m. [ma 'gi, ri ri,]
n. ['Gi Ma Gi Ri] ['Sa ni da pa]
o. ['ma ni da pa] ['ma gi ri sa]
[k–o] Koluvayyunnaaḍee: Aadi: Tyaagaraajaa
p. ['ni ,] ['Gi Ri Sa ni,]
q. ['ma, ni di pa di ni di ni,]
Upacaaramu I: Aadi: Tyaagaraajaa
r. [ma 'ni, da da pa]
Tanayuni broova: Aadi: Tyaagaraajaa
s. [ri ma 'gi, ri]['ri sa]
Upacaaramu II: Ruupakam: Tyaagaraajaa[203]

These examples are by no means exhaustive. But they suffice to prove my point that a learner/listener can actually start the process of constructing a free flowing text with the help of these phrases culled from these commonly encountered compositions.

To recall our earlier discussion (pp. 216–217), the last cited instance is of considerable theoretical interest. Although Ayyangar 'precisely' notates the phrase in (13s) as 'gi ma gi, ri' (I: 395), it is very often rendered as I have indicated it ((13s) above). Now, according to 'text book definitions', Bhairavi is not allowed the sequence 'ri ma' as it will elicit a *AMBSEQ violation with Mukhaari as the latter has the scalar definition 'sa ri ma pa...'. But not only do performers usually render the phrase as I have indicated when they render the composition, they also include the phrase in their aalaapanai etc. It actually vindicates a point I made in the previous chapter about *AMBSEQEMPH >> *AMBSEQ. In other words, what is important is the emphatic/prominent note, which is 'gi', and the focus thus shifts from the offending 'ri ma' to the highlighted/focused 'ma 'gi, ri' making it grammatical in the final count. Notice that had the prominence been on 'ma' (accompanied by length) instead of 'gi', the phrase will be ungrammatical for Bhairavi. This example also helps prove the point that phrases are actually culled from often heard/rendered compositions and are ready for real time access, so to speak.

While on the topic of construction of musical phrases in the I Set, recall that in chapter 7 while discussing Musical Phrase Construal, I said that one of the functions of Musical Phrase Construal was checking for clichés and clichés were defined as typical, often occurring musical phrases associated with particular raagas. Clichés are only a small part of the stock of musical phrases that are collected over time from several sources, namely well-known compositions, favourite performers, crafted as part of an attempt at forging one's own style, etc. On the one hand, clichés are the phrases which are the easiest to perceive as they are the most commonly encountered phrases in a raagam, on the other hand their use is an indication that the mind is not actively forging musical phrases but falling back on commonly used ones. Of course, as in great literature, greatness does not lie in avoiding commonly used words and expressions but in the way words, including common words, are used. The drift of the argument is that the process of de-composition also involves classifying the de-composed elements as different types of musical notes and musical phrases, some of which are proto-typical and other less so of a raagam. It is the former which normally elicits a *AMBPHRASE or cliché violation. Of course, as in many things in Carnatic music, since the lexicons of individuals are not necessary congruent, what constitutes a cliché for one performer may not constitute a cliché for another because of variable listing in the respective lexicons. This explains the fact that matters of taste are so divergent in Carnatic music. Another related issue is the fact that an audience nurtured on clichéd, stereo-typical music sometimes finds it difficult to recognize and appreciate some of the rare ideas painstakingly crafted and sometimes gathered from infrequently heard compositions etc. Unfortunately, it is not uncommon for the 'law of the lowest common denominator' determining taste in some groups of the Carnatic music fraternity.

The point that the entire discussion on musical phrases leads to is the characterizing of the I Set. As opposed to the S Set, members of the I Set are positively characterized by specifications for individual notes and they are refined over time with increasing exposure. And unlike members of the S Set, a raagam of the I Set never encountered before cannot be rendered by musicians however well-trained.

Of course, the impossibility of interpreting a raagam of the I Set is only hypothetical and cannot be actually tested at any given point of time. But diachronically, it is far from hypothetical. Many members of the I Set have gone out of use and attempts to revive them are bound to be tentative, at best. Take the case of the the raagam Ghaṇṭa. Its scale according to Ayyangar is 'sa gi ri gi ma pa da pa ni Sa / Sa ni da pa ma gi ri sa' and according to Ayyangar its demise is due to the prevalence/popularity of the raagam Dhanyaasi (Kritimanimalai III: 82). From this statement I deduce that this raagam belonged to the I Set. A few musicians have attempted to 'reconstruct' the raagam, but one person's guess is as good as another's as to how this raagam was actually rendered originally.[204] But it must have once been a fairly popular raagam for Tyaagaraajaa has six compositions in it.[205]

8.4. The idiomatic and the scalar sets of raagas

In this section, I will now take a closer look at the two sets of raagas. As membership of raagas to the two sets is a matter of usage/personal taste etc., it may turn out that whereas a raagam belongs to the I Set for one musician, it may very well belong to the S Set for another. Let me illustrate the point with two raagas, namely Hamsadhvani and Moohanam. I am describing these two raagas the way I render them and hence their affiliation to the sets as I describe them. The facts may be different for other performers (more of that in chapter 9).

(14) Musical demonstration

Hamsadhvani[206] [⊙ 8.152]
Sa ri gu pa nu Sa/ Sa nu pa gu ri sa
RenScale and
ri, rendered as a note pitch curve [ri gu ri];
gu, rendered as a note pitch curve [gu pa gu];
pa, rendered as a note pitch curve [pa nu pa]
[gu 'ri, sa nu pa]

Moohanam [⊙ 8.153]
sa ri gu pa di Sa/ Sa di pa gu ri sa
RenScale and
ri, rendered as a note pitch curve [ri gu ri];
gu, rendered as a note pitch curve [gu pa gu];
pa, rendered as a note pitch curve [pa di pa]
di, rendered as a note pitch curve [di Sa di]
and
Note pitch wave rendering of ri, gu and di
e.g.,
// ; ; ; di, - ; di ; di ; / di pa ; ; ; - ; ; di, pa, di pa // gu, ...
mo: ha na ra: ma:
ri, gu, and di rendered as pitch waves between adjacent notes on the scale.

While for Hamsadhvani the renderings of notes are restricted to RenScale and note pitch curves between adjacent notes, Moohanam allows red.tone pitch waves for 'ri', 'gi' and 'di' in addition. I assume that this is a pointer to the former belonging to the S Set and latter to the I Set in my lexicon. But only barely so, perhaps.

This brings us to the next issue regarding membership to the I Set. Not all raagas of the I Set are equally 'idiosyncratic'. While Moohanam has just one characteristic of the I Set in that it allows red.tone pitch wave renderings of some notes (for me and many others), a raagam like Madhyamaavati allows a range of pitch value interpretations for the notes 'ri', 'ma' and 'ni' (musical demonstration [8.150] above) and finally a raagam like Bhairavi in addition to allowing a range of pitch values for notes also has several, intricate sequencing possibilities established through extended usage. Thus, while all raagas of the S Set share similar characteristics, the raagas of the I Set are not all alike as they may attest a) different types of raagam-specific tonal constraints to varying degrees and b) attest specific sequential possibilities in their musical phrasing acquired through use. Thus there are different layers of idiosyncrasies associated with them. Musicians and music teachers know intuitively the different levels of difficulty of the members of the I Set and select raagas for teaching depending on the attainment level of the student. But more of this in the next section.

8.5. Distinct learning strategies

I had demonstrated in section 1 how the prior acquisition of some raagas from the I Set would enable the learner to tackle any member of the S Set almost effortlessly. While this is true, it is also true that, by their very nature, members of the I Set are more marked than the members of the S Set because of the tonal realizations of notes. Thus it will be more effortful for beginners to attempt any member of the I Set than any member of the S Set.[207] In this section I shall briefly review the teaching strategy that is adopted widely in Carnatic music circles and show the correctness of my assumption regarding the relative markedness of tonal values in the two sets of raagas. I show that while the rationale of the method is sound, the actual practice is problematic. I then go on to show case the teaching practice of the school of music I belong to,[208, 209] in order to advance a viable solution to the problem of markedness of tonal realizations in Carnatic music.

The wide spread practice in Carrnatic music circles is backed by the (commonsensical) reasonable assumption that the less marked elements would be easier to learn prior to the acquisition of more marked elements/structures. Since, on the whole, RenScale is definitely easier to render than the complicated pitch waves and curves, beginners are sometimes taught only RenScale versions of *all* raagas. I have heard beginners rendering the Tooɖi varɳam in Aadi taaɭam composed by Paʈʈaɳam Subramaɳya Ayyar in (15) when it should be at least as in (16) to be minimally grammatical.

(15) Musical demonstration
RenScale version of Tooɖi varɳam in Aadi [⊙ 8.154]
// [Sa ;] [Sa - ni da] [pa da / ni] [ni da pa] - [ma gi ma ni]
e: ra: na: pai in ta
// [ni da pa] [ma - gi ra sa ra] / [gi ma pa] [gi - ma pa da ni]
cau ka se: ya

(16) Musical demonstration
Minimally grammatical version of Tooɖi varɳam
[⊙ 8.154]
// [Sa ;] [Sa - ni da] [pa da / ni] [ni da pa] - [ma gi ma ni]
e: ra: na: pai in ta
// [ni da pa] [ma - gi ra sa ra] / [gi ma pa] [gi - ma pa da ni]
cau ka se: ya

For Tooɖi to be minimally grammatical, the notes 'gi' and 'ni' in this musical line have to be rendered as red.note pitch waves at least. Now, if a scalar raagam like Malahari (17a) or a border line scalar raagam like Vasantaa (17b) are rendered as RenScale, then there is minimal grammaticality violation, if at all. But if raagas of the I Set like Shankaraabharaɳam (17c) or Kamaas (17d) are rendered as RenScale, the grammar of Carnatic music is severely violated.

(17) Musical demonstration
a. RenScale Malahari [⊙ 8.155]
Sa ra ma pa da Sa / Sa da pa ma gu ra sa
b. ?RenScale Vasantaa [⊙ 8.156]
sa ma gu ma di nu Sa / Sa nu di ma gu ra sa
c. *RenScale Shankaraabharaɳam [⊙ 8.157]
sa ri gu ma pa di nu Sa / Sa nu di pa ma gu ri sa

Minimally grammatical rendering
Note pitch curve for ri, ma and di. Aug.ma and aug.nu pitch curve for ma and di and note pitch curve for ri

d. *RenScale Kamaas [⊙ 8.158]
sa ma gu ma ni di ni pa di ni Sa
Sa ni di pa ma gu ma, ri gu sa
Minimally grammatical rendering
Pitch wave for ni and a pitch wave for long ma

Thus the common syllabus for music begins with a reasonable assumption about the markedness of tonal rendering but ends up teaching plain ungrammatical texts. This is the first cause of frustration in beginners who clearly see their own output as something different from Carnatic music. The second cause of frustration is the next stage of learning when they have to unlearn whatever they have learnt, abandoning RenScale renditions and picking up the difficult task of learning inter-tonal variations. Small wonder more than seventy five percent of learners quit music lessons at this stage in sheer disgust.

The alternative to this approach is to judiciously mix S Set raagas like Bauḷi, Vasantaa, Hamsadhwani with border line I Set raagas like Deevamanoohari, Bahudaari, Keedaaram etc. so that *at no stage is the learner ever learning ungrammatical texts in the name of simplification*. This approach satisfies the learners need in many ways. The learner has the satisfaction that she/he is not learning ungrammatical music and, more importantly, his/her communicative needs are also satisfied as she/he is likely to come across compositions she/he has learnt in music concerts rendered fairly close to the way she/he was taught.[210]

(18) Musical demonstration

a. S Set RenScale Bauḷi
sa ra gu pa da Sa / Sa nu da pa gu ra sa

b. S Set RenScale Vasantaa
sa ma gu ma di nu Sa / Sa nu di ma gu ra sa

c. S Set RenScale Hamsadhwani
sa ri gu pa nu Sa / Sa nu pa gu ri sa

d. Notes in italics are rendered as pitch waves
I Set Deevamanoohari
sa ri ma pa di *ni* Sa/ Sa ni di ni pa ma *ri*, sa

e. Notes in italics are rendered as pitch waves
I Set Bahudaari
sa gu ma pa di *ni* Sa / Sa ni pa ma gu sa

f. Notes in italics are rendered as pitch waves
I Set Keedaaram
sa ma gu ma pa nu Sa
/Sa nu pa ma gu ri sa *ri*, sa

The transition from the S Set to the I Set will be smooth and gradual and the beginner would have learnt his/her first lesson in Carnatic music about the tonal values of notes being raagam-specific. Finally, the stages of transition from RenScale to Pitch waves to Pitch curves will reflect the increasing markedness of pitch realizations of notes in Carnatic music.

8.6. Distinct performance strategies

In the previous section, I said that the beginner could benefit enormously if the teaching proceeded from the *S Set* to the border-line *I Set* as the transition from RenScale to Pitch waves to Pitch curves would be smooth and, more importantly, painful re-learning could be avoided and the learner's interest could be sustained as he/she would be learning to produce 'real' Carnatic music right from the beginning.

Let me now turn to performance strategies of musicians. Performing a composition as it has been taught is one thing (though it is no mean achievement) and interpreting it creatively is quite another thing. But performing an aalaapanai requires a leap of imagination. While rendering a text, there are props all over the place for the performer to hold onto as he/she can go from one musical phrase to another and so on. But in an aalaapanai, there are no fixed props to hold onto. I find that there are broadly two strategies available for performers attempting an aalaapanai. Keep the scale in mind (with or without the raagam-specific pitch specifications) and/or access the musical phrases gathered from compositions. In some circles, it is fashionable to render an I Set member as though it were an S Set raagam, supposedly signaling greater creativity, ability to innovate radically, etc. Here is a sample of Dhanyaasi aalaapanai rendered as an I Set member (in a fairly orthodox manner) and also rendered as though it were a member of the S Set (with RenScale values exclusively) modeled on a performance at a prestigious organization in Chennai in the year 2003.[211]

(19) Musical demonstration
Dhanyaasi aalaapanai as an I Set raagam [⊙ 8.159]
['ni sa gi;] ['ma, pa ma gi, ra sa] ['sa gi ma pa] ['ma pa]
['pa ni,] [ni 'da, pa] ['ma, pa ma gi ; , ,] [gi ma pa 'da, pa]
['ma pa ma pa da pa, da] [pa ma 'gi, ra sa]
Danyaasi as an S Set raagam with RenScale values exclusively [⊙ 8.160]
['ni sa gi;] [pa ma 'gi, ra sa ni] [sa gi ma gi 'ra, sa]
[sa gi ma pa ni 'da, pa] [pa ni Sa 'ni, da pa ma] ['gi, ra sa]

Now, my grammar just does not allow RenScale 'gi' if long, and RenScale ni if long in the descent. It is not that this raagam does not allow RenScale values at all. In fact, as I have pointed out several times, being the least marked pitch value, RenScale values cannot be totally prohibited for any raagam. According to my grammar, this raagam requires a sparing, judicious use of RenScale value for 'gi' and 'ni' to be used only in the ascending phrases.

Apart from the fashion of rendering I Set raagas as though they belonged to the S Set, it should be mentioned that very often such renderings use sequences of notes and fast paced idioms to the exclusion of musical phrases gathered from compositions. Therefore, in the literal sense too, the renderings can be said to be 'unidiomatic'. Finally, such a rendition invokes *Amb violations because these tonal values and sequences signal another raagam, namely Sindu Bhairavi. The generalization then is that if a member of the I Set were to be rendered as though it belonged to the S Set, then *AmbTone and *AmbSeq, to some extent, become redundant. But more of this in the following section.

There is yet another tradition where the notes of an I Set member are altered mid course sometimes to RenScale values (this is the relevant part here) or to the values of a totally unrelated raagam. This practice is called ʃruti bheedam/graha bheedam/modal shift where the fundamental tone is shifted from 'sa' to any other note in the scale. I will illustrate in (20) below one such possibility which performers have exploited in the past.[212]

Almost all pitch values and lengthened notes are contrary to the grammar of the base raagam Tooḍi. The notes second and fifth of the original scale which now function as the fourth and the seventh of the shifted scale have higher pitch values; the notes 'ra' and 'da' are lengthened in the descent contrary to the grammar of Tooḍi. While rendering ʃruti bheedam, performers generally stay close to the RenScale values of the shifted raagam though it may too belong to the I Set. But in contemporary Carnatic music, for many performers, this is accepted practice; it is something clever and exhilarating to be attempted as the 'piece de resistance' in the main raagam in a concert.

(20) Musical demonstration
Tooḍi with ʃruti bheedam on ra to render the scale of Kalyaaṇi.
The musical phrases rendered as ʃruti bheedam are enclosed in curly brackets and in italics.
Tooḍi ʃruti bheedam [⊙ 8.161]
['sa ra gi ma pa da] [ma 'pa, da pa ma gi,] ['gi ma pa da]
[ni Sa Ra 'Gi, ra]
{['*ra*; sa ni dada,] ['*da*, *pa ma gi*, *ra*]}
[ra gi ma pa da 'ni, da] [pa da ni sa Ra 'Gi, Ra]

The example of ʃruti bheedam just given is no doubt a 'real' sample. But, subtler versions of the concept are also possible where the musician remains true to the pitch values of the base raagam even while shifting the first note. A more accurate ʃruti bheedam is possible when the original pitch values are not abandoned but carefully accommodated in the shifted scale. Here is an example of such an exercise. But in such an exercise, extended full octave exposition of another raagam is not possible; only phrases suggestive of another raagam are possible. Moreover, all the possibilities in the newly hinted raagam cannot be utilized as some of the notes/sequences may require pitch values which are at variance with the base raagam. I give below an example of ʃruti bheedam on Kalyaaṇi subtly suggesting Suraṭṭi. However, the musical phrases of Suraṭṭi which are given below with an '!' cannot be integrated into the ʃruti bheedam because of pitch value violations to the base.

(21) Musical demonstration
ʃruti bheedam on Kalyaaṇi suggesting Suraṭṭi
The passage rendered as ʃruti bheedam is enclosed in curly brackets and in italics. The phrases of which cannot be integrated into the ʃruti bheedam are enclosed by exclamation marks.
Kalyaaṇi ʃruti bheedam [⊙ 8.162]
['gu mi pa di] ['mi pa di nu Sa Ri]
{['*Ri*,] ['*Sa nu Ri*,] ['*Sa nu di*,] ['*pa mi di*,] ['*pa mi gi*,]
['*gu pa*, *mi di*,] ['*di Sa nu Ri*,]}
Played on Ri as Sa
![ri ma pa ni Sa], [ni, ni, ni Sa ni di pa]...!

It must be said that even here, only the least marked of pitch values are taken for both raagas for doing ʃruti bheedam once again vindicating our stand regarding two major types of interpretation of notes in Carnatic music.

In the fifties of the previous century, there arose a new style of Carnatic music which became very popular and later, initiating a major school of Carnatic music. This style of singing was the first to explore the bold, unorthodox (then) method of rendering many I Set raagas as though they belonged to the S Set. It freed the performer from orthodox gamakkam and set the voice racing up and down the octave in torrents of cascading notes, providing great excitement to the listener. Here again, the trick was to switch to RenScale values avoiding/minimizing raagam-specific phrases, and ignoring raagam-specific constraints on lengthening of notes etc. It was really an exhilarating saga of exploration which signaled a kind of romanticism/a spirit of rebellion in Carnatic music. In hindsight, perhaps, we could say that it helped clear the cobwebs of mindless orthodoxy in Carnatic music. As the shock value of the rebellion diminished, more mature experimentation (or at least more restrained exploration) followed.

In the contemporary scene, one can safely comment that the unbridled RenScale exploration of the previous century is definitely not a major phenomenon any more (not withstanding a few performers here and there, namely cases like the Dhanyaasi aalaapanai cited above). But what has replaced it for some performers is yet another version of RenScale exploration, this time mimicking the north Indian variety of Indian music. It is not uncommon to come across a Carnatic raagam rendered as though it has been imported from the north, as the notation below illustrates.

(22) Music Notation
Kalyaaṇi rendered with 'over long' RenScale/minor pitch wave rendering. [⊙ 8.163]
Mi; gu mi, gu, ri sa ṇụ; ri gu,

The RenScale long 'mi' and overlong RenScale 'nu' (almost RenScale versions) are not at all characteristic of the Carnatic Kalyaaṇi but perhaps more reminiscent of its north Indian cousin (and specially the sequence nu ri gu). Switching from such a style to a kriti in the raagam is almost like switching dialects while speaking; but the oddness does not seem apparent to many performers, listeners and even critics. Perhaps, like the previous fashion of RenScale wilderness this too would pass, being a passing phase which fulfills a need to explore new pastures.

Whatever that may be, the conclusion that I wish to draw from the entire discussion is that there are two distinct strategies in Carnatic music – the idiomatic usage bound exploration and the RenScale, S Set strategy which allows the performer great freedom in interpreting raagas.

8.7. Distinct evaluation strategies of *AMB

As I have said earlier (more than once), *AMBTONE violations are possible only in I Set raagas as raagas of the S Set select only unmarked pitch values for all the notes in the scale. And I had implicitly assumed that sequences are checked for *AMBSEQ violations within the musical phrase (though see chapter 7, pp. 213–214, musical demonstrations [7.133–7.135] for a discussion of wit in Carnatic music). We need to revise this simplistic assumption in light of the bipartite division of the Carnatic music lexicon advocated here. Members of the S Set, in principle, will violate *AMBTONE as well as *AMBSEQ. If two members of the S Set share the notes of a part of the octave, the individual notes as well as the sequential possibilities in musical phrases in that part of the octave will be ambiguous between members of the S Set. Take the example of the raagas Bahudaari and Naagasvaraaḷi. Both have identical member notes in the first half of the octave, namely 'sa gu ma pa'. Since they share the notes and their pitch value realizations, musical phrases constructed using these four notes will definitely be ambiguous between the two raagas invoking *AMBSEQ violations within musical phrases.

I propose that *AMBSEQ violation is computed differently in I Set and S Set raagas. While the former evaluate musical phrases for violations, the latter take on the entire musical line for computing violations. This results in performers adopting different strategies for composing musical lines in the two sets of raagas. In typical I Set raagas, an entire musical line can cover a part of the octave leaving out many notes as the identity of the raagam will not be in question. The rendered notes will have marked pitch values to announce the intended raagam clearly. Here is an example of an I Set raagam Bhairavi where all the notes in the musical line are between 'sa and pa'.

(23) Musical demonstration
Bhairavi (lower octave) [⊙ 8.164]
// [ri, gi ma gi ri sa] [ri gi <u>ma, pa ma ma gi</u>][gi, ri sa]
[ri gi, ri]... [gi ma, gi]... [ma pa, ma] [gi, gi ri ri sa]
[ri gi ri gi sa ri,] //

The pitch values of 'gi' and length of notes announce clearly in every musical phrase the identity of the raagam. Therefore, checking for *AMBTONE and *AMBSEQ can take as their domain the musical phrase in the I Set member.

On the other hand, as we said earlier, *AMBTONE is irrelevant in the S Set and *AMBSEQ cannot take musical phrases as the domain for computing violation. Instead of the musical phrase, if *AMBSEQ takes on the musical line, then one has to make sure that every musical line has at least one instantiation of every note of the scale, either as a fully articulated note or as a hinted note.

(24) Musical demonstration
Naagasvaraaḷi [⊙ 8.165]
// [gu ma gu, ma gu gu sa] [gu ma,][gu ma pa,]
[ma pa di Sa di, pa] [pa ma ma, gu sa gu,] //

In this musical line, the first two musical phrases are ambiguous between Naagasvaraaḷi and Bahudaari. But within the musical line, there is no ambiguity as the sequence 'di Sa' in the third phrase clearly establishes the identity of the raagam, signaling Naagasvaraaḷi. Thus we see that *AMBSEQ has to take the entire musical line as its domain in S Set raagas to compute *AMB violations. So, *AMBSEQ violations are computed differently for I Set and S Set raagas, vindicating the bipartite structure of the Carnatic music lexicon advanced at the beginning of this chapter. Also notice that, as I explained earlier, *AMBSEQ does not actually look at strict linear sequencing but at presence versus absence of notes. While in I Set raagas, *AMBSEQ looks for membership of notes in musical phrases in non-vakra raagas, in S Set non-vakra raagas, the task of looking for the presence of a note applies in the extended domain of the musical line rather than the musical phrase. Turning to vakra raagas, however, the same strategy is operative in both types of raagas, i.e. looking out for specific sequences of notes to be branded as ungrammatical.

8.8. Predicting the direction of change

In this section I show how the direction of change in contemporary Carnatic music can be predicted given this partitioning of the Carnatic music lexicon. And the change is from more marked to less marked membership, i.e. from the I Set to the S Set in line with language change where also the direction of change is from more marked to less marked segment/structure etc.

Take the case of language change, for example. While the parent language Sanskrit allowed consonant clusters like /gr/ and /sn/ as in words /grahaɳa/ 'eclipse' and /sna:na/ 'bath', one of its derivative language, e.g. Punjabi disallows consonant clusters in the beginning of the word/syllable changing the pronunciation of the words accordingly, e.g. /garant/ 'holy book' and /sana:n/ 'bath'. Similarly, in Tamil a marked segment of Sanskrit like /b^{h}/ as in /b^{h}akti/ 'devotion' becomes /b/, i.e. /bakti/. These are instances of language change where the change is always in the direction from more marked to less marked segment/structure etc.

I may not be too off the mark in assuming that centuries of practice in isolated/insulated communities of practitioners had rendered Carnatic music a richly diverse entity. This richness and diversity was evident even in the golden age of Carnatic music, i.e. the age of the great composers of Carnatic music. There are innumerable instances where the grammar of the same raagam is ever so slightly different for the great composers (going by the notation in Ranga Ramanuja Ayyangar). Take the case of Mukhaari and the composers Tyaagaraajaa, Muttuswaami Diikshitar and Subbaraaya Shaastri (the son of Shyaamaa Shaastri and a great composer in his own right). While Tyaagaraajaa is the most conservative of the lot, he has the marked preference for exploiting the note 'da' as the illustration below, the anupallavi of the kriti Kaarubaaru in aadi, demonstrates.

(25) Musical demonstration
Anupallavi: Kaarubaaru: [⊙ 8.166]
Mukhaari: Aadi: Tyaagaraajaa
Aaroohaɳam: sa ri ma pa di Sa
Avaroohaɳam: Sa ni da pa ma gi ri sa
(Kritimanimalai I: 437)
// ; nidi - ni, <u>da ; nida</u> / da, da, - pa ; ni - da pa pa ma // pa ; ,
uu ri va ru dee sha

Here, the composer seems to be exploiting the note 'da' in the descent to the maximum. Consider next the unusual treatment of both 'da' and 'di' in the composition Eemaninee by Subbaraaya Shaastri in Aadi.

(26) Musical demonstration
Eemaninne: Mukhaari: [⊙ 8.167]
Aadi: Subbaraaya Shaastri (Kritimanimalai IV: 112–113)
a) chittaswaram/saahityam
// [pa di,] [sa - ri ma pa di/,] [Sa ni da - pa ma pa di] //
pa daabja muleesa daa vi nu ti sa lu pi tee
b) Third line of the charaṉam [⊙ 8.167]
// ; , ri - ma pa dini, di / di Sa, ni Sa, Ri Sa ni - , da pa, //
cha ra ṉa ma hi ma pọ ga
c) middle of the last line of the charaṉam
// - / - Sa, Sa ni di // pa, di pa pa ma pa di -
sri pa ra dee va tee

Normally, the note ‘di’ in the ascent is generally not subject to extra length and is also not favoured in the phrase final position (a and b). And ‘di’ is not favoured in the descent (c). Both these conditions on the use of ‘di’ are disregarded in the charming composition Eemaninee by Subbaraaya Shaastri in Aadi above (at least in the notation used in our school).

Finally let us consider an unusual use of ‘di’ in the Diikshitar composition Paahimaam ratnaachala in aadi.

(27) Musical demonstration
Paahimaam ratnaachala: [⊙ 8.168]
Mukhaari: Aadi: Muttuswaami Diikshitar (Kritimanimalai III: 304–305)
Fifth and sixth lines of the charaṉam
// ; pa, dama - pa; di / ni di ni di - nidi pa di ni di
vi dyaat ma ka sri
// ni di di, Sa ni - ni da, pa pa, / ma pa da ppa ma -
cha kraa kaa
pa; da pa; da ma pa
ra
// ; , ma - pa, pa, Sa di - Sa, Sa ni - ni di di ma
vi ci tra na va ra
// ma, ni di - di, Sa ni ni di di, / Sa ; Ri Sa ni di, - di Sa ;
tna gi ri vi haa ra

Clearly, the three composers had slightly variant grammars of the same raagam Mukhaari. It is a debatable issue whether they inherited this difference from their respective schools or they forged their own grammars as they went along.[213] But contemporary Carnatic music with its broad based, eclectic learning/listening avenues is certainly on the way to losing such subtle variations. This is what I call the process of simplification. This process of simplification is driven by the twin criteria of prescriptivism and the need to reduce the tonal markedness of raagas. Prescriptivism dictates change if the desire to maintain the aaroohaṇam – avaroohaṇam overrides notation and usage as the cases discussed above indicate (see endnote 21). The last two illustrations are not widely popular in the contemporary scene (and the reasons are not far to seek).

Now I turn to the second criterion of raagam change, i.e. reduction in markedness. I have already discussed the change pertaining to Pantuvaraaḷi earlier in this chapter, musical demonstration [8.148], where the change is from the raagam-specific specification of pitch wave 'gu' to the unmarked specification as RenScale 'gu' for many contemporary musicians. Here I give two more instances of raagam change, one involving a total change from an I Set to an S Set and another a partial change in an I Set raagam reducing the markedness of the raagam considerably.

The first case is that of the raagam Janaranjani the scale being /sa ri gu ma pa nu Sa/ Sa di pa ma ri sa/. The discourse I am referring to is a recording of this raagam rendered by a much admired musician of the sixties and an accompanying violinist who is also a widely admired musician in Carnatic music circles. The raagam is a marginal I Set member for the vocalist with a very idiosyncratic rendering of 'nu' which is markedly close to 'ni'. For the violinist, however, it is clearly a RenScale 'nu' and, for sensitive ears, it is very much like speakers of different dialects conversing. Here is a musical demonstration of the two versions of the raagam.

(28) Musical demonstration
I Set member Janaranjani I & II [⊙ 8.169]
[gu ma pa di, pa] [<nu Sa Ri,] [Sa di pa ma ri,]
[gu ma pa <nu,] [pa ma ri gu ma ri, sa]
S Set member Janaranjani
[gu ma pa di, pa] [nu, Sa Ri,] [Sa di pa ma ri,]
[gu ma pa nu, Sa] [di pa ma pa ma] [ri gu ma ri, sa]

The idiosyncratic value for 'nu' (indicated as <nu) has changed to the less marked, RenScale 'nu' for many contemporary musicians. It would not be wrong to say that the change in this raagam is driven by both prescriptiv-

ism and markedness. Prescriptivism demands that a raagam be classified as an unambiguous derivative of a full scale. Therefore, prescriptivism demands that the niʃaadam be unambiguously either 'ni' or 'nu', not somewhere in between. Having decided that Janaranjanai should be a derivative of Shankaraabharaɳam with 'nu' as the niʃaadam, the reduced 'nu' is suppressed in favour of a full-fledged 'nu'. The change also reduces the markedness value of the niʃaadam by changing a reduced 'nu' to a RenScale 'nu'.[214]

The next example I give is of a raagam that has changed for many musicians from a very marked I Set member to a less marked member of the same Set. The raagam in question is Saaveeri and its two 'dialects' which I describe below. While dialect A requires Grammar A, dialect B is best described by Grammar B. Both dialects are presented below.

(29) Musical demonstration
Saaveeri [⊙ 8.170]
Dialect B: janya of Maayaamaaɭavagauɭa
sa ra ma pa da Sa / Sa nu da pa ma gu ra sa
[sa ra ma pa da,] [ma pa da nu, pa da,] [ma pa da,] [da pa ma gu, ra] [sa ra gu sa ra,]
Saaveeri
Dialect A: janya of Maayaamaaɭavagauɭa
with italic nu and gu rendered almost as ni and gi respetively (like Tooɖi)
[sa ra ma pa da,] [ma pa da *nu*, pa da,] [ma pa da,] [da pa ma gu, ra] [sa ra *gu* sa ra,]

I had been exposed to dialect B all along and had not learnt any composition in the raagam directly from Ayyangar. However, Ayyangar (1967) notes that there was a popular saying (roughly translated) "if 'nu' occurs after Sa it is higher and if it occurs by itself it is lower".[215] Thus in a phrase like [pa da nu pa da,] the 'nu' should be much lower than elsewhere, almost like Tooɖi. And applying the law of symmetry, in a phrase like [sa ra gu sa ra,] the 'gu' will be rendered much lower, almost like 'gi', making it like Tooɖi. This quotation from Ayyangar had remained an abstract, curious observation that I did not know how to put to practice till I heard the recording of this raagam and the Muttuswaami Diikshitar composition Sri Raajagoopaala rendered by a well respected vocalist duo of great musical lineage. It was then that Dialect A came alive for me.

It is not very difficult to guess which of the two varieties is older. Dialect A must have been the original version of the raagam and the other dialect a case of simplification. A change from dialect A which has more raagam-specific pitch value definitions, specially the definitions of 'gu' and 'nu' in specific contexts to dialect B is a clear case of simplification. However, dialect B is still not unmarked enough to be classified as an S Set raagam, as it still retains other raagam-specific pitch definitions on other notes.

Thus I have shown in this section the usefulness of my new classification of raagas demonstrating its predictive power with respect to the way raagas change over time.

8.9. Raagam-change and the networked Carnatic music lexicon

In this section, I take up the problem of a number of raagas shifting their affiliation from Meeḷakartaa Naṭabhairavi (no. 20 – sa ri gi ma pa da ni Sa) to Meeḷakartaa Karaharapriyaa (no. 22 – sa ri gi ma pa di ni Sa) with either the raagam completely replacing 'da' with 'di' or adopting 'di' as the major exponent and 'da' as the accidental (minor) exponent over a period of time. Though Carnatic music text books and books on music theory continue to list many of the raagas as derivative of Meeḷakartaa Naṭabhairavi, current practice is fairly uniform in the large scale use of 'di' as the major daivatam. Of the derivative raagas of Naṭabhairavi, fifteen for Tyaagaraajaa and thirteen for Diikshitar, only two raagas, namely Hindooḷam (with sa gi ma da ni Sa - Sa ni di ma gi sa) and possibly Saaramati (with sa ri gi ma pa da ni Sa - Sa ni da ma gi sa) which may be considered major raagas (in the sense that performers render aalaapanai, niraval and swaram) have retained their affiliation to Naṭabhairavi with the exclusive use of 'da'. The rest of the major raagas (in the sense spelt out above), namely Bhairavi, Mukhaari, Huseeni, Aabeeri[216] and Aanandabhairavi (and even Maanji) have a predominant 'di' in their usage. And what is uniformly avoided in all the raagas is the use of 'da' in the ascent. The offending sequence is rather 'pa da ni' which even Hindooḷam does not allow (as the raagam does not select 'pa' at all) and the other raagam which selects only 'da', namely Saaramati, selects only RenScale 'ni'. The common factor thus is the sequence 'pa da ni' which is selected by the preeminent Carnatic raagam, i.e. Tooḍi.

My hypothesis is that the dominant presence of Tooḍi in the Carnatic music network of raagas actively militated against another *major* raagam of the I Set selecting 'pa da ni' with pitch wave and pitch curve rendering of 'ni' (reduced and augmented 'ni'). The crucial factors here are a) major and b) member of the I Set. As scalar possibilities are always open for exploration and can never be disallowed by the network, the question here is only that of members of the I Set raagas.

Before we take a closer look at the range of raagas which have undergone re-affiliation, let us consider the 'conceptual space' associated with the notes 'ra gi ma' and 'pa da ni'. Taking up the former sequence first, if we look at the number of major raagas which exploit these three notes, we find that there is only one I Set raagam, namely Tooḍi. On the other hand, the number of major raagas selecting the notes 'ri gi ma' are many, namely Bhairavi, Karaharapriyaa, Kiiravaaṇi, Aaboogi, Kaanaḍaa, Sriranjanai, Aanandabhairavi, Riitigauḷa and many more. The question to ask is "Why is it that whereas if 'ra' and 'ma' are selected the selection of 'gi' leads to just one raagam which is a member of the I Set, namely Tooḍi, if 'ri' is selected so many raagas of the I Set are possible?" Even the ancient raagam Bhuupaaḷam which must have been a member of the S Set and which selects 'sa ra gi pa da Sa' has fallen into disuse now.[217]

My explanation is that even RenScale 'gi' is contextually marked when 'ra' is selected and hence the mariginality of S Set raagas which select these notes and pitch wave or pitch curve rendering of reduced 'gi' will invoke an *AmbTone violation with Tooḍi and hence the absence of any major raagam other than Tooḍi selecting the sequence 'sa ra gi ma'.

Similarly, if 'pa' and 'da' are selected only one major raagam which belongs to the I Set is possible with 'ni', i.e. Tooḍi (as RenScale 'ni' is contextually marked in the vicinity of 'da' just as RenScale 'gi' is contextually marked in the vicinity of 'ra'). This is the reason why many of the raagas switch over to 'di' from 'da' when they select 'ni'. Thus the explanation is that 'gi' and 'ni' are contextually marked when they occur after 'ra' and 'da' respectively and reduced 'gi' and reduced 'ni' after 'ra' and 'da' are strong indicators of Tooḍi and hence avoided by other I Set raagas because of *AmbTone and the Carnatic music network of raagas. As a corollary, we now have an explanation for why we have a raagam Bhairavi but not a raagam *Anti-Bhairavi which switches the use of the 'di' from the ascent to the descent, i.e. while 'sa ri gi ma pa di ni Sa; Sa ni da pa ma gi ri sa' is attested, 'sa ri gi ma pa da ni Sa; Sa ni di pa ma gi ri sa' is not (see chapter 2 and the musical demonstration of the scales of Bhairavi and Anti-Bhairavi [2.13 and 2.14] respectively).

Consider now the raagam Riitigauḷa which was most probably a derivative of Meeḷakartaa Naṭabhairavi for Muttuswaami Diikshitar.[218, 219] Any attempt to render his compositions in the contemporary scene with 'da' as daivatam is, at best, of academic interest. So, this raagam would constitute another example of a raagam which has moved away from 'da' to 'di' because of the selection of 'ni' as a member of the scale.

Another, perhaps, equally strong reason for the raagam to select 'di' over 'da' is symmetry which is a very powerful driving force in Carnatic music. If we look at the majority of popular raagas in Carnatic music, we find that they allow symmetrical sequences of notes/similar ways of handling notes in the lower and upper parts of the octave. The musical demonstration below illustrates this point with examples from a range of raagas.

(30) Musical demonstration
Symmetry in the selection of notes [⊙ 8.171]

a. Shankaraabharaṇam
sa *ri* ... pa *di*

b. Kalyaaṇi
Sa nu *di* ... pa mi *gu*

c. Beegaḍaa
ni, di pa ... *ma*, gu ri

d. Sahaanaa
ma di ... ni Ri

e. Kaanaḍaa
ri pa ... ma di

f. Varaaḷi
nu Sa Ra (gi) Ra Sa ... mi pa da (nu) da pa

g. Kaamboodi
pa ma gu pa di ... Sa ni di Sa Ri

h. Aarabhi
Sa Sa, nu di, ... ma ma, gu ri

i. Yadukulakaamboodi
gu, ma pa, ma gu ... Di, ni Sa, ni di

j. Suraṭṭi
ri *ma*, ... pa *ni*,
ni ni, di pa ... ma ma, gu ri

One can go on and on illustrating the law of symmetry in Carnatic music. But surely, these examples from a range of raagas would suffice to convince even the skeptical reader of the importance of symmetry in the selection of notes and the tonal pattern of notes in popular raagas in Carnatic music.

Having established the importance of symmetry in Carnatic music beyond reasonable doubt, it would now be clear that the choice of 'sa' and 'ri' in a raagam would automatically favour the choice of 'pa di' over 'pa da' in a major raagam. Thus we have two really strong reasons for the historical change which is a fait accompli in contemporary Carnatic music (academicians not withstanding), namely the Tooḍi factor in the raagam network and the criterion of symmetry. Of course, I do not deny that there are many raagas which do not obey the laws of symmetry which belong to the I Set as well as the S Set of raagas. But, nevertheless, symmetry is a strong driving force in the shaping of major raagas in Carnatic music.

Let us now take a closer look at some of these raagas which were originally affiliated to Naṭabhairavi with 'da' as the only or the major exponent of the daivatam which have over time switched the major affiliation to 'di'. Let me illustrate the use of 'di' in many of these raagas which continue to be listed as derivatives of Naṭabhairavi in contemporary music books and books on Carnatic music theory. The number of occurrences of 'da' is minimal in the musical lines in the illustrations showing its minor affiliation. The raagas I choose for illustration are Bhairavi, Mukhaari, Aanandabhairavi and Aabeeri.

(31) Musical demonstration

a. Bhairavi aalaapanai [⊙ 8.172]
// [ni di ni ni, da pa] [di, ni Sa, pa] //
// [pa Gi, Ri] [Ri Sa ni, da pa] //
// [ma, ni di <u>pa di ni di ni,</u>] [da ma,] [pa di ni Sa] [ni, da pa] //
// [pa,] [di pa di,] [ni di ni,] [Sa ni Sa,] [Ri Sa Ri,] [<u>Sa, Ri Sa</u> ni, da pa]

b. Mukhaari aalaapanai [⊙ 8.173]
// [pa ni <u>di, ni di di</u> Sa, Ri] [Sa ni, da pa] [da pa da ma] //
// [pa di,] [pa di Sa,] [di Sa,] [di Sa Ri,] [Sa ni, <u>di, ni di</u> di,] [<u>Sa, Ri Sa</u> ni, da pa ma,] //
// [ma,] [pa, ni, ni da, pa] [pa da, ma]
[pa di <u>Sa, Ri Sa</u> ni di Sa Ri,] //
// [Sa Ri, Sa ni, di,] [<u>Sa,Ri Sa</u> ni di ma,] [pa di, <u>Sa, Ri Sa</u> ni, da pa] //

c. Aanandabhairavi [⊙ 8.174]
// [pa, ni pa] [pa ma gi, ri] [gi ma pa ni pa] [pa, ni di pa] //
// pa, di ni di, ni] [<u>pa, di pa</u> ma] [<u>ma, pa ma</u> gi, ri] [gi,] //
// [gi ma pa da,] [ma pa, gi, ri] [gi ma pa ni pa Sa,] //

d. Aabeeri aalaapanai [⊙ 8.175]
// [pa ni Sa gi,] [Ri, Gi Ri Sa ni di pa] [gi ma pa ni,]
[di, ni di pa ma gi ri] [sa ri, sa] //

Notice that in Bhairavi, the occurrence of da cannot be stated as 'followed by pa or ma' as the second phrase in the last musical line has the sequence 'di pa di,'. Such occurrences of 'di' in the great varṇam defy all simplistic, prescriptive laws. Whatever the problem with defining the occurrence of 'da' in Bhairavi, it is a minor note occurring in restricted phrases only and 'di', is beyond doubt, the major exponent of the daivatam in the raagam.

Clearly, 'da' is more pronounced in Mukhaari than in Bhairavi. But once again it is not easy to define the occurrence of 'da' and 'di' precisely as both notes can be followed by 'ma', though only the former can be followed by 'pa'. Thus it would not be incorrect to say that whereas Bhairavi is primarily a derivative of Karaharapriyaa with the caveat that 'da' occurs before a 'pa', Mukhaari really straddles two meḷakartaa raagas Naṭabhairavi and Karaharapriyaa equally.

Turning to Aanandabhairavi, we find that 'da' plays even more of a minor role in this raagam than in Bhairavi – as it occurs in only one context, namely after 'pa' phrase finally. Therefore, it would be quite appropriate to classify it as a derivative of Karaharapriyaa.

Finally, the contemporary, popular version of Aabeeri does not ever use 'da' anywhere in the discourse and therefore must not be listed as a derivative of Naṭabhairavi at all, contrary to music books and music theory.

In this section we saw that raagas do change over time and the change is shaped by four criteria, namely

(32)
a. Tonal Markedness,
b. Shifting a raagam from the I Set to the S set,
c. *AMBTONE in the raagam network, and
d. Symmetry being a driving force in raagam change.

Of the four criteria listed above for Raagam change in Carnatic music, a), b) and c) all point in the same direction, i.e. a bipartite structure of the Carnatic music lexicon governed by the principle of markedness. Therefore I claim that raagam change is mainly driven by markedness and consequently the validation of the bipartite structure of the lexicon that I proposed in this chapter (though I must admit that considerations of symmetry are of fairly high priority).

A conclusive argument for symmetry as a criterion for raagam change can be constructed if we can show that a raagam can allow a reduced 'nu' if and only if it selects a 'ma' and not if it selects a 'mi'. Take the case of Janaranjani. It selects 'sa ri gu ma' in the lower half of the octave, and 'pa nu (reduced)' in the upper half in the conservative tradition. If there is a 'pratimadhyama' counterpart to Janaranjani which selects the same set of notes as Janaranjani but selects 'mi' instead of 'ma', let us call it pseudo-Janaranjani, intuitively, I feel that such a raagam will not select a reduced 'nu' like Janaranjani as symmetry will force it to have higher pitch values for 'nu' to correspond with that of 'mi'. Had such a raagam existed then we would have had a very strong argument for symmetry as a driving force in Carnatic music. But even then, the existence of asymmetrical I and S Set raagas of great beauty like Kiiravaaṇi (sa ri gi ma pa da nu Sa) (I Set), Suddhasaaveeri (sa ri ma pa di Sa) (I Set), Lataangi (sa ri gu mi pa da nu Sa) (S Set), Heemavati (sa ri gi mi pa di ni Sa) (S Set), Gauḷa (Sa ra ma pa nu Sa - Sa nu pa ma ra gu ma Ra sa) (I Set)[220] with more notes in the lower half of the octave than the upper half and Valaji (sa gu pa di ni Sa) (S Set) with more notes in the upper half of the octave than the lower show that 'symmetry' is not an inviolable criterion but merely a high ranking one. The constraint based theory of linguistics which I am trying to use for the description of the grammar of Carnatic music allows me to re-word the role of symmetry in Carnatic music thus. Augment Symmetry is a family of constraints that are high ranked in styles of Carnatic music which value microtonal details and are not unduly pedantic and the constraints are active only in scales which have scope for their application. In other words, these constraints examine a scale to evaluate the tonal relationships between notes which are in symmetrical relation in the scale. For example, 'ra' and 'da', 'ri' and 'di', 'gu' and 'nu' are in symmetrical relation with 'sa' and 'pa' and 'ma' and 'ni', 'mi' and 'nu' and 'gu ma' and 'di ni' are in symmetrical relation with respect to 'pa' and 'Sa'. The schematic representations below may help clarify this concept of symmetry. While Figure 1 captures some symmetrical relations with respect to 'sa' and 'pa', Figure 2 captures some of the symmetrical relations with respect to 'ma' and 'Sa'.

The two figures do not exhaust all the possible symmetrical relations that can and do exist in Carnatic music. Firstly, some more relations can be extracted out of these 12 notes. Secondly, recall Carnatic music has a 16 notes scale and not a 12 note scale (see chapter 4 section 4.2, p. 76). Therefore the four 'new' notes can also, in principle, enter into symmetric relations and they do. Thus for instance, the notes 'ru' and 'du' and 'ga' and 'na' too will be considered symmetric.

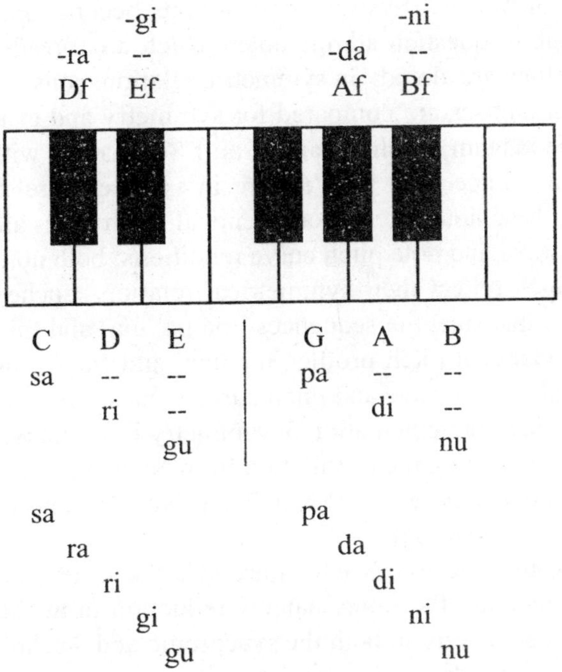

Figure 1.

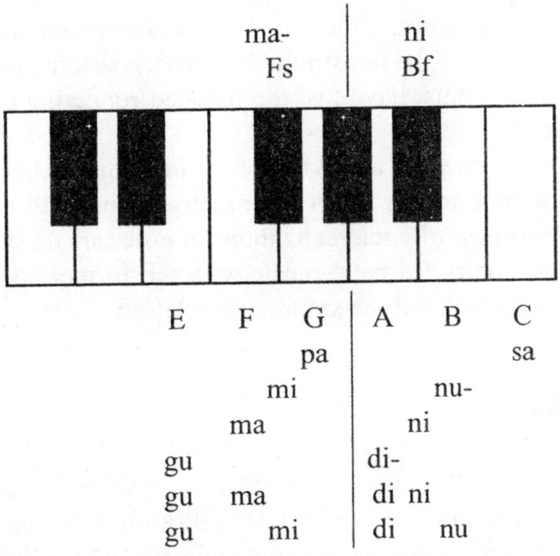

Figure 2.

The family of AUGMENTSYMMETRY constraints become operational if and only if the scale in question admits notes which are already in symmetric relation. Once they are already in symmetric relation, consideration of pitch values, musical phrases are compared for symmetry and evaluated. For example, take the raagam Madhyamaavati an I Set raagam with the scale [sa ri ma pa ni Sa]. Since 'ma' and 'ni' are in symmetric relation, the pitch realizations of these notes are almost identical; both notes allow, RenScale, red.tone pitch wave and note pitch curve renditions; both notes permit musical phrases which reflect their symmetrical relation couched in symmetrical phrases. For instance, the sequences [ma pa, ma] and [ni Sa, ni] can be rendered with identical pitch profiles for 'ma' and 'ni' in musical phrases, namely RenScale, pitch wave and pitch curve values.

The most radical implementation of symmetry is, of course, the diachronic case of raagas changing their affiliation from Naṭabhairavi with an unsymmetric *[sa *ri gi* ma pa *da ni* Sa] to Karaharapriya with a perfect, symmetric scale [sa *ri gi* ma pa *di ni* Sa].[221]

Thus we see that the forces which are at work in lexicon construction and raagam change are the same, namely reduction in markedness and an augmentation of symmetry in both the synchronic and diachronic grammars of Carnatic music. Further, it is symmetry which predicts that, for instance, the change that affected Saaveeri changing it from dialect A to dialect B [8.158] must have affected the notes 'gu' and 'nu' simultaneously and not sequentially changing either of the notes first and affecting the other note at a later point of time. It is the constraint AUGMENTSYMMETRY that tells us that dialect B of Saaveeri must have lost the reduced rendering of 'gu' and 'nu' at the same time.

While symmetry may be a driving force in raagam change in the diachronic grammar of Carnatic music, symmetry along with concern for decreasing the markedness of pitch realizations of notes are the defining factors of style in contemporary Carnatic music with the former operative only in scales where notes are already in symmetric relation.

8.10. Conclusion

In this chapter, I argued for a new classificatory system for raagas based on the principle of markedness – a principle well-known in linguistics. While the unmarked set is the S Set where notes in a scale have the least marked pitch values for notes, the members of the I Set are not all of equal complexity. Whereas raagas like Tooɖi, Bhairavi, Karaharapriyaa, Kiiravaaɳi, Shankaraabharaɳam, Beegaɖaa, Kaamboodi and Kalyaaɳi are of maximal complexity with many specific pitch values associated with notes and specific musical phrases sanctioned by usage from the body of compositions and due to frequency of handling by great musicians, raagas like Vasantaa, Keedaaram, Bahudaari, Suddhasaaveeri are on the I Set periphery as they are minimally specified for special pitch values. And a large number of raagas fall in between these two groups with varying degrees of complexity. Of course, it is possible to quantify precisely the degree of complexity of a raagam and rank the raagas in the I Set, but that is a task I leave to others.

The amazing fact that needs to be noticed is that two groups of major raagas of the I Set which share the lower half of the octave, namely [sa ri gi ma] and [sa ri gu ma], show such minute distinctiveness in pitch values and usage. The raagas in question are Bhairavi, Karaharapriyaa, Kiiravaaɳi, Mukhaari, Riitigauɭa, Aanandabhairavi, Aaboogi, Sriranjani, Kaanaaɖaa of one group and Shankaraabharaɳam, Kaamboodi, Harikaamboodi, Beegaɖaa, Bilahari, Keedaaragauɭa, Suraʈʈi, Kamaas, Naaʈakuranji and Keedaaram of the other. While the latter group may have gathered all the idiosyncratic pitch values and specific sequencing possibilities over centuries of usage, the first group owes its colour and distinctive variety to the greatest composer South India has known, namely Tyaagaraajaa, also referred to as Tyaaga Brahmam with reverence in Carnatic music circles. He was single-handedly responsible for writing the definitive grammars of Karaharapriyaa and Kiiravaaɳi, composing many compositions in the former but only one in the latter.[222] This is truly a remarkable feat. It goes without saying that any one can create a raagam of the S Set but no other composer has, till today, created a raagam of the I Set complete with specific idioms announcing the individual raagam.

(33)	Musical demonstration	[⊙ 8.176]
	[ma gi gi, ri,]	Karaharapriyaa
	[sa ri gi, ri ri sa,]	Karaharapriyaa
	[ma (di,) ri gi,]	Karaharapriyaa
	[ma, gi gi ri sa]	Kiiravaaɳi
	[ma, pa ma ma, gi gi,]	Kiiravaaɳi
	[ri (RenScale) gi ma pa, da,]	Kiiravaaɳi

Having set up a bipartite classification of raagas, I then went on to show how the criterion of markedness of pitch values used for this classification is useful independently. Firstly, precise ranking of markedness of pitch values is an important pedagogic tool for teaching Carnatic music. Secondly, I demonstrated how the distinct characteristics of these two sets are used as distinct performance strategies. Thirdly, I showed how the two sets of raagas require different domains for *AmbSeq evaluation with the I Set taking the musical phrase as its domain and the S Set the Musical line. Fourthly, I argued that the direction of change is always from the I Set to the S Set, though the change may be partial or total, once again supporting the assumption in linguistic theory about change being always in the direction of greater simplicity/ loss of markedness. Finally, I examined the historical problem of many raagas changing their affiliation from one parent raagam to another driven by the twin concern of *AmbTone in the raagam network and the need for symmetry. I submit that the tools tentatively suggested in the preceding chapters will enable a detailed, precise description of the raagam system of Carnatic music which I leave for future work.

Chapter 9
Accounting for variation in Carnatic music

9.1. Introduction

I have said several times in the course of this book that Carnatic music is inherently variationistic, i.e. variation-oriented. In this, the last chapter, I will consider in some detail the parameters along which styles can vary leading to an examination of two distinct styles in some depth. Let me begin by reiterating once again a point that will bear repetition. As in language, in Carnatic music too dialects/variations abound. Just as in language, where no dialect is *inherently* superior to any other dialect, so too in Carnatic music, all varieties are inherently of the same standing. A dialect acquires the status of the standard not because it inherently possesses superior qualities but because of the social, political and economic prestige of its users. Just as in matters pertaining to language, as people evaluate dialects with adjectives like 'elegant', 'precise', 'educated', 'upper class' etc., so too in Carnatic music, practitioners tend to defend their own styles using adjectives like 'authentic', 'emotive', 'mellifluous', 'popular' etc. The fact remains that from the descriptive standpoint, one dialect/style is as good as another. Of course, it is quite another matter when it comes to native speakers/practitioners and their subjective points of view. Each user continues to use her/his variety because she/he is convinced of its innate superiority/appeal etc. In my case too, though as a theoretician I 'know' that all styles are of equal standing, as a practitioner I 'feel' and am convinced of the superiority of my own style. The rather delicate issue that this discussion is leading to is that when I take on the task of comparing two contemporary styles of Carnatic music, I should pick out styles I am sympathetic to, which are comparable and worthy of close examination (in my view). Keeping my own preference in mind, I have chosen to compare my own style, which I call 'Chamber Music Style A' (henceforth CMA for Chamber Music A) with that of an established, contemporary vocalist, Sanjay Subrahmanyan which I call 'Concert Hall A' (henceforth CHA for Concert Hall A). I will show that the distinct styles are born of distinct strategies driven by distinct expectations from the audience. While the chamber music style caters to an intimate audience, a small group of more or less homogenous taste, the concert hall style caters to a large audience whose taste is usually not homogenous. While the former can expect its audience to respond to every nuance, detail, the latter cannot do so. Further, the former being addressed to a closed, small group, constrains the performer to be truly 'classical' – in the sense of avoidance of emotional/intellectual excess. In other words, a chamber music performer is more like a miniature artist who revels in subtle details. The concert hall performer, on the other hand, is like an artist who works on a large canvass, so to speak, and she/he must address every segment of the large audience, avoid unnecessary subtlety, keep the melodic line uncluttered, rhythmic statements loud and clear, etc. Finally, I have called both varieties as style 'A' keeping in mind the fact that other possibilities exist in both types.

Getting back to the idea of dialectal variation in language, all of us know that dialects can vary along all and any of the following parameters: sounds, the way words are pronounced, differences in lexical items, newly coined words and sentence construction. Here are a few examples of dialectal variation across varieties of English that we commonly come across. While American and Canadian English admit the flapped pronunciation of 't' and 'd' in words like 'letter' and 'madder', other varieties do not. Similarly, while many of us pronounce the word 'route' as [ruut], the Americans prefer to pronounce it [raut]. The word 'momentarily' means something different in American English than it does in most other varieties. In a similar vein, the object referred to as 'pavement' and 'sidewalk' is the same in British and American English respectively. Finally, people on the west of the Atlantic say "so and so lives on X street' and others say "so and so lives in X street".[223]

As in language, in Carnatic music too, variation can arise from the use of particular tones/notes, phrases and sequences. As I said in chapter 8, the lexicon of Carnatic music is the repository of de-composed notes/phrases etc. and one can attribute the differences across styles of Carnatic music to the differences in the corresponding lexicons. However, before I take up the issue of distinct lexicons of Carnatic music, let me summarize briefly the core ideas in the concept of the grammar of Carnatic music and the definition of style in Carnatic music; see figure 1 below.

The grammar of Carnatic music is a mediating box that interprets tones as notes and assigns grammaticality and style/ stylistic evaluations to the input submitted to it.

But the mediating device itself is shaped by two major criteria, namely the internal constraint set FAITHLEX (be faithful to the lexicon) and RENSCALE (render as a precise pitch on the scale) and two sets of 'external' factors, namely PERFSTYLE (Performance Style) and MUSMED (Suit the Music to the Medium). The figure (Fig. 3, p. 34) given in chapter 2 is reproduced below for ease of reference.

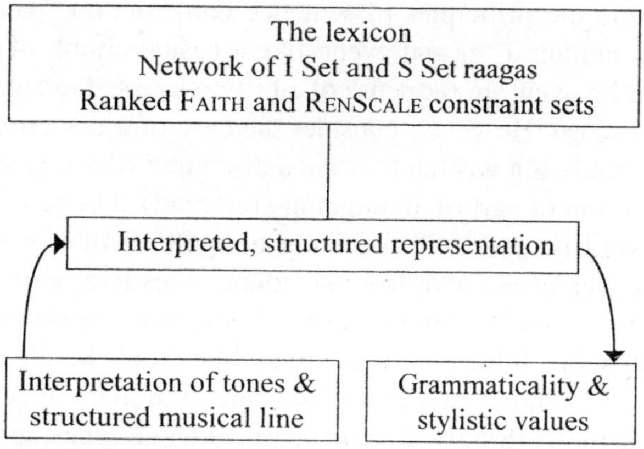

Figure 1. The grammar of Carnatic music

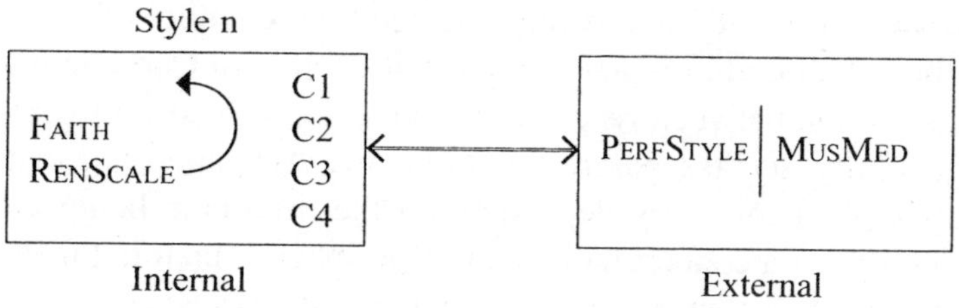

Figure 2.

As I said earlier, a style is defined by the set of 'internal' constraints FAITHLEX and RENSCALE. These two sets are defined by two external sets of constraints, namely PERFSTYLE and MUSMED. I term the latter sets 'external' as they define performance factors/criteria. We will see by and by in what ways these so-called 'external' criteria can determine the grammar, in other words, the ranking of the set of FAITHLEX and RENSCALE constraints. The box lexicon in Figure 1 is in fact made up of the networked raagas and the details in Figure 2 above. The lexicon is made up of the constraint set and the networked I and S Set raagas.

9.2. Performance style and the medium

At first blush the statement that 'external' factors determine the grammar seems a bit odd. In language we do not normally expect 'external' factors like lack of adequate control over one's breath, laryngitis, memory lapse etc. to determine the principles of sentence construction. Well, a Carnatic music event is neither a 'casual event' like a casual chunk of conversation nor a fully 'public event' in the sense of a fully rehearsed event, an art object in the Western sense. However, consider the case of a discourse meant as a formal lecture read off a written text and a discourse which is meant to be an informal discussion (a part of an ongoing argument). The sentence construction in the two discourses will definitely be quite distinct with the former attesting longer sentences with 'formal' connectives like 'nevertheless', 'on the other hand' etc. and the latter attesting shorter and sometimes incomplete sentences with more informal connectives like 'look here', 'hey, I didn't mean that', etc. It could be argued that the core grammars of both discourses are really the same with only the choice of sentence types and connectives being different. The point of difference between language and Carnatic music, it could be argued, is that in language, every user has occasion to choose from both types of discourse (among others) and hence it could be claimed that the grammar is not significantly affected by the nature of the discourse and that the actual output is only a matter of choice. In Carnatic music, this kind of distinction between types of discourse does not seem to exist. A performer, generally, sets the parameters of his/her style and once that is done, only peripheral factors vary depending on the discourse being a chamber music discourse or a concert hall one. By 'peripheral' factors I mean factors like the choice of compositions to be rendered, the decision to render a pallavi (an item involving mastery over rhythm), etc. The style has been set, so to speak, and the performer is not free to make major changes as it would involve issues pertaining to the identity of the artist.

Actually, a more relevant point of comparison for the idea of 'external' factors impinging on the grammar in language and Carnatic music would be pragmatic factors shaping the grammar both in language and Carnatic music. If we can show that pragmatic factors can and do shape the grammar of language, i.e. determining the constraint ranking of its grammar, then we would have shown that 'external' factors can and do determine the shape of the grammar of language and that the grammar of Carnatic music is no different from that of the grammar of language in allowing 'external' criteria to shape its grammar. Take the example of aspirated plosives in Sanskrit, Hindi,

Bangla and Tamil. As I have mentioned several times, aspiration in plosives (p, t, ʈ, c, k) and [b, d, ɖ, ɟ, g/ is a marked feature, i.e. it is more difficult to pronounce /p^h/ than /p/ and /b^h/ than /b/. This difficulty in pronunciation is a *pragmatic* markedness constraint. As this constraint is very high ranked in Tamil, a Sanskrit word like /p^hala/ is pronounced /paẓam/ 'fruit' and the word /b^hakti/ is pronounced /bakti/ 'devotion' by Tamilians. Here, markedness is ranked higher than faithfulness. Apart from this general markedness, comparatively speaking, aspirates are more difficult to pronounce at the end of words than when followed by vowels (when they are released fully). This type of markedness is called context-sensitive markedness. Sanskrit and Hindi rank faithfulness above this context-sensitive markedness and so aspirates are always fully articulated everywhere in these languages. However, in colloquial Bangla, while aspirates are faithfully pronounced when followed by a vowel, they are not pronounced when they occur at the end of a word, e.g. /bag/ 'tiger' but /bag^{h}er/ 'tiger (genitive)'. Notice that the total suppression of aspiration in Tamil and the partial suppression of aspiration word finally in Bangla are determined by pragmatic features, namely difficulty in pronunciation/perception of aspirates. Thus, we see that even the grammar of language can and is determined by 'external' (i.e. performance) factors. Now the case of Carnatic music is no different. I have given several examples in the previous chapters of raagas losing some of their marked features as part of the process of simplification and change. I had cited the example of raagas like Pantuvaraaɭi, Janaranjani and Saaveeri which have lost (some of) their raagam-specific features for many contemporary performers veering towards more RenScale renditions from earlier pitch wave or lowered pitch target value curves etc. These are examples of the pragmatic factor – the markedness constraint set RenScale determining the grammar of these raagas for contemporary performers.

I had mentioned briefly the role of external factors in determining the grammar of Carnatic music specially how the choice of performance style could set various aspects of the grammar of a performer. Let me take up the two factors for more extended discussion. Taking up performance style first, let me try and enumerate the distinct features of some of the styles that come to mind. To begin with, it would be reasonable to assume that at the two ends of the spectrum we have styles which can be classified as 'authentic' and 'light classical'. While the former is a serious attempt at maintaining many of the values of earlier varieties passed on from 'renowned' musicians of the past, the latter is an attempt at capturing large audiences with 'modern' taste – meaning an audience whose taste is very eclectic to include film music, north Indian classical music and sometimes even jazz. The latter attempts to woo more and more people to Carnatic music by playing down many of its arcane, outdated orthodoxy, eschewing unnecessary complex pitch variations, trying to hold the attention of the audience with fast (and faster) tempo rendering, more of feet thumping rhythm, etc. While many of these styles are anathema to many performers (including myself), the important function these performers play in making Carnatic music accessible to larger and larger audience groups cannot be denied. But for the service they render Carnatic music, the Carnatic music fraternity may very well drop below the critical threshold and eventually disappear as a living language (recall the earlier discussion in chapter 1, p. 10).

As for the former style, I reiterate the point that I have made several times, Carnatic music being an oral tradition, no claim to authenticity is to be taken at face value. Though the line of guru-siʃya (teacher-disciple) could be unbroken, change is something that is inevitable (see discussion in chapter 2). There are far too many instances of schools acquiring idiosyncratic tonal interpretation, musical phrases and 'distinct' rendering of compositions (see below, pp. 276–281) for one to believe implicitly in 'authenticity'. Despite the fact that claims of authenticity should be taken with a pinch of salt, nevertheless, it is quite obvious that in many cases the effort to preserve what was learnt is well-intentioned and therefore to be respected and taken as instances of 'authenticity' or at least, attempts at 'orthodoxy'. In this context, we can interpret the so called authentic style as an instance of ranking FAITHLEX above RENSCALE in particular lexicons without assuming that this particular instance of FAITHLEX to be *absolutely authentic*. Notice, FAITHLEX is a relative term, what the performer is faithful to is what he/she thinks is authentic (irrespective of his/her lapses of memory/incomplete learning/unintentional variation etc). I take it that a style is authentic/orthodox to the extent that it has that many FAITHLEX constraints in the de-composed lexicon of the performer, specially, in the I Set raagas. No more, no less. Keeping this discussion in mind, if we consider the 'authentic' style (though there are ever so many of these), we find that this style can never be fast paced as faster the tempo the lesser the details and claims to authenticity have to be substantiated with details. Thus we see that the so called 'authentic style' is a careful style, replete with details (read complex pitch movements), subtle rhythmic distinctions, etc. Thus we see that these two major classificatory heads define the orthodox and the liberal boundaries of contemporary Carnatic music.

Within this broad spectrum bounded by orthodoxy on one side and liberal thinking on the other, we have quite a wide variety of styles available to performers/listeners. One can aim to do one of several things with the audience, namely educate them, move then to tears, whip up their religious fervour, make them stamp their feet to the rhythm, soak them in sweetness, impress them with an aggressive rendering, etc. Let us look at each one of the above factors in some detail. If a performer takes on the role of a teacher, then he/she is aiming at demonstrating new techniques/ideas/compositions and at guiding the audience's taste. The performing style will have to be slow and deliberate, with perhaps, ideas/ new elements structured from the simple to the more complicated as the performance progresses and important ideas/elements may be repeated at regular intervals to reinforce them, etc. If the performer aims to move his/her audience to tears, once again, his/her rendering will be slow and deliberate with maximum emphasis on the emotive aspect of tonal renderings. To increase the emotive appeal, certain notes may be lengthened in an exaggerated fashion (with or without an emotional tremolo on the note) etc. If a performer aims to arouse the religious feelings of the audience, then he/she selects the kind of compositions that are amenable to such interpretation, conceives a religious theme for the performance with items selected and arranged in a specific order. Of course, for overt religious feelings to overflow, this planning must be combined with the kind of rendering that evokes emotional excess too. If a performer wants to get the audience to be energetically involved in the performance, the performer selects fast paced, familiar compositions, keeps the melodic lines as simple and uncomplicated as possible and the rhythm bold and obvious. Finally the last two styles namely the sweet/mellifluous styles and the aggressive style seem to have a gender bias with their own characteristics in contemporary Carnatic performances. While the former achieves an almost 'convent school educated style' of enunciation of the language text, the latter allows the language text to be mutilated (sometimes beyond recognition), the former is self-conscious, avoids emphasis and, specially the singers perform with a controlled voice (to be precise, avoiding a full throated rendering), the latter revels in creating thick and thin effects by punctuating the musical lines with loud emphatic prominence. In the contemporary scene, the former style is predominantly feminine and the latter masculine (broadly speaking, including instrumental styles). However, if we look back on the practices of the last fifty years, we find that this kind of gender polarity was not so obvious with many women singers of genius exhibiting a remarkable range of distinct styles. It is a pity that what women singers had gained when they had to literally take by force what was considered the male fortress in the past fifty years, producing a wide variety of remarkable women's style, is now being lost in unnecessary type casting of gender-based performance styles. One only has to consider the distinct styles of great women performers like M. S. Subbulakshmi, M. L. Vasantakumari, D. K. Pattamal, T. Brinda, Mani Krishnaswamy, Srinrangam Gopalaratnam to acknowledge the fact that women performers had carved a fairly large space for themselves which the women performers of the contemporary scene are gradually relinquishing. But fortunately, the tribe is not altogether lost as there are a few women singers who sing with a majestic voice, in a full throated manner.

I now turn to the other pragmatic criterion which determines style, namely MusMed. While discussing this criterion I will examine the nature of the performer's voice as well as the nature of instruments (and their social settings) which determine style. If a performer has an 'intractable' voice, then naturally complex pitch manoeuvers are ruled out automatically in favour of RenScale renderings. In addition, if he/she cannot render fast passages, what we have on hand is a stately, majestic style which has the gait of an elephant both in terms of speed and flexibility.[224] I am not denigrating this style; all I am saying is that this style is strictly determined by the limitations of the performer's voice. In fact, we must appreciate the genius of Carnatic music and the intelligence of the performer to create something positive and beautiful against all odds. I now turn to the instrumental aspect of MusMed. I will take up two distinct styles (there may be more) which arise as a consequence of the capability/limitation of the instrument (and in one case the social setting as well).

Let us look at the style of naadaswaram playing to begin with.[225] This reed instrument was really meant to accompany temple rituals. As temple rituals are very elaborate, lasting for several hours, this instrument had to be played over extended periods of time and to an audience which was ever changing, preoccupied with matters other than music. Because of this ambience, the naadaswaram players, I advance the tentative hypothesis, developed an 'expansive' style. The hallmarks of this 'expansive style' are lack of logical structuring of the entire discourse, phrases and even lines are allowed to be repeated several times over a period of time within the discourse, a grand disregard for the 'narrow' constraints of the rendering of notes/phrases and finally, the instrument allowed renderings at great speed over three octaves, a tremendously fast paced coverage of all the three octaves several times in a musical line. Musical discourses like aalaapanai and kalpanaa swaram cannot be assigned any logical structure as a) they are meant to be taken up for extended periods of time from a quarter of an hour to an hour and b) any structure will be lost to the ever changing audience. Similarly, if the discourse is to be extended for long periods, repetition cannot be avoided and finally, at great speed, complex tonal renderings had to be sacrificed.[226]

I will show how the typical naadaswaram style disregards the constraints governing the construction of musical phrases in I Set raagas and how in S Set raagas random RenScale combinations are attempted in this expansive style. The samples I demonstrate are based on a recording of a pre-eminent player of the first half of the twentieth century.

(1) Musical demonstration   [☉ 9.177]
  Kaamboodi aaroohaṇam:
  sa ri gu ma pa (di) ma gu pa di Sa
  Naadaswaram style
  // sa ri *gu ma pa di Sa* // // pa̤ di̤ sa ri *gu ma pa di Sa* //
  Kaamboodi avaroohaṇam
  Sa ni di pa ; Sa nu pa
  Naadaswaram style
  // [sa di̤ pa̤] [ri sa di̤ pa̤] [sa di̤ pa̤ di sa ri gu, ma gu]

(2) Musical demonstration   [☉ 9.178]
  S Set raagam Chaarukeesi
  Aarohaṇam: sa ri gu ma pa da ni Sa
  Naadaswaram style
  [sa gu pa ni]
  [pa ni Sa] [ni pa ni Sa] [ni pa ma gu]

Thus we see that the naadaswaram style of playing sets the performer free from many of the restrictions in the lexicon of I Set raagas and allows fast renderings and RenScale values to be camouflaged in fast tempo phrases. In fact, the naadaswaram style was such a liberating influence on vocalists in the mid twentieth century giving rise to several styles which are popular, vocal styles till date. In fact, the RenScale of Dhanyaasi that I demonstrated in the previous chapter (p. 248) owes its inspiration to the naadaswaram style of playing.

I next turn to a fretted instrument, namely the veena. If naadaswaram playing sacrificed complex pitch values at the altar of speed, the average veena playing sacrifices pitch complexity to the easier method of playing *on the fret*. As it is easier to play on the fret rendering RenScale tones than deflect the string to produce complex pitch patterns, many veena players sacrifice FAITHLEX to RENSCALE. The illustration below is based on authentic practices encountered in many styles of veena playing.

(3) Musical demonstration [⊙ 9.179]
Shankaraabharaṇam
scale: sa ri gu ma pa di nu
Fretted style of veena playing
[pa di ri sa] [di nu gu ri] [ri gu pa ma]
[ri gu ma di nu] [gu ma di nu Ri] [ma di nu Ri Gu]

In some cases, even orthodox veena players resort to such fretted playing in their aalaapanai and taanam. Since this style is accepted practice in contemporary Carnatic music, all that is being said here is that the style in this case is dictated by the nature of the instrument. I am not saying that these renderings are ungrammatical; but they find no place in my style. There is yet another technique which many veena players attempt, namely playing on two strings at the same time. Needless to say, such renderings allow only RenScale values and that my style does not allow such experiments.

9.3. Lexical differences

So far we saw the choice of style and the limitations of the medium determining the grammar of the performer. I now turn to the differences arising from the lexicon of Carnatic music. In language, speakers have distinct preferences with respect to pronunciation of words (e.g. words like 'schedule', 'economic' etc.), choice of lexical items (e.g. 'search/look for', 'return/hand in' etc.) and also syntactic structures (e.g. 'Ram gave Seetha a book' vs 'Ram gave a book to Seetha'). As in language, in Carnatic music too, users may access non-overlapping lexicons. I demonstrate below some musical phrases which are distinct to schools of Carnatic music, not necessarily attested in all styles of contemporary Carnatic music. The examples I give below (ten in all) are by no means exhaustive. They merely vouch for the differences between different styles of Carnatic music. The point that needs to be laboured is the one regarding grammaticality. As in dialectal differences, it is not a point of grammaticality for two dialects to have non-overlapping dictionaries, so too in Carnatic music, one should not assume any of the examples given below to be 'ungrammatical' or contrary to Carnatic music theory (which any way has no authority to consider any current usage ungrammatical). A particular phrase, or tonal contour may not be attested in all schools of Carnatic music; but that does not make it less grammatical in any sense of the word. As long as a school/style which is practiced/has a listener following which endorses a particular usage, that usage is grammatical in that particular context. No performer/listener/authority has the right to brand it as ungrammatical (following the practice in the language science). Therefore, the instances I list below are not cases of 'deviant' behaviour; merely behaviour not attested in all schools of Carnatic music.

Another point that needs to be made is that these are not instances of what I have called 'minor phrases' in chapter 7 (p. 187). The sequences which I have termed 'minor phrases' are those which are attested across schools and which are allowed to be rendered only once or twice in the entire musical discourse. The instances I give below are, first of all, not attested across schools. Secondly, they may or may not be 'minor' phrases allowed to be rendered only once or twice in the entire discourse. They are, rather, practices which do not find sanction in all schools and hence not attested in all schools of Carnatic music.

Here are a few (precisely ten) examples of such school specific practices. I assume that they are entered in the lexicons of the schools which attest them and not in the lexicons of other schools. All the examples given below are backed by either documentary evidence in the form of a commercially available prerecorded cassette or a public broadcast on the All India Radio by an established artist or attested in my own practice.[227]

I begin with a musical phrase from the raagam Aahiri.

(4) Musical demonstration [⊙ 9.180][228]
Raagam Aahiri
[pa di ni Sa,] [Sa ni, da pa]

The use of the dhaivatam 'di' is not generally attested for the raagam Aahiri in many schools as the dhaivatam that is sanctioned for this raagam is 'da'. But some schools of music allow the use of the dhaivatam 'di' in the ascent, in particular, this sequence. Thus this is an instance of a style/school-specific entry that is part of the lexical entry of the raagam Aahiri for the style/school in question. However, even in such styles the choice of 'di' in the ascent is limited to a few phrases.

Here is another musical phrase which is attested in some schools of Carnatic music in the raagam Bhairavi.

(5) Musical demonstration [⊙ 9.180]
Raagam Bhairavi
[Sa, ni pa ma gi ri]

The raagam Bhairavi for most practitioners does not allow one to skip the dhaivatam 'da' in the descent. This phrase is attested in a vocal style, also in the accompanying violin playing (in the pre-recorded cassette of an established artist who was popular till the seventies and eighties) and can be traced to the earlier naadaswaram style of playing (which, as I said earlier, has scant regard for rules of ascent and descent in raagas). This instance of a 'liberal' interpretation of the raagam is a part of the 'liberal/expansive' naadaswaram style which influenced this school of vocal music in the early half of the twentieth century.

I next turn to a phrase which is attested in my own style in the raagam Tooḍi.

(6) Musical demonstration [⊙ 9.180]
Tooḍi
[da pa ma gi ri gi, ra sa]

This is an instance of a truly minor phrase in my style as it is attested only once (near the end) in a discourse. For the raagam Tooḍi, generally, only the riʃabham 'ra' is allowed and not 'ri'. Allow me to hazard a guess as to how this phrase crept into this raagam to begin with. The last saṅgati (variation) of the pallavi of the Tyaagaraajaa kriti Koluvamaragada, in my view, attests this riʃabham although in fleeting.

(7) Musical demonstration [⊙ 9.181]
Koluvamaragada: Tooḍi: Aadi: Tyaagaraajaa
// ; , ni - ni da ma, / <u>ma gi *gi*</u>, gi da - <u>da pa pa ma pa da pa da</u>
ko lu va ma ra ga da
// ma pa...

The note transcribed as gi in italics is actually a RenScale ri (the pitch values can be easily ascertained in my own playing); but no one in his/her right senses will transcribe it as 'ri' as 'ri' is not a part of the scale of this raagam. But what has happened is that the two interpretations of 'gi' played from 'ri' are the reduced 'gi' and the RenScale 'ri' from which the following glide starts. This practice has been transferred to the 'minor' musical phrase that I mentioned above.

Turning next to the raagam Aṭaaṇaa here are two distinct sets of phrases belonging to my school and another school.

(8) Musical demonstration [⊙ 9.180]
Aṭaaṇaa
['di Sa,]
The grammatically sanctioned phrase 'ni Sa' is rendered almost as red.ni which may be interpreted as either 'di' or 'ni'.

(9) Musical demonstration [⊙ 9.180]
Aṭaaṇaa
Sa Ri Gu, Ma Ri]

The normative phrase attested in many performers with respect to the raagam Aṭaaṇaa is [Sa Gu, Ma Ri]. But this particular player rendered this phrase as notated above in (9) several times during the course of the aalaapanai. First of all, this is deemed to be a 'minor' phrase and hence to be rendered only once (or minimally) during the entire discourse. In this discourse, this particular, renowned, player renders this phrase several times attesting to its major status for this player.

(10) Musical demonstration [⊙ 9.180]
Sahaanaa
[pa ma <gu ma ri]

The lowered 'gu' in the descent for Sahaanaa is a beautiful practice that I encountered in the playing style of an elderly veena artist I much admire. Distinctly, this lowered 'gu' occurs only in the phrases which are in the descent thus allowing the raagam three different 'gu's, a RenScale gu, a lowered 'gu' (which must be actually an aug.gi) and an aug.gu as well.

(11) Musical demonstration [⊙ 9.180]
Kamaas
['nu Sa] [Ri 'Gi, Ri Sa]

The raagam Kamaas usually selects the scale [sa ma gu ma ni di ni pa di nu Sa / Sa ni di pa ma gu ma, ri gu sa]. But this unusual phrase occurs in a rare jaavaḷi (a fast paced love song) popular in our school attesting the accidental note 'gi'.

(12) Musical demonstration [⊙ 9.180]
Karaharapriyaa
[Sa (nu) di ni di] [ma (gu) ri gi ri]

The raagam Karaharapriyaa selects only [sa ri gi ma pa di ni Sa] as its members. Yet many performers (my style included) indulge in a rare shadow occurrence of (nu) and (gu) in phrases like the ones indicated above.

(13) Musical demonstration [⊙ 9.180]
Beegaḍaa
Sa Nu di pa

The ultra-orthodox statement of Beegaḍaa would include only phrases like [Sa nu pa di, pa], if at all.[229] In my school, this phrase is sanctioned because the great Veena Dhanam has included this phrase in her rendering of the varṇam.

(14) Musical demonstration [⊙ 9.180]
Suraṭṭi
[ri ma pa di; ni (Sa) ni di pa]

The raagam Suraṭṭi, normally does not allow 'di' to occur after 'pa' in the ascent. But this distinctly long 'di' in this phrase is attested in the renderings of padams (love songs rendered in slow tempo) in this raagam in a certain style of Carnatic music.

The differences in the lexicons of different styles, it must be noticed, are all with respect to I Set raagas. I cannot think of such lexical differences for genuine S Set raagas across schools. For instance, there are no such differences with respect to genuine S Set raagas like Lathaangi, Naagasvaraaḷi etc. The reason is not far to seek. S Set raagas lack specific construals for Tone, Sequence and Phrase and so no 'innovation' can be entered in their lexicons which are really empty idiosyncratically being merely networked scales. However, in I Set raagas the lexicons are richly specified for specific tonal, sequential and phrasal phenomena in addition to the *Amb constraints shaping the construals actively. And, innovations, new ideas can be entered in a lexicon only if the structure of the lexicon permits them. This is why, innovative pitch renderings are attested only in I Set raagas and not in S Set raagas. However, even within a style, it cannot be predicted on the basis of any I Set raagam admitting an innovation that such innovations will be allowed in other I Set raagas too. For instance, in my style, while Karaharapriyaa admits the fleeting notes 'nu' and 'gu' as discussed above, fleeting 'nu' and 'mi' are not allowed in Moohanam (which other styles allow). Thus while only I Set raagas initiate innovation, the actual occurrences of innovations cannot be predicted.

Thus we see that there is strong documentary evidence for distinct musical phrases in the lexicons of different styles. So far we have seen differences in style arising out of different performance strategies or the constraints of the medium (voice or instrument) and differences in the lexical entries of different styles. So differences in styles can be accounted for in terms of the lexical differences or the differential ranking of the constraints that are a part of the grammar of Carnatic music.

In the following section, the last section of the book, I take a yet closer look at two distinct styles which I call Concert Hall A and Chamber Music A being the style of the renowned singer Sanjay Subrahmanyan and my own style respectively.

9.4. A tale of two styles

In this section I take up the task of comparing two distinct styles of Carnatic music, namely the concert style of Sanjay Subrahmanyan and my style which is a chamber music style. Before taking up the detailed analysis of our two styles of rendering aalaapanai and taanam in the raagam Kaanaḍaa, I wish to lay out the framework of the comparison, the rationale of the prototypes of the two styles etc. I claim that there are broad, irreconcilable, differences in the two styles which make them distinct in the first place. I wish to establish these differences to begin with.

Let us go over the broad differences between the Concert Hall Style (CH) and the Chamber Music (CM) Style which are attributable to the venue of the recitals. While performing for a large audience, the performer cannot afford to address his/her music to any section of the audience but must make an attempt at reaching out to all the sections of the audience. A CH recital must have pace and variety, as it must cater to the tastes of all the sections in the audience. The moment an artist begins to pay more attention to any one aspect of Carnatic music, he/she will begin to lose some sections of the potential audience. For instance, if the artist likes to specialize in rare compositions, a large part of the audience will cease to attend his/her recitals. Similarly, if an artist is occupied with mathematical exploration, once again, a large section of the audience will feel left out. Therefore, a performer who wishes to reach out to a large audience has to plan his/her recital with care. Selection of compositions must be drawn from well known ones with occasionally an unknown piece thrown in; a mix of languages, largely well known raagas with an occasional rare raagam selected just once perhaps, etc.

A CM recital, on the other hand, has a more intimate ambience. The performer can address his/her music to people who show their appreciation more openly and something like a musical soliloquy becomes possible. Since the audience's undivided attention is there for the performer, she/he can afford to make the structure of the musical discourse more complex in all respects. Depending on the audience, the performer can plan the recital to include rare compositions, rare raagas, rare taaḷas, etc. A CM recital can be a teaching experience, exposing the audience to new ideas.

Thus the objectives of the two types of recitals are fairly distinct and therefore, in principle, the two types of musical discourses ought to be distinct in approach and execution. However, as I said earlier, not many artists start out as CM artists as almost all artists have ambitions of CH exposure. It is a simple matter of economics and social success. Thus, in the contemporary scene, there are not too many genuine CM artists – there are only the not so successful artists who do CM since that is better than not performing at all. This being the case, we do not see much of a difference in the thinking, planning and execution in the so-called CH styles and the so-called CM styles now a days.

However, I can say with justifiable pride that I am fortunate that my musical lineage can be traced to an artist who chose to be a chamber music artist, deliberately moulding her style to the requirements of her musical genius. It is not purely accidental that the practitioners of this school have also chosen to take up Carnatic music not as a profession but as an object of non-professional dedication. Therefore, the original objectives laid out by the founder of this style – Veena Dhanam – have not been lost till date.

I will now take up the issue of what constitutes the difference in the *prototypes* of the two styles when it comes to the content of a musical line. As in a Carnatic music recital, we start our discussion with the varṇam. Listen to the renderings of the first line of the great Beegaḍaa varṇam by Veenai Kuppayyer in aadi Taaḷam, first in the prototypical CH style and then in the CM style.

(15) Musical demonstration[230] [⊙ 9.183]

Beegaḍaa varṇam: Concert Hall Style

// di pa ma, gu ri sa, - sa nu di, di pa sa, sa,

in ta jaa la

/ sa, sa nu gu ri gu, - ma ma pa gu ma ri gu ma

mu jee

// pa, ma di, pa Sa nu - di pa Sa ni di Ri Sa,

si tee

/ pa di pa ni, di, pa - ma, gu, ri gu ma pa

ma ni daa ḷu du ra

Beegaḍaa varṇam: Chamber Music Style[231]

// di pa pa pa ma, pa - ma gu ri, sa sa

in nta

/ Sa; ri sa nu di di - pa di, pa sa,

ja la

// sa, pa sa sa nu - sa, gu ri gu, ;

mu jee

/ ma ma pa, di pa ma; pa - ma gu ri, gu, gu ma

si tee

// pa, pa ma pa - di pa Sa nu

ma ni

/ di pa Sa nu - di Ri Sa,

taa

// pa di pa di - >ni di; ni di pa

ḷu

/ ma gu ma; pa ma gu gu ma - ma ri gu gu ma pa,

du ra

A cursory look at the notation is sufficient to arrive at the conclusion that the musical line of the CH style has flow, in the sense that the melody is not impeded with too many complex note interpretations/musical phrases allowing it for speedier renderings. On the other hand, the musical line of the CM style is rich in details which can never get rendered in faster tempo. What is lost by way of over all tempo of a musical line is more than made up, in my opinion, with many more pitch 'events', complexities/details and subtle differences of rendering, etc. For instance, take the several occurrences of the note 'ma' in this musical line, the number of pitch interpretations of this note are undoubtedly greater in the CM style than in the CH style. Take the instance of the first occurrence of this note in the musical line, for example.

While the CH style has the standard, normal aug.ma pitch curve for this note, the CM style has a flat, RenScale ma which is surprising for this raagam. To dare to start this varṇam with a RenScale ma when the expectation is that of an aug.ma pitch curve is typical of a musical style where you expect the audience to pay minute attention to details which will be lost on a large audience. In a manner of speaking, this varṇam sets the standard for our style. Of course, we the present practitioners do not have genius to match her phrase for phrase. My thinking has been heavily influenced by her rendering but, I am fully aware that my rendering must be but a poor shadow of her brilliance.

We can safely say that the two styles have different range of expressions starting from the tone, to the sequence, phrase and musical line. There is a world of difference in the output that is aimed at in the two styles. Each one is moulded by its own concerns and limitations. While the CH style aims at pleasing a large audience, the CM style aims at making its small audience sit up – pay attention to every nuance that is rendered.

(16) Musical demonstration [⊙ 9.184]
Shankaraacaaryam: Shankaraabharaṇam: Aadi: Subbaraama Diikshitar: Version Concert Hall A

```
                                             *     *
// ; , pa - pa ma ma, gu, / ; ri gu ri, - sa du ; nu ;
     sha nka          raa                          caa

  *
// sa , ; - ; ri sa / nu sa ri gu - ma, ; // ri gu ma
  ryam      sri              mad
```

Shankaraacaaryam: Chamber Music Style A

```
// ; ; , pa, du pa - pa ma ma, gu gu ri gu,
        sha        nka         raa
/ ma gu, ri ri sa - sa sa, nu di nu
                    caa
// sa, nu sa nu sa - ; , ri; gu
      yam                 sri
/ ri, gu ri sa sa, nu sa ri - gu ma, pa, di pa
                                       mad
// ma, pa ma gu ri gu ma
```

Once again notice the difference in the contents of the musical lines. While the CH style has a flowing musical line with minimal musical idioms, e.g.

'pa ma ma,', the CM style is replete with musical idioms. Another point worth noting is the emphatically marked rhythmic break in the middle of the line in the CH style where the three instances of emphatic prominence (marked with asterisks) make the nature of the rhythm loud and clear. This ending of two notes of three moras each taking off after two moras of a beat with the final note on the beat (the part of the line in italics) is a well known rhythmic device which is obligatory in a pallavi (the main piece in a concert where after an elaborate aalaapanai and taanam a line of music is taken up for elaborate rendering). In a pallavi where rhythmic criteria are of primary importance, this is necessary. But if this device is employed elsewhere, it signals an unsubtle approach to rhythm in compositions. Notice that in the CM style this device is eschewed altogether. However this does not mean that this style does not employ rhythmic devices at all. It does as can be seen in the ending of the musical line where a three mora excess (as the line starts after three moras) is made up with the interesting rhythmic phrase in bold which starts one mora before the beat giving us an interesting 1+1+2 sequence of rhythmic phrases in fast tempo. The point worth noting is that the rhythmic sequence in the CM style requires close listening for appreciating the rhythmic subtlety.

Table 1. Prototypical differences between the two styles

	Concert Hall	Chamber Music
a.	Smooth flow of the musical line	Eventful musical line
b.	Standard interpretation of pitch values	Critical of orthodoxy at every level
c.	Limited range of pitch interpretations	Fully exploiting the pitch ranges
d.	Minimize idioms	Idioms are the staple of musical thought
e.	Rhythmic phrasing boldly executed	Subtlety in the execution of rhythmic phrasing

To sum up my analyses of the two prototypes, what we have is the characteristics of the two styles laid out as a table above. Once again, I would like to reiterate the point made earlier that these differences are prototypical differences, over and above the choice of performing style, musical medium and individual lexical differences.

Thus we see that the irreconcilable differences in the two approaches towards musical content is firmly established on the basis of the nature of the musical discourse. One is like a dramatic soliloquy or an aside and the other is like an overheard piece of introspection; one is like a painting on a large canvas and the other is like a miniature painting.

Now I take up two individual styles, namely Sanjay Subrahmanyan's and mine, which I call CHA and CMA respectively. Listen to the Kaanaḍaa aalaapanai done by Sanjay Subrahmanyan and me.

(17) Musical demonstration [⊙ 9.185]
Kaanaḍaa aalaapanai: CHA: Sanjay Subrahmanyan

(18) Musical demonstration [⊙ 9.187]
Kaanaḍaa aalaapanai: CMA: K. G. Vijayakrishnan

The two factors which are strikingly different in the two styles are the intensity range displayed and the way the note 'gi' is handled. While in CHA the intensity range is fairly high ranging from barely audible 'thin' effects to fairly loud emphatic effects in certain musical phrases, the intensity range is narrow in CMA with the intensity modulation being very subtle. This can be directly attributed to the ambience of the two styles, a large hall allowing greater loudness effects and a smaller hall not requiring such effects. A further implication is that this style allows greater scope for exploiting expressive effects with repetition, greater emphasis etc. Here are a few examples of this in this instance of CHA.

(19) Greater intensity/emphatic effects in CHA

a.
     *   *   *
[ma ma, ma] [di di, di] [ni ni, ni]
[Sa Ri Gi,] [Ri Sa ni pa]

b.
                      *
[ri gi ma pa] [ni, pa gi,]
RenScale gi

c.
*   *   *
[ni Ri Sa] [ni Ri Sa] [ni Ri Sa] [ni pa ma]

Such effects are systematically absent in CMA.

But with respect to everything else, the two styles are different not because of the nature of the venue but because of the details that go into the two styles. Here are a few stylistic differences between the two styles highlighted.

(20) Stylistic differences between the two styles

a. The note 'gi is handled differently in the two styles. While CHA has a tendency to use a higher pitch value for 'gi' or a RenScale value or a 'gi' pulled down from 'ma', CMA uses a pitch curve gi and also pitch spike gi to exploit the different 'gi's allowed in the raagam

b. CHA has a very beautiful pitch realization of the note 'ma' as illustrated in the musical line given below:

  *
  [*ma* ; ;] [pa, di pa, di] [ma pa di pa] [ma gi,]
  {'ma' interpreted as a note pitch curve on 'ma' roughly as [ma, pa ma]}

c. CMA has several unorthodox practices. Firstly, it attests the use of the shadow notes 'nu' and 'gu' in several phrases.

d. CMA also attests an unusual interpretation of the note 'pa' with an inverted note pitch curve on 'pa' starting from 'di' in the phrase [pa ; ;] [di, ni, Sa ni ni, pa].

Finally, a very important point for me is the lack of clichés in both styles. For instance, an often encountered phrase in Kaanaḍaa is [gi ma pa ; ri] which is conspicuously absent in both styles. It must be clear to every one by now why I chose this particular CH style. Though the differences are irreconcilable, it is a style that has much that I admire.

I now turn to the taanam in the two styles.

(21) Musical demonstration [⊙ 9.186]
Kaanaḍaa taanam: CHA: Sanjay Subrahmanyan

(22) Musical demonstration [⊙ 9.188]
Kaanaḍaa taanam: CMA: Vijayakrishnan

Listening to the taanams, we find the same distinctions that were in place for the aalaapanai attested, only in a more emphasized manner. Actually, as is well known in the Carnatic music fraternity, the taanam is meant specially for the veena. This is exemplified in CMA by the sheer variety of phrasing and the flow of different rhythmic patterns in different tempos succeeding each other in a most unpredictable manner.

The stylistic differences between the two styles are presented below in a systematic manner as was done in the case of the aalaapanai.

(23) Stylistic differences between the two styles in the taanam

Concert Hall A:

a. All the differences noticed in the aalaapanai are attested here too. For instance, here too, while CHA has a slightly higher value for 'gi' than CMA which has an aug.gi rendering with a pitch spike 'gi' thrown in occasionally. And, here too, CMA attests unorthodox shadow notes 'gu' and 'nu' in some phrases.
b. The range of emphatic effects in CHA is much wider than in CMA, as expected. The interesting factor is the range of strategies employed to carry out these effects.
   Here are a few:
   i. several iterations of short phrases, e.g. [ri sa ri]
   ii. using the 'jaṉṯai' type of emphasis specific to taanam, e.g. [ma 'ma, pa] {[ni sa ni *ni*] [pa ni pa *pa*] [ma pa ma *ma*]} with extra emphasis on the phrase final notes (in italics)
   iii. adding an emotional tinge to emphatic phrases rendered as unadorned RenScale notes in combination with shadow notes (chaaya swaras), e.g.

   *　*　*
   [Ga; (Ma)] [Ri ; (Gi)] [Sa ; (Ri)]
c. The taanam is spiced with unexpected new, untypical phrases, e.g. [ri sa ri gi ma] [ri sa ri pa *pa ma ma*,]
d. The finale is a long drawn out sequence of phrases around 'Sa', 'pa' and 'sa' done four times each time slower than the previous one – truly dramatic.

Chamber Music A:

e. The common place iterative taanam phrases are altogether absent or kept to the bare minimum, e.g. [gi gi ri,] [ri sa ri,]
f. The rhythmic phrases are never repeated several times at a go and the phrasing is ever changing, necessitating very close listening.
g. The tempo of rhythmic phrases also change unpredictably, e.g. [pa di ni, Sa ni ni pa ma gi] [[pa di ni] pa, ma]
h. Rendering of parallel phrases in the upper and the lower register of the octave.

i. As expected, the finale is less dramatic than in CHA with just two rounds of phrases around 'Sa', 'pa' and 'sa'.

9.5. Consequences of raagam music

The major thrust of this book was the argument that Carnatic music is a language-like system with a comparable architecture of its grammar and similar concerns with respect to the role of the individual in the collective system. Just like language, we said in chapter 2, Carnatic music too admits two different kinds of creativity, namely the type mentioned in linguistics circles which we may call the *every day miracle of creativity* which enables every user to produce and comprehend sequences never before attested. But in addition to this kind of creativity, Carnatic music, like language, admits the poetic type of creativity. I would like to sum up the argument for this book by taking a closer look at these two types of 'creativity'.

Let me take up the issue of the 'every day miracle of creativity' in language and Carnatic music first. As in language where every language event is a 'new' event; every discourse is new; so in Carnatic music too every musical event/discourse is 'new'. In language the newness of the event/discourse is signaled by the individual user's idiolect characteristics (the peculiar way in which sounds are articulated – the intonational melody characteristic of the user etc.)/her/his dialectal characteristics besides his/her world view. In fact, in day to day life, we go by these factors to classify individuals/recognize voices etc. In Carnatic music too, one recognizes the individual in an event by the voice/phrasal idiosyncrasies/mannerisms/special ideas etc. Thus every accredited performer is like the user of a recognized dialect. Carnatic music being an art form, this 'dialect' is the creative effort of an outstanding individual. But, unlike the Western notions of 'art', this is still an ephemeral musical event – not a self conscious object of art created for posterity. Every musical event is an ephemeral event, ever changing – like the dialogues of every day life and not sacred or quotable, unlike the objects of Western art. That is why the Carnatic music events can never be governed by copyright laws. Every member of the Carnatic music fraternity has the right to borrow (without acknowledging) any idea, phrase, sequence, composition, etc. In fact, in the true spirit of Carnatic music, an event is ephemeral and its reproduction is valueless.[232]

But then, just as in the public domain elsewhere, in Carnatic music too, artists are ranked by listeners. What could the basis for this ranking be? Why is one musician ranked higher than the other? The answer lies in our total constraint ranking advanced in chapter 7. The ranking is based on distinct features of the performer, the style – popular/academic/orthodox/...medium pleasant/fast paced/slow/intractable/etc. Once these preferences are set, the overall evaluation automatically produces the ranking for that particular user of Carnatic music. And ranking is based on collective evaluation. But fortunately, evaluation is not always only quantitative. Evaluation could be based on qualitative responses to artists by the 'more' knowledgeable of the Carnatic music fraternity. But whatever the nature of the evaluation, qualitative or quantitative, the event itself is ephemeral and not quite equivalent to the Western canon of an 'art object' which is a self-conscious object standing in relation to the art tradition. The idea of an artist defining herself/himself 'against' a tradition which is so typical of Western Art is totally alien to the world of Carnatic music. In the Carnatic music world the artist does not have to break with the tradition/redefine the tradition as the artist has to in the Western world. That is why the typical Carnatic musician is not a rebel (as the typical Western artist is – if he/she is to be taken seriously) but one who creatively re-interprets tradition – in the sense of a dialect being a creative re-interpretation of a language. The creativity of the artist in Carnatic music lies in the fact that, unlike language where this dialectal difference is a collective/unconscious process, in Carnatic music, it is a product of a creative individual's self-conscious effort. Here lies the artistic greatness of an S. Balachnder (veena player) who forged his own style, a G. N. Balasubrahmanyan who started a school of music (although it was heavily indebted to the naadaswaram style of playing etc.). I shall assume that every Carnatic musician of 'standing' has forged his/her own dialect of Carnatic music and therein lies his/her call to greatness.

It must be noted that what is enthroned here is not any specific *art event* but the 'competence' of an artist. Just as in language, a user is evaluated on the basis of his/her competence (abstract, unconscious knowledge of his his/her language) and not the actual performance. The performance could be marred by several performance factors like 'nervousness', unpreparedness', 'hostility of the interlocutor', etc. Thus we see that a genuine Carnatic music event is an ephemeral event which is evaluated by a set of ranked constraints where the ranking changes from individual to individual (style-to-style) as in dialects in language.

Thus we see that an object of Carnatic music is not really comparable to any object of Western art. While the former is an ephemeral event, the latter is a self-conscious object for exhibition; while the former is an overheard event, the latter is a public statement; while the former has a continuous link with tradition, the latter has to make a conscious break with tradition. Questions of creativity are not major landmarks of break up of communication in Carnatic music as they are in the Western tradition. As in language, generations of Carnatic music users do not break away from established practices just to establish their individuality as artists do in the West. Artists in the Carnatic tradition have a continuing tradition to uphold which is greater than any individual ego. Thus we see that the first type of creativity – the every day event of creativity – is no mean achievement. Keeping in mind the twenty first century Western canons of art, the fact that Carnatic music has stood up firmly *against* the standard Western canons of art – unlike the other art forms of modern India is to be noted with a special word of appreciation. Thus, a Carnatic music recital does not warrant a scrutiny on the lines of a Western music recital (mere interpretation); and at the same time it does not warrant a critique as an object of art (a new composition) in the Western canon of art. I am very happy to say that there exists at least one major art domain in India where the hegemony of Western/colonial canons of art do not hold sway.

Let us now turn to the second type of creativity in Carnatic music. Recall our earlier discussion in chapter 7 regarding Content Construal. Specifically, the construals 'checking for new sequences', 'checking for new phrasing', 'wit' and 'imagery' are relevant for the discussion here (chapter 7, section 7.6, pp. 207–214). The first place where we would have to look for these is in compositions (as there are no recordings of earlier performers). Even among compositions, one finds creativity of this type which attests one of the above mentioned construals mainly in the great composers, namely Uuttukkaaḍu Veenkaṭasubbayyar, Pallavi Goopalayyar, Tyaagaraajaa, Muttuswaami Diikshitar, Shyaamaa Shaastri and Subbaraaya Shaastri and also Ksheetragnya. In their oevre, as we know of it today, both in terms of musical structure and musical ideas we find sufficient examples of the poetic type of creativity. Each composer has a unique musical structure of the composition (as I have observed earlier) and there are many instances of distinct musical phrasing in their compositions. Taking up the distinct types of compositions first, it is stating the obvious that each of these composers had a unique approach to the structure of the composition vis-à-vis the musical line, the parts of the composition, etc. The examples cited below are a proof of this statement. It is unfortunate that I am not able to substantiate this statement with matching musical demonstrations for two reasons. Firstly, this section of the book was an after thought. Secondly, even if I had thought of it earlier, we could not have managed to demonstrate all of them in our MP3 musical demonstrations as they would have taken up too much time/space.

(24) Compositions in the raagam Kalyaaṇi by the major composers
a. Maadhava Aadi Uuttukkaaḍu Veenkaṭasubbayyar
b. Niiducaraṇa Aadi Pallavi Goopalayyar
c. Sundari ni Aadi Tyaagaraajaa
d. Abhayaambaa Aadi Muttuswaami Diikshitar
e. Tallininnu nera Tisra Tripuṭai Shyaamaa Shaastri
f. Kaantimatiim Rupakam Subbaraaya Shaastri
g. Kaddarivagalamaa Tisra Tripuṭai Ksheetragnya

The structure of the composition is different in each one of the compositions above and, not only that, musical phrases are also distinct in each one of them. Thus the closest that Carnatic music ever got to the Western canon of signaling the individual artist is in the remarkable output of these great composers. In addition to creating different musical structures, each of these composers had added something to the lexicon of Kalyaaṇi as their unique contribution in terms of musical phrasing/the way the note is held, etc. This is a topic of another book and I will not go into further details here. The point that I am trying to make is that this intense degree of creativity where every artist was conscious of all the other artists' output brought out an intense self awareness in the composers. This artistic endeavour clearly underlined the role of the individual artist in the artistic tradition and even without any clearly spelt out canon, they had forged their own form and their own idiom. It is a credit to the Carnatic music system that they did not have to lose any of the fraternity in the process of establishing their own style. My understanding of the situation is that the Carnatic music system allowed individual artists to take liberties where there was a lacuna in the system or where the system was silent about a certain practice. For instance, the composition in (24f) attests a new way of rendering the note 'ri' not attested in any other composition.[233] As I see it, these great composers were great thinkers, who were aware of current practices, and they made their own statements where they felt that the raagam would allow such an addition. One must be clear that even here, what one has is not quite a Western canon of art where the individual has the right to deal in any way he/she chooses with the tradition – clean break, stand it on its head, etc. What we have here in the Golden age of Carnatic music is a composer creating his own dialect of composition and the raagam as well. That is why, even this type of creativity is not contrary to the grammar but an extension. Poetic creativity becomes possible when the artist is intensely aware of the artistic scene and when there is scope for the individual to manipulate the lexicon of Carnatic music.

The post-trinity stage set in an orthodoxy which duly stamped out this kind of creativity in Carnatic music. This is a thesis that is worth a separate dissertation or a book. But what I would like to say here is that, subsequent to the Golden Age of Carnatic music what we had was an age of orthodoxy which went strictly by the aaroohaṉam and aavaroohaṉam, which lacked imagination, and which stamped out individual differences that went against it. Unfortunately, this is the voice of the majority which dictates the norms. The freedom that the individual artist had as a genuine member of the Carnatic fraternity is now lost because of this hegemony of 'prescriptive grammar'. And the true nature of Carnatic music as a language-like system is under attack. Unless artists wake up and throw their collective gauntlet challenging orthodoxy, nothing meaningful will be achieved.

However, I would like to point out that it was in the one and only genuine chamber music style that all these prescriptive dictats were challenged. Veena Dhanam took on the entire orthodoxy in her 78 rpm recordings facilitated by Ranga Ramanuja Ayyangar. One just has to listen to her rendering of Beegaḍaa varṉam, her Tooḍi slookam, her Kamaas jaavaḷi to understand what her engagements with the orthodoxy was. Take her Gauḷa rendering as part of the Gana raagamaalika taanam; the niʃaadam that she renders is unique. Similarly her rendering of a miniscule aalaapanai for Broovabaaramaa in Bahudaari is very revealing; she creates her own idioms – no questions asked.

The point that I wish to make is that while we, the Carnatic music fraternity, do not toe the line of the Western artistic canons, it would be desirable to evolve our own critical norms for evaluating creativity in Carnatic music. We just have to look at the post-trinity output, by and large, to see how the system has succumbed to sycophancy. All the post-trinity composers follow blindly the Tyaagarajaa format of composition with or without the added fast tempo lines on the lines of Muttuswaami Diikshitar (and that too without the finesse of that great composer.) That there has been no major re-thinking on the nature of the composition for the last one hundred years is a sad reflection on the Carnatic music scene. The post-trinity scenario was a major imitative scenario. Tyaagaraajaa's disciples/grand disciples etc. saw to it that his model was adopted for new ventures. Ever since the trinity and the major composers, no new ideas have been added to the lexicon.

As opposed to the Western, fractured view of tradition where every generation has to define itself anew, in Carnatic music, the need to be different is not so overwhelming. Just as in language, every generation of language users would be changing the language in ever so many small ways, so too in Carnatic music, every user (of standing) would be doing that in ever so small ways; however this act of creativity should not be devalued vis-à-vis creativity in the Western framework of art. But sadly, in the field of Carnatic music, there has been a very serious attempt at stamping out any effort to rebel against a prescriptive tradition.

In the final count, I would like to sum up the scene thus: Composers, who should exemplify 'poetic creativity' in Carnatic music have not been visible in plenty; performers who can defy orthodoxy are almost non-existent. In such a scenario, how is it possible for creativity to flourish in Carnatic music? There is no room for creativity, only scope for polishing one's concert hall poise. Thus we see that, of late, the performance/presentation factors of Carnatic music have come to the fore; what matters is the packaging, not so much the content/the competence of the artist. Carnatic music becoming more performance-oriented is indeed an unfortunate development. It means that it is no longer a spontaneous event like everyday language, but a well rehearsed performance where every detail has been pre-meditated, thoroughly rehearsed and the attention is more on performance values like stage appearance, sound enhancement (more often than not over-enhancement), a mechanical (almost factory line) approach to concert planning and execution. Thus, along with prescriptivism, this concern for performance values have stamped out creativity of both kinds from the contemporary scene.

9.6. Conclusion

In this chapter we saw that the differences between any two styles can be captured as a consequence of several interacting factors, namely performance style, performer style, medium, lexical differences and finally ranking/reranking of constraints both grammatical and stylistic. The brief comparison of two distinct styles bore out this claim in every way, listed in (20) and (23) above. For instance, if the set of constraints pertaining to emphatic prominence are reconstituted to include new strategies mentioned in (20) and (23) above and ranked high, then that would explain the CHA discussed above.

Thus, I have managed to cover the range of topics I had set out to do, perhaps just barely so. I had taken on the task of determining the contents of the grammar of Carnatic music from the level of the tone, sequence, phrase and the line and at the same time establish the mechanism which will evaluate the style and the stylistic functions of a line of Carnatic music. At the same time, having applied the ranked constraint-based approach I was able to explain the nature of variation across users in Carnatic music.

However, what I have managed to accomplish is only to lay the groundwork for a future Grammar of Carnatic music and hinted at what this grammar of Carnatic music would look like, more or less. At the practical level, the framework established here can be applied to detailed analyses of raagas, composers, performers etc. which would then constitute the body of research on Carnatic music that would then feed research programmes on Universal Musicology, comparing Carnatic music with other musical systems. Such a research programme on Universal musicology would, hopefully, throw light on the music faculty in humans. Needless to say, these are merely speculative at this point of time.

Appendix 1
A note on the Roman notation

It has not been possible to supplement the Roman notation of Carnatic music samples in the book with staff notation due to unforeseen circumstances. Therefore, I shall provide a detailed guide to the interpretation of Roman notation used in the book for the convenience of Western scholars. To begin with, as I had explained in the text, we must begin with the names of notes. I repeat below, for ease of reference, the keyboard diagram and the names of the notes in Carnatic music that I will be using throughout the book.

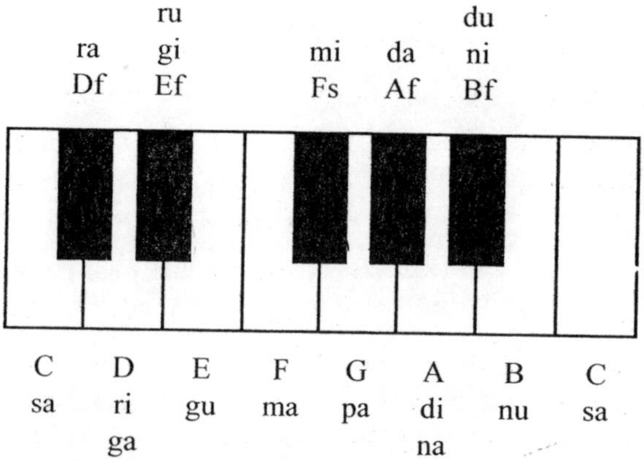

Figure 1. The Carnatic 16 tone system

With four of the twelve notes performing dual functions, we have a sixteen note octave in Carnatic music and the names of the notes other than sa – C, pa – G, ma – F and mi – F sharp, all the other notes have three versions each, namely Xa, Xi and Xu where 'X' stands for 'r'– D, 'g' – E, 'd' – A and 'n' – B as a prototype and not the specific note of the scale.

Take the first sample of Carnatic music below: The raagam Madhyamaavati selects the notes 'sa, ri, ma, pa, ni Sa' (upper case indicates upper octave and under-dotting the lower octave). A word of caution at this point. The notation whether Roman or staff is only a rough skeleton and will not match the music in exact pitch values as has been explained at great length in chapters 4 and 5. The 'ni' will not match the exact note B flat as it will be a minor pitch deflection from a point slightly lower than

B and targeting a pitch value higher than B in this particular phrase. Similarly the last note indicated as 'ri'- D will not be a steady pitch value of the note 'ri'- D but a pitch wave going a bit higher than 'ri'. Thus the notation does not reflect exactly the way the music is rendered. The notation in the book is adequate for those trained in Carnatic music for interpretation but a mere prop for the music demonstration audio clips in the accompanying MP3 collection.

(1) Raamakathaa Madhyamaavati [⊙ 1.6]
Tyaagaraajaa Aadi
// ; sa, - ṇi sa ri sa / ri,
ra: ma ka tha:

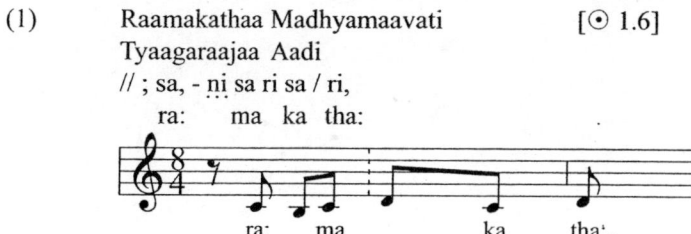

Apart from the keys to individual notes the point that needs to be explained in some detail is the nature of musical timing, the beat and the beat cycle in Carnatic music. The part of the line above if represented as a structured line of music will have to be represented as shown below:

(2) // [; 'sa, - ni] ['sa ri sa / ri,]...

where brackets enclose musical phrases, ' stands for musical prominence and the slant lines and hyphens stand for beats of the rhythm cycle. It will be noticed that musical prominence need not coincide with the beat of the rhythm at all – a notion of considerable amazement to Western musicians and hence rather difficult to capture in Western staff notation. Although the literature on rhythm in Western music and poetry do bring up the issue of musical or linguistic rhythm not attested on every beat or beats falling on adjacent elements, the issue is rather different here in Carnatic music. It is not just the case that musical prominence may not occur on the beat, but it may occur elsewhere, before, on or after the beat and that too at minutely specified timings from a beat that is intriguing to the uninitiated.

Every taaḷam can be rendered with two moras to an even beat, and also three, four, five, seven and nine moras to a beat in complex rhythmically set 'pallavi' passages. The music demonstrations in the book attest only two and four moras to a beat. In addition to the even timed rhythm cycles of eight beats to a cycle (Aadi taaḷam) and three beats to a cycle (Ruupaka taaḷam), Carnatic music also attests beats of uneven duration, e.g. the tisra tripuṭai as a caapu (shortened version) has three beats of three, two and two moras (or their double). Even in the demonstration version above, though the entire sequence 'sa ri sa ri, belongs to one phrase with prominence after the beat, the Western notation does not allow a beat to occur in the middle of a phrase and so the phrase has to be split as [sa,] [ni sa] [ri sa] contrary to the musical structuring in Carnatic music. Thus the notation is only a rough and ready reference and not to be taken as God's truth. And definitely, the Western notation is still farther removed from real phrasing and prominence in Carnatic music.

Appendix 2
Another take on the mathematics of the twelve notes

This appendix is informed by the extensive comments from Paul Kiparsky (p.c.). The pitch values of my veena are amenable to yet another explantion. Setting aside both the precise and equal tempered cent analysis of Western music (due to orchestral compulsions) and the values postulated by Indian musical theory, if we take a closer look at the actual pitch values of my veena, it is possible to offer a simpler, mathematical explanation for the twelve note boundaries in an octave. I reproduce the notes, their pitch values on my veena and the mathematical ratios that they reveal.

Note	Pitch value	Ratio
sa	164	1/1
ra	172	16/15
ri	184	10/9
gi	195	6/5
gu	207	5/4
ma	220	4/3
mi	233	11/8
pa	248	3/2
da	261	8/5
di	277	5/3
ni	294	16/9
nu	311	15/8
Sa	330	2/1

The simpler the ratio the less marked the note in the scale.

Thus the notes in the increasing order of markedness are as shown below:

sa > pa > ma > di > gu > gi

This scale of markedness may presumably be reflected in the pentatonic scales found in the far eastern music systems. The notes with more complex ratios, i.e. ra, ri, mi, da, ni and nu are more marked than the notes listed above. While this reflects our intuition about the greater markedness of the notes ra, mi, ni and nu there are several probems raised by the markedness rankings. Firstly, the intuitively felt lesser markedness of ri is not reflected here. Secondly, the relative markedness of da does not get reflected correctly. Thirdly, the predicted lower markedness of gi seems counter-intuitive, presumably because of my Carnatic music bias. However, this ties in partially with the interpretation of the first four notes of Saama Veedaa scale (see Ayyangar (1972)), namely [ni sa ri gi]. But notice that ri is not part of our lesser marked set. Fourthly, intuitively, one of the notes ni or nu should have been in the less marked set. Going by the relation [ni sa ri gi] we can expect the four note follow up sequence [ma pa di ni] which is supported by one interpretation of the Saama Veeda scale (Ayyangar). However, if we go by the least marked set and look for symmetry, the set [sa (ri) gu ma] allows us to expect [pa (di) nu Sa], giving us the Western major scale. Only a more nuanced exploration of scales employed by diverse music systems across the world will enable us to take the issue to the next level of research.

Appendix 3
An annotated selection of Carnatic music webpages

Ahiri

Artist: Ramnad Krishnan
http://www.sangeethapriya.org/~/svasu/085-Sri%20Ramnad%20Krishnan/
Artist: M. S. Subbulakshmi
http://www.sangeethapriya.org/~/svasu/166-Smt.M.S.Subbalakshmi/

Arabhi

Artist: M. L. Vasantakumari
http://www.sangeethapriya.org/~/svasu/151-Dr.M.L.Vasanthakumari/
http://www.sangeethapriya.org/~/tvg/041.MLV/

Begada

Artist: O. S. Thyagarajan
http://www.sangeethapriya.org/~/svasu/219-Sri%20O.S.Thyagarajan/

Bilahari

Artist: D. K. Pattammal
http://www.sangeethapriya.org/~/hariharan/DKP/07-DKP-MA1967/
Artist: M. L. Vasantakumari
http://www.sangeethapriya.org/~/tvg/036.MLV-KANYAKUMARI-MANI%20IYER%20(103)/

Chakravakam

Artist: Oleti Venkateshwarlu
http://www.sangeethapriya.org/~/svasu/205-Sri%20Oletti%20Venkateswaralu/

Dhanyasi

Artist: D. K. Pattammal
http://www.sangeethapriya.org/~/tvg/304.SMT%20D%20K%20PATTAMMAL/

Harikambodhi
Artist: D. K. Pattammal
http://www.sangeethapriya.org/~/hariharan/DKP/18-DKP-Unknown/readme.txt

Hemavathi
Artist: T. Brinda
http://www.sangeethapriya.org/~/tvg/022.T.BRINDA/

Kedaragowla
Artist: M. S. Subbulakshmi
http://www.sangeethapriya.org/~/svasu/166-Smt.M.S.Subbalakshmi/

Mayamalavagowla
Artist: T. N. Seshagopalan
http://www.sangeethapriya.org/~/tvg/290.MADURAI%20SRI%20T.N.SESHAGOPALAN%20-%20THIRUVAIYYARU/

Poorvikalyani
Artist: Sanjay Subramanian
http://www.sangeethapriya.org/~/asokan/CARNATIC/095.TNS-SDS-RAMAN-Ananthapur%20SEP76/
Artist: Oleti
http://www.sangeethapriya.org/~/tvg/030.VOLETTI%20SRI%20VENKATESWARALU/

Ragam: Anandabhairavi
Artist: G. N. Balasubramanian
http://www.sangeethapriya.org/~/ranganathan/Music_Audio/Vocal/03_GNB_AIR_2004/

Ragam: Bhairavi

Artists: M. L. Vasanta Kumari, M. S. Subbulakshmi, D. K. Pattammal, K. V. Narayanaswami, T. N. Sheshagopalan, Ariyakudi Ramanuja Iyengar, Ramnad Krishnan. Semmangudi Srinivasa Iyer, Sanjay Subramanian, D. K. Jayaraman, Madurai Mani Iyer.

http://www.sangeethapriya.org/~/hariharan/57-Bhairavi/

Ragam: Devagandhari

Artists: K. V. Narayanaswami, T. N. Sheshagopalan, Ariyakudi Ramanuja Iyengar, Ramnad Krishnan, Semmangudi Srinivasa Iyer.

http://home.sprynet.com/~dsivakumar/music/intromus.htm

Ragam: Dhanyasi

Artists: T. V. Sankaranarayanan, D. K. Jayaraman, K. V. Narayanaswami, Alathur Brothers.

http://home.sprynet.com/~dsivakumar/music/intromus.htm

Ragam: Kalyani

Artists: M. D. Ramanathan, M. S. Subbulakshmi, G. N. Balasunramanian, D. K. Pattammal, K. V. Narayanaswami, M. L. Vasantakumari, Dr. M. Balamuralikrishna, Ramnad Krishnan, Semmangudi Srinivasa Iyer, Brinda and Mukta, Alathur Brothers, Voleti Venkateswarlu, Madurai Mani Iyer.

http://www.sangeethapriya.org/~/gvr/kalyani/

Ragam: Kambodhi

Artist: Oleti Venkateshwarlu

http://www.sangeethapriya.org/~/murthy/048%20%20Oleti%20Venkateshwarulu%20-%20AIR-18.01.2007/

Artist: K. V. Narayana Swamy

http://www.sangeethapriya.org/~/murthy/078%20%20K%20V%20Narayanaswamy-Evarimata/

Ragam: Kambodhi (*continued*)

Artist: M. S. Subbulakshmi

http://www.sangeethapriya.org/~/ranganathan/Music_Audio/Vocal/01_MSSubbulakshmi/01_MSSubbulakshmi_%20Radio_TVRecordings/04_MSS_Madras_TV_25MAR1987_Sri_Rangam_Samprokshanam/

Ragam: Keeravani

Artist: M. L. Vasantakumari

http://www.sangeethapriya.org/~/murthy/003%20%20M.L.Vasantakumari/

Artist: Semmangudi Srinivasa Iyer

http://www.sangeethapriya.org/~/ksj/Semmangudi%20R%20Srinivasa%20Iyer/SSI%20%23033%20(@Sengotta)/

Ragam: Kharaharapriya

Artists: M. S. Subbulakshmi, D. K. Pattammal, K. V. Narayanaswami, Nedunuri Krishnamurthy, Dr. M. Balamuralikrishna, Ramnad Krishnan, Semmangudi Srinivasa Iyer, Brinda and Mukta, Alathur Brothers, Voleti Venkateswarlu, Madurai Mani Iyer, Sanjay Subranmanian, T. M. Krishna

http://www.sangeethapriya.org/~/gvr/KharaharaPriya/

Ragam: Mohanam

Artists: Nedunuri Krishnamurthy, M. D. Ramanathan, M. S. Subbulakshmi, G. N. Balasunramanian, D. K. Pattammal, K. V. Narayanaswami, M. L. Vasantakumari, Dr. M. Balamuralikrishna, Ramnad Krishnan, Semmangudi Srinivasa Iyer, Brinda and Mukta, Alathur Brothers, Voleti Venkateswarlu, Madurai Mani Iyer.

http://www.sangeethapriya.org/~/gvr/Mohanam/

Ragam: Mukhari

Artists: M. S. Subbulakshmi, D. K. Pattammal, K. V. Narayanaswami, Nedunuri Krishnamurthy, Dr. M. Balamuralikrishna, Ramnad Krishnan, Semmangudi Srinivasa Iyer, Brinda and Mukta, Alathur Brothers.

http://www.sangeethapriya.org/~/hariharan/55-Mukhari/

Ragam: Sankarabharanam

Artist: K. V. Narayana Swamy

http://www.sangeethapriya.org/~/murthy/051%20%20K%20V%20Narayanaswamy-ChaturRTP%20-%2028.12.2007/

Artist: Ramnad Krishnan

http://www.sangeethapriya.org/~/murthy/049%20%20Ramnad%20Krishnan-LGJ-PMI-Tagging%20Project%20%20-%2022.01.2007/

Artist: Semmangudi Srinivasa Iyer

http://www.sangeethapriya.org/~/ksj/Semmangudi%20R%20Srinivasa%20Iyer/SSI%20%23MA58%20(VVS-TS)/

Ragam: Saveri

Artists: Nedunuri Krishnamurthy, M. D. Ramanathan, M. S. Subbulakshmi, G. N. Balasunramanian, D. K. Pattammal, K. V. Narayanaswami, M. L. Vasantakumari, Dr. M. Balamuralikrishna, Ramnad Krishnan, Semmangudi Srinivasa Iyer, Brinda and Mukta, Alathur Brothers, Voleti Venkateswarlu, Madurai Mani Iyer.

http://www.sangeethapriya.org/~/gvr/Saveri/

Ragam: Todi

Artist: K. V. Narayana Swamy

http://www.sangeethapriya.org/~/murthy/018%20%20KVNarayanaswamy-AIR%20FM%20Gold/

Artist: Semmangudi Srinivasa Iyer

http://www.sangeethapriya.org/~/ksj/Semmangudi%20R%20Srinivasa%20Iyer/SSI%20%23MA61%20(MSG-PMI)/

Sankarabharanam

Artist: T. N. Seshagopalan

http://www.sangeethapriya.org/~/tvg/290.MADURAI%20SRI%20T.N.SESHAGOPALAN%20-%20THIRUVAIYYARU/

Shanmukhapriya

Artist: M. L. Vasantakumari

http://www.sangeethapriya.org/~/tvg/017.MLV-RTP-SHANMUGAPRIYA%20(LIVE)/

Thodi

Artist: Aruna Sairam

http://www.sangeethapriya.org/~/svasu/095-Smt.Aruna%20Sayeeram/

Artists: Alathur Brothers

http://www.sangeethapriya.org/~/svasu/334-Alathur%20Brothers%20Sri%20Srinivasa%20Iyer%20&Sri%20Sivasubramaniya%20Iyer/.

Varali

Artist: T. N. Seshagopalan

http://www.sangeethapriya.org/~/asokan/CARNATIC/095.TNS-SDS-RAMAN-Ananthapur%20SEP76/

Artist: K. V. Narayanaswami

http://www.sangeethapriya.org/~/tvg/009.KVN-16-08-1%20&%202/

Artist: D. K. Pattammal

http://www.sangeethapriya.org/~/hariharan/DKP/07-DKP-MA1967/

Appendix 4
Carnatic music glossary

Aaroohaṇam: ascending scale
Avaroohaṇam: descending scale
Aalaapanai: free exploration of musical ideas within the space allowed by a raagam.

Composers (a select few only):

Aadiappayyer, Paccimiriam: this composer is known only for one great masterpiece – viribooṇi, the Bhairavi Raagam Aṭa taaḷa varṇam. He was also Shyaamaa Shaastri's guru.

Diikshitar, Muttuswaami (1775-1835): The youngest of the Carnatic music trinity; musically, he was the most adventurous of the three; he liked to explore new possibilities in old raagas, redefine their peripheries, so to speak; he was open to experiment with raagas from the north; however, the large majority of his experimentation with new raagas in the Maayaamaaḷavagauḷa scale are not all that successful as they remain of academic exercises (at least for me). In contrast, Tyaagaraajaa's experimentation with the Harikaamboodi and Shankaraabharaṇam scales have produced an enormous number of new raagas which have been accepted by the Carnatic music fraternity widely.

Goopalayyar, Pallavi: A senior contemporary of the trinity; has a few great varṇams to his credit and an entirely different approach to composition though not a prolific composer.

Ksheetragnya: Varadaiah, later known as Ksheetragnya was the author of a great many padams – love songs of which only less than a hundred are available to day with notation and text. This model of an erotic text set to music in a leisurely pace set the trend for later padams in Tamil in the times of royal patronage to Carnatic music and dance (late eighteenth and nineteenth centuries).

Shaastri, Shyaamaa (1763-1827): One could say that this was a composer closest to pure musical expression as his language text was clearly of secondary importance; he did not explore a great range of raagas and his output is meager when compared to the other two; still, his approach to raagas and taaḷas was unique and his style of composition was also unique.

Shaastri, Subbaraaya (1803-1862): The son of Shyaamaa Shaastri had the distinction of learning from his father and also Tyaagaraajaa. He incorporated many features from all the three great composers.

Shivan, Paapanaasam: a twenty-first century composer; called modern Tyaagaraajaa, he was a prolific composer in Tamil (a few compositions are also in Sanskrit); he composed in a range of raagas in simple style sometimes incorporating the fast tempo finale passages that Muttuswaami Diikshitar was justly famous for.

Tyaagaraajaa (1767-1847): unarguably the greatest composer of Canatic music; contributed immensely to the development of 'creative' music "manoodharma sangiitam" in the realm of sangati – variation on a line of music leading to niraval, swara singing, etc. But he was rather orthodox when it came to exploring raagas.

Veenkaṭasubbayyar, Uuttukkaaḍu: A clearly pre-trinity composer of a distinct tradition; he must have been one of the earliest to compose in Tamil; he seems to have had a distinct approach to well known raagas and has many new raagas to his credit (going by the claim of his twenty-first century descendent).

Gamakkam: the systematic exploitation of inter-tonal pitch frequencies. In this context, in this book I make the systematic distinction between the terms 'tone' and 'note': while the former refers to the pitch rendering, the latter refers to the interpreted note of a scale/raagam.

Guru-siʃya: teacher-disciple; the relationship between the teacher and the taught is 'supposed' to be more than a mere teacher-student relationship; it was a kind of live-in studentship with all the resultant hardship/exploitation which nobody wants to talk about.

Raagam/raagas: a melodic exploration of a set of notes (with or without a prohibition on specific note sequences). Through use, raagas can and do acquire idiosyncratic tonal/phrasal specifications.

Sangati: variation on a line of music in a composition.

ʃruti: 1. alignment with the pitch; 2. microtone; a pitch interval approximately 20/25 cents above or below a semi-tone or a tone but never exploited as a static pitch target.

Swaram (ciṭṭaswaram): A set rhythmic piece composed by an artist (not necessarily the composer) appended to the anupallavi and caraṇam (if present) of a composition.

Swaram (kalpanaaswaram/swarakalpanai): Extempore rendering of notes with or without rhythmic planning appended to a line of music of a composition or the pallavi. The point of interest is that each exercise of kalpanaaswaram must end at a point which is determined by the take off point of the line of the composition. More orthodox styles insist on more stringent conditions, e.g. "the ending of the kalpanaaswaram should always lead to the end in an upward movement of notes" etc. Of course, this is not a sacred rule that all styles respect. Therefore, depending on the style, we could find a diversity of views on this matter. Further, we also have mathematical schools which revel in complex mathematical formulae being tested in the arena.

Types of composition:

Bhajana: a musical composition of simple, repetitive structure which is rendered in chorus with simple lyrics with devotional content.

Jaavaḻi: a quick witted, nimble paced, love song.

Janya: a derivative raagam of a full scale, i.e. meeḻakartaa. It can be full scale either in the ascent or descent and also a vakra raagam avoiding some linear sequences of notes. It can also have accidental notes drawn from outside its parent meeḻakartaa's scale.

Kiirtanai: this composition type was first set in place by the father of Carnatic Music – Purandaṛa daaasaa and refined by the later composers. The norm of the kiirtanai is a three part composition: the pallavi – introduction; the anupallavi – the antithesis; and the charaṇam which is a resolution of the musical theme, in a sense. However, there are great compositions which go against this prototype. We have compositions which have multiple charaṇams; we have compositions which do not have an anupallavi (but only a samaʃṭicaraṇam) and finally we have great swarajatis which have a great many charaṇams.

Niraval: a melodic/rhythmic exploration of a line of music in a composition or the line of a pallavi.

Padam: a lovely, slow, seductive melody framing a love song.

Pallavi: a line of music such that the syllables of the language text are arranged according to rhythmic principles; this line is elaborated (as niraval (see above)) and then rendered in double tempo and also sometimes three moras to a beat tempo known as tisram (three) and then kalpanaaswaras are rendered in the slow and fast tempo leading to kalpanaaswaras in different raagas (optional). This is usually the piece de resistance in a Carnatic music concert. The taaḻam selected may be moderate to very complex, with difficult take off points at specified points after the beginning of the taaḻam cycle or even before it.

Taaḻam: a beat cycle; a taaḻam may consist of several parts, e.g. a beat with the down turned palm, counting of beats with the fingers starting from the little finger to the thumb (and there could be more than one cycle of finger counting) and the beat denoted by the upturned palm. The interval between beats may have one to four moras depending on the naḍai 'gait' whether the kriti is in the slow tempo or fast tempo etc. Longer intervals between beats allow sub-beats to emerge as a possibility. And pallavis also admit beats of 5/7/9 moras to a beat.

Aṭa taaḻam: this particular rhythm cycle is a fourteen beat cycle of two rounds of 5 beats (one down turned palm and four finger counting) and two rounds of beats with the down turned palm and the upturned palm.

Types of composition: Taaḻam (*continued*):

Jampai: a three beat cycle of uneven beats of 2, 1, 2 moras (or their double).

Kaṇṭa caapu: Kaṇṭa means that a rhythm cycle of five or ten beats is shortened to three beats of 2, 1, 2 moras (or their double).

Misra caapu: Caapu means a shortened form and misra means seven; thus this name refers to the Tisra Triputai which is performed as a three beat cycle.

Ruupakam: a three beat rhythm cycle of even beats.

Aadi: an eight beat rhythm cycle of even beats.

Tisra Triputai: a three beat cycle of uneven beats of 3, 2 and 2 moras (or their double).

Tillaanaaa: a rhythmic composition with a bare minimum of language text in the charaṇam. It has passages set to rhythmic syllables.

Varṇam: A two-part composition rendered at the beginning of the recital; it has a pallavi anupallavi two-in-one first movement with a solfa/note/passage and second movement – charaṇam with a line of music followed by four to five solfa passages. There are several kinds of varṇam which have a slightly different make up which need not concern us here; in the kind of varṇam that is relevant for our discussion the language text is kept to the minimum (and kept to the arcane undemanding level) and therefore, this is one of the instances of 'abstract music' in Carnatic music.

Taanam: exploration of semi-rhythmic ideas within the domain of a raagam [2.87 & 2.89].

Tone vs. Note: in this book by tone I mean the actual pitch rendering; by note I mean the interpretation of the actual pitch rendering as a note of the raagam.

Notes

1. "The language of the book and the material in it indicate that Brihaddeesi belong to the 9th century and not earlier." R.R. Ayyangar (1972: 51).
2. Or Old Tamil to contemporary, colloquial Tamil for that matter and the musical practices described in ancient Tamil texts to contemporary Carnatic music.
3. T stands for taaḷam (the beat cycle), A for Aadi taaḷam, R for Ruupaka taaḷam, MC for Misra Caapu taaḷam.
4. Listen to these compositions in the MP3 collection. The numbering allows you to listen to the specific piece of music demonstration that is under discussion. The first number refers to the number of the chapter and the second number to the particular piece of music demonstration.
5. The point at issue here is not whether other systems of music are legitimate and of equal standing as Carnatic music. The point I am making, perhaps, a bit too emotionally, is the gradual depletion of the Carnatic music fraternity.
6. Whether other forms of art are also equally 'cognitive' is a large issue and I do not wish to get into the discussion.
7. N.S. Srinivasan's inaugural address at the Ranga Ramanuja Ayyangar Centenary Celebrations, 30th March, 2002, Hyderabad. However, not all practicing musicians pay attention to such minute details. It is amusing to note that there is a commercially available audio recording where the vocalist carefully follows the notation of the composition Raamakatha after every line of kalpanaaswaram and the violinist keeps playing the first line of Paalintsukaamaakṣi after his kalpanaaswaram assays. This shows the level of sensitivity of the accompanying artist.
8. The modern bhaktas deserting Carnatic music to other systems of music is a comparable case.
9. The teevaaram and tiruppugazh are an exception as they are of amazing musical and rhythmic complexity. But they were really esoteric disciplines.
10. A two part composition performed at the beginning of a concert, said to be excellent for training the voice.
11. Improvisation on a line of the composition.
12. Also called swara kalpanaa. It is generally attempted from a unique line of a composition where strings of rhythmically designed musical phrases (sung as 'notes') are composed on the spot to merge with the starting point of the chosen line of composition after each attempt at kalpanaaswaram. In some cases, minor variations of the starting point of the line of the composition can also be attempted such that the point at which the kalpanaaswaram ends and the line of the composition starts vary minimally. For example, in the composition Bhajaree of Muttuswaami Diikshitar in the raagam Kalyaaṇi, if the line "deevi shakti biijoodbhava" is selected for rendering niraval (rhythmic variations on the line)

followed by kalpanaaswaram, it is possible to match the end point of the kalpana-aṣwaram such that one smoothly starts the musical line "deevi..." which occurs at the beginning of the rhythmic cycle (taaḷam being tisra triputai of three beats of six, four and four moras) or "...shakti..." which occurs after 12 moras into the cycle or two moras before the new cycle.

13. The gems in the raagas Naaṭai, Gauḷa, Aarabhi, Sri and Varaaḷi.
14. Set rhythmic lines tagged on to the second and third movements (if present) of the composition.
15. It will be noticed that there is basically a conflict of interest here between the music 'theorist' and the music practitioner. While the former stands for the principle of 'non-judgmental acceptance of variation', the latter is committed to the interests of particular styles (for purposes of continuity etc.). The shrewd reader will gradually discover that this book has a hidden agenda supporting the latter's interests.
16. But I shall not define the terms 'competent' performer and 'intelligent' listener and leave it to the imagination and understanding of the Carnatic music fraternity.
17. For the time being, ignore the absence of ru, ga, du and na. The logic of the labels will be explained in chapter 4 section 4.2, pp. 76–79.
18. I am grateful to Francois Dell for the discussion on the scale as an unordered set.
19. Of course, this is too simplified a statement and is not accurate.
20. I am grateful to Geetha Durairajan, Deepti Ramadoss and Saumya (p.c.) for bringing the issue of structure dependence to my attention.
21. The reason is that this phrasing will signal another raagam. See chapter 6 for an extended discussion of ambiguity and how it is a sign of ungrammaticality in Carnatic music.
22. The pronoun in (13b) allows other interpretations too.
23. Perhaps the practice of ʃruti bheedam – 'modal shift' in Carnatic music where during the elaboration of one raagam another raagam is hinted at is an instance of displacement, although limited. I am grateful to Professor Saskia C. Kersenboom for bringing this to my notice. It seems in Bharatanaatyam it is possible to quote someone or refer to an event outside the domain of reference of the dance using special gestures. See chapter 7, pp. 223–225.
24. Padma Varadan and N.S. Srinivasan have confirmed this for me (p.c.).
25. Due to oversight, the music demonstration was grouped with those in chapter 6.
26. The evidence is in a pre-recorded cassette rendering by a famous musician I admire very much.
27. These are obviously performance oriented constraints. But it is not difficult to give them a listener orientation and reformulate them slightly.
28. Current approaches to the phonetics-phonology interaction is markedly pragmatic/functional.

29. See chapter 9 for a fuller discussion.
30. My concern in exploring the grammar of Carnatic music too has the same ultimate goal, namely to discover the universal principles of pitch and rhythm that make music possible in humans (see the last sections of chapters 5 and 7 for a fuller discussion).
31. And in spite of the teachers' efficiency/insistence etc., for more than a decade, many children just do not manage to learn a second language (or the standard variety of their first language, if it is very different from the variety that they speak at home) that efficiently. Certainly food for thought.
32. Of course, this principle does not work in second language learning situations. The reason is that by the time the child takes on the second language, he/she has already learnt the first language and fixed many of the generalizations in a certain way. These old habits die hard and hence the persistence of these first language traits in the second language.
33. See Vihman (1996).
34. The commonly encountered observation about people with different language backgrounds not being able to produce certain sounds of certain languages being attributed to genetic traits, in fact, has nothing to do with the anatomy of the oral tract of distinct linguistic communities. It is purely a matter of language habit. Take the case of the supposedly difficult Tamil sound 'z̨' in the word 'paz̨am' 'fruit'. In fact, the American English pronunciation of the 'r' in 'car' is fairly similar to the sound in Tamil. But the context in which the sound occurs in American English is very different from the context in which it occurs in Tamil and that is the reason for the difficulty for Americans. It has nothing to do with the supposedly 'superior' lingual anatomy of the Tamils.
35. Not to ignore the part that lip rounding plays in the production of vowels.
36. The last sound stands for the vowel in the standard British pronunciation of the word 'dog'.
37. Also conceptually complex.
38. Southern Tamilians and Malayalam speakers will vouch for this as they pronounce English words like 'temple' and 'wrinkle' as 'temble' and 'ringle' respectively.
39. The question that might arise at this stage is "why should languages select marked elements at all?" This question is prompted by the assumption that we have marked and unmarked elements and that only a 'funny' (impractical?) language would choose to select marked elements.There are several problems with this assumption. First of all, markedness is a relative term. A supposedly marked element may turn out to be unmarked in certain contexts, with respect to some other segment set. Secondly, we have to consider markedness in a holistic way. We may reduce markedness at the level of the segment but increase it at the level of the word. Take the hypothetical case of language X. Assume that X selects just three consonants /p, t, k/ and three vowels /i, a, u/ and only CV (open) syllables,

i.e. nine syllable types only. For this language to build a reasonable vocabulary of nouns and verbs of say 10,000 words, a large number of words would have to be very long. To be precise, it will have a miniscule vocabulary of mono-, di- and trisyllables but its quadrisyllables would come to 6561 words, 65.61% of its total vocabulary. This is not taking into account morphologically complex words like verbs inflected for tense, mood and person, number and gender and nouns for case markers. When these endings are added, the inflected verb may turn out to be several syllables longer (Ramadass p.c.). Therefore, including these morphological indicators, this hypothetical language would end up having words of great length, say words of eight, nine syllables or even longer. However, if the language decides to add two vowels and two consonants to its inventory, it would not have to have any quadrisyllables but its trisyllables would still constitute 93.5% of its total vocabulary and its inflected vocabulary be five or six syllables long. However, most 'normal' languages have a larger vocabulary than 10,000 words and a fairly large part of the vocabulary is made up of short words, i.e. mono- and disyllables. This is why languages prefer to select marked segments to overcome the problem of having marked word length. However, language types fall into different groups when it comes to their preference for word length. Take the case of most of the languages of the Far East which prefer monosyllables and consequently have to select many marked segments (e.g., voiceless nasals, voiceless liquids [l and r] etc.) and also tones as distinct elements in vocabulary building. Markedness is not a simple uni-dimensional matter. Complexity has to be computed at different levels, segmental, syllable structure, number of syllables in a word etc. There is a trade-off between markedness at different levels. If segmental markedness is low and syllable markedness is also low (i.e. the language selects only short, open syllables), then the pressure of vocabulary building would force the language to choose polysyllabic words and markedness at the level of the word would be very high. Further, markedness is a complex issue which needs to be computed holistically – in the areas of phonetics, phonology, morphology and syntax.

40. For ease of presentation I ignore the details of disyllabic loan words like /guru/ 'teacher' and even native words e.g. /paru/ 'pimple', disyllabic words which have a rounded vowel in the first syllable e.g. /koʃu/ 'mosquito' and hypocoristics (short forms of proper names like /paddu/ for /padma/ etc.) which can and do end in the vowel /u/, at least in my dialect.
41. Morpheme-initial syllables. We do have suffixes like -um] 'conjunctive suffix', -um] '3rd neuter singular suffix etc. which attest the vowel /u/.
42. For ease of presentation, I simplify the constraint as *ASPIRATION. Actually the constraint would have to be spelt out in terms of articulatory/acoustic characteristics.
43. This is not the actual constraint that has been proposed in the literature. This simplification has been done keeping the lay reader in mind.

44. Of course, across generations of Tamil speakers, since aspirates have never been pronounced anywhere, Tamilians would have assumed the input representation of a word like /b^hakti/ to be actually /bakti/. Since aspirates are never found in output representations, the question of IDENTIOASPIRATION (FAITHASPIRATION) playing a role in the grammar of Tamil does not arise. The inviolability of *ASPIRATION renders the feature aspiration totally invisible in the grammar of modern Tamil.
45. Another major difference between standard theories of linguistics and OT is the latter's claim to non-derivationality. Suffice it to say for our purposes that unlike standard theories where representations are taken step by step through several stages of derivations, OT takes an input and arrives at the optimal output by evaluating all the logically possible representations simultaneously.
46. Unless otherwise specified, by Tamil I mean contemporary, colloquial Tamil, specially my own dialect – the Brahmin dialect spoken in Chennai.
47. Further, the final /m/ is deleted rounding the preceding low vowel and making it nasalized and /n/ is also deleted nasalizing the preceding vowel. That leaves /ɳ/ which is protected by faithfulness. Therefore even the final nasal deletion is driven by the constraint which prefers final vowels in words.
48. Even the final /ɭ/ in the feminine suffix is deleted to satisfy the requirement that words end in vowels. Interestingly, while the present , singular feminine /r-aaɭ/ ~ /kkr-aaɭ/ and the past singular feminine ending /d-aaɭ/ ~ /nd-aaɭ/ ~ /tt-aaɭ/ delete the final /ɭ/ without changing the quality of the preceding vowel, the future tense /v-aaɭ/ and /pp-aaɭ/ delete the final /ɭ/ concomitantly rounding the preceding vowel (and raising it to /oo/). These details are excluded from the discussion for ease of presentation.
49. For ease of presentation, I will not integrate constraints specific to vowel quality into the ranking here.
50. Notice that the transcription is that of my own dialect where /s/ is sometimes pronounced /ʃ/.
51. The analysis offered here is not fully satisfactory and it requires another constraint specifying the nature of the edges of words/morphemes. But as that will take us into details which do not generally concern us here in this book, I will not discuss this issue any futher.
52. Lexicon optimization applied to music implies that among several possible interpretations of a musical phrase, the one that is closest to the 'optimal' rendering will get recognised as the lexical entry listed in the lexicon.
53. Chapters 4 and 5 deal with this notion of 'the intention of achieving reduced/augmented targets' vis-à-vis Carnatic music theory and practice.
54. I have benefited enormously from discussions (email exchanges) with Srinivasan Pichumani and Arvindh Krishnaswamy and the latter's papers posted on his website and wish to acknowledge their intellectual contribution to the writing of this chapter. Of course, errors of understanding, if any, are my own.

55. By 'tone' I mean the actual pitch frequency and by 'note' I mean the 'swaram' or the interpretation that performer/listener imposes on the physical realization. Therefore the term 'tone' is equivalent to the phrases 'pitch realization/pitch value' etc.
56. The quality of the preceding vowel is also different. I have ignored these differences for presentation purposes.
57. Of course, when asked to pronounce them differently, all of us can oblige by exaggerating the former (as it is supposed to be the 'big 'r'). Historically, the two sounds were pronounced differently and, perhaps, in some dialects like Sri Lankan Tamil they still are.
58. I suppose that in Western tonal music also, the mode can be established only with reference to a changing fundamental.
59. A scale, in principle, is an unordered set of notes (I am grateful to Francois Dell p.c. for bringing this to my notice). In the Carnatic system, ordering of notes gets imposed from two sources. The first is by explicit prohibition of certain note sequences in 'non-linear' scales. The other kind of ordering restriction is implicit in the system. As each raagam is required to be different from every other raagam, certain note sequences are avoided. More of this later.
60. See Krishnaswamy (2002a) for slightly different values, specially for F sharp and A.
61. This table is adapted from Sambamurthy (1999, V: 41).
62. I am grateful to Ramadass (p.c.) for sorting out this mathematical puzzle for me.
63. See appendix 2, "Another take on the mathematics of the twelve notes", p. 299–300.
64. Unless of course, one is interested in applied work like automatic transcription or computer synthesis of Carnatic music.
65. This is obviously incorrect.
66. The situation is no different in language where minute differences in real pitch values are interpreted accurately in context, for instance, signaling a statement or a question, the most important word in an intonational group pronounced in a neutral setting or in a corrective/contrastive setting. In these cases the real differences can be ever so minute in certain styles of speech and yet there is no misperception in discourse.
67. Preferably by speakers with standard British pronunciation where the rounding effect can be observed dramatically.
68. The actual facts are a little more complicated.
69. Not counting the release of a consonant into another consonant e.g. from 'l' to 'p' as in 'help' and from 'p' to 'l' as in 'apple'.
70. Specially the 'minor' tones, namely 'ra' D flat, 'gi' E flat, 'mi' F sharp, 'da' A flat and 'ni' B flat.

71. Though the actual m.tones that are required for contemporary Carnatic music may be slightly different from the 'postulated ones', marginally. More of this in the next chapter.
72. Due to oversight, this piece of music has not been included in the music demonstration.
73. The obligatory selection of red.gi and red.ni for raagas which select 'gi' and 'ni' is easily proved. The most awkward renderings of Carnatic music on a keyboard instrument are of those raagas which select these two notes.
74. However, experiments have shown that infants are able to perceive subtle distinctions between prerelease, post release and extended VOT and this ability gradually decreases as their exposure to their mother tongue skews their perception in favour of their mother tongue.
75. Another fact that argues in favour of a specific tone interpretation mechanism in Carnatic music is that what the theory terms aug.gu is, in fact notated as 'ma' (red.ma) which is attested in raagas like Beegaḍaa and Harikaambooji.
76. It could work in both directions, i.e. converting tones and pitch ranges to notes from the perception point of view and from notes to tones and pitch ranges from the production point of view.
77. While 'ethnomusicology' will be satisfied merely recording differences across cultures, my incipient theory of 'Universal Musicology' will force one to ask strict questions and set the paradigm for future research, hopefully.
78. This is the commonplace assumption in Carnatic music theory (cf. Ayyangar (1972).
79. See appendix 2, "Another take on the mathematics of the twelve notes", p. 299–300.
80. The early lessons in Carnatic music based on the raagam Maayaamaaḷavagauḷa with 'ra' and 'da' is actually quite difficult for learners and hence quite inappropriate. The practice in north Indian Classical music of using the major scale is much more sensible.
81. There is a commercially available recording of an established singer rendering these 'vivaadi' raagas in quick succession in the manner described above.
82. There is a commercially available pre-recorded cassette of an established singer performing a composition in the raagam Naaṭai which will vouch for my observation. It must be noted that I am not, in any sense, branding such renderings as 'ungrammatical'. All I am saying is that for these performers the markedness constraint prohibiting these sequences is higher ranked than the sequences sanctioned by the raagam and so their altered rendering.
83. However, for the same performers, if the 'nu' is long in the sequence 'pa nu, Sa', the difficulty is considerably reduced and there is no intrusive 'di' in their rendering.
84. The two hypothesized m.tones red.ri and red.di in italics are of questionable standing. I advance the view that while 'ri' and 'di' have no m.tones, and unlike the other

notes 'gi' and 'ni have two m.tones each a reduced version and an augmented version each and so does, perhaps the note 'ma'. See below for evidence and discussion.

85. But an ambitious theoretical group has advocated 53 tone boundaries in an octave in Carnatic music. This proliferation of tone boundaries is the result of a mistaken notion that there are many more incarnations of the notes of Carnatic music. For instance, the claim is that if we apply the law of consonance, mathematically, we can arrive at distinct frequencies for the 'ra' of Gauḷa, Maayaamaḷavagauḷa and Saaveeri. But, this can easily be shown to be incorrect taking samples from any established performer and splicing the note 'ra' from these raagas and subjecting them to pitch analysis.
86. Or utmost three with the addition of a Mid tone.
87. This can be tested on any vocal rendering. The only point that I would like to make at this point is that only my school of music recognized this 'fact' without any prejudice and it is evident in our school of veena playing also, thanks to the musical insight of Veeena Dhanam.
88. Of course, in slower, deliberate styles this phrase can be rendered with 'ma' as the anchor but that is certainly not the normal practice.
89. All these figures are pitch values on my veena and my playing.
90. To be sure, enormous doubt.
91. I believe that the note 'ni' will mimic the pitch graphs of 'gi' to a large extent and hence all the generalizations that I have made for 'gi' may be extended to 'ni' as well. I am a bit unsure of the note 'ma'. Like these two notes, 'ma' also does admit a reduced variety exemplified in raagas like Asaaveeri and Madhyamaavati thus allowing two m.tone variations like 'gi' and 'ni', namely a reduced and an augmented one. I have an intuition that red.ma is executed with 'gu' as anchor no matter what the preceding designated note is for the raagam, 'gu' (Harikaamboodi), 'gi' (Aanandabhairavi), 'ri' (Madhyamaavati) or even 'ra' (Saaveeri). Thus whatever the designated previous note, 'gu' is the designated anchor for red.ma; of course this statement is subject to empirical verification. Thus we see that the Carnatic music octave has 23 ʃrutis rather than 22 as postulated by the theory – one each for 'sa', 'pa', 'ri' and 'di' and two each for 'ra', 'gu', 'mi', 'da', 'nu' and three each for 'gi', 'ma' and 'ni'. Surely an inelegant number.
92. However, some performers take the meeḷakartaa schema literally and they render 'ru' and 'du' as RenScale 'gi' and 'ni' respectively.
93. Since this idea occurred much after the recording for the book was over there is no audio demo for these observations. This oversight is regretted.
94. Unfortunately, I cannot display the pitch graph of the pitch wave rendering of aug.gi in a vivaadi raagam as my veena has been reset after the recording and all the values would be different.
95. It is truly unfortunate that I am unable to include these in my music demonstration.
96. See discussion above.

97. As I said earlier, going by my ear, I have heard some performers target even 'pa'.
98. The systematic difference between an aug.m.tone driven pitch wave and pitch curve is the target note. While pitch waves tend to have nearby targets, pitch curves have farther targets (specially in ultra-orthodox styles).
99. More or less. The actual pitch realizations can be more tricky, more unpredictable as there is considerable variation across users in Carnatic music.
100. Perhaps not unachievable.
101. I am grateful to R.Amritavalli (p.c.) for explaining this concept to me.
102. And if asked to disambiguate the two 'r's, speakers will happily oblige, rendering the second instance as a rolled 'r' to the satisfaction of the unsuspecting phonetician.
103. The non-inclusion of this phrase in the music demonstration is an oversight.
104. Specially in scalar raagas (see chapter 9 for details), not all raagas allow note pitch curve between notes which are at least a note away from each other. I am not quite prepared to take on this issue at the moment. This is an issue which has to be researched in detail.
105. I do not have in mind solo instrumentalist accompanied by several percussionists in mind when I think of orchestrated music but several melodic instruments playing together as in Western music trios, quartets and quintets etc.
106. See chapter 6 and the discussion of musical phrase and musical line in Carnatic music for a statement of the problem.
107. It may be quite different in musical systems where harmony is a major guiding principle. My total ignorance of the principles of tonal music forces me to say no more.
108. The imagery is even more dramatic in my rendering where the second ascent is once again from 'ri' like the first and not from 'ma' as in the rendering here. The rendered sequence is ['ri, ma ri] ['ma, pa ma...] but the way I render it is ['ri, ma ri] ['ri, pa ma...].
109. Talking of texts, this part of the composition is normally rendered at a fast pace. The same text is rendered very differently, at a much slower pace, with more details, in the Veena Dhanammal school of music. See chapter 9 for a detailed discussion of style in Carnatic music.
110. To introduce a point that I make later while discussing the issue of checking the sequence of notes in a musical phrase, though this raagam is a vakra raagam, the sequence that is absolutely prohibited is *pa di ni Sa.
111. It is another matter that the rendering will continue to be awkward as the phrase 'ni, di pa' occurs again just a beat away.
112. It must be pointed out that in contemporary Carnatic music, because of eclectic listening/learning practices, the styles of many performers are sometimes not homogenous. There are numerous instances of performers selecting one style for aalaapanai and another for niraval and kalpanaaswaram and yet another for

rendering a composition. Strikingly, it may be observed that many performers adopt very different styles for rendering different types of compositions in the same concert. This reflects their mix and match approach.

113. Due to an oversight these demonstrations are not included in the demo MP3 collection.
114. We will see later on that (in chapter 8) that sometimes *AMB cannot be satisfied at the level of the note and we need to take into consideration the minimal phrase and still further, there are times when it can be satisfied only at the next higher level, i.e. the musical line, specially in raagas which belong to the scalar set. Thus *AMB is really a constraint set encompassing the note, the sequence, the minimal phrase and the musical line.
115. Here is another example of a tonal rendering of the note 'ni' where the targets are almost the same, i.e. aug.ni, and yet two raagas, namely Aṭaaṇaa and Madhyamaavati, bring out the distinct characteristics with the help of a glide from the preceding note. Though the target is the same for these two raagas, namely aug.ni. Madhyamaavati's double pitch curve on 'ni' with a glide from 'pa' and Aṭaaṇaa's double pitch curve on 'ni' with 'di' as anchor help disambiguate the two raagas. At first blush it might seem that *AMBNOTE is not resolved at the level of the single note as both raagas allow 'ni' to be rendered as a double pitch curve with aug.ni as a specified note. But closer examination of the actual pitch curves reveal that the pitch curves are, in reality, quite distinct with Madhaymaavati eschewing any trace of 'di' (as anchor) even in passing (for me and many more practitioners) by choosing an anchor slightly above 'di' while, Aṭaaṇaa requires 'di' as anchor very clearly. Due to oversight, this piece of music demonstration was left out both from the MP3 collection and the pitch analysis.
116. Unfortunately, since this topic of shades of ambiguity was an after thought, brought up only at the time of revision (prompted by the discussion group), the entire discussion has no music demonstration to accompany it. The omission is regretted.
117. The note in parenthesis is a fleeting note, which is just hinted at in passing.
118. However, we will see in chapter 8 that the lexicons of raagas list some phrases as 'minor' phrases which may not be iterated very often in a discourse as such iterations will reflect a general deficiency in the performer.
119. As mentioned earlier, the entire discussion is an afterthought and so, unfortunately, no audio music demonstration to accompany this discussion.
120. Yet for linguistic theory, the word is notoriously difficult to define. Are inflected forms different words; are compounds single words or a two word sequence? The issue is irrelevant for our purposes as we would be taking the stand that musical phrases are comparable to the notion phonological word. I am grateful to R. Amritavalli for this insightful suggestion (p.c.).
121. I will revise this assumption shortly.

122. This is the term that Arvindh Krishnaswamy uses.
123. But one implication of this hypothesis is that one must stop branding people as 'tone deaf' as is the common practice now in music circles. True tone deafness would imply an inability to acquire and use the intonation patterns of the first language which is easily identifiable from the use of flat intonation similar to robotic speech. As everyone knows, such cases are almost non-existent in the case of language. Unsuccessful or inadequate learning/teaching strategies must be the reason for people not being able to perceive differences in tunes etc. However, unsuccessful execution of musical phrases must not be attributed to tone deafness. Of course, I have nothing to say about the perception of 'absolute pitch' which is an artifact of Western music. It has been suggested that lesions in certain areas of the right hemisphere may result in difficulty in perceiving differences in intonation patterns and perception of musical notes (Nicholson et al. (2003)). I observed that my mother, who was my music teacher, progressively lost her ability to recognise raagas after she suffered a stroke of the right hemisphere.
124. This is not as far fetched as it may seem at first blush. In fact, all these characteristics, i.e. identifying phrase boundaries, phrasal prominence, intonation group, nucleus of an intonational group, the specific intonation tones used are required for the successful learning of the intonation patterns of a language where the pitch range is narrower than an octave and hence calls for greater subtlety. The PAD thus is definitely required for the acquisition of language and once in place, music may as well make finer demands on it
125. The proof for prominence on the second syllable is in the reduction of the first vowel in casual speech. The prominence facts of Tamil have been simplified for ease of presentation.
126. Notice that the absolute final note in a musical phrase is not prominent, though long.
127. Notice the taanam like phrasing.
128. However, see chapter 2 pp. 23–25 for a discussion of poetic license in Carnatic music.
129. The fact that this model requires parallel evaluation becomes even clearer at the end of the next chapter when the constraint sets and their ranking are laid out as a general schema. Unquestionably, this strategy of parallel evaluation where all elements of the musical line starting from the tone, to the sequence, to the musical phrase, to the rhythmic phrase, to the musical line are evaluated simultaneously is just not feasible in a derivational model of the grammar of Carnatic music which works in a bottom-up fashion.
130. But in some cases, the intonational phrase may contain more than one tonic/nucleus. But more of this later.
131. Not surprisingly, this habit carries over to the English of Tamilians as well.
132. Unfortunately not included in the music demonstration.

133. And too much attention to words and their pronunciation can at times result in destroying the flow of the musical line. While mutilating the language text beyond reconstruction should be avoided, the other extreme of cutting up the musical line in odd places for the sake of the language text is also not desirable.
134. The first half of this line has been lost because of an editing mistake.
135. I am grateful to N.S. Srinivasan for bringing this interesting fact to my attention (p.c.)
136. See discussion below for a probable reason for such a type of change.
137. The take off point in the rhythmic cycle is also altered in many styles of rendering. I ignore this fact for making the presentation simpler.
138. It is not uncommon for musicians to change even the notation of a line to suit their preconceived notions of grammar. Sanjay Subrahmanyan (p.c.) tells me that the notation of some of Muttuswaami Diikshitar compositions by his grandson Subbaraama Diikshitar has been altered by twentieth century musicians as some of the composer's idioms do not fit into the grammar of the performers.
139. See the references cited for the alignment of stress and rhythm in metre in poetry and in Western and modern music.
140. All the beat cycles admit twice the number of moras in slower paced compositions.
141. In larger cycles of beats other fingers also come into play, sometimes including more than one cycle of all the five fingers.
142. This beat cycle also admits two or four moras to a beat. The second beat is normally indicated by a repetition of the gesture with the palm. But technically speaking, there are other variations of this cycle where finger counting becomes necessary.
143. Misra means 'seven' and caapu means a shortened version of a cycle.
144. Kaṇṭa means 'five'.
145. The notation and the rendering do not match. This happened because I had my own style in mind while notating but later got Sanjay to sing it for me. This should give one a flavour of what Carnatic music is all about – not notation and precision but the individual's freedom to interpret. I am not going to apologize for this.
146. I ignore emphatic prominence which is optional anyway.
147. This composition is played at a brisk tempo with four moras to a beat (and no half beat). This is the second sangati of the first line of the pallavi.
148. As I said in chapter 1, it was Tyaagaraajaa's innovative approach to sangati in compositions which proved be the corner stone of manoodharma sangeetam, i.e. developed the communicative aspect of Carnatic music (in this case aalaapanai and niraval), once again we see that it is the genius of Tyaagaraajaa which guides the rhythmic principles at work in Carnatic music performances.

149. Logically speaking, three mora phrases should be similarly eschewed in three/six mora beat too. But as this is much harder to achieve, the rule is relaxed in the unusual three/six mora or five mora beats.
150. This tension between rhythmic and musical prominence is reminiscent of the similar tension between linguistic prominence and metrical beat noted in metre in poetry. I refer the reader to the enormous literature on stress and metrics and modern music given in the bibliography. I am grateful to K.A. Jayaseelan (p.c.) for bringing this to my attention.
151. As my previous footnote may have hinted, rhythm is Carnatic music is eminently analyzable in a constraint based approach with grid based representation. (with or without more enriched representations).
152. Speaking of overplayed emotion, tremolo, i.e. mini vibrations on every note (including the fundamental and the fifth which is actually quite contrary to orthodox theory) can also be encountered in certain styles which are to be interpreted as renderings with extreme religious fervour/devotion etc. Needless to say, such uncontrolled display of emotion is quite contrary to the spirit of classicism.
153. I have nothing to say about interpretation of emotion in other systems of music.
154. This is a dialogue spoken by the character Jaṭaayu to Raavaṇaa in the Raamaayaṇa opera Raamanaaṭakam composed by Aruṇaacala Kavi (1712–1779).
155. This is a beautiful example of the missed beat style where alternate beats in a rhythm cycle which is already irregular aligning with musical prominence (see chapter 6, pp. 173–178 for a discussion of the missed beat style in Carnatic music.)
156. Due to oversight, this piece of music does not have a matching recording in the MP3 collection. The inconvenience caused is regretted.
157. Phrases which are commonly used in the taanam are some times used elsewhere too. Known as 'jaṇṭa' they receive non-initial prominence as in phrases like [sa 'sa] etc. Examples of this kind of musical phrase are found in this musical passage. They invariably also receive emphatic prominence. Also notice that syllables of the language text are not always aligned with prominent notes in the musical phrase.
158. It is not uncommon to come across performers who switch styles following one style in the aalaapani, niraval and kalpanaa swaram and another while rendering the composition. In such cases, we need to partition the performance into two distinct musical discourses for evaluating them correctly.
159. See Prince and Smolensky (1993) for a discussion of the evaluation of gradient constraints.
160. See chapter 8 for a full discussion of the lexicons of Carnatic music and their organization.

161. Of course, the ultra-orthodox who go by the letter of the aarooha ṇam/avaroohaṇam may not subscribe to these minor phrases.
162. This is one of the reasons why Carnatic music cannot be satisfactorily rendered on a keyboard instrument or any other instrument which allows only the strict RenScale values. I leave it to the intelligent reader to actually list the instruments on which Carnatic music cannot be/ought not to be rendered.
163. In fact 'prescriptivism' in Carnatic music with rigid views of Raagam classification has lead to just that.
164. It could be the case that the tolerance level for clichés among Indians is rather high because of our literary traditions where the same similes can be trotted out time and again.
165. I am grateful to R. Amritavalli (p.c.) and Geetha Durairajan (p.c.) for the discussion on clichés in Carnatic music.
166. As there was a problem in recording the singer in the 'madhyama ʃruti', i.e. with F as the fundamental, I had to skip these two pieces while doing the recording.
167. Listen again to music demonstration [1.10] and [1.11] which are two versions of a song of Tyaagaraajaa.
168. I am grateful to R. Amritavalli (p.c.) for bringing this to my notice.
169. Line final syllables (closed or light) are allowed to be aligned with the final note sequence in the musical semi-line, a semi-line being a part of a line which is amenable to repetition or break in the rendering etc.
170. In addition to this, this composer had a different approach to some of the common raagas and had the distinction of creating many new ones. The greatest tribute one can pay the great composers of Carnatic music is to analyze each of the styles in depth and write their grammars.
171. This is a beautiful example of the missed beat style where alternate beats in a rhythm cycle which is already irregular aligning with musical prominence (see chapter 6, pp. 173–178 for a discussion of the missed beat style in Carnatic music.)
172. As this piece of music notation was added later, it was not possible to include it in the demonstration MP3 collection.
173. See chapter 8, pp. 262–263 for a discussion of 'symmetry' in Carnatic music as a source of raagam change.
174. The second sangati of this composition is one such sangati (Ayyangar (1965 II: 155)) which I personally avoid.
175. It is not accidental that all these variations are missing in Ayyangar's Kritimanimalai (1965 II: 262).
176. Albeit a minuscule minority (a fast dwindling tribe).
177. Take a musical phrase like [Sa Ri Sa] [nu Sa nu] [di ni di] with three notes to a rhythmic group each. If all the three phrases are rendered alike the sequence may sound a bit monotononous. One can, however, lengthen the initial note a

bit and compensatorily shorten the second note in one of the phrases to avoid monotony. The absence of an accompanying demonstration is regretted.

178. It is not desirable for Carnatic music performers to perform with a piece of notated text. Critics come down heavily on performers who do so. It is understandable in the context of Carnatic music, as performers are not really expected to 'parrot' a musical text but interpret it creatively and freely. If a performer is dependent on a written text it proves his/her lack of control over the text inhibiting his/her ability to interpret creatively.

179. Not only is there no such thing as copyright in the Indian context, one way of expressing one's admiration for a great composer is to take an entire composition and compose a new language text to go with it. The original composer, far from feeling angry or hurt ought to feel flattered. (See also chapter 1, p. 7 for a discussion on lack of copyright in Carnatic music just as in everyday language use.)

180. I am aware that the use of general labels like 'pattern', 'balance', 'symmetry', 'coherence', 'wit' may evoke consternation in linguistics circles where constructs have to be defined formally. But I am convinced that musical content cannot be discussed without reference to these constructs. Apart from a general definition with respect to all art, I am certain, these constructs can be defined strictly with reference to Carnatic music, as I have done for 'wit' and 'symmetry' later on in the chapter (pp. 218–221) and in chapter 8. For lack of space I have not been able to define the other constructs in a similar manner.

181. At least for me, this is one of the chief attractions of Muttuswaami Diikshitar's style where in many of his great compositions he makes sure that the performer/listener sits up at least once and runs to the lexicon to redefine it. Of course, the entire exercise happens if and only if careful attention is paid to musical phrasing in his compositions. Unfortunately, most performers go through his compositions, specially the charaṇam, as though they want to reach the second tempo passage so that they can rush through the composition and wind it up.

    And it is rather strange that on the one hand we have Muttuswaami Diikshitar who is perhaps a conservative when it comes to the language text of the composition eschewing emotion altogether but musically, he dares to expand the horizon of the raagam, to tease the listener (if he/she is willing to pay attention), in short be revolutionary. On the other hand, we have Tyaagaraajaa, who revolutionized Carnatic music as far as spontaneous improvisation (the realm of sangati, aalaapanai, niraval and kalpanaaswaram etc.) is concerned, is a conservative when it comes to defining the raagam. He chose to take the regular, beaten path to musical phrasing.

182. A few of her 78 rpm records are accessible to the listener. While her rendering of the Begaḍaa varṇam and the Kamaas Jaavaḷi are specially full of wit in this sense, her Tooḍi viruttam is truly experimental in its approach to musical content.

183. Listen to the last item in musical demonstration [8.151]. For another interpretation see endnote 203.
184. It must have become amply clear by the discussions in chapters 4 and 5 that pitch values are not as precise in Carnatic music as they may be in other systems of music as a range of values are often attested in practice. However we may interpret the pitch value in this case, they will definitely be closer to ri than gi.
185. The music discourse I have in mind was broadcast on the music channel Worldspace and I assume it may be available commercially.
186. The pitch specifications on ri and di is another instance of symmetry. If one considers the scale, another interpretation of symmetry emerges; alternating notes in the scale, i.e. ri, ma and di admit identical pitch manipulations (though the inter note intervals may not be identical).
187. This style, at its best, can be very moving, expressing an austere, expansive grandeur. But it can also degenerate into empty rhetoric resembling the incoherence of a drunk.
188. The perfect ʃruti bheedam, i.e. according to (61) is the one done on the note ma in the raagam Yadukulakaambodi where one gets the same raagam (RR Ayyangar p.c.). Even here it will be seen that the partitioning of constraints must be done though the mapping is not between two raagas but between different notes of the same raagam.
189. This is why the eminent musicologist late Harold Powers (p.c.) suggested the title "A Grammar for Carnatic Music" for this book. Unfortunately, it was too late to change the title when he made this suggestion.
190. Books on Carnatic music theory discuss several types of classification of raagas depending on the possible origin of the raagam, the number of notes in the ascending and descending scale, whether the raagam has any accidental notes etc. (see Sambamurthy, Ayyangar and others for details).
191. Another possibility is classification based on acoustic parameters.
192. Recall the discussion of the pitch values of 'gi' and 'ni' in my rendering (and many other musicians) where even the RenScale pitch value is lower than the steady pitch value of 'gi' and 'ni' and also the rendering is a mild or flattened pitch wave (specially when 'ra' and 'da' are selected). I ignore this wrinkle when I broadly generalize that all notes can be rendered as RenScale.
193. It is true that in most styles of Carnatic music, 'gi' and 'ni' in S set raagas do not admit note pitch curves freely/at all.
194. This scale is not listed among the 2116 scales listed in Ayyangar (1972).
195. However, I am quick to point out that several artists are quite comfortable with phrases like [gu pa da;] and [da Sa Ra;] in this raagam.
196. In short, the difference between Pantuvaraaḷi and Puurvikalyaaṇi, in traditional styles, can be attributed to the fact that while the former selects aug.gu thus

sanctioning pitch wave gu, the latter does not thus allowing only RenScale gu and note pitch curve gu.

197. In styles where these notes can be rendered as RenScale, obviously, this constraint is lower ranked and becomes invisible. But the presence of the constraint may appear later.
198. Once again, there are styles where these notes are attempted as RenScale renderings, but personally, I find these renderings over-dramatic.
199. However, raagam-specific constraints that demand RenScale interpretation for long, emphatic notes takes precedence over this constraint.
200. In fact, Sanjay Subrahmanyan (p.c.) bemoaned the fact that the contemporary Carnatic fraternity has lost its ability to invest new values /forge new sequential possibilities to notes in raagas thanks to the conformist, prescriptivist contemporary scenario.
201. Notice I did not say that all notes are un-interpretable.
202. Sometimes such identification is not accurate in the contemporary scene as the traditional method of learning is supplemented with or replaced by different modes of learning like distance learning, learning from different teachers, learning from recorded music etc. These new methods have enabled learners to mix and match styles, some times producing musical discourses which lack internal consistency.
203. Additionally, recall that 'gi' generally is resistant to a RenScale rendition and being a very short note, red.gi interpretation is also not possible and hence the execution of 'ri' but notated as 'gi'. See discussion chapter 7 pp. 216–217.
204. The renderings of compositions in this raagam sound more like Dhanyaasi gone 'bad' as broad generalisations are not extractable from the renderings across different schools.
205. Sanjay Subrahmanyan makes a similar point for the demise of the raagam Naaraayaṉagauḻa in his observations on Raaga lakshaṉa in the website www.sangeetham.com.
206. It is possible that this scale was invented by Raamaswaami Diikshitar, father of the great composer Muttuswaami Diikshitar based on the major chords in the Western major scale 'sa gu pa' 'pa nu Ri'. I am grateful to N.S. Srinivasan (p.c.) for this piece of information.
207. Even S Set raagas can be stressful for beginners particularly with the rendering of note pitch curves.
208. For more details about the school of music I belong to and its approach to Carnatic music see Sruti, Winter, 1991.
209. My guru, Ranga Ramanuja Ayyangar, had arrived at this approach in the 1940's when even in language teaching circles structuralism was the only method. He was truly way ahead of his times. If only he had written about his teaching practices in detail, it would have been one of the first to raise the issue of communicative learning/teaching in general and specifically in Carnatic music.

Further, he had decided that texts meant for beginners was unnecessary baggage and so his music syllabus began with small compositions of the trinity and other composers, i.e. 'real' music, i.e. the equivalent of 'authentic texts' in communicative methods of language teaching.

210. I am told that many teachers have slowly changed their teaching methods in this direction (Sanjay Subrahmanyan p.c.)
211. To be fair to the performer, the entire aalaapanai was not rendered as RenScale but only the climactic part of the rendition.
212. Recall discussion chapter 7 pp. 224–225.
213. It was Sanjay Subrahmanyan's observation (p.c.) on current practices which set me thinking on this section of the chapter. He was observing how senior musicians adopt prescriptive positions regarding what is permitted in a raagam and consequently go against the clearly laid down notation in Subbaraama Diikshitar's Sampradaayapradarshiṉi. The example he gave was the notation 'ni di ni Sa' in Muttuswaami Diikshitar's compositions like Kamaḷaambaa and Tyaagaraajayoogavaibhavam in Aanandabhairavi. Such tampering with notation would have been labeled 'vandalism' in the Western art set up. He lamented that the practice of composers/performers stretching the raagam to its very limits was now almost extinct.
214. Notice that there is no such thing as red.nu. The decision to classify this raagam as a derivative of Shankaraabharaṇam with a reduced 'nu' must have been a well thought decision based on accurate perception of pitch values. The reasoning must have been that this 'reduced nu' is different from the augmented 'ni' found in Madhyamaavati.
215. This aphorism sounds interesting in Tamil: "Saniyeevarum meelee, taniyeevarum kiizḫee".
216. Diikshitar's Aabeeri is neither popular nor can be considered a major raagam.
217. Many mistakenly assume that Bhuupaaḷam and Bauḷi refer to the same raagam.
218. Only in his system of raagas and not for other Carnatic music practitioners.
219. A couple of performers do make this attempt, in my view, unsuccessfully.
220. Perhaps, because of the famous reduced 'Gauḷa rishanbham' this raagam was an I Set raagam to begin with. But for most contemporary performers it is only a marginal I Set raagam with no other indication of I Set membership other than the reduced riʃabham Curiously, for Veena Dhanam, in her recording of the Gana Raaga pancakam, a lower 'nu' is attested arguing for another feature of its I Set membership. Also see Sangeetham (www.sangeetham.com) archives on Papa Venkatramaiah on Veenam Dhanam's Gauḷa.
221. There is comfort in numbers and the die-hard sceptic may be convinced by the facts presented as an additional argument. A cursory look at 42 I Set raagas covering all the 72 meeḷakartas reveal that though 50% of the raagas do not have scales which are symmetrical, only 14% of them have no pair of notes in

the two halves of the octave which are not in symmetrical relation. From this generalisation we see that though there is freedom to construct unsymmetrical scales in Carnatic music through usage, notes which are in symmetrical relation develop symmetrical pitch specifications and/or phrasal possibilities. Therefore AUGMENTSYMMETRY is a family of constraints which is active in the grammar of Carnatic music.

222. Uuttukkaaḍu Veenkaṭasubbayyar, possibly a pre-trinity composer has a great composition in the scale Kiiravaaṇi. But it is composed in the S Set raagam Kiiravaaṇi, in my view, and not the I Set raagam Kiiravaaṇi as in the case of Tyaagaraajaa.
223. I am grateful to S. Upendran for this example (p.c.).
224. Recall the discussion of this style in chapter 7, pp. 219–222.
225. I have deliberately kept the pronunciation of raagas, technical terms and instruments at the popular, non-formal level. For a discussion of the origin of these terms, their supposedly 'correct' pronunciation etc. the reader has to look elsewhere.
226. There is another, micro aspect to naadaswaram playing and temple rituals. As these instruments were also involved in more time-bound rituals inside the temple where precise, set compositions had to be rendered, the ingenuity of the players was addressed to rhythmic matters. Here, rhythmic passages of amazing mathematical complexity are attested, involving fractions etc. What is truly amazing here is that many of these players lacked/lack formal education and all their mathematical complexities had been arrived at through ingenious, mental calculations with abstract time. (I am grateful to Sanjay Subrahmanyan (p.c.) for bringing this to my attention).
227. It is unfortunate that all the ten instances are grouped under one music demonstration. I had to work within the limitation of one CD not allowing more than 99 citations.
228. This is with the archives of All India Radio, Hyderabad.
229. Even the composer Tyaagarajaa apparently did not seem to go with this orthodoxy as he sanctioned the line // Sa, (Ri) Sa nu di pa gu ma, gu ri sa... // in his great composition 'Naadoopaasanaa'.
230. In the notation, the bow denotes a pitch glide bridging two notes, the > denotes a pitch spike.
231. I recall a music connoisseur Srini Pichumani expressing his surprise at this interpretation of the note 'ma' in our style years back. That is precisely the point. The style set forth by our paramaguru 'great guru' is full of wit which challenges many of the standard assumptions. The rendering of this varṇam, thankfully preserved for posterity, is full of wit in this sense. Many standard assumptions are called into question in her rendering.
232. I realize the irony of these claims as pointed out by Kiparsky (p.c.). Throughout the text I have quoted approvingly from Veena Dhanam's recording, elevating

it to the status of a classical art object invested with permanence. And the thriving music industry also runs counter to this claim.

233. There is a commercially available audio recording of Sanjay Subrahmanyan rendering this composition which attests this 'ri'.

Bibliography

Amritavalli, R.

1999 *Language as a Dynamic Text: Essays on Language, Cognition and Communication.* New Delhi: Allied Publishers.

Ayyangar, Ranga Ramanuja

1965 *Kritimanimalai: I–IV.* 2nd ed. Mumbai: Vipanci Cultural Trust.

1972 *The History of South Indian (Carnatic) Music.* Mumbai: Vipanci Cultural Trust.

1973 *Sangeetha Ratnakaram: A Critical Study.* Mumbai: Vipanchi Cultural Trust.

1977 *Musings of a Musician: Recent Trends in Carnatic Music.* Bombay: Wilco Publishers.

Bhagyalekshmi, S.

1990 *Ragas in Carnatic Music.* Trivandrum: CBH Publication.

Chomsky, Noam

1993 A Minimalist Program for Linguistic Theory. In *The View from Building 20*, Kenneth Hale and Samuel Jay Keyser (eds.), 1–52. Cambridge, MA: MIT Press.

Durga, S. A. K.

1991 *Research Methodology for Music.* Chennai: Centre for Ethnomusicology.

Feld, Stevens and Aaron Fox

1994 Music and Language. *Annual Review of Anthropology* 23: 25–53.

Gautam, M. R.

2001 *The Musical Heritage of India.* New Delhi: Munshiram Manoharlal Publishers.

Gilbers, Dicky

1992 Phonological Networks: a theory of segment representation. PhD thesis, University of Groningen.

Gilbers, Dicky and Maartje Schreuder

2002 Language and Music in Optimality Theory. Rutgers Optimality Archives 571. roa.rutgers.edu

Gussenhoven, Carlos

2004 *The Phonology of Tone and Intonation.* Cambridge: Cambridge University Press.

Hayes, Bruce

1984 The Phonology of Rhythm in English. *Linguistic Inquiry* 15 (1): 33-74.

Hayes, Bruce and Abigail Kaun

1996 The Role of Phonological Phrasing in Sung and Chanted Verse. *The Linguistic Review* 13: 243–303.

Hayes, Bruce and Margaret MacEachern

1998 Quatrain Form in English Folk Verse. *Language* 74: 473–507.

Higgins, John

1975 From Prince to Populace: Patronage as a Determinant of Change in South Indian Music. *Asian Music* 7 (2): 20–26.

Hockett,Charles

1960 The origin of speech. *Scientific American* 203 (3): 88–96.

Jackendoff, Ray

1989 A Comparison of Rhythmic Structure in Music and Language. In *Phonetics and Phonology I: Rhythm and Meter*, Paul Kiparsky and Gilbert Youmans (eds.), 15–44. San Diego: Academic Press.

Jackson, William

1991 *Tyagaraja: Life and Lyrics.* Madras: Oxford University Press.

Kager, René

1999 *Optimality Theory.* Cambridge: Cambridge University Press.

Kaufman, Walter

1976 *Ragas of South India.* New Delhi: Oxford and IBM Publishing Company.

Kersenboom, Saskia

1995 *Word, Sound and the Tamil Text.* Oxford: Berg.

Krishnaswamy, Arvindh

2003a Application of Pitch Tracking to South Indian Classical Music. arvindh@ccrma.stanford.edu

2003b Pitch Measurements versus Perception of South Indian Classical Music. Proceedings of the Stockholm Music Acoustics Conference: Sweden. arvindh@ccrma.stanford.edu

Kritimanimalai

see Ayyangar (1965).

Lerdahl, Fred and Ray Jackendoff

1983 A Generative Theory of Tonal Music. Cambridge, MA: MIT Press.

Lieberman, Philip

1984 *The Biology and Evolution of Language.* Cambridge, MA: Harvard University Press.

McCarthy, John and Alan Prince

1993 Prosodic Morphology: constraint interaction and satisfaction. Ms. University of Massachusetts and Rutgers University.

Menon, Indira

1999 *The Madras Quartet: Women in Karnatak Music.* New Delhi: Lotus Books.

Menon, Narayana

1957 The Impact of Western Technology on Indian Music. In: *The Bulletin of the Institute of Traditional Cultures*, 70–80. Madras.

1987 *Music of India*. Mumbai: Bharatiya Vidya Bhavan.

Menon, Raghava

1976 *The Sound of Indian Music: A Journey into Raga*. New Delhi: Indian Book Company.

1995 *Penguin Dictionary of Indian Classical Music*. New Delhi: Penguin Books.

Mukherjee, Nirmalangshu

2000 *The Cartesian Mind: Reflections on Language and Music*. Shimla: Advanced Centre.

Nicholson, Karen G., Shari Baum, Andrea Kilgour, Christine K. Koh, K. G. Munhall, and Lola L. Cuddy

2003 Impaired processing of prosodic and musical patterns after right hemisphere damage. *Brain and Cognition* 52: 382–389.

Oehrle, Richard

1989 Temporal Structures in Verse Design. In *Phonetics and Phonology I: Rhythm and Meter*, Paul Kiparsky and Gilbert Youmans (eds.), 87–119. San Diego: Academic Press.

Parthasarathy, T.S.

1981 Ragas of Karnatak Music. In: *Journal of the Music Academy Vol. LII*, Chennai.

Pesch, Ludwig

1999 *The Illustrated Companion to South Indian Music*. New Delhi: Oxford University Press.

Peterson, Indira

1984 The Kriti as an Integrated Form: Aesthetic Experience in the Religious Songs of Two South Indian Composers. *South Asian Literature* 19 (2): 165–179.

Prince, Alan and Paul Smolensky

1993 Optimality Theory: constraint interaction in generative grammar. Ms. Rutgers University.

Ramakrishna, Lalitha

1991 *Varnam: A Special Form in Karnatik Music*. New Delhi: Harman Publishing House.

Ramnarayan, Gowri

1997 *Past Forward: Six Artists Speak about their Childhood*. Madras: Orient Longman.

Reck, David
1984 India/South India. In: *Worlds of Music: An Introduction to the Music of the World's Peoples*, Jeff Todd Tinton (ed.), 209–265. New York: Schirmer Books.

Sambamurthy, P.
1939 Madras as a Seat of Musical Learning. In *Madras Tercentenary Commemorative Volume,* 429-437. Madras and London: Oxford University Press.
1999 *South Indian Music I–VI.* (7th ed.) Chennai: The Indian Music Publishing House.

Seetha, S.
1981 *Tanjore as a Seat of Music.* Madras: Madras University Press.

Shankar, Vidya
1983 *The Art and Science of Carnatic Music.* Madras: The Music Academy.

Subba Rao, T.V.
1962 *Studies in Indian Music.* Madras: Vasantha Press.

Subramanian, Lakshmi
1999 The Reinvention of a Tradition: Nationalism, Carnatic Music, and the Madras Music Academy. *Indian Economic and Social History Review* 36 (2): 131–163.

Vihman, Marilyn M.
1996 *Phonological Development*: *The origins of language in the child.* Oxford: Blackwell.

Vijayakrishnan, K.G.
1991 The RR School of Music. *Sruti* Winter 1991. Reproduced in *The Saga of a Legend*, Padma Varadan (ed.), 2001. Mumbai: Vipanci Cultural Trust.

Weidman, Amanda
2001 Questions of Voice: On the Subject of "Classical Music" in South India. PhD dissertaion, Columbia University.
2003 Guru and Gramaphone: Fantasies of Fidelity and Modern Technologies of the Real. *Public Cultures* 15 (3): 453–476.

Yip, Moira
2002 *Tone*. Cambridge: Cambridge University Press.

Author and composer index

Subject index

Raagam index